The MOMENTS WE MADE Ours

SWIFT RIVERS SERIES

A HATLEY FAMILY SPIN-OFF

LJ EVANS

The MOMENTS WE MADE Ours

LJ EVANS

LJ EVANS BOOKS
www.ljevansbooks.com

Cover Design: © River Briar Designs
Cover Couple Photo: © Getty Images
Cover Design Photos: © iStock Gearstd | © Depositphotos bhphoto
Chapter Title Images: © Creative Markets Lana Elanor | Depositphotos mykef | iStock Ekaterina Lanbina; Elen11
Developmental & Line Editing: Lycanthrope Media
Copy Editing & Proofing: Jenn Lockwood Editing, Karen Hrdlicka, and Stephanie Feissner

Library of Congress Cataloging in process.

Playlist

https://geni.us/TMWMO-Play

Prologue – Skip This Part by Kelly Clarkson
Chapter One – thank you aIMee by Taylor Swift
Chapter Two – Man Down by Kelsey Hart
Chapter Three – Second Wind by Kelly Clarkson
Chapter Four – Legendary by Bon Jovi w/ James Bay
Chapter Five – monsters by Ella Langley
Chapter Six – Life as We Knew It by Lonestar
Chapter Seven – broken in by Ella Langley
Chapter Eight – Letter to a Friend by Bon Jovi
Chapter Nine – Chances Are by Lee Ann Womack
Chapter Ten – Keep Up With A Cowgirl
by David Adam Brynes
Chapter Eleven – Alright by Lady A
Chapter Twelve – Burn My Summer by Kelsey Hart
Chapter Thirteen – Ruin the Friendship by Taylor Swift
Chapter Fourteen – Love This Pain by Lady A
Chapter Fifteen – Chemistry by Kelly Clarkson
Chapter Sixteen – Mercy by Shawn Mendes
Chapter Seventeen – i hate love
by Kelly Clarkson w/ Steve Martin
Chapter Eighteen – love you tonight by Ella Langley
Chapter Nineteen – I Want to Be the One by Lonestar
Chapter Twenty – favorite kind of high by Kelly Clarkson
Chapter Twenty-one – Crazy 'Bout You by Kelsey Hart
Chapter Twenty-two – Save Your Love by Great White
Chapter Twenty-three – Without You In It by Kelsey Hart
Chapter Twenty-four – Be That For You by Lady A
Chapter Twenty-five – Life With You by Kelsey Hart
Chapter Twenty-six – Honey by Taylor Swift
Chapter Twenty-seven – I Can Love You Like That
by John Michael Montgomery
Chapter Twenty-eight – You're Still the One by Shania Twain
Chapter Twenty-nine – Out Go The Lights by Lonestar
Chapter Thirty – Let Your Tears Fall by Kelly Clarkson
Chapter Thirty-one – Softly by Lonestar
Chapter Thirty-two – how much a heart can hold by LeAnn Rimes
Chapter Thirty-three – With My Eyes Open by Lonestar
Chapter Thirty-four – Cassandra by Taylor Swift
Chapter Thirty-five – We Don't Run by Bon Jovi
Chapter Thirty-six – Opalite by Taylor Swift
Chapter Thirty-seven – Worst Way by Riley Green
Epilogue – Workin' On This Love by Lady A

Dedication

*To anyone who has ever felt like they weren't enough.
Duckling or swan, you are beautiful just as you are and
worthy of love just as you are. Don't settle for someone who
doesn't make you feel like a princess every day.*

To my love, for always making me *feel like a beautiful
princess.*

Please note: content warnings are available on
https://www.ljevansbooks.com/books/content-
warnings

Prologue
Maisey

SKIP THIS PART
Performed by Kelly Clarkson

FOURTEEN YEARS AGO

HIM: Where are you? Thought we were celebrating by finishing The Hunger Games *in the tree house?*

HER: Not tonight.

HIM: What? Why?

Minutes passed.

HIM: Maise?

More minutes passed.

HIM: That's it. I'm coming over.

I wound the tire swing as tight as I could before letting go. The branches and leaves of the oak tree became a dark whirl as I spun, wishing with all my might that I could actually take off and sail somewhere else. Anywhere else.

In the shadowy twilight descending over our small town in the foothills of the Sierra Mountains, the crickets sang in full chorus, the frogs croaked their symphony by the river, and the chicken coops murmured with the soft rustle of the roosts settling down. Yet, I could still hear my parents over it all. The sound of their argument streamed through the screen door, reaching out to me like a specter stretching its hands.

My stomach clenched, as it always did when they fought.

It was the same argument—money.

At least, this time, it wasn't about the boatload they were spending to fix me or the cost of my classes at the Western Riding School. Instead, they were arguing about the summer acting camp Chelsea wanted to attend. If she wasn't allowed to go, I'd feel even more selfish than normal for hogging all the extra money our family had available.

Mom was trying to squeak out the funds, but Dad was digging in his heels. He didn't want Chelsea to go, and it wasn't just because of the exorbitant fee. Dad didn't think it was healthy for my stunningly beautiful sister to want a famous life so badly that it had already carved itself into her soul.

I wasn't one to judge. I already had things carved into my soul too.

Not the least of which was how ugly I was compared to her.

It was like, when we'd been born, she'd been granted all the beauty, while I'd been handed all the deformities.

The alarm on my phone went off, and I shoved my hand into the front pocket of my oversized hoodie to silence it, hoping Mom hadn't heard. But that wasn't to be my luck. The argument in the house stopped briefly, and the kitchen floor creaked as footsteps crossed the cracked linoleum.

Mom called out from the screen door, "It's time to come inside, Maisey."

"I know. I'm coming," I called back.

She didn't wait. She knew I'd come in. She knew I'd do the right thing.

Except today, I really didn't want to.

I let the swing continue to unwind as tears leaked out and traveled down my cheeks. I didn't want to go in. I didn't want to put on the stupid facemask. I didn't want to go from ugly Maisey to hideously freaky Maisey.

I'd thought I'd finally broken free of the reverse-pull headgear, only to be told today I had to go another summer wearing it. So instead of celebrating the trashing of the face mask with Beckett in his treehouse tonight and finishing our latest book, I'd be stuck inside again. Alone.

I'd been giddy at the idea of reading with Beckett at night for the first time since we'd started reading together four years ago. It had felt…romantic…hopeful… Which was stupid, because Beckett had never looked at me that way. We were friends. Nothing more.

Suddenly, the tire swing jerked to a stop, and the screech that tore from me was as horrendous as my mouth. My heart slammed against my ribs as I twisted around, panic flaring. The wild rhythm only quickened when I saw who it was.

Usually, I heard Beckett land after jumping over the barbed-wire fence that separated our two small farms on the edge of downtown Swift Rivers—or just Rivers, as the locals affectionately called it. But tonight, I'd missed the sound, too distracted by my parents' argument and the mess of thoughts twisting through my head.

I had to look up—way up—to meet his eyes. Beckett had shot up nearly three inches over the winter, and the rest of him hadn't quite caught up yet. He was downright skinny these days, despite the lean muscles he'd built from endless chores on his family's goat farm and the long hours he put in at the Harrington Ranch, where his dad worked full time.

Beckett's dark-brown hair was on the longer side, curling about his ears and around his neck. He was constantly pushing the floppy mass out of his eyes—deep, warm, chocolate eyes that rested under thick brows he'd gotten from his dad.

"Thought we were celebrating," Beckett said. His voice had changed two years ago. It sounded like a man's voice, even when he still looked like a scraggily fourteen-year-old.

My body hadn't started to change at all. When Chelsea had been twelve, like me, she'd already been wearing a bra and had started her period. My body looked like I was still eight. How was that fair? But then again, Chelsea would say it wasn't fair that I hogged all our family's money simply because my jaw stuck out too much.

Beckett studied me closely. And even though the sky had slid just beyond the hills, and the oak tree cast shadows over me, there was still enough light for him to see the glimmer of tears streaking down my face.

"Maise?" Worry coated his voice.

Beckett and Fallon were the only ones I didn't mind calling me "Maise." They said it softly, like it actually meant something good. Everyone else turned it into a joke. Once the kids in school found out it was the Native word for corn, they started calling me Corny the Deformed Corncob. And Chelsea calling me Cornlette hadn't helped, no matter how sweetly she intended it.

"I have to go inside, Beckett."

And with that handful of words, he got what I meant.

"Shit. The orthodontist wants you to wear the facemask for longer?"

Beckett liked cussing these days. It was as if being a few weeks away from graduating eighth grade and moving on to high school had suddenly made it essential that he become familiar with every curse word in existence.

"Yep," I said with an extra pop on the P. "Another entire summer where I'll be stuck indoors after seven p.m."

"You don't have to be stuck inside, Maisey."

Technically, I didn't. No one said I couldn't leave the house with the facemask on. The hideous contraption, slowly shifting my jaw into a more "appropriate" position, didn't require darkness and solitude, but I didn't want anyone to see me in it.

I didn't even want my family to see it.

After I put on the mask, I hid in my room, where I devoured the books Beckett had helped me master, until sleep found me.

Beckett rested his hands on my shoulders, and even at twelve, even though my hormones hadn't really found me yet, I felt something deep inside me swoosh at his touch. It had been that way since the very first time we'd touched. From the moment I'd stuck my hand out to help him up after he'd fallen out of a tree and landed in our yard. It felt like…coming home after a long trip. Like…I'd found the place I truly belonged.

But tonight, the gentleness I always received from Beckett only made the tears flow harder.

"Don't cry, Maise. Please don't cry." His voice was thick,

choked with emotions that mirrored mine.

"I hate being me. I hate my jaw and my teeth and my parents fighting over the money I'm costing them."

Beckett yanked me out of the swing and wrapped his arms around me. I was so short compared to him after his growth spurt that my nose ended up in his armpit. I didn't care. He didn't smell like the other stinky boys at school, who hadn't figured out how to use deodorant yet. Beckett smelled like bonfire smoke and pine trees. Like some of my best childhood memories. Sometimes it felt like the only memories that really mattered were the ones made after he moved in next door six years ago.

"I refuse to stand by and let anyone, including you, hate on my Maisey-girl," he growled.

And my sick little preteen heart swooped again. I loved it when Beckett called me *his* Maisey-girl, even though I wasn't really his.

He'd actually been "going out" with Chelsea's frenemy, Delilah, most of the school year. But after his dad's fiancée had broken up with Kurt and taken off for South America, Beckett had broken up with Delilah and said he was over dating, just like his dad.

Beckett tugged gently at my plain, long brown hair. I wished I could wear it in the fishtail braid Fallon had taught me, but when I pulled it back, my jaw and teeth were all anyone focused on. At least with my hair down, I could hide behind it.

My second alarm went off, and it made me want to cry even harder. I didn't ever want to leave Beckett's arms. But the reminder warned me I was dangerously close to not putting on the facemask in time for it to do its job. My orthodontist told me that every minute I was late was why I had to wear it for longer than they'd expected. Except, I'd rarely been late. I'd been diligent for four years. Four years… It felt like a lifetime already.

"We can still camp out in the treehouse and finish *The Hunger Games* trilogy this summer. I don't care about the facemask. You know I won't laugh at you."

"You haven't ever seen me in it, Beckett. It's so…" I shook

my head. I couldn't even explain it. With the front of it suctioned to my forehead, the contraption hanging down over my nose and mouth and hooking to my teeth, I looked like a robot gone wrong. A mistake not even fit for the Island of Misfit Toys. "It makes me even uglier."

"You're *not* ugly." He said it fiercely, as if he were swearing. Like he meant it. "When I met you, it was your green eyes I noticed first. They made you look like…an avenging angel or something."

I missed his embarrassment at the compliment in the midst of my self-indulgent whine.

"Guys don't kiss eyes! They kiss mouths." I waved at my teeth covered in braces. "And this hideous mouth isn't ever getting kissed."

"You're wrong."

I moved to brush past him, but before I got even a step, Beckett grabbed my arm and hauled me to him. The next thing I knew, he'd placed his perfectly formed, cupid-bow lips on mine. His mouth was warm and insistent, the pressure gentle and yet firm. Shock held me still, and then my body went limp.

Beckett was kissing me.

Beckett.

My Beckett.

He'd given me my first kiss.

And it felt so right. Sweet and gentle and perfect.

The world spun around me just as it had when I'd been on the tire swing, everything beyond us a blurry mirage. It was as if we were in a bubble where nothing could touch us. Where nothing mattered but this—the two of us, at twelve and fourteen, somehow finding our other half.

I couldn't help the smile that started to replace the frown I'd been wearing since coming home from my appointment. But it was the smile that ruined everything because it allowed my braces to connect with his soft skin.

I felt him flinch.

Felt him try not to jerk back.

But I did it for him, wrenching myself free. My face flamed, and my insides rolled when I saw the blood that appeared on his beautiful lips. Lips I'd stared at for far too many hours in the last year as we'd taken turns reading aloud to each other.

He pushed a knuckle against the cut while his eyes remained locked on mine. I couldn't read his expression. But I wasn't sure I needed to.

Disgust. I was disgusted enough for both of us.

He'd done something nice and paid the price. More tears welled. The embarrassment would keep me in my room this summer more than even the stupid mask.

"Maisey, Mom is going to have a coronary if you don't come in and put on your headgear," Chelsea said, stepping out onto the small wooden deck at the back of our house.

The last thing I wanted was for Chelsea to find out about this embarrassing situation.

My overprotective big sister would flip out. She already thought my friendship with Beckett was weird.

I fled, whirling around and running up the trio of steps onto the deck, pushing past my beautiful sister with her wavy auburn hair and green eyes and perfect jaw and perfect figure. I ran through the galley kitchen to my bedroom just beyond it. I slammed the door and locked it but didn't flip on the light.

My heart beat wildly again. Those heavenly few seconds with Beckett's lips pressed against mine disappeared in a sea of humiliation.

Through my open window, my sister's voice easily carried to me.

"What happened to make Cornlette take off like she'd seen a ghost?" She sounded mad. Like she always did when defending me.

"Nothing," Beckett said.

"You're bleeding."

Silence.

"Did you kiss my sister?" she demanded, and when he still didn't respond, she continued, "She's a sixth grader, for heaven's sake."

It was the same baffled tone she used when he'd started

reading with me when I was eight. Up until then, reading had been yet another thing Chelsea had done with ease that I'd struggled with. I wasn't stupid, but my grades made it seem like I was.

Everything had changed the day I'd seen Beckett reading a book about horses. When I'd asked him about it, he'd started reading it to me, and then, he'd had me take a turn. He'd been patient with my mistakes and never once given up the way everyone else in my life did after a few bumbling sentences. Ever since then, reading had seemed fun, not only because of the books Beckett chose, but because it meant I had more time with him.

"I was just trying to help," Beckett finally responded. "She thought no one would ever kiss her."

"So it was, what? A pity kiss?" My heart fell. My cheeks, that had already been flaming, lit more. "Our poor little Maisey was sad, and you had to step in to help once again? You're such a sap."

My entire insides tightened at that word—sap. Beckett had sworn he'd never be a sap like his dad, loving women who didn't stick.

"You're such a bitch, Chelsea. You don't have the first clue about what friends will do for one another."

My stomach leaped. It wasn't the first time he'd called her a name like that. It was the one thing Beckett and I fought over. He insisted Chelsea wasn't the defender I'd always seen her as. But he hadn't been around when I was five, and the kids on the street made fun of my weird jaw and teeth. She'd thrown rocks at them.

"If it means having to kiss a twelve-year-old, I don't need friends." Her tone sounded disgusted, even angry. "If it happens again—"

The rest of her sentence faded away as they moved deeper into the yard. All I could hear was a murmur of voices that sounded uncomfortably like my parents arguing.

When the hum stopped, I could imagine Beckett jumping from the boulder by the chicken coop onto the wooden fence post between the barbed wire dividing our yards. He'd leap like a superhero through the air, land gracefully on his feet, and still end up startling the goats.

And just like in my imagination, the bleat of the herd sounded through the air, followed by Chelsea's feet pounding up the porch steps.

The noise unfroze me. I didn't want her to know I'd overheard their conversation. I didn't want her telling me that Beckett had only kissed me out of pity while warning me, again, that my crush on Beckett was going to get me hurt. She'd already told me kids at school made fun of me, not only for my looks, but because of the way I tagged after Beckett like a stray dog. Like the Hunchback in that animated movie, fawning over the Romani girl.

Beckett was kind to me, but that didn't mean he was going to fall head over heels in love with me. No one would ever fall for the freak show who'd barely learned to read.

I grabbed the bag with my facemask in it and hurried into the tiny bathroom I shared with my sister.

There was only one thing to do from here—pretend Beckett Romero had never kissed me at all. I'd put the entire memory in a box, lock it away, and forget it had ever happened.

And maybe in a few weeks, I'd be able to look at him again without embarrassment swarming through me like gnats on an apple core.

Chapter One
Maisey

THANK YOU AIMEE
Performed by Taylor Swift

FOURTEEN YEARS LATER

HIM: Are you coming to One-Eyed Frank's tonight?

> *HER: Nope. I have leftover enchiladas and a new book calling me.*

HIM: I need protection, Maisey-girl. Your protection.

> *HER: You're six foot four and roughly the size of a barn. What kind of protection could I possibly provide that you couldn't give yourself?*

HIM: If I'm with you, other women stay away. I don't risk offending someone and getting slapped. You're protecting my cheeks from taking a real beating.

> *HER: It isn't your cheeks but your ego that needs a beating.*

PRESENT DAY

I opened my locker door and stared at the woman who appeared in the mirror inside. I scowled at her. "You are *not* going to Frank's."

Especially not looking like this—like I'd just gotten off a twelve-hour shift that had started at seven this morning. With my plain brown hair pulled back in a ponytail, makeup all but worn off my long, narrow face, and in scrubs with unicorns on them, I looked like I was sixteen instead of twenty-six.

I locked my sage-colored eyes on the reflection. "Maisey Campbell, you will not go to One-Eyed Frank's. He will not crook his finger, and you show up."

It was a battle I'd been waging for two decades when it came to Beckett. Sometimes I won. Sometimes I lost. And every time I lost, it reminded me I was the same idiot girl who'd fallen for the heroic boy-next-door, who'd patiently taught her to read.

If he'd been hard to resist as a beanpole of a teen who'd shared his deepest, darkest wounds with me, it was impossible to resist the muscle-bound fire captain he'd become, especially with that perfect dimple in his right cheek and his confidence the size of the entire state of California.

I ripped the band out of my hair and tried hopelessly to fluff it up. It didn't cooperate, especially without any of the multitude of products I usually used to help it. The strands had always been straight as a board and were a generic brown that no one asked their hairdresser to repeat. I'd tried highlights and different colors over the years, but it had ultimately ruined the fine texture and made things worse. So these days, I stuck with plain brown. I stuck with who I was.

Maisey the sidekick to two best friends.

Maisey the helper.

Maisey the nurse.

I'd never been *hot Maisey,* who had equally hot guys drooling after her.

I'd stopped expecting any sort of miracle like that in college. One too many "hot guys" had made it clear I should be grateful they'd "chosen me" for sex, but I shouldn't expect anything more. I shouldn't expect dates and romance.

Even still, I hadn't given up on love and companionship the

way Beckett had. I still felt like it was out there for me, somewhere, with someone. But I also wasn't going to let some disappointing-in-bed guy make me feel bad about the hardly noticeable scars on my jaw from the surgery that had finally and permanently corrected my severe malocclusion.

I snagged my reusable water bottle off the shelf, shoved my bag onto my shoulder, and slammed the locker door. A horrifying screech escaped at the face that appeared in front of me.

"Holy potatoes, Meredith, you scared the hell out of me."

Her face remained serious as she said, "I need you to cover Lisa's shift tomorrow."

Part of me groaned at the idea of working another shift, while another part of me was excited at the thought of being in Labor and Delivery. I'd loved working L&D at my first hospital after college. But when I'd joined Swift Rivers Community Hospital, they'd only had a job in the floater pool available, and due to liabilities, floaters rarely got to work in specialty departments.

"What's wrong with Lisa?"

Meredith frowned. "She took off to Vegas with her new boyfriend and isn't coming back. With that summer cold flying through the staff, the last thing we need is to be down another body."

If Lisa was gone, it would mean a permanent position in Labor and Delivery had opened up. That vicious bitch, otherwise known as Hope, leaped through me, but she was just as likely to crush me as she was to give me what I wanted.

And as tempting as it was to say yes at the chance it would help me get the permanent job, I'd just worked five twelve-hour shifts in a row, instead of my usual three, covering for people at Meredith's request. I needed a break and had planned on spending the morning on my horse at the Harrington Ranch, training for the Fourth of July show, and then binge-reading a new cowboy romance.

I sidestepped Meredith and headed for the exit. "Ask Wendy."

"Wendy is going to a wedding. If you want the spot on the

Labor and Delivery team, this is your opportunity to show you can handle it. Plus, you promised when I hired you that you'd pull every shift needed." Meredith pouted.

I felt that old, familiar twinge deep inside—guilt at being the reason others didn't get what they needed or wanted. My therapist had almost yanked the tendency out of me, but it still surfaced now and again. I inhaled deeply and let it out slowly before responding.

"That was three years ago, Meredith. I've proven my loyalty and my willingness to be a team player since then. I've proven I can handle any ward you've thrown at me. If the managers here don't think I'm ready for a position in Labor and Delivery, perhaps I should consider looking for a job elsewhere. I hear County is hiring."

"That isn't what I said," she backpedaled, knowing the hospital couldn't afford to be down two nurses, and I felt another pang of guilt at pushing her. But damnit, I'd paid my dues.

As I headed for the door, I did something I rarely did—I made a demand on my own behalf. "I want the Labor and Delivery spot. If you and Becka can guarantee I'll be the first person in line for the job, then I'll cover tomorrow. Otherwise, find someone else."

My heart was pounding, but I didn't look back as I left.

A weird mix of pride and remorse surged through me. I'd earned the spot. I'd put in the time and done what I could to help the hospital, and yet I could still hear Chelsea's voice in my head, telling me I was being selfish for demanding more. She wasn't right, but she also wasn't wrong. As a kid, I'd taken so much of our family's time and resources that it had scarred my sister almost as much as it had scarred me.

Outside, I took a deep breath, surprised at the heaviness in the air. It had been nearly ninety today, normal for summer at the base of the Sierra Mountains, but the humidity was unusual. It had hung over the town for a week now, as if a storm was brewing somewhere out past the mountains, waiting to break. Or maybe that was just the thriller novel I'd finished last night getting to me.

The sky was still light, but the shadows were stretching toward my faded-blue pickup as I climbed into the driver's seat and started the engine, hoping it would start. When it coughed to life, vibrating my seat with its deep shudder, I sighed with relief.

I just needed it to last a few more years, at least until a pay raise and more savings gave me some breathing room to purchase a car. And even then, I'd rather buy back my horse Dad had sold off first.

Even though it had happened over a decade ago, just thinking about how I'd almost lost Titan was enough to make my chest contract. My friend Fallon and her billionaire family had stepped in to save the day, buying my horse and letting me treat him as if he were still mine. I was even more thankful for that gift than I'd been for the college scholarship they'd given me, and I was overwhelmingly and deeply grateful for the funds that had let me graduate debt-free.

My phone buzzed, a welcome interruption to the spiral into my troubled childhood that threatened to ensnare me. But when I saw it was Beckett calling, I almost didn't answer.

If I talked to him, I'd weaken. I'd head to Frank's like he wanted.

Except, Beckett rarely actually called—he was strictly a texting kind of guy—so what if something was wrong? What if he needed help?

I hit the accept button, confronting any request for me to show up head-on. "I'm not going. I'm dead on my feet."

Loud chanting greeted me on the other end. "Maisey. Maisey. Maisey."

Deep voices mingled in with a few female ones, and my cozy night at home all but disappeared. If all my friends were all at the bar, asking me to come, I'd never be able to say no.

"That's low, Beckett, even for you."

He laughed. A slow, deep rumble that I felt all the way down to the pit of my stomach. Dangerously delightful. Dangerously off-limits.

"Fallon and Andie are attempting to pull off a trivia win.

They need you, darlin'," Beckett taunted. "You don't show up, and you'll be the sole reason the Femme Fatales lose tonight."

On the other end, I heard Fallon demand, "Let me talk to her," and two seconds later, she came on the line, pleading. "We're down twenty, Maise. *Twenty*. And I've got something big riding on this with Parker."

I couldn't help the chuckle that escaped. "Stop betting sexual favors with your husband, and then you won't have to worry about winning or losing."

Her voice turned quiet and muffled, as if she was using her hand to cover her mouth so the others wouldn't hear. "It's not sex. Well… Not sex, per se. This is a *very important* bet. You remember what I talked to you about the other day?"

She'd been talking about having another baby. Her little girl, Lila, was just over two years old now, and Fallon had gotten it in her head it was the perfect time to start trying for baby number three. This time, one she and Parker created together, rather than one they'd adopted or the one she'd had with the loser who'd knocked her up.

I sighed. "I need to go home and change. I'm still in my scrubs."

"No one here cares what you're wearing."

But I cared. I'd lived too many years of my life feeling like the ugliest person in the room not to at least try to look good before heading into a bar full of beautiful people.

"If you want me to come, then you need to give me a few minutes to clean up."

Fallon let out an exasperated sigh. "Fifteen minutes, Maise! I need you." The phone shuffled, and from somewhere in the distance came her muffled shout, "Intermission! Andie and I are waiting on our relief pitcher!"

There was a mix of cheers and groans on the other side of the phone.

Then, Beckett's voice was back in my ear, tantalizing me. "I'm wounded, Maise. Wounded. Not only are you showing up because Fallon needs you, when you wouldn't show up because I did, but now you'll be playing for the wrong team."

"It'll do your ego some good to be knocked down a peg or two."

"You have to beat us first."

"We will."

"I like your confidence." I could hear the amusement in his voice before it dipped low. "Care to place a bet?"

My heart skittered, stomach swooshing, but I was glad my voice didn't reflect it. "Nope. You know I don't bet."

"Someday, darlin', that'll change."

"Today isn't that day."

He laughed, told me to hurry, and then hung up.

Twenty minutes later, I was back downtown, feeling just as tired as before but at least a little more put together. I'd slipped into a yellow summer dress to combat the sticky humidity, touched up my makeup, and pulled my hair half-up in a messy, beachy twist.

It was nearing eight o'clock, but Main Street was still humming with the kind of easy energy that made evenings here feel like they stretched a little longer than anywhere else. Cars edged the curbs where the shops and restaurants kept their doors propped open late, hoping to catch the last of the tourists drifting by.

Swift Rivers, built during the old Gold Rush days, still proudly wore its forty-niner heritage, with weathered wood siding, hitching post–style parking meters, and wrought-iron lampposts dangling baskets of bright blooms. Framed by snow-capped peaks, the whole town looked like it had been lifted straight from a movie set. And when night fell and the neon signs flickered on, they washed the Old Western streets in a kaleidoscope of color that felt part Nashville honky-tonk and part vaudeville magic.

When I was a kid, Swift Rivers had been like so many fading small towns, its storefronts emptying out as families traded mom-and-pop shops for box stores and theme parks. But then Fallon's family transformed their ranch into a five-star resort, drawing the wealthy at first, and then the everyday vacationers. Now the place thrived through every season—

skiers carving paths through the snow in the winter, hikers and rafters chasing sunlight in the summer.

I slowed for a laughing group of twentysomethings wandering across the street before turning into the Emporium lot. Part souvenir shop, part grocery, part pharmacy, it was Swift Rivers's own homespun version of a box store. It had something for everyone, just like the town itself.

I locked my truck and joined the throng crossing Main to the bar. Music and people spilled out of Frank's, stalling my feet as doubts winged back in. I wasn't sure I had the energy required to put on my happy face and keep it there tonight.

But before I could retreat, a man emerged from the bar, and my feet automatically unlocked, moving toward him as if they had a mind of their own. I swore I could be lost in a sea of people, and my body would still gravitate to Beckett. It had been that way from the moment we'd met at six and eight years old.

Beckett studied me as I crossed the street, his look strolling down my body and back to my face, causing my heart to stop for several long seconds before restarting with a bang. A smile lifted the corners of his mouth, showcasing the dimple on one side and turning him from one of the most handsome people I knew to the kind of handsome the world idolized.

He rubbed a hand down his sharply angled jaw while his chocolate eyes twinkled at me.

"You look like a sunflower," he said, his smile growing with each syllable.

I fought the old tick that insisted I draw my hair over my face whenever I was under scrutiny and tried not to blush at his compliment.

"How much have you had to drink tonight, Captain Romero?" I asked.

He chuckled, and if it had made my stomach flip over the phone, up close and personal, the vibration traveled through me like a lit fuse. All it would take was a simple touch, and I'd go off like a firecracker.

"Not nearly enough, Nurse Maisey. I think you should prescribe me at least two more rounds."

I tried not to cringe at the name. Nurse Maisey sounded like a bad cartoon. Or like I was about to go all Nurse Ratched and lobotomize someone for standing up to me. While it was better than being called Corny the Deformed Corncob, it was a far cry from my favorite nickname—one I'd never admit to another living soul I still craved hearing.

Our shoulders brushed as we turned toward the bar, and I ignored the spark that came with the simple touch. I deserved a medal for all the years I'd pushed those feelings aside.

"So, who is it you need protection from tonight?" I asked. "Any of the repeat offenders?"

Growing up in a small town had its distinct advantages and disadvantages. Having only a limited pool of single people near our age was one of the downsides. Beckett had already blown through the majority of the local females, resorting these days to tangling with the tourists. His preferred M.O. was one night and one night only, and not just because he was a typical guy in his twenties who wasn't ready to settle down. Beckett had scars from his childhood that made him determined to remain single for the rest of his life.

"Delilah is here," he said with a frown. "But she's been distracted by some hot influencer who is filming by the pool tables."

If I hadn't also struggled with keeping my feelings for Beckett at bay, I'd wonder why Delilah hadn't given up hope of snagging him after nearly a dozen years of his denying her. But if she was focused on someone else tonight, it meant I wouldn't have to play middleman while she flirted with Beckett and simultaneously ignored I existed.

Stepping into the bar, the noise and smells slammed into me, and my feet stalled once more. As if sensing my reluctance, Beckett snickered. His hand went to my elbow, preventing me from retreating, instead guiding me farther inside. My skin lit up from my elbow to my shoulder all over again. The heat spread through my chest, landing dead center in my heart. I wanted to hate it. Just like I wanted to hate my weakness for this man, but I couldn't. The warmth was too enticing to hate.

"No backing out now, my Maisey-girl. Work is done and

playtime has arrived."

And his nickname, the *my* before it, did exactly what it had always done—had me secretly longing for my own playtime with him. Solo time in the dark with just our bodies twined, even if I knew it would likely end in the same humiliation as our ill-fated, tween kiss had. I wanted a happily ever after with someone, and Beckett wanted nothing to do with love and marriage.

It meant Beckett and I would forever be friends with absolutely zero benefits.

Chapter Two
Beckett

MAN DOWN
Performed by Kelsey Hart

ELEVEN YEARS AGO

HIM: How about Island of Doctor Moreau?

> *HER: Yuck. No. I need something lighter.*

HIM: I've suggested a dozen books. You're up to bat.

> *HER: You don't want to read what I do these days.*

HIM: I absolutely can't read porn with you, Maise.

> *HER: Romance books aren't porn.*

HIM: So why do you hide them from your dad?

> *HER: Because he turned purple when he saw the cover of my last one. I'm saving him from having a heart attack.*

HIM: How about a bet? If you can show the romance book to your dad without blushing, I'll read it with you.

> *HER: I don't bet.*

HIM: Bawk. Bawk. Bawk.

PRESENT DAY

I shouldered and elbowed a path through the Saturday night throng, propelling Maisey with me before she could back out. The throng of people meant she was practically pressed up against me, and the scent of her washed over me. She smelled light and airy, as always, like the water lilies on the pond near our childhood homes. A smell I would forever associate with comfort. With home and acceptance and friendship.

Next to Maisey was where I always felt settled. At peace.

The two of us were more than friends and neighbors who'd seen each other through tough times. We were all but family.

And tonight, my job as her family was to ensure she let loose and had some fun that didn't involve a book. She wasn't escaping Frank's without a few drinks and some laughter.

While the rest of Swift Rivers had traded its rough edges for a bit of shine, Frank's had stayed true to its roots as a hometown dive, where everyone knew each other and nobody minded the scuffs on the floor. The river-rock walls and oak-beamed ceiling carried the weight of a thousand stories, and the hand-carved chairs and nicked-up tables had seen generations of laughter, spilled drinks, and long nights. Aside from the modern touches—some updated wiring, a tin-tile backsplash that caught the light, and a few TVs humming in the corners—Frank's was still the heart of the town's nightlife.

"I come delivering your pinch hitter, ladies," I said to her friends as we made it to the cowhide-covered stools we'd commandeered at the back of the bar.

Fallon rose and hugged her friend.

The two women were as different as night and day. With a vivacious attitude and flashing hazel eyes, Fallon was a striking blonde who commanded a room just by walking into it. She was a lightning bolt, while Maisey was the rolling thunder that accompanied it. Maisey's brown-haired beauty snuck up on you, slowly surrounding you and lingering in ways that a sudden burst of light never could.

The women had been friends for as long as I'd known Maisey, helping each other through traumas that teenagers and young adults should never have to go through. Or at least helping each other as much as two independent people would allow anyone to help them.

"We had a bet, Wife, and you're altering the terms with this last-minute team change," Parker said, eyeing Fallon with a smirk. Even though he was retired, the dark-haired former Navy SEAL—with his broad shoulders and calm disposition—still had a look that screamed special forces. Sweeney, his mammoth-sized business partner sitting a couple of stools down, had the same unmistakable vibe.

Fallon stuck her tongue out at her husband. "You're just afraid I'll win."

"Let them bring in Maisey. The sweet little thing only adds to the challenge," Sweeney said, winking at the woman standing next to me and patting the empty stool on his far side. "I call dibs on her sitting next to me. It's been far too long since her sunshiny light has graced me with its beautiful presence."

It was far from the first time the black-haired, dark-skinned Hulk had flirted with Maisey in my presence. I swore, he almost made a game of it, each time hoping it would be the time she took a bite, so I wasn't sure why his words brought a bad taste to my mouth tonight.

I glanced down at Maisey to see a blush coating her cheeks. Her yellow sundress was glimmering around her like sunrays, and the ethereal glow turned her into exactly the magnificent, avenging angel I'd always considered her to be. Strong and brave and ready to champion others. Like a fierce blow to the chest, it hit me just how right Sweeney was. She was one of the most stunning women I'd ever met, more so because her beauty radiated from the inside out.

"She's fine right here," I growled, practically shoving her onto a stool next to the one I'd been sitting on all night.

"I guess I can't really complain about the change in players," Parker said with a heated look directed at his wife. "Either way the cards fall, I'll still be the luckiest man here tonight."

Sweeney choked on his beer, and the woman sitting between him and Parker laughed.

Fallon's hotel manager, Andie, was always a bit too

buttoned up for my taste—too tailored, too precise, too everything. Her deep-copper hair was always twisted into a tidy bun, and she clung to business attire like it was armor. Even on a Saturday night, she'd shown up in tailored gray pants and a sky-blue silk blouse, both so crisp they looked fresh from the dry-cleaning bag. Yet somehow, that prim-and-polished image had the men under my command lining up to ask her out. As far as I knew, she hadn't said yes to any of them, or anyone else, since she'd moved to Rivers.

"What can I get you, Maise?" I asked as Dee, the bartender, headed in our direction.

"Just iced tea, please."

"No. Absolutely not," I said, shaking my head. "You just worked an obscene number of days in a row. You need to blow off some steam."

"I might have to go in tomorrow, so I need a clear head."

Irritation with Meredith filled me. After three years, she still had Maisey rotating around departments, covering all the empty holes and gaps. But the one time I'd told Maisey she was being taken advantage of again, she'd bit my head off and told me to mind my own business.

Truth was, Maisey was perfectly capable of fighting for herself. I'd seen her do it, but it would take being trampled nearly to death before she'd take the stand. It was her nature to help first. To make everyone else's lives easier, regardless of what it did to her own.

"You need at least one shot to even the odds," I insisted, waving a hand between her and the group. "We've all had a couple. Your clear mind would give you an unfair advantage."

Maisey tugged at a tendril of hair.

I didn't wait for her to argue more. I simply ordered the group a round of tequila shots that Dee delivered with lime and salt. When Maisey's tongue darted out to lick her hand before tossing back the shot, heat hit my gut, and visions of pulling her to me and replacing her tongue with my own filled me.

And that was just all sorts of wrong. I didn't think of Maisey that way. Not ever.

It had to be the alcohol making me see and think things I shouldn't. The alcohol and the long-assed time it had been since I'd had sex.

One thing was certain—kissing Maisey was *not* in the cards.

She was my best friend and nothing more. I wouldn't sacrifice what we had for a night of pleasure that wouldn't last beyond a few hours. I wouldn't risk Maisey for anything. She was one of the best things in my life, just as she was.

When the trivia game resumed, I was grateful to replace tormenting thoughts of kissing my friend with smack talk, as the three of us testosterone-driven men battled it out with the three whip-smart women. We'd purposefully broken up the seating in guy-girl order so that we couldn't share answers with our teammates. It left me with Fallon on one side, Maisey on the other, and an empty stool beside her.

As the night progressed, that empty seat became my nemesis. Several of the firefighters in my crew and a handful of other single men in town stopped by, using the stool as a perch to do their flirting with the women. One scowl from Parker had the guys leaving Fallon alone. And sandwiched as she was between two He-men and with her rejection-prone reputation following her, Andie only received a few shallowly placed offers, which left Maisey open to the remainder of the shots.

Our newest recruit, Leon, was one of the first, stammering out, "H-hey, Maisey. You sure look pretty tonight."

The bad taste I'd had with Sweeney complimenting Maisey returned. I was about to give him a huge setdown and send him on his way, but all it took was one quiet, "Thanks, you look good tonight too, Leon," from Maisey to send him running for the back with his pale skin turning the same color as his carrot-red hair.

It was Tejas who caused the most problems as he slid up to the bar to order a drink.

My second-in-command was dark-haired, tan-skinned, and had a reputation as the most charming firefighter at the station. He had a wide mouth that never shut up, earning him the Motor-mouth nickname with the crew, but he was also famous for popping out smooth lines that had women dropping their panties right into his hand.

"Maisey, it's been far too long since you've been out," Tejas said, leaning into her space.

Maisey didn't notice. She was more focused on the trivia question on the screen above the bar than on Tejas as she responded. "I've been working extra shifts, covering for staff brought down by that summer cold winging through town."

"Sounds like you're long overdue for a good time," he said, voice dropping low. "I know how to deliver a good time."

I envisioned pushing him off his stool and barely stopped myself before biting out, "Back off, Motor-mouth. Maisey is here to spend time with friends, not get laid."

She inhaled sharply and shot me a glare. "Since when is it your job to decide who ends up in my bed?"

Tejas chuckled, and my stomach turned to pure acid. "Trust me, Maise, you don't want Tejas anywhere near you. You know that saying about an ego writing checks a dick can't cash? That's him."

"That isn't the quote at all, Captain, and I've never had one complaint lodged against my dick or my ego." Tejas looked over Maisey's head at me with a raised brow. "You offering Maisey an alternative?"

Maisey choked and turned a delightful shade of red that made me want to chase the color with fingers and tongue— What the actual fuck?

What was wrong with me tonight?

There'd been a brief period, after Maisey's mom had died and before I'd graduated high school, where my teen hormones had tempted me to make something more of our friendship. But that had been a temporary pubescent insanity that had lasted no more than a handful of months, ending abruptly after the one horrible night that had solidified every belief I'd ever had about myself and relationships.

Maisey was my friend.

An attractive, sweet, caring friend.

I wouldn't ruin twenty years of friendship to appease my

dick for a single night.

When neither Maisey nor I responded, Tejas's smile grew wider. He leaned in, tucking a strand of her hair behind her ear, and the intimacy of the move made me long to punch him in the face.

"If Romeo won't man up tonight, Maisey, just remember, my door and my bed are always open to you."

"Get out of here before I fire your ass," I snapped.

Tejas's expression grew smug and knowing as he picked up the pint Dee had slid in front of him and sauntered away.

"You're taking the protective-best-friend gig too far tonight, Fireball. I can field my own offers," she said.

"You want forever after, darlin', and he isn't someone who'll give it to you. He's got years before he settles down."

I softly rubbed her arm, in way of apology for overstepping, and watched with sick delight as her skin pebbled. The goosebumps were completely at odds with the heat of the room, and the reason for it—the attraction it insinuated—landed yet another fierce blow to my chest. Sharp and fast and brutal.

"Sometimes, while waiting for forever after to finally show up, a woman deserves a fast, fiery moment of passion to tide her over." Her eyes met mine, and the fire I saw there tore right through me, all the way down to my overactive libido.

I hadn't seen that look in a long time. Definitely not since she'd come back to Swift Rivers.

The Maisey who'd returned home wore a bit of a mask, giving me a blank face more often than she showed her cards. She'd earned more scars while away at college, internal ones instead of the almost invisible one that lingered on her jawline, so I hadn't taken it personally. But I'd also be kidding if I said I didn't miss the Maisey who'd once worn her heart on her sleeve.

I tore my gaze from her heated one and ordered more drinks for the group.

I needed to cool off, to cool us both off and put aside this unwelcome barrage of thoughts and feelings.

While I didn't want to think about Maisey sleeping with

anyone, it was obvious I needed to get laid—and soon. In an effort to clean up my player image with the town's bigwigs before it prevented me from getting my next promotion, I'd abstained for too long. That was the problem tonight. It had nothing to do with my friend and everything to do with my dick begging for action.

As the trivia round ended, Maisey slid off her barstool and headed for the restroom.

I kept an eye glued to the hallway she'd disappeared through, waiting to ensure she made it back unmolested. But when she finally returned, my discomfort only grew as I watched Leon, Tejas, and even a couple of tourists try to make their move on her. Every time one of them scanned her body in that flirty dress or even smiled at her, the viselike grip on my gut ratcheted tighter.

By the time she made it back to us and Sweeney shot her another flirtatious tease, touching her shoulder as she went by him, I was ready to start a fight. To pound a few faces into the ground.

And I simply didn't understand it.

Protecting her wasn't anything new, but what I felt tonight, the uncontrollable anger at any man who even looked at her, was absolutely new. New and uncomfortable.

I needed to get the hell out of here.

When the trivia game ended an hour later, relief coasted over me, even with the men losing. I needed to walk Maisey home, have a long talk with my dick, and get my head on straight.

As Maisey leaned around me to whisper to Fallon, "You owe me. I get naming rights now," I got another whiff of that uniquely Maisey scent. The normal comfort I got from it was replaced with a different reaction. One I felt all the way down to my balls.

Before Fallon could reply, Parker stood, grabbed his wife off the stool, and tossed her over his shoulder.

"Time I pay my debt, Wife."

Fallon laughed, pounding him playfully on the ass.

"Have fun, you two," Sweeney bellowed as they made their way through the crowd to the door.

"And with that sickening display of love, I'm out," Andie said, gathering her belongings.

"I'll walk you to your car," Sweeney told her.

"I'll come with you," Maisey said. As she reached for her bag, the look of hope that crossed Sweeney's face had me grinding my teeth.

Two seconds ago, I was ready to duck and run, but now there was no way I was letting her walk out with him. I grabbed her wrist, stopping her.

"Nope. Not leaving yet, darlin'. You owe me one more drink."

She rolled her eyes. "I don't owe you anything."

"Fair is fair. I asked you to come out first, and you turned me down only to show up for Fallon. You owe me a drink to soothe my hurt feelings."

"As if that dead muscle in your chest could actually be wounded," she huffed.

Even though my heart did have a thick layer of scar tissue built up around it, I could tell she immediately felt sorry for saying it. She'd witnessed firsthand how that stupid muscle had received most of its scars. Still, I wasn't above using the guilt against her if it meant I could get her to stay, rather than walking out that door with a man who wanted nothing more than to take her to bed.

"You've hit me dead center several times tonight," I said. "I'm not sure my ego can stand it."

Seeing our debate was just getting started, Andie and Sweeney waved and made their way out of the bar before Maisey had even realized they'd left.

"Your ego could use a bit of trimming."

I waggled my brows, lowered my voice, and said, "I promise, there's nothing on me that needs trimming."

She flushed, her pale skin turning a fiery red in that delightful way that suddenly tempted me to chase it with fingers and tongue.

"It's always the ones who talk up their penises who are the biggest disappointment."

I leaned over the bar, grabbed one of the plastic swords Dee used for cocktails, and plunged it at my heart. Dee growled at me to get my hands off her supplies while Maisey laughed.

The delightful sound was still reverberating through the air when Delilah slid into the stool Fallon had vacated beside me. I barely bit back a groan.

Del's Saturday night outfit was the complete opposite of the business wear she wore during the week. The slouchy blue tank put her cleavage on display, tight black shorts barely covered the curve of her ass, and spiked cowboy boots added a few more inches to her height, putting her at nearly six feet. Her makeup was perfect, if a bit overdone for my taste, and her dark hair, dyed a deep mahogany, was teased and styled to accentuate her best feature—a pair of royal-blue eyes.

She was classically pretty, and once upon a time, I'd fallen for it. But I wasn't a thirteen-year-old boy with hormones raging any longer, regardless of the lack of self-control I'd had around Maisey tonight. Well over a decade had passed since I'd allowed myself to actually date Delilah, but the way she talked and acted, you'd think we'd just broken up last week.

I always handled her cautiously because I'd seen in brutal clarity what my rejection could do to her, which meant I was continually walking a fine line, keeping her at bay while trying not to wound her further.

"If you'd needed a third person for trivia, I would have happily played," Delilah said, a small pout forming over her heavily glossed lips. "You didn't need to pull Cornlette from her senior-citizen bedtime."

From the corner of my eye, I saw Maisey stiffen, and when I turned my head slightly, I watched all the lightness disappear from her.

"You know, funnily enough, Delilah," Maisey replied dryly, "most senior citizens sleep less than the average adult, which means midnight is pretty normal for them. You must have meant to say toddler bedtime. But then again, you were never known for your ability to land an insult."

My dick went semi-hard all over again. I loved it when Maisey defended herself. The rarity of it happening didn't make it any less powerful.

Delilah's mouth popped open before snapping shut again, and I had to fight back my laugh.

Maisey slid off the stool. "And with that, I really will call it a night."

I reached into my pocket, grabbed some cash, and threw it on the counter to cover our tab. I called after Maisey, "Hold on. I'll walk you home."

"I'm good. No need for you to leave."

As I started after her, Delilah put a hand on my arm, halting me. "Let her go. I have important news to share. News you've been waiting for."

"I'm not letting her walk home alone."

"What about me? Who's going to walk me home?"

My stomach clenched, and that line I balanced on warred with me. "I don't know, Del. Maybe your boyfriend."

"Carter isn't my boyfriend. You know that. We just use each other to scratch an itch now and then."

She paused, as if waiting for a reaction she'd never get from me. I couldn't care less who she scratched her itches with, as long as it wasn't me.

My eyes were still on Maisey, who was already at the door. I'd have to sprint to catch up with her, but there was no way I was letting her walk home alone in the dark with a few drinks in her and the tourists flooding the streets.

"Daddy is retiring." Delilah's words did precisely what she'd hoped, ripping my gaze away from Maisey to her.

"What? When?"

She smiled coyly. "Well, that is what I wanted to talk to you about." She patted the stool I'd vacated. "Come on. I'll buy you another shot."

For two seconds, indecision warred. Fire Chief Nattingly's decision to finally step down from his post after nearly four decades was breaking news. It proved at least one of the rumors circulating through the town about the city's leaders was true.

After decades of service, the chatter was that the chief, mayor, and sheriff might all be ready to pass the baton to the next generation.

I'd been chomping at the bit for this moment to become a reality. In my eight years with the Swift Rivers Fire Department, I'd earned my bachelor's and master's, aced every fire service exam I could, and packed my resume with experience. I'd put in extra hours with the county fire marshal and even used vacation time to train at the CAL FIRE schools. I'd done everything I could to prove I wasn't just hungry for the job, but that I was ready for it.

If it was true, if Nattingly was retiring, sitting next to Delilah might get me information I needed, but it would be at the cost of her thinking she'd gotten her hooks into me, and that wasn't something I could afford. I'd played that game once and lost. We'd both lost.

When I glanced toward the exit, Maisey had already disappeared. My need to protect her overcame any remaining temptation to stay with Del.

"I'll talk to you tomorrow," I said, starting for the door again.

"They're not going to hire you," she called after me, and her words halted me once more. "And I know why."

My chest tightened, the alcohol in my stomach turning sour. She would know. Not only because she still lived at home with her parents, but because she had an ear for gossip. An ear and a mouth that could spread news like a wildfire burning through dry brush.

I was also smart enough to know she was using this not just to get me to sit back down, but specifically to keep me from going after Maisey. Delilah's beef with the Campbell sisters would likely live until she took her last breath.

"I'm not up for your games tonight, Del. If you got news you feel like sharing, I'll hear about it tomorrow. Otherwise, I'll figure it out myself."

I didn't wait for her response. I just jogged through the crowd and onto the street, determined to catch Maisey before she wandered too far on her own.

Chapter Three
Maisey

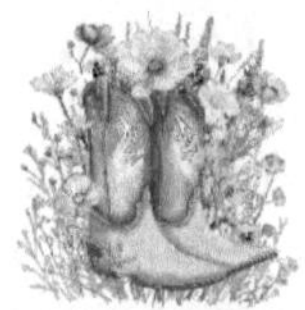

SECOND WIND
Performed by Kelly Clarkson

ELEVEN YEARS AGO

> *HER: She left me taking care of the chickens by myself...AGAIN. When I asked if she'd be back to collect the eggs, she just shrugged.*

HIM: You need to tell your mom she's been sneaking out and not coming home.

> *HER: Mom's been really preoccupied lately. I think she and Dad are having more than their usual troubles. And you know I can't tell on Chelsea. She barely talks to me anymore. If I got her in trouble now, it would be the end of our relationship.*

HIM: What relationship? The one where she uses your unjustified guilt to get what she wants?

Moments passed.

HIM: Don't be mad at me for telling you the truth. We agreed we'd always be honest with each other.

> *HER: We'll just have to agree to disagree when it comes to my sister.*

PRESENT DAY

I cursed the disappointment that welled through me as I made my way out of Frank's alone and stood staring across the street at the Emporium where my truck was parked. I wasn't really much of a drinker, and the couple I'd had tonight meant I was in no shape to drive. My apartment building was on the opposite side of town. I could walk it, but it was at least twenty minutes on foot, and I was even more exhausted now than I'd been before.

So instead of heading toward my apartment, I crossed the street, starting in the direction of the neighborhood behind the Emporium and my childhood home.

A voice rang out from the parking lot. "Hey, Maisey, hold up!"

I turned, trying not to wince as I saw the last person I'd expected jogging toward me. Carter Smythe had a finger hooked in the suit jacket he'd thrown over his shoulder. His shirt sleeves were rolled above his elbows, and his tie was loosened. These days, he was all slick businessman, the complete opposite of when I'd made the unfortunate mistake of going with him to the homecoming dance in high school. Back then, he'd been more of a blue-collar man in work boots and plaid shirts—at least that's what I'd thought of him whenever he'd been at our house, hanging out with Chelsea and her crew.

Since graduating, Carter had turned his family's construction business into a high-powered real estate development company. Smythe & Sons had a hand in almost every change happening in Swift Rivers, no matter the size, from the fancy new streetlights on Main Street to the entertainment complex being built just past my apartment.

He came to a halt a few inches from me, running a hand over his icy-blond hair and giving me a good look at the expensive watch slipping out from his shirt sleeve.

"You're just the person I wanted to talk to," he said.

Surprise shifted through me. Not once in the three years I'd been back in Swift Rivers had Carter looked me up. He hadn't even acknowledged me. Not at Frank's, not at Jack's, the town's favorite Italian restaurant, and not at the Emporium when we'd crossed paths shopping.

He chuckled. "I know. We haven't really gotten a chance to catch up, but I needed to talk to you about your dad's place."

Wariness eased in. "What about it?"

"I wanted to make sure he considered my offer before the bank got its hands on it."

The alcohol in my stomach turned nastily. "What do you mean, the bank?"

His brows lifted. "You didn't know? They're going to foreclose. He hasn't been making the payments."

I was spun right back to that horrible moment eleven years ago after Mom's death, when I'd been faced with losing the home I'd grown up in. Dad hadn't been paying any of the bills, hadn't even known what bills to pay because Mom had always handled their accounts. If it hadn't been for Beckett's dad stepping in to help me sort through it all, we would have lost everything.

But that had long since changed. Before I went away to college, I'd set everything up online so Dad didn't have to do much more than check that everything was going through. He'd been handling it just fine…

Or at least I'd thought he had been.

"I'm sorry you didn't know," Carter said, voice softening. "The bank won't give him what it's worth. You know they won't. But I have ideas for that entire section of town, and I can offer him top dollar."

"Maisey! Wait up!" From outside the bar, Beckett's voice rang out.

Emotions swelled in my chest—happiness as I watched Beckett jog across the street toward me mingled with worry about the bomb Carter had just dropped.

Carter glanced in Beckett's direction, and his lips formed a grim, straight line before he looked back at me. "I gotta go. But call me so I can explain what I have in mind."

He slipped me a business card and was already halfway across the parking lot before Beckett slid in beside me. He darted a frown in Carter's direction before turning a stunning smile on me. A smile that made me ache from my head all the way down to my toes.

Why did he have to be so handsome that it physically hurt?

"Heading to my place, I see," he teased, nudging my arm.

I scoffed, "As if."

He sobered. "Seriously, I'm glad you're not driving. I don't have any beds in the guest rooms yet, but you can have mine, and I'll take the couch."

After the city had changed its livestock ordinances, making it illegal for Kurt to keep his goat herd on their land, Beckett's dad had moved out to Fallon's ranch with them, and Beckett had taken over his childhood home. Since then, he'd slowly been remodeling it. So far, he'd gutted the kitchen, knocked down a few walls, and added a brand-new main suite that jutted out into the backyard. The work he'd done on the 1920s Craftsman had made Dad's matching one on the lot next door seem more pitiful than ever.

My stomach knotted. If Carter was telling the truth, Dad had done far more than ignore the maintenance on the house.

I swallowed over the lump that had formed in my throat and said, "Thanks, but I'll just stay at Dad's. He got back from a month-long job earlier this week, and I wanted to check in on him anyway."

Shoulder to shoulder, Beckett and I headed down the street into my old neighborhood, leaving the noise of Main Street behind. Crickets chirped, an owl hooted, and the rush of the river filled the air.

"What did dickhead want?" Beckett asked.

For a moment, I was tempted to tell him exactly what Carter had said, but then, I bit my cheek. If Dad had gotten himself into another financial mess, Beckett would want to help, just like Fallon would. But I wasn't relying on my friends again. I was incredibly grateful for all they'd done for me growing up, and I refused to take more from them. I wouldn't be my dad. I wouldn't be an adult who had to rely on others, or a teenage daughter, to hold my shit together.

"Nothing important," I answered with a shrug.

"You aren't thinking of dating that imbecile?" I knew better than to think the growl in his voice meant he was jealous. Beckett would never want to date me. He'd never want a long-term relationship with anyone. His mother, his dad's fiancée, and Delilah had all ensured it.

"And give Delilah even more reason to hate the Campbells? No." It went deeper than that. After what had happened in high school, I'd never give Carter another shot at my heart. Delilah could have him. Although, everyone in town knew she'd drop him in a hot minute if it meant Beckett decided to ante up.

As we reached the end of the cul-de-sac, the sights and sounds of our childhood greeted us. The houses closer to downtown sat on small suburban lots, but the last three, belonging to Beckett, Dad, and the Helmers, were large plots from when the town had first been founded. Each stretched over five acres, long and narrow, with the houses close together at the front, and the lots growing wider the farther back they went until they crossed the river and climbed into the hills.

As kids, Beckett and I had spent our mornings helping with farm chores before tearing off to roam the land like it was our kingdom. We'd played along the riverbank, cooled off in its rushing water every summer, and chased each other through the hills in endless games of hide-and-seek. After Beckett and his dad had built a treehouse in the live oak that stretched over the river, it had become our secret haven. We'd spent hours reading there, and once I'd finally been freed of my nightly facemask, we'd lain shoulder to shoulder, watching the stars bloom across the sky.

Some of my very best and very worst memories had happened on this street.

"I'm surprised you escaped the bar without blood being drawn," I said, shoving Beckett's shoulder with my hand.

"It was a near miss," he teased. "She nearly got a hook into me this time."

Shock flickered through me. "Really? I thought you were never playing in that sandbox again."

He made a disgusted noise. "Give me some credit, Maise. No, Del almost hooked me with news about her dad."

"What's up with the chief?"

"She says he's finally going to retire."

My feet ground to a halt. When I looked up at Beckett, the gossamer glow of the moonlight washed over his face, transforming him into a beautiful black-and-white drawing. A vampire hero. Dark and gorgeous. Mesmerizing. Hard to resist.

"That's awesome news. Congrats, Chief."

His smile turned triumphant.

"Stoney is going to put up a good fight for the job. He's got me beat, hands down, in the experience category."

"Stoney isn't a leader, Fireball. You and I both know it, and so does Chief Nattingly." His grin widened, exposing his dimple, and it turned him from vampire to superhero just like the one I'd nicknamed him for.

"The city council has to approve the candidate, and I'm not sure how many friends I have on it."

I tucked my arm in his, and we continued walking.

"Well, Fallon has friends, and we both know she'd rather see you as the fire chief than Stoney."

Like me, Fallon was only twenty-six years old, but her resort was the town's largest employer and most prominent donor. It meant she held considerable sway with the city leaders.

We finally reached the end of the court where our family homes stood almost shoulder to shoulder. The cement pathway from the street to my dad's steps was cracked and buckled from the roots of an overgrown oak tree. Clumps of dirt peeked out of grass that needed reseeding, the porch roof sagged slightly over the tapered columns, and one of the decorative shutters was hanging askew.

No sign remained of the perfectly maintained house Mom had taken so much pride in.

Next door, Beckett's house gleamed. He'd painted it a pretty forest green that complemented the dark-brown shutters and stone foundation. The front door was a beautiful cerulean color that highlighted the four stained-glass squares built into it. His porch was in perfect condition, just like his yard. He'd replaced the grass with eco-friendly plants, giving the yard an English-cottage vibe.

The difference between the two houses was heartbreaking.

"She'd hate this," I whispered before I could take it back.

I felt Beckett scouring my face for tears, but they were all locked up. I rarely cried over Mom anymore. I'd done enough crying the first summer she'd been gone that I'd foolishly thought it had drained me of tears forever. But life had proven me wrong, and Beckett had had a first-row seat to those times too.

"I'm almost wrapped up with the remodel on my place. I can start helping out here," Beckett offered.

"I'm not sure he has the money to do anything right now, but I'll talk to him."

I didn't have the guts to say he might not even own the house for long.

"Whose car is that?" Beckett asked, drawing my attention to the shiny red sports car parked across the street by the Helmer's mailbox. It was so new it didn't even have an official license plate yet.

I shrugged. "Probably holiday renters."

When Mrs. Helmer had passed not long after her husband, their kids had come home and cleared out anything of value before listing the house on an online vacation rental app. Then, they'd promptly returned to the lives they'd built elsewhere. Dad griped about the traffic on the street sometimes, but for the most part, the guests came and went without him even noticing.

I stepped backward toward the house, careful not to trip over the roots peeking through the sidewalk.

"Thanks for walking me home, Chief Fireball Romero."

"Don't jinx it," he huffed before adding, "Thanks for coming out tonight. I know you didn't want to, but it was good to see your face, my Maisey-girl. It's been too long."

I rolled my eyes at him. "You saw me on Wednesday at the Emporium."

Amusement lifted his lips once more. "Passing in the fruit aisle doesn't count."

It had been a long time since we'd really hung out one-on-one. But being with Beckett was always a double-edged sword—joy and pain. The truth was, it would be better if I spent even less time with him. Maybe then I'd actually get a date with someone who might make my dreams of a home and children come true.

I ached for a love and a permanence Beckett insisted didn't exist.

I gulped at the cool air and forced lightness into my voice as I said, "Night, Beckett."

"Night, Maise."

I turned around and didn't look back as I made my way up the porch steps, slid the key into the lock, and quietly opened the door. Once I'd shut it behind me, I leaned against it, only to be assaulted with memories of sneaking in just like this as a kid. Not from any rebellious teen adventures like Chelsea, but from reading books by flashlight with Beckett in his treehouse.

Surprisingly, it had been my sister who'd given me the hardest time when she'd caught me. She'd told me she couldn't protect me if I was stupid enough to continue to dog after Beckett. She reminded me that I'd always be the deformed little girl next door whom he took pity on and not someone he wanted to date.

And I'd known she was right. I'd heard him say it himself after that horrible attempt at a kiss when I'd been twelve. Ever since then, he'd simply treated me as a friend. Someone he shared his secrets with, but not a woman he wanted to devour and claim.

And that was exactly what I wanted—to be devoured and claimed in a way that left no question as to whom I belonged to—so I could claim someone right back with equal ferocity. Unfortunately, all my experiences with men had been with jerks who couldn't be bothered to keep me. Men who'd run just like Carter had after a failed makeout session in high school.

I pushed myself off the door and made my way through the living room, trying not to let the house's hollowness unravel me.

The neutral-colored, microfiber furniture, cream walls, and dark wood flooring were the same as they'd been before Mom had died, but the jewel-tone colors she'd splashed around the room had slowly dwindled over the years. The only remains of our happier days were the pictures piled in the dark wood built-ins. They showed my family stuck in a time before I'd turned fifteen, when Mom was still here. But even those bright images had faded now.

As I made my way to the kitchen that was stuck in time like the set of a canceled '90s sitcom, the absolute neglect I found hit me in the gut. It wasn't because of the chipped counters or cracked cabinets, but because of the stack of empty take-out containers and the smell coming from the sink full of dishes.

More guilt slammed into me. Dad had been home almost a week, and I hadn't been by to see him. If I had, I would have been able to help him keep up with some of it. He'd never been good at cooking or cleaning, but as my therapist would gladly have reminded me, I wasn't responsible for looking after an adult father. It should have been the other way around. He should have looked after his daughters when they needed him most.

Instead, after Mom's death, he'd done what he thought he had to do, which was get behind the steering wheel of his semitruck and drive. He'd loved us, but he'd thought providing for us monetarily was the best way to support us, when what we'd really needed was him. Chelsea and I had been mere teenagers, left alone to keep up with Mom's egg business, maintain the house, and hold everything together, while trying not to fall apart.

I shook my head. The alcohol and the memories my childhood home always brought back weren't a good combination. I'd wash up, fall into bed, check on Dad in the morning, and then head out to the ranch to train with Titan. I'd use the fresh air and exercise to shake the haze of regrets and memories trying to stick to me like the humid air was clinging to our town.

Chapter Four
Beckett

LEGENDARY
Performed by Bon Jovi with James Bay

FIVE YEARS AGO

HIM: Bow down to King of the Pranks.

> *HER: Your ego has no limit. Who was on the losing end of your latest hijinks?*

HIM: Just so you don't think I have no heart, this was revenge. Stoney got me first, with the whole clear-plastic-wrap-on-the-toilet-seat prank. So, technically, he started it.

> *HER: And what did you do?*

HIM: Ground up chocolate stool softener and put it in his latte.

> *HER: *** barf face emoji *** That's just gross…and mean.*

HIM: The only person I feel bad for is Mrs. Stone. I didn't realize they were going out on a date last night.

> *HER: That's awful!*

HIM: She made him swear on Saint Florian that he was done with the pranks…hence me winning the final round and the crown.

> *HER: Someday, someone is going to take it from you.*

HIM: How much you want to bet I keep it?
HER: You know I don't bet.

PRESENT DAY

It felt like I'd barely closed my eyes when Vader pounced on my chest and licked my face. This would have been fine if he weren't a sixty-five-pound, black Labrador and greyhound mix with the friendliness and muscle of the former and the litheness and speed of the latter.

"No. Just no," I growled.

He whined, lying down full length on my body and covering a good portion of my six-foot, four-inch height. When I pushed him off and threw an arm over my face, he used his nose to nuzzle under it and slobber all over my cheeks.

"Is this payback for leaving you on the porch while I went to the bar?" I groused.

His yip was an impassioned yes if I ever heard one.

I rolled out of bed, hissing when I landed on the heel of a cowboy boot I'd lazily yanked off before falling on the mattress last night. That's what I got for not putting things away properly. As a firefighter, I knew better.

But I'd been distracted last night with unexpected thoughts of Maisey in that sinful summer dress awash in the moonlight. Those images had followed me into my room, forced me to take myself in hand to ease the tension, and left me feeling guilty. Maise deserved better than some asshole jacking off to thoughts of her. She deserved romance and rose petals and lingering kisses that drew out her pleasure until it crested like a tidal wave.

And shit, I was hard all over again just thinking about it.

I needed to lose these unwelcome thoughts about my best friend before they turned into something that would ruin our friendship.

As I picked up my carelessly discarded clothes, Vader decided it was time to play, instigating a game of tug-of-war with my socks. I ended up spending a good ten minutes chasing him around the house before I could slide into my workout clothes and grab my go-bag for the next four days.

"I get it. I get it. You need exercise. Well, so do I," I told the mutt as I looked down into his big golden eyes. "Let's go to the station. You can take a run in the hills and zap out your energy while I hit the weights and pound away this stupid craving."

Vader barked, and I swore it was in agreement again.

Heading to the station early also meant I might be lucky enough to catch Chief Nattingly before the shift change. I'd weasel the truth out of him so I wouldn't have to rely on his daughter for the news.

If I'd taken a job in a big-city fire department, it would've taken another decade before I would've been considered for a fire chief position—just like it would've taken longer for me to promote to captain. But that was part of the reason I'd chosen to work in Swift Rivers, even though it meant a lower salary. Here, I'd had the chance to prove myself, and I had. My crew's record spoke for itself.

But stepping into the chief's role would be a whole different challenge than getting my captain's bugles. Nattingly deciding to retire now wouldn't exactly help my cause. If he'd waited a few more years, I would've been in my thirties, which would've sounded a lot more reassuring to the city council than turning the department over to a twenty-eight-year-old known around town for his player ways, which was exactly why I'd curbed my extracurricular activities in the last year.

I just had to hope it had been soon enough.

Locking up the house, Vader and I jogged over to my SUV. I opened the back passenger door for him and hooked him to the seat belt before sliding into the driver's seat. In my peripheral vision, I caught a glimpse of movement in a window next door. The curtain in Chelsea's old bedroom fluttered down as if someone had dropped it, just like when Chelsea used to spy on Maisey and me as kids.

Just thinking about Chelsea was enough to make a man's balls curl up. That woman was cold, hard, and brutal. She used people and tossed them aside like they were disposable cups.

Maisey had never been able to see the full extent of her sister's viciousness because of the unnecessary guilt she held on to from their childhood. Then again, I wasn't exactly the poster kid for resolved childhood traumas. I was just glad Chelsea wasn't around anymore to continue to pick at Maisey's conscience and self-worth.

I backed out of my drive and headed down the street just as my phone rang.

"Morning," I greeted.

As early risers growing up, Dad and I had spent many a predawn moment in the kitchen, talking about our plans for the day over breakfast. It had been a comforting routine we'd continued all the way through my adulthood, but once he'd moved permanently to the Harrington Ranch with the goats, we'd had to exchange our in-person talks for phone calls.

"You on your way to the station?" Dad asked, his twang coasting over me like a warm blanket.

Spending the last twenty years in California hadn't beaten the drawl out of him. Even though I'd only spent the first eight years of my life in the South, I'd held on to bits of it too, and it was always more prominent when I talked to my dad.

"Yep," I answered. "Going to hit the gym before shift change. What's on your schedule today?"

"Castrating cows."

My stomach turned. As a kid, I'd been happy to do every chore at Dad's side, even this ugly one. I'd wanted nothing more than to be just like him, but the fire in Alabama had changed everything. And once a firefighter had saved my life, all I'd wanted to do was pay it forward by saving others.

"Castrating cows, huh? So, you had a hearty breakfast of sausage and eggs over easy," I teased and was rewarded with a choking sound from Dad.

"Bastard. How'd I raise such a bastard?"

I chuckled, imagining Dad's bushy eyebrows furrowing together as he tipped his cowboy hat back and angled his leathery face toward the morning sunshine.

"Just for that, I'm tempted to *not* tell you the rumor I heard," Dad taunted.

"You can't keep a secret to save your life, old man."

"Now that's just a flat-out lie. I know how to hold my tongue when it's needed. I'm just smart enough to know when to let it wag too."

A smile stretched across my face, but I felt a tug deep inside. I missed him.

"We need to get together soon. It's been too long."

"Now that's what a father really wants to hear. Guess you've earned that rumor after all," he said. "Mumblings around town are that Nattingly is turning in his fire hat for good."

The same mix of excitement and anticipation I'd felt when Del had mentioned it last night returned. "I might've heard something similar. Think it's true?"

"Don't know the man well, but when people get to be my age, we start thinking about how to get up and spend more time lounging in the sun than breaking our backs sweating in it."

"Are you talking about yourself now, old man? What would you do if you hung up your cowboy hat? Sleep in a hammock all day?" When I didn't get the immediate laugh I'd been expecting, I continued, "Really, Dad? You considering retirement?"

"I'm sixty-five, Beckett. This work is hard on these brittle bones. I've been thinking about doing some traveling before I can't carry my own bag."

My throat clogged, partly at the thought of Kurt Romero struggling to pick up anything and partly at the idea of his wanting to travel. It had been one of the main breaking points in his relationship with Liza.

What am I supposed to do, Liza? Drag Beckett away from the friends and family we've made here so we can trot around the globe after you? For how long? Years? I can't do that. Not when my son has finally found his feet after that crap Camila pulled.

Dad never knew that I'd heard their argument before she'd

left. I hated knowing I was partially responsible for the demise of their relationship.

I cleared the lump that had formed in my throat and said, "You make a list of the places you want to go, and we'll hit them up together during our vacations."

"If you get the fire chief position, you aren't going on vacation for another twenty years," he scoffed.

It soured my anticipation for the job just a hair. Taking it would absolutely mean I had less time for Dad and friends like Maisey.

When I didn't say anything, Dad's voice got serious. "You know how I'd really like to spend my retirement years, Beck?"

"Getting laid on a beach in Maui?"

He snorted. "I'd like to play with my grandkids the way Teddy gets to play with his. Never thought I'd be jealous of the man, but there it is."

Surprise shifted through me as I pulled into the parking lot behind the station. Dad had never pressured me to find love, get married, and have kids. Never even hinted that he hoped to have grandbabies.

"Dad—"

"No, no. Don't say anything. I'm sorry I even let it slip. Truth is, Fallon and Parker treat me like family. Their babies are all but mine in name. You live the life you want, Beck. The only people you ever need to answer to are God and yourself."

After everything we'd been through, all the losses, I couldn't rely on faith the way my father still did, just like I didn't believe in past lives or soulmates like Maisey. People weren't fated to *be* anything or to *be with* anyone. Screw ordained destiny if it meant having people tear your heart out by abandoning you.

Because my mood had turned decidedly for the worse, and I didn't want him to know it, I signed off. "I love you, old man."

"Love you too, son. Go get that job you want, make it yours, and kick some fire ass. Just be safe doing it."

"Will do. You watch the hooves directed at your balls today. I don't want to have to send *you* to get castrated."

He was still chuckling as we hung up.

I parked, grabbed my bag, and opened the back door to unhook Vader. As soon as he leaped out of the SUV, he sprinted for the hills behind the station.

"Stay out of the skunk den!" I hollered after him, striding toward the back door.

Usually, talking with Dad had me starting my day on a good note. Today, it had rattled me in multiple ways. I felt unsettled as I jogged up the back stairs.

The old firehouse had been fully renovated just before I was hired, bringing the building into this century while holding on to its earlier roots. The first-floor equipment had been upgraded, with a full gym and showers being added, and the second-floor living quarters had been completely refreshed in a way that perfectly blended the work we did with the family we'd created here.

Upstairs, most of the budget had gone into the great room, where the kitchen had been modernized and the living area outfitted with a solid gaming and entertainment setup. The designer had kept as much of the original brick and stone as possible, pairing it with modern tones of steel and granite. The little money that had remained had been used to put a fresh coat of paint on the bedroom walls and wax the wood floors in the two offices at the back.

The chief took one of those offices, leaving Mike Stone and me, the shift captains, to share the other, which was where I headed first, flinging my bag onto the leather chair behind my desk. I'd just reached for the stack of messages waiting for me when Nattingly's voice drifted in from the open doorway across the hall.

"We'll post the job on the state and national fire service websites, and by the end of the month, we'll have more applicants than we know what to do with."

A pause.

"No, no. I'm sure. Stoney doesn't have the educational requirements, and Romero isn't settled down enough yet. Give him another five years, add a wife and a family to his list of qualifications, and he'd be the perfect candidate. But I can't wait any longer. Rose and I have given enough to this town. We need to start checking things off our bucket list while we still can."

My stomach bottomed out, not only because the conversation sounded so much like the one I'd just had with my father, but because of the chief's words about me.

I wasn't in the running for the job. They weren't even going to consider me. They were planning on hiring externally because they'd sized me up and found me wanting.

Not because I lacked the education or experience, but because I was missing a fucking wife?

Fury welled.

An old and familiar smoke filled my lungs, stealing my breath.

What in the hell did a wife have to do with being able to run this department?

Absolutely nothing.

Especially a wife who would only end up leaving. A wife who wouldn't stick when things got tough but would take off to follow her own dreams at your and your son's expense. A wife who nearly murdered your son by setting fire to your home for the insurance money. And then, when it couldn't be proven she'd done just that, she took you for half of everything you owned in the divorce, including the small farm that had been in your family for three generations.

That's what a wife had done to my dad, what a mother had done to me.

I coughed, trying to clear ash and fumes that were nothing more than residues of childhood trauma.

Dad had barely recovered, barely found what he thought was love again, when Liza had torn out our hearts all over by giving up her life in Swift Rivers to build schools in Bolivia. She'd chosen hundreds of kids over me. Over Dad.

Our story wasn't the only example of marriages and relationships that ripped apart more than they healed. Maisey's mom had died, and her dad had failed to pick up the pieces for her and her sister. Fallon's parents had all but abandoned her until murder had pulled them together. Hell, even Nattingly's marriage had almost come apart at the seams when he'd been caught one too many times with his pants down in someone else's bedroom.

Who the fuck was *he* to tell *me* I couldn't do the job because I didn't have a woman with my ring on her finger standing next to me?

Screw. That.

I almost stormed into his office and spewed those angry words. Almost threw my shield on his desk and told him to find another stupid guinea pig to twirl in a cage. I'd find another department. Another place to get the job I wanted.

But just the thought made that bile in my stomach roil. Starting over somewhere else meant being back at the bottom of the seniority ladder. Meant I'd be the last considered for an internal promotion rather than the first. It meant leaving the town I'd grown to love and my dad.

It meant leaving Maisey.

Just thinking her name had my mind coming to a full stop. Had a crazy-ass idea leaping into my head. One that caused every breath to leave my body once more.

It was an impossible, stupid, fraught-with-pitfalls idea I knew I'd regret.

That might end up costing me the one friend who'd never abandoned me.

But did I have another option?

Delilah would happily offer herself up as a "sacrifice." But the thought of giving Delilah what she'd always wanted, of potentially ending up repeating that horrific night from our teen years, was enough to make me want to hurl up the breakfast I hadn't eaten.

But Maisey… Waking up with her in my house? That wasn't at all vomit-inducing.

But it would end badly, just like every relationship did. And who would I turn to when it did? Who would Maisey turn to? She had Fallon. She had other friends. But me? I had a crew I'd separated myself from to be a leader, a father who was talking about retiring, and Maisey.

No. I couldn't ask Maisey to do something stupid like this with me.

No way, no how.

Which just meant, if I stayed, I'd have to suck it up and report to some external hotshot they hired.

Unless I could somehow convince them I didn't need a wife on my arm to run this station—and run it better than Nattingly had been doing in the last few years.

But damned if I could think of how to accomplish it.

Chapter Five
Maisey

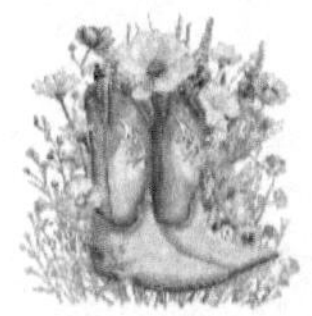

MONSTERS
Performed by Ella Langley

THREE YEARS AGO

HIM: You're home!

> *HER: Yep!*

HIM: I got promoted, and you finally got a job in town. This calls for a celebration.

> *HER: You got your captain bugles?! Why didn't you tell me?*

HIM: I'm telling you now. Meet me at Frank's. Stat.

> *HER: I'll be there in an hour. I need to clean up, and I'm at the good part of my book where the hero is making a grand gesture to win the heroine back after his stupid mistake.*

HIM: I'll happily give you a grand gesture. You just gotta come get it.

> *HER: *** puke emoji *** How is it possible for you to turn every single sentence into a sexual innuendo?*

HIM: Practice. Years of practice.

HIM: But seriously, put the book down now, or I'll show up on your doorstep and drag you out of the house.

> *HER: You'd have to find me first. I got my own place.*

> *HIM: Maisey, this is Swift Rivers. It'll take me two minutes to find you. Get your ass down here.*

PRESENT DAY

I wasn't sure exactly what had woken me because when my eyes dragged open, the house was still silent. No sounds drifted through the wall my room shared with the kitchen, which meant Dad wasn't awake and fumbling with the coffeepot.

Even with Mom having been gone for eleven years now, he still hadn't quite gotten the hang of making his own coffee. She used to make it for him, just like she'd filled his thermos and cooler, so he'd have as much homemade food as possible before he started eating at fast food chains and diners on his long-haul jobs.

The sun was drifting weakly through the old fabric blinds Mom had made, casting my childhood room in early morning shadows. The dresser and shelves were full of old knick-knacks and trophies from my riding days, and the closet held a barrage of out-of-fashion clothes. I needed to clean it all out. Dad had refused to get rid of most of Mom's things, but I could stop hanging on to objects from a childhood that had been mixed with joy and pain.

The great purge would have to wait for now. At the moment, I needed to shower away the haze of a night spent tossing and turning, so I could tackle the most critical tasks. I needed to set the kitchen to rights, order Dad some groceries, and get to the bottom of Carter's accusation all before I headed out to the ranch for a practice session with Titan.

Thinking about Dad losing the house had guilt swarming through me like termites in wood. When I'd returned to Rivers, I could have moved back in with him. I could have ensured he was keeping it together, paying his bills, and eating healthy when he was home.

Selfish. The sound rippled through me in Chelsea's voice.

I pushed it away. My therapist had insisted the boundaries I'd put up were healthy. Refusing to be sucked back into caring for a father who'd failed to care for his children was a necessary step in my own healing. I'd needed to put distance between teen Maisey, who'd done everything to soothe everyone's pain but her own, and the Maisey who'd finally faced most of her demons.

Except, here I was, at home, wondering how to right the mess Dad had made.

I sighed, eyeing the crumpled yellow sundress laying by the closet. I threw back the cover and went to the closet, scanning the leftover mishmash of clothes left from my childhood. My hand reached almost automatically for a faded-pink terrycloth robe.

I pulled it on and rubbed my nose against the collar. Even after all these years, I swore it still held a hint of Mom's perfume. A spicy, almost masculine, scent of pine and sandalwood layered with a hint of magnolias. A strong and sturdy smell, just like her, until cancer had eaten away at the very fiber of her.

By the time we'd found out about the lung cancer, it had already metastasized to her brain. It had already started to eat away at her personality, making her short-tempered and grumpy when she'd never been anything but patient. It had pulled her apart from the inside out.

Less than six months later, she was gone.

The doctors had been surprised she'd lasted that long.

During those last weeks, the hospice nurses had become my friends, staying with her during the day while I was at school, and being on call for me when I needed them at night. I would have been on my own without them, because Chelsea…

I shook my head, cutting off the spiral before it could start.

That was all in the past. I needed to live in the *now*.

I headed for the tiny bathroom Chelsea and I had shared growing up and had just put my hand on the doorknob when it opened from the inside.

I couldn't help the screech that escaped as a man emerged on the other side. A stranger. A black-haired, blue-eyed, good-looking stranger.

My heart pounded so furiously I thought it would leap out of my chest.

Behind me, the door to Chelsea's room opened, and my sister's dry voice said, "Leave it to Cornlette to panic at the sight of a man."

I whirled around to face her. My sister was wearing a silk pajama set. A tiny camisole edged with lace that bared her stomach and a pair of shorts so small they might as well have passed for underwear. And although it wasn't even seven in the morning, she was completely made up, looking like she was ready to step onto a runway in her sleepwear. Her deep-auburn hair, which Delilah had spent a lifetime trying to mimic, was wound in long, lazy curls past her breasts. Her skin glowed, dusted with a powder that made it sparkle even more than normal. Eyeliner outlined her vivid green eyes, and mascara coated her dark lashes in an old-starlette fashion.

Her eyes and hair were our dad's, but the rest of her was our mother. A stunningly beautiful combination that had turned heads, even when we'd been kids. I'd gotten Mom's straight, brown hair, but the rest of me was our board-like father. Shorter. Flatter. All my limbs and proportions were just a tad off what society considered elegant or graceful or beautiful. Not Chelsea. She was the embodiment of perfection.

My sister examined me, taking in Mom's robe, and her lips twisted in disapproval. "It's like you haven't left this house in a decade. Have you moved back in to take care of Daddy? I worry about you, Maise. Will you ever stop being the dutiful daughter long enough to actually have a life of your own?"

As always, I was uncertain about how to take her comment. If you listened to just the words, you'd think she was actually worried about her little sister. But they also had an edge to them, a hint of criticism. For most of my life, I'd believed the concern. When I was little, she'd spent years standing up for me. I had dozens of moments, when she'd ripped my tormentors to shreds with her sharp tongue, burned into my brain.

But those times had gotten fewer and fewer as I'd gotten older, and by the time Mom had gotten sick, Chelsea had nearly vanished from my life.

"Thought you said your sister was ugly," the man behind me said, drawing my memories and my gaze away from my sister and back to him.

His forearm was on the doorframe above his head, and the position put his naked chest on display. He was cut and carved in all the right places. Muscles flexing, eight-pack looming. Other than the thick waves on his head, he had no hair on any other part of his body. It was like he'd been wiped clean. It made him seem like a computer-generated image instead of a real person—an idolized male model crafted to play a part on a screen.

He studied me, taking me in from the top of my disheveled bedhead down to my bubblegum-pink painted toenails. Chelsea would say the color was boring, but I liked that it added a splash of color without screaming, "Notice me."

"She could be hot if you gave her some fashion tips."

Without being able to control it, I flushed at the almost compliment—one I'd heard many times before from good-looking men. I *almost* stacked up. I was *almost* what they wanted. And sometimes, I was what they tolerated when perfect wasn't available. But I wasn't a keeper. I wasn't the one they wanted on their arm when it really counted.

"Hot is overrated," I said, scanning his hairless chest before meeting his eyes that were too unnaturally blue to be anything but contact lenses. "Real is something I strive for, but I'm not sure you'd understand that. Fake seems to be your mantra."

Instead of getting angry, he laughed, crossing his arms over a broad chest. "Down, girl. It wasn't an insult. No need to get your grandma panties in a wad."

I refused to tighten the belt on the robe. If he'd gotten a look at my underwear, so what? They weren't grandma panties. They were cute boy shorts with tiny yellow flowers. I wasn't ashamed of them.

Unhappy to have his attention focused on me, Chelsea eased in next to him and wrapped an arm possessively around his waist. "Cornlette, meet Gavin Acres. Current lead on a film I can't tell you about without killing you afterward."

Typical Chelsea, describing him by his most notable role. Acting school and life in Los Angeles hadn't helped my sister's personality. If anything, it had amplified all her worst characteristics.

These days, we kept in touch, mostly by text and an occasional call, but I hadn't seen her in person in almost two years. She hadn't been home in much longer. She hadn't set foot in Dad's house since he'd told her not to come back until she could talk to him with respect. It had been the last straw in their already torn relationship that had only shredded more after Mom had died.

Chelsea taking off had left me holding all the threads of our lives here, trying to keep them from unraveling completely. My therapist said I was allowed to be angry about it. That I should verbalize my feelings to them about what their departures, physically and emotionally, had done to me. But I hadn't brought it up to either of them, because doing so wouldn't change anything, even if it made me feel momentarily better.

I inhaled slowly, counted to five, and then exhaled. "What are you doing here, Chelsea?"

Her eyes narrowed. "We're due on set for a movie we're filming in the Sierras. I thought it would be nice to stop by and see my family on the way."

Meaning she'd wanted to rub our noses in the fact she was working on some important movie while showing off her newer, more famous boyfriend. I couldn't keep up with the men in her life. She'd gone through more than I could count when she'd been at the California Institute of the Arts. And since graduating with her MFA in acting and moving to LA, she'd gone through even more.

I was pretty sure Chelsea saw each guy as a stepping stone to something bigger. Something she was working her way up to. Maybe Gavin would be the pinnacle, or maybe she'd move on to someone else by this time next year, especially if his movie flopped.

I whirled around, heading for the kitchen. I didn't need this.

I could shower at my own house later. I just needed to see Dad, get dressed, and get out of here.

Over my shoulder, I tossed back, "I doubt Dad has anything for breakfast. So, you'll have to hit the diner if you're hungry."

I'd expected the kitchen to be empty, but instead, Dad was sitting at the tiny table shoved in the corner with his head in his hands. It drew attention to the bald ring at the crown of his auburn hair. For all my life, Dad had been a sturdy and robust man. Solid and tough. Today, he looked unexpectedly thin. Almost frail.

He didn't look up as I approached, hadn't even registered I was in the room, until I put a hand on his shoulder. He startled, turning to look at me with a face that shocked me to the core. His green eyes that had always been as vivid and bright as Chelsea's were pale, empty, and glassy. The wrinkles on his face weighed the skin down like an aged hound dog's. His beard looked ragged rather than neat and clipped, unlike how he usually wore it, and the white seemed to have completely taken over the warm brown, like weeds in the yard.

Something was wrong. Something far worse than the house mortgage. I hadn't seen him look this devastated since Mom had died.

"Dad? What is it? What's the matter?"

His eyes shot to a stack of papers in front of him. He tried to fold them up, but I yanked them from under his hand before he could stop me.

The first was a statement from the bank. Just like Carter had insinuated, Dad was behind on the mortgage, and they were threatening to foreclose. I forced back the panic that threatened like it had when I was fifteen and I'd seen a similar statement. This wasn't my home anymore. I wasn't going to lose the roof over my head. But my father might.

"Why would you let this go so long?" I demanded. "You have money in your checking account." I knew because we both still received the statements. So why had he stopped the automatic payment for the mortgage? He didn't have enough in there now to pay back all the mortgage with interest, but he could have kept up with it monthly.

Damn him for making me feel guilty for not holding his hand and making sure he did what every grown-up was supposed to do.

He was the father. I was the kid!

Dad rubbed a hand over his face, and it pulled my eyes to a bruise on the back of his hand and a scab I recognized. Painful marks left behind by an IV that hadn't been put in properly. A new fear settled over me.

He was sick.

I sat in the chair next to him, brought his hand to mine, and gently rubbed the bruise. "Dad. What's going on? You were in the hospital?"

He looked down at my touch, avoiding my eyes. "Had a mild stroke on the road. Crashed my rig."

Shock slashed through me. "What happened? Where were you? Why didn't you call me?"

He didn't answer any of my questions. Instead, he looked away, out the screen door to a porch in desperate need of refinishing. "They pulled my commercial license until I can pass my DOT cert again."

Meaning, he was grounded. The Department of Transportation wasn't going to approve his medical certificate with a stroke on his record. He'd never drive a semi again. He'd lost his job just as he was about to lose his house.

Tears filled my eyes. Fury and sadness. Not just for him and his losses, but for me and what it said about our relationship that my father had been in the hospital somewhere, alone, and hadn't even thought to call his daughter.

"Nothing really has changed, has it?" Chelsea's sharp voice ripped our attention to her as she glided into the kitchen.

She was wearing a navy dress with side cutouts, that probably cost as much as I made in a month, and stiletto heels with red soles I knew she couldn't afford. Not with the debt she'd racked up paying for college on her own.

When Chelsea didn't get the reaction she wanted from either of us, she dug deeper. "Dad is still an incompetent ass, Maisey is still the lost little saint who needs saving, and I still don't belong."

Finally, I let the irritation and hurt get the better of me.

I rose from the chair and crossed my arms over my chest. "You chose not to belong, Chelsea. Just because my friends had the heart to step in to help hold us together when you left, doesn't mean I'm some weak flower that would have died if someone didn't water me."

For two seconds, her face softened, and I saw a Chelsea I rarely saw anymore. The one who'd played dolls with me and biked along the creek and created make-believe worlds where we were both princesses who married princes and had entire kingdoms at our beck and call. Where I was the ugly duckling who turned into a swan.

"Neither of us should have had to hold our father together. *He* was the adult." Chelsea's words mirrored my therapist's, and the anger in them, the frustration and hurt, were the first real feelings—other than scorn—I'd seen from my sister in years. As quickly as she'd shown the emotions, they disappeared. She became the actress she most craved, doing what she did best—only giving the world the pieces she wanted them to see. "You deserve more than a life picking up his mess, Maisey. Someday, I hope you realize that."

"Ready, babe?" Gavin said, coming into the kitchen from the hall, carrying two oversized suitcases. He took one look around the room and then quirked a brow. "Heavy in here. Guess you've found that fuel you were looking for after all." He winked at my sister. "You're going to nail Miranda's disgust of her family."

"Get out," Dad said softly. "I told you before, you're not welcome until you can show this family some respect."

"Believe me, *Dad*. I regret the spur-of-the-moment decision to stop by more than you can imagine."

She walked out of the kitchen. Gavin shot us one last, interested look and then followed her.

I stood for far too long, trying to catch my breath, trying to tame my anger, before I went scrambling after them. They were already on the street past the broken walkway by the time I got out the front door.

"Why? Why did you really bother coming?" I called after her.

Chelsea studied the house before settling her cold gaze on me. I wanted to believe it was sadness I saw there. Regret. But I was pretty sure I was just projecting.

"I thought maybe I'd see things differently after all this time. Hoped I'd find something worthy of my time." She gave a careless shrug. "But all I see is a weak man and a little girl wasting her life trying to hold him up. Let him fall, Maisey, because this time he might take you with him when he crashes."

Gavin stuffed their suitcases into the back of the red sports car I'd thought belonged to renters. He slid on a pair of dark sunglasses and scanned my childhood home one more time before getting into the driver's seat.

Chelsea didn't say goodbye. Didn't apologize. Didn't even glance back at me or the house. Instead, she purposefully avoided looking in our direction as she climbed into the passenger seat. Gavin peeled away from the curb, and they disappeared around the corner.

And all I could think was that I'd never disliked my sister this much, because, for the first time ever, I was afraid she might be right. I was afraid if I didn't walk away from the mess that was our father, I'd either have to depend on others to save us yet again, or I'd end up drowning right along with him.

Chapter Six
Beckett

LIFE AS WE KNEW IT
Performed by Lonestar

SEVEN YEARS AGO

HIM: I don't care what you say, Tolkien was a genius.

> *HER: If you like pages and pages of war and death and depression.*

HIM: Bravery, courage, and good winning over evil.

> *HER: Did they really win, though? At least at the end of a romance novel, you know they'll have a happily ever after.*

HIM: They end your books at the high point because if they continued, over fifty percent of the relationships would be destroyed by jealousy, selfishness, and death.

> *HER: Cynic.*

HIM: Dreamer.

> *HER: Someday, I'll prove you wrong.*

HIM: ...

> *HER: And no, before you even ask, I don't want to make a bet.*

PRESENT DAY

I loved my job. I loved everything about fighting fires. Not only the actual time spent taming the beast but the preparation required to do it right. The training. The time spent cleaning, repairing, and ensuring our equipment was in tip-top shape for when the call came. It was comforting. Soothing. And today, I was grateful for every task that kept me occupied.

After pounding out some of my fury in the station's gym over the chief's call I'd overheard, I'd showered and dove into the list of things my crew and I needed to do. That included running drills with our probie.

I was manning the stopwatch as Leon rolled up the lines, when Vader came sauntering in the large roll-up doors. I barely shot him a look, keeping my focus trained on the time.

"'Bout time, dog. You almost missed a meal."

Leon glanced over at my dog, and his grip on the hose loosened. "What's he got? A dead animal?"

I stopped the watch and said, "That's your worst time yet, probie. Do it again."

I'd just turned to look at Vader as a mewl escaped his mouth—one emanating not from my dog but the animal he held tenderly between his teeth.

"Oh fuck, no," I said, shaking my head.

Vader just sauntered over, plopped his butt on the cement next to me, and looked up at me with sad, sad eyes. The short-haired, gray-and-white striped kitten meowed again.

"You can't keep doing this, shithead," I told the dog.

"Is that a cat? Is he going to eat a cat?" Leon's voice rose in panic.

"He isn't going to eat it," I said in disgust.

Somehow, the greyhound, hunting-prey instinct in Vader's DNA had been mangled with the protective, caring instinct of his Labrador ancestors so that my dog was routinely bringing home abandoned animals, mostly kittens. But there'd also been a baby chipmunk and an illegally kept ferret. People found it endearing, but that was because they weren't the ones who had to find families to take in the strays.

"Let me see what you got there," I grunted, squatting down to take the kitten from him.

Slobber mixed with dirt coated the kitten. It barely looked old enough to feed itself, which had my stomach falling all over again. My last attempt at bottle-feeding had not ended well.

"Stretch the line, probie, and run the drill again," I ordered before heading up the cement and metal stairs to the kitchen.

Vader followed on my heels, looking as proud as a father in a delivery room. "You're a pain in the ass, dog. You're lucky I don't send you to the shelter along with this thing you dragged in."

Kasey and Tejas simply watched, not even attempting to hide their amusement, as I dunked the cat in the sink. I washed the animal with Dawn dish soap, while the kitten complained viciously, and Vader whined in concern.

"Thanks for the help, assholes," I groused, looking over at my crew.

Kasey's cropped blond hair and broad shoulders shook with the force of her laughter. Once she got a hold of herself, she said, "Your dog, your responsibility."

My good deed of cleaning the cat was rewarded with scratches up my arms and a set of teeth marks on my thumb, which I was certain would leave a scar. I wrapped the kitten in one of the soft towels we used for waxing the wagons and placed it in a plastic crate. Vader stuffed his nose inside it, sniffed in apparent approval, and then curled his body around it while I called Sheila at the shelter.

When she said she was full up and couldn't take in another animal, I groaned.

"I'll call around to my volunteers who foster litters and see if anyone has room," she promised, but I knew how that went. At this point, I was pretty sure Sheila considered me one of her foster families.

While I'd been on the phone, Tejas had dug through our cabinets and come up with a can of soft cat food from the last time Vader had dragged in a pair of kittens. He placed the disgusting glob of goo in a bowl and put it inside the crate. I was relieved to see the cat lap at it with little growling noises. At least I wouldn't have to repeat the bottle-feeding nightmare.

Vader's tail thumped on the floor, and I swore the dog smirked at me. Tejas did the wrong thing by pulling a dog treat from the cookie jar and handing it to him. My dog would never stop bringing animals home if he got snacks out of it.

"Well, you'd better be prepared to share your bed with this one for a few days," I told my dog, running a hand over his smooth head. "You old softie."

It tugged at something inside me. Old memories. Old worries. My dad had been a softie too. He may not have brought home strays, but he'd had his heart crushed multiple times. Good thing my dog wasn't out on the prowl for a mate, or he'd end up in the same shape as my father—old, single, and with a scarred heart.

The tap of high heels drew my attention to the stairs.

Delilah stepped into the kitchen in what I considered her work uniform. The gray pencil skirt and pale blue button-down covered every curve in a classy, old school sort of way. Her hair was up in a messy bun, and she'd slid a pair of tortoise-shell eyeglasses on her slender nose I was ninety percent sure she didn't need.

Delilah was good at playing roles. Her personality flipped with a speed that made my head spin, rotating between wounded ex, sexy siren, and strict professional. All of those were usually easy for me to ignore. It was when she wore the depressed-friend role that I ended up sitting next to her at the bar.

The crew greeted her warmly. She was well-liked at the station. In truth, she was well-liked just about everywhere she went because she made friends easily. It was a skill she'd learned from her parents, the mayor and the chief. Only the Campbell girls and Delilah didn't get along.

Del had valid reasons for hating Chelsea. But her reasons for disliking Maisey were as skewed as her beliefs about me.

"Your dad isn't here," I told her.

"I know. I'm dropping off the latest budget proposal for you and Nancy to look at," Delilah said, waving a stack of papers at me.

It wasn't really a secret around town that Rose Nattingly was grooming her daughter to take over as mayor someday. But what I wasn't sure many people knew, and what I wasn't sure even Del herself remembered these days, was that politics had been the last thing Delilah had wanted to do growing up. Even in college, when we'd carpooled to Fresno and back, her heart had been in her art classes, not business lectures.

"I'll just go through the numbers with you," Delilah said when I hadn't moved.

The anger I'd spent an entire morning and early afternoon trying to tame after overhearing the chief's decision about me flared back to life. Billie Nattingly hadn't even looked at the budget in the last eighteen months. That had all been me and Nancy.

The truth was, I hadn't minded taking it on because it had been one more item for my resume. One more reason I'd be qualified for the fire chief role when it became available. Now, I wondered exactly why he'd handed me the responsibility if he hadn't believed I was ready for the actual job.

"Nancy isn't here today," I reminded her. As our department's admin, HR representative, and accountant, Nancy worked purely Monday through Friday, eight-to-five, unless there was an emergency that required all-hands-on-deck.

"You can pass on what I share to her next week."

Delilah headed for the hall leading to the offices, and I sighed before going after her. A soft whistle followed me and a quiet, "Have fun with that," from Tejas.

I flipped him off over my head but didn't look back.

The team thought Delilah and I were doing the horizontal mambo on a regular basis, mostly because of the innuendos she dropped. Even her dad had to have heard the rumors. But the more I'd protested, the more my crew gave me shit, so I just left them to their own beliefs while holding on to the knowledge I'd never be sliding beneath her sheets.

My feet stalled, nearly causing me to trip, as an ugly thought slammed into me. Was the chief putting this new requirement on the job because he was pissed? Did he think I was slipping it to Delilah without asking her to marry me? That idea was followed by an even worse one. Were the chief and the mayor hoping that marrying us off would also help put their daughter in office? Perhaps this entire scenario wasn't about me and the fire chief position at all, but some mastermind plan to help make Delilah the next mayor.

A bitter, ugly taste coated my tongue.

By the time I got my feet working again and joined Del in my office, she'd already slid the papers onto my desk and turned to lean against the edge of it.

Her gaze skimmed my uniform, she bit her lip, and then said, "You ran out before we got to finish our talk last night."

I stuffed my hands in my pockets and leaned a shoulder up against the wall by the door, careful not to smudge the schedule Stoney and I had written on the whiteboard.

"I'm not sure we really have anything to talk about, Del."

"He's not going to hire you. He's looking externally."

"I know."

Surprise flitted over her face. "You do?"

She pushed off the desk and took a step toward me. "Do you know why?"

"I've heard a little something on the topic."

She tilted her head. "I can fix it." She stopped and cleared her throat. "We can fix it. Together."

She ran her hand along her arm from her elbow to her wrist. It was an old habit. A tick. Her thumb lingered on the old scars.

Wounds from a night that had marked me almost as much as it had scarred her.

Life had piled up on her at seventeen. Vicious rumors. Cruel names. Things that had nothing to do with me, and yet I'd added a brick to the pile already weighing her down. The guilt still haunted me.

"If Daddy thought you and I might actually make it official, I know he'd reconsider his position on the matter," Delilah said. She stared for a few beats before her eyes dipped to my mouth and back.

My neck broke out in goosebumps. Not the good kind. The ones that felt like someone had walked over my grave. A biting remark was on the tip of my tongue before I caught it.

I wouldn't hurt Delilah on purpose—never again if I could help it—but I also felt an overwhelming need to shut this door once and for all. Not just for Del but for the entire town. I was exhausted from having to prove there was nothing between her and me, and I was pissed everyone was trying to back me into a corner and force my hand.

So fine. Fucking fine.

They'd force it, but it wouldn't be in the direction Delilah and her parents had wanted.

"The thing is, Del, it would be impossible for you and me to ever be anything," I said it gently, but it didn't stop the annoyance from flickering across her face.

"Only because you're too stubborn to see what's right in front of you."

What flashed in my mind wasn't Del. It was another woman with hair like chocolate silk and pale-green eyes. A woman who understood the dead muscle in my chest and my inability to commit. A woman who understood the revulsion I felt at relationships wasn't just temporary but necessary. I may not ever have told Maisey about the smoke that filled my lungs when I thought of marriage, but she accepted I couldn't do forever after.

Delilah would always wish for more than I could give. As if proving my point, her hands landed on my chest, sliding up seductively.

I caught them, trapping her wrists and ignoring the flare in her eyes at the action.

Self-preservation and anger had me spewing words I had no right to spill, especially without at least having a conversation about them first. "No. It's impossible, Del, because I'm already engaged to someone else."

Her entire being went still, shock rolling over her face. She yanked her hands away from me and took a step back. "Liar. You haven't dated anyone seriously in years."

I was going to hell. I was going to hell, and my best friend was going to be the one to send me there. And I'd deserve it. But the truth was, Maisey would cover my ass while she did it. She'd step up to the plate because that was the core of who she was—she took care of others.

It made me hate myself a bit more, knowing Maisey had already spent a lifetime picking up after other people and I was giving her one more mess to handle. But it didn't stop me from continuing the lie.

"We've been keeping it quiet on purpose," I insisted. "We weren't ready to tell anyone yet."

Delilah's lips tightened. "Who? Because you seriously haven't been seen with anyone in months besides…" Her mouth popped open as realization settled in. "Maisey? You're talking about Maisey?"

I didn't have time to respond as the alarm sounded, roaring through the station and echoing out into the street. Grateful, for the first time in my life, for a fire, I whirled and raced down the hall, sliding down to the lockers where our turnout gear waited. My crew was already there, feet sliding into their boots. I was not even two seconds behind them, but seconds mattered when it came to fire.

Vader bounded onto the stairs with an excited woof, and I shouted at him to stay with the stupid cat before I launched myself into the engine with Kasey chauffeuring.

Sliding into my seat and throwing my phone into the compartment in the dash as we roared onto the street, I asked, "What have we got?"

The crew exchanged a look, and my stomach sank. It was the probie who answered, not understanding what it would mean to me.

"Structure fire. Residential. 501 Meadow Lane." Sensing the tension in the air after he'd blurted out the address, Leon asked, "What? Do we know who lives there?"

Memories hit me like a reel gone viral—hard and fast and on repeat. Jumping over the fence into Maisey's yard. Playing tag and hide-and-seek amongst the chicken coops. Mrs. Campbell fixing us sandwiches and cookies at the rickety table with a piece of cardboard under one leg to even it out. Maisey curled up in a ball on a twin-sized bed, sobbing after her mother died, while I slid in behind her, simply holding her because I didn't know what else to do.

Maisey in that damn yellow dress, picking her way over the roots in the cracked path as she made her way to the steps of a porch that sagged and needed replacing.

The heart I often thought was dead flexed in its cage of scars, slashing out at me.

She wasn't at the house. She would have left hours ago.

She'd talked about picking up a shift at the hospital or going to the ranch to practice with Titan.

She was not in a burning house!

The cars on Main Street parted for us, and as we flew by the Emporium, I saw the smoke rising from the neighborhood beyond it. Black and insidious, it curled into the unusually heavy summer air. Kasey spun the wheel, and we turned the corner at speeds that had the rookie cursing behind me.

The engine hadn't even stopped before I'd jumped out to assess the situation at the Campbell house. The fire was at the rear. Likely the kitchen. My crew sprang from the engine, and I issued commands. "Leon, stretch the pipe. Tejas, do the initial investigation and make sure it's contained to the kitchen while I conduct the primary search. Kasey, alpha provides the easiest egress. It's a straight shot through the front door to the kitchen. You and Leon follow me in."

I dragged my lid and SCBA on as I headed up the steps. Tejas ran to the left, sweeping the property clockwise, while Leon and Kasey went to work on the plug and pipe.

I had my hand on the front door as a body came tumbling out. I might not have recognized Maisey's dad if I'd passed him on the street. Not because he was covered in black ash but because he seemed half the man I'd grown up around.

He coughed horribly, and the kitchen fire extinguisher he held banged against the doorframe.

"Is there anyone else here?" I demanded.

He looked at me, dazed and confused. I doubted he

recognized me, not with the breathing apparatus altering my voice and my turnout gear covering me from head to toe.

"Mr. Campbell, are you alone in the house?"

"I…I tried to stop it." He looked down at the fire extinguisher. His hand was raw and red. Burnt. Shit.

Into my radio, I said, "Engine 2 requesting bus at 501 Meadow Lane. Resident needs medical."

My gut fell, hoping Maisey wasn't in the ER today, hoping she wouldn't hear the callout, but even more, hoping she wasn't inside.

Instead of wasting time moving Lewis off the porch and away from the house, I raced inside, chest tight and breathing shallow. I ached to head straight for the bedrooms, but I forced myself to rely on my training, clearing the rooms one by one from front to back.

When I got to the kitchen, the fire danced a vicious beat. It had already melted plastic, ripped through wood, and was working its way along the wall Maisey's room shared with the kitchen. My heart nearly exploded with fear as the blaze crawled through the wood and Sheetrock, a beast eating its way through its prey.

In my headset, I heard Tejas say the fire had taken the porch on the Charlie side. He was knocking it down with his handheld. Behind me, Kasey and Leon filed into the house, dragging the pipe across the hardwood with Kasey at the tip.

I shoved several burning dinette chairs out of my way, storming toward the hallway and calling Maisey's name. The words echoed eerily in my mask.

I slammed the door of Maisey's bedroom open, scanned the interior, and felt the pain and pressure in my chest ease slightly. No one. The room was empty except for the fire licking through the hole it had formed in the wall. I turned, clearing the bathroom she'd shared as a kid with her sister before opening Chelsea's room.

But that room was empty too. Not only empty of people but stripped clean. Nothing on the walls, nothing in the closet. Just a bed with an ancient mattress and a dresser with the drawers open.

Thank God.

Thank fucking God.

Maisey wasn't here.

I sprinted back to the kitchen, mind clearing so I could focus on the work. Tejas had doused the porch and busted through the back door, taking the blaze from the rear. Kasey was attacking from the front. I took over the tip and ordered Leon to return to Mr. Campbell and assess his injuries while we waited for the EMTs to arrive.

It took less time to put the fire out than it had taken us to get there.

Less time than it had taken for me to panic and clear the house.

I gave the command to kill the water and then stood there for a brief second, assessing the disaster.

The kitchen was gutted—nothing salvageable—and a hole now tore through the wall to Maisey's old room. Even from this angle, I could see her bed had been torched, and the dresser was black with streaks.

Fuck.

But it hadn't spread to the rest of the house. It hadn't spread to mine next door.

"Engine 2. Structure fire under control," I said into the radio.

What the hell had happened?

I handed over the overhaul to Tejas and Kasey and stepped outside.

A bus had arrived, and Bugsy, the lead EMT for the ambulance company, had Mr. Campbell sitting in a peeling old chair on the porch while she wrapped his hand.

I ripped off my lid and SCBA before squatting next to him. "Mr. Campbell, have you called Maisey? Does she know about the fire?"

His eyes were glossy and distant when he looked at me. "Maisey is at school. She's at school. But Chelsea." He shook his head. "She left again. Not coming back this time." He looked at the dark-haired Bugsy working on his hand and said,

"I miss my girls. Marjorie, tell the girls I miss them, okay?"

My stomach sank at his mixed-up jumble of words.

It had to be the shock that caused him to flip back in time and act as if his wife were there. As if Maisey was going to stroll home from the school at any minute.

Bugsy and I shared a look. She'd grown up in town too. She knew Marjorie Campbell was dead, knew Maisey was not at school—high school, college, or otherwise.

"Will you stay with him?" I asked. "I'm going to call Maisey."

Bugsy nodded, and I jogged to the wagon, searching for the phone I'd tossed aside. I didn't want to call her through the emergency channels. I didn't want her to panic and assume the worst.

She'd be distraught.

What I wanted to do was go pick her up and drive her here myself, but I couldn't. I had a job to do. Mop up to continue. An investigation to start.

Most likely, it was a kitchen accident gone wildly wrong. But they'd need the paperwork completed for the insurance. Maisey had already mentioned her dad didn't have the money to fix the place up. This would hurt more.

I didn't have to scroll to find her name. It was already at the top of my list. Still, I paused before hitting the call button.

How was I going to break it to her that her dad was okay but that he wasn't all there?

That he'd made a mess of their home while I'd been making a mess of her life with a lie.

I promised I'd fix it all the best I could.

Somehow, I'd make everything right.

Chapter Seven
Maisey

BROKEN IN
Performed by Ella Langley

ELEVEN YEARS AGO

> *HER: I don't know what to do.*

HIM: What's wrong?

> *HER: Dad left this morning. Chelsea didn't come home. And Mom is gone.*

HIM: What?

> *HER: I came in to check on her before I went to sleep. But she's...*

> *HER: She's...God. I can't type it.*

HIM: Dad and I are coming over. We'll be right there, Maise. We're coming.

PRESENT DAY

As I closed the door on Titan's stall after rubbing him down, I reached into the bag I'd hung on a hook by his door and pulled out an apple. He softly nuzzled my palm as he took it, eyes bright with affection.

My emotions had been a problem for us in the corral today. I'd missed tricks I shouldn't have, and it wasn't just because I was rusty from lack of practice. If Titan hadn't been as steady as a rock, I'd be leaving the ranch with a lot more bumps and bruises.

If I didn't get my act together, I was going to fall on my ass during the Fourth of July show. I'd have to double my practices between now and then because I refused to embarrass myself or Fallon. Neither of us got to perform much anymore, mostly for special occasions, but that didn't mean I couldn't make it the best show we'd done since we'd started performing as teens.

I ran a hand over Titan's silky mane. The American Paint's white-and-chestnut design that ran down his neck, over his body, and down his fetlocks was smooth and healthy. He'd never once missed a meal or day of training, and that was all due to Fallon and her family taking him on when Dad had sold him.

The ranch had saved my horse while Fallon and Beckett had saved me.

I hadn't thought of it as *saving*, not until Chelsea had rubbed it in my face that I was always being rescued. At the time, I'd simply seen it as friends helping friends. Family helping family. And I'd been eternally grateful.

Not only for the way Beckett had taught me to read and lifted my spirits when I was a kid, or for how Fallon had stood up for me at school, but for how both of them had stepped in to take care of the household chores when Mom got sick. With Dad on the road, everything at home had landed on me, because Chelsea hadn't lifted a finger. Instead, she'd escaped the house, running wild with her fast crowd of friends that included Carter, Randy Cleaver, a few cheerleaders, and her theater groupies, while leaving me to care for our dying mother.

Even after Mom had passed, when I'd been drowning and I'd finally had the courage to ask for help, Chelsea had refused.

You've always gotten whatever you wanted, Maisey, while I stood empty-handed. I won't be your latest victim, letting you bleed me dry like you've bled our parents. But I'm sure if you turn your tear-streaked face toward your friends, one of them will come running to save you.

That was when I finally realized my sister had stopped protecting me years before. She'd gladly handed off the duty to Fallon and Beckett. She'd let the bitterness of a childhood spent getting less of our family's limited resources drive a wedge between us.

What I'd told Chelsea this morning was the truth. I wasn't some fragile flower who couldn't figure out how to save herself. I'd survived things in my childhood a lot of grown-ups couldn't handle. But I had leaned on my friends to do it. Had it been selfish? Had I greedily gotten what I'd needed at some greater cost to the people I loved? Or were Chelsea's words just digging up old worries and wounds?

Reading my emotions, Titan pushed his nose into my shoulder, blowing air out his nostrils in a soft snort as if to tell me to knock it off.

"You're right. You're right. I can't let Chelsea get to me. But what am I going to do about Dad's mess?"

Dad wasn't rich, by any means, but he'd earned enough to pay his bills, just like when I was growing up. It had only been the extravagant costs that had us really pinching pennies. If my parents hadn't already bought Titan before the costs from my orthodontic work kicked in, I never would have had my horse.

Once the budget had gotten really tight, Mom had arranged a deal with the riding school, bartering my classes and Titan's food and board in exchange for our work. She used her handyman skills to handle routine maintenance, while I helped feed the horses and muck the stalls. But after Mom was gone, I couldn't keep up the arrangement on my own, and that was when Dad sold him.

The gratitude I'd felt back then overwhelmed me all over again. Since I'd returned to Rivers, I'd started paying for Titan's board and upkeep, even though Fallon fought me on it. And I'd promised myself that, someday, I'd pay the Harringtons back for all of Titan's costs and buy him back, even if I'd never be able to pay back the college tuition they'd handed me.

"We're pretty lucky, Titan. Aren't we?" I whispered, and he nudged me in agreement.

My phone buzzed, and I looked down to see a message from Meredith. She'd been unable to find anyone to cover the L&D shift and was begging me to come in. I'd planned on stopping in to see Fallon before I left the ranch, but after the way my morning had gone, I could use the distraction a shift would bring.

I kissed Titan's star, gave him another good rub, and then headed out of the barn, waving to some of the staff. I skirted a group of guests waiting for their guided horseback ride and headed for my truck in the parking lot.

The Victorian Gothic Revival castle Fallon's ancestors had built in the 1930s stood tall and proud, casting long morning shadows over the vehicles parked there. The curls and flourishes along the golden gables and towers gleamed in the sunlight, thriving just like the expansive pools and grounds did since the renovations. Fallon's dad had even brought a bit of his Vegas casinos to the ranch by adding an animated centaur fountain to the circular drive that came alive each night with music and lights to entertain the guests.

I'd barely driven past the fountain when my phone rang, announcing Beckett.

"Two calls in two days," I greeted. "That has to be a record. But I can't talk long. I'm heading home to get cleaned up for my shift."

"Maise," his voice cracked with deep emotions, and my heart lurched. "First, I want you to know, your dad is okay. I'm looking at him right now, and he's okay."

My palms turned clammy, and my pulse raced as my mind spiraled through a host of ghastly scenarios. Had Dad had another stroke? Was he even now lying on a stretcher, struggling to talk and move? Or had there been a fire? At the house?

Oh God…was it gone? Had we lost everything?

I choked out, "Wh-what happened?"

"A fire. It started in the kitchen, but we contained it."

The house. My stomach cramped, bile rising to the back of my throat.

Dad was okay. Beckett wouldn't lie. He was okay.

But he'd nearly lost the house.

I bit back a hysterical laugh because hadn't he already lost it to the bank? That thought spurred an even more terrifying one. Had Dad done something on purpose? In desperation?

A horrible sense of foreboding filled me.

This morning, he'd looked… defeated. Even more so after the encounter with Chelsea. More so after I'd told him I'd come by later and work through the bills with him.

But there was no way he'd risk the last faded memories of Mom we had left by purposefully setting a fire. He wouldn't. He just wouldn't.

"How…" My voice shook. "How bad is it?"

"We're still mopping up, but the kitchen is gutted and part of your old room. The back porch is toast."

I thought of the teenage leftovers I'd just considered clearing out of my room this morning. My stomach rolled again. At least it wasn't the scrapbooks Mom had made. Those were all in a cabinet in the living room.

"I'm on my way," I said and then hung up before he could respond.

Dad could have died.

I could have lost my father.

My hands on the steering wheel trembled so badly I had to fight to keep the truck on the road.

When I finally turned onto our street, my breath evaporated. A fire truck blocked the road, with a fire hose running from the hydrant through the front door. I winced, thinking of how much time and effort Mom had once put into the wooden floors, making sure they were waxed to perfection. Now, they'd be a mess.

More of a mess than they'd already been. The house had suffered Mom's absence the most. While my dad and I hid our fractures behind practiced masks, the walls had surrendered, every faded corner and peeling edge marking the truth in ways we couldn't deny. She was gone, and I'd failed to keep her legacy alive.

In my desperate attempt to put boundaries up between childhood Maisey and adult Maisey, I'd let her down. I'd let Dad and the house disintegrate before me.

I parked down the street from the Helmers' house and ran the rest of the way. The smell of burnt plastic and wood slammed into me, a terrifying nightmare playing out in front of me.

But there was no smoke coming from the house, and I reminded myself that Beckett had said they were mopping up. They'd put it out. The fire wouldn't continue to eat away at wood and childhood memories.

I didn't see Beckett when I got to the porch, but Dad was there, sitting in the old Adirondack chair Mom had once sanded and painted a bright blue but was now nothing more than chipped paint. Dad's elbows were on his knees, head in his hands, much like I'd found him this morning, except this time one hand was wrapped in gauze.

Bugsy was standing over him with a hand on his shoulder.

The EMT's face was so grim that tears pricked my eyes, and I had to fight them back. I fell on my knees next to Dad, drawing his injured hand closer. It was the same one he'd had the IV marks on.

"You're hurt," I said quietly, glancing up at Bugsy, hoping for more information.

"The burn is second degree. It's gonna hurt like a bitch, but other than that, physically, he's okay." Her tone was the same clipped one she used when handing off a patient to us in the ER.

"I don't know what happened." Dad's words drew my attention back to him.

His voice was thick with years of smoking. Dad wasn't much of a drinker, and he hated drugs with a passion, but he lived off caffeine and cigarettes to ease the boredom of long days stuck behind the wheel of a semitruck. He hadn't stopped smoking once in my lifetime, not even after Mom's cancer diagnosis. Not even after the disease had stolen her from us. Not even when I'd cried and told him I was scared of losing my only remaining parent.

"I don't understand. What happened?" Dad's brows furrowed together until they were one long, thick line, and my worry grew.

"It'll be okay, Dad. Beckett said it was just the kitchen. It could have been worse," I tried to soothe.

He looked away, seeming to disappear right before me as he said, "I just don't know what happened, Marjorie."

The world blurred in front of me. A ringing sounded in my ears.

He thought I was Mom?

Heavy steps behind me had me whirling around to find Beckett emerging from the house. His facemask and helmet were gone, but he still wore his turnout gear with the SRFD logo emblazoned on the chest and back. His gloves were shoved into the pockets of the jacket, and there was black ash coating his face. He looked like a superhero. A savior.

My savior. God… Chelsea was right. I'd let my friends save me. And here he was, saving my family again.

Cleaning up a mess we'd made.

Beckett's warm brown eyes met mine, concern written in them as he glanced from me to Dad and back. He watched me closely, like he could pry my emotions out of me if he stared long enough, but I hid them behind the blank face I'd gotten good at showing him over the last few years out of pure self-preservation.

"Mr. Campbell," Beckett stepped closer, looking down at my dad. "I think we're almost done inside. We just need your statement about what happened so we can file the report for the insurance company."

Oh God. Did Dad even have insurance? If he hadn't been paying the mortgage, I somehow doubted he'd kept up with that either. What were we going to do?

Dad frowned, looking at Beckett, down to his gauzed hand, and then at me. "What happened, Marge?"

Beckett's eyes snapped to mine, and neither of us looked away for a few painful seconds.

A new fear stabbed at me. Not because of the fire or the physical damage that had been done to the house, but because of my father.

And right on its heels, another selfish, awful thought followed. I didn't want to do this. I didn't want to spend the rest of my life taking care of my father after I'd given up the dregs of my childhood caring for Mom and keeping my family afloat. I didn't want to drown while attempting to fix things I'd had no hand in creating.

I ground my teeth together, and pain shot through my straightened jaw right to my temple. It brought me back from the edge of a panic attack. It reminded me of what my family had sacrificed for me.

There was no way I was walking away from Dad now.

I'd made it through worse. I was an adult now and could handle these new problems far more easily than the ones I'd coped with as a kid. But this time, I wouldn't drag my friends down with me while I did it.

♫ ♫ ♫

Dad had fallen into a fretful sleep in the hospital bed, and seeing him there only exasperated the frailness I'd seen in him this morning. The panic I'd forced back earlier threatened to overwhelm me again, and my vision blurred with unshed tears.

"Maisey?" Meredith called.

I turned to find her concerned eyes looking at me from the doorway. She'd been kinder than she'd ever been before when I'd shown up at the hospital, not to start my shift but to get my dad checked out in the emergency room.

"Is it okay for me to let Beckett in?" she asked.

Beckett ignored her question and strode into the room anyway.

Meredith huffed even as I said, "It's fine. Thank you."

She left, and I took Beckett in as he made his way to me. He'd showered and changed but was still wearing his Class B uniform and had a radio on his shoulder. He was still on call. Still saving people.

The tears rushed in again, and I turned away quickly so he wouldn't see them.

In two long strides, he was at my side, grabbing my hand and trying to pull me to him. I resisted, putting the chair I'd been sitting in between us. I couldn't let him hold me. If I did, I'd break. If I did, I'd forget my vows to go this alone. To not drag the people I cared about into yet another mess the Campbells had made of their lives.

Beckett frowned. "What did the doctor say?"

"She wants to keep him for a day or two at least. He came around a bit. He knew who I was and the current date, but then he faded again when I asked about the fire. He kept mixing things up and grew agitated. The doctor doesn't think he had another stroke, but he has a knot on the back of his head, so his memory loss could be because of that."

"*Another* stroke? He had a stroke? You never—"

"I just found out this morning that he crashed his rig after having one. He didn't tell me. Didn't call." Hurt and anger and guilt all swarmed inside me like an insidious bug.

"Maise." Beckett tugged at my arm, once again trying to draw me to him, but I pushed him away.

"Don't. I can't handle it right now, Beckett. I can't fall apart."

The noise he made at the back of his throat was close to a growl, and the look he gave me was intense—almost angry.

"All you've done is take care of him. It isn't on you if he didn't call. Maybe he was actually trying to do the right thing by handling things on his own for a change."

I thought of the stack of bills on the kitchen table. It seemed impossible that I'd be able to get my arms around it. Dad certainly wouldn't be able to do it on his own. What on earth was I going to do with him if he lost the house? Have him move into my studio with me? Figure out a way to draw on his retirement and Social Security early to get him his own apartment?

I tugged at my hair, drawing it across my jaw before realizing what I was doing and dropping it. "Do you know what started the fire?"

Beckett looked up and away before clearing his throat and saying, "Something on the stove."

"The stove!" Shock slammed into me. "He was cooking? Dad never cooks."

Beckett scratched the back of his neck and then shoved his

hands in his pockets. "I don't know what to say. The fire definitely started on the stove. Ron can tell us more after he finishes the investigation."

My stomach lurched uncomfortably, and I pressed my hand against it.

If he'd called the county fire marshal, it had to be serious. Normally, Beckett performed the basic investigations.

"Why…why did you have to call Ron?"

His throat bobbed. I'd spent two decades learning everything there was to know about Beckett Romero, including all his tells, and now I knew he was nervous, holding back.

"I just want to make sure all the T's are crossed and I's are dotted so you don't have an issue with the insurance claim."

His reasons were solid, but I didn't feel the relief I should have at his words, because I knew Beckett was holding back.

"If he even had insurance," I said, rubbing my forehead in frustration.

"What?" Beckett's voice dropped in surprise.

Dad let out a moan in his sleep, and I turned back to him, adjusting the IV line. In his agitation earlier, he'd tried to tear it out. He'd even threatened the staff, so we'd decided the benefits of a sedative had outweighed the possible complications after his recent stroke. It would take a few hours for it to wear off, but hopefully, when it did, he'd be back to the calmer father I'd always known.

I straightened his blankets and then turned and tilted my head toward the hallway. I didn't want to talk about my father where he could hear it, even in his subconscious.

Moving toward the door required stepping around Beckett, and when I did, my arm brushed against his. As always, the simple touch of skin on skin curled through me. Longing and desire. What would I give to lose myself in those feelings, if only for a few hours? To forget for a few moments the way my life was crumbling around the edges once more?

But I wouldn't. I'd figure this out. I'd stand on my own and take care of my family.

As we left the room, Tina glanced up from the nurse's

station. I didn't want her to hear this conversation any more than I wanted my dad to in his subconscious, so I kept moving in the direction of the exit, and Beckett followed.

The trees on the hills behind us cast long shadows over the staff parking lot as we stepped out the rear entrance. The hours had slipped away while I'd been waiting for Dad's test results, for him to recover his sanity, and for me to find answers to problems that had no easy solutions.

"What's going on, Maisey?" Beckett asked.

I debated how much to tell him, but if Carter knew about the bank foreclosing, it would be all over Swift Rivers soon enough. So, I explained what I'd learned this morning about the mortgage and Dad's stack of bills while I paced the pebbled pathway from the hospital door to the parking lot and back. Beckett watched, hands in his pockets, eyes penetrating and watchful.

"If, by some miracle, he paid the insurance, there's a slim chance I can right the ship. I'll talk to the bank, figure out a way to get him caught up on the mortgage. It'll mean giving up my apartment and moving in with him so I can use my rent money to help with the bills."

Beckett made a frustrated sound. Fury? Disgust?

They were all emotions I was feeling too. But they were coated with a healthy dose of guilt and a bucket of resignation.

Chelsea's words this morning now felt like they'd been a premonition, because I would be moving back home. I'd be everything my sister had said—the dutiful daughter taking care of a father who might just take her down with him.

But I wouldn't walk away from our dad.

Mom had sacrificed everything, even her relationship with Dad at times, to make sure I had whatever I needed. She'd hate that he'd been left to struggle on his own as much as she'd hate that the house had fallen down around him. Maybe it did make me a ridiculously dutiful daughter, or maybe I was simply showing loyalty to a dead parent and what she would have wanted. Or maybe I was just doing the right thing for the person I loved, regardless of his flaws. I wasn't sure which of those things was true. Maybe all of them were.

Chapter Eight
Beckett

LETTER TO A FRIEND
Performed by Bon Jovi

TEN YEARS AGO

HIM: I bought a Stephen King book today. Bring the popcorn, and we'll see if this one can actually scare us silly.

> *HER: No can do. I'm spending the night with Fallon. We're working on our routines for the Fourth of July show.*

HIM: We haven't read anything together in a long time. Are you avoiding me?

> *HER: *** eye-roll emoji*** Don't be ridiculous. You've been busy with your summer semester, and I've been busy helping out at the ranch.*

HIM: I miss my Maisey-girl.

> *HER: Stop by Jack's, and you'll be swarmed with at least a dozen females willing to be my stand-in.*

HIM: No one can take your place, Maise. You're irreplaceable.

PRESENT DAY

Maisey's eyes were flashing as she paced. Fury, frustration, and responsibility all mixed into a potent cocktail that I thought might just explode. It was better than the glazed, what-the-hell-just-happened look she'd had when she'd shown up at her dad's house—the look most fire victims had when we arrived at the scene of a residential fire.

But I'd gladly take the fury over the blank face she'd gotten good at showing me lately. The one she'd shown just now in her dad's hospital room.

As she flew back and forth over the sidewalk, the fading sunlight surrounded her, and I swore it cast a halo around her. She shimmered and sparkled with a crusading angel-type glow.

Instead of a yellow sundress tempting me as it had last night, it was how her small, tantalizing curves were on display in her riding outfit. Curves that made me crave things I'd never wanted before last night. Impossible things. Like how she would feel wrapped around me in the middle of the night... Hell, the middle of the day. Any time of day.

Fuck.

I had to get a grip on this new obsession. Because those thoughts, the places my brain and body went just as she was drowning, proved exactly why I wasn't cut out for a relationship. Not with her. Not with anyone. Here she was, stressed and hurting, and I was thinking about what she'd sound like if I were deep inside her.

Disgust filled me.

I was a bastard.

A selfish bastard who'd done things to her today she didn't even know about yet.

The lie I'd told Delilah.

The evidence I'd handed over to Ron.

I'd debated for longer than I should have about calling Ron after I'd found the empty Sterno can sitting next to what was left of her dad's stove. Ron trusted me to make the call on most cases, and I could have just pretended I hadn't seen it. But if it ever came out that I'd hidden evidence in a fire, my career would be over. Forget the job as fire chief, forget *any* firefighting career. And I couldn't save Maisey's dad at the cost of my future.

As Maisey paced by me once again, I caught her arm to stop her. She resisted my touch just like she had in the hospital, but this time, I refused to back off. I just yanked her to me. She put a hand out to slow the collision of our bodies. The heat of her palm burned through my chest, settling over the cold heart that beat beneath it and zapping it with the strength of a defibrillator.

"If he loses the house, that's on him," I said. "You don't owe him a goddamn thing."

Lewis Campbell hadn't completely fallen apart after his wife died, but he hadn't kept his shit together like my dad had when the worst struck. Not once had my father abandoned me, physically or emotionally, after any of the hits he'd taken. He'd stuck around while Maisey's dad had escaped to his rig, using money as an excuse for leaving her and Chelsea to shoulder the real loss on their own.

Maisey tried to pull away, but when I didn't let go, she gave in, resting her forehead on my chest. My hands went to her shoulders, kneading at the stiffness I felt there. She didn't deserve more heavy burdens landing on her. She'd already had enough for a lifetime.

When she lifted her face, the look of devastation I saw made me want to strangle someone.

"He's lost his wife, his job, and his pride, Beckett. If he loses his house too..." her voice cracked. "I can't let that happen. No matter his failings, no matter our past, I love him too much to let him lose the last bit of himself...of Mom...he has left."

The tightness in my chest grew at her tortured words, wishing I could ease them. I was as helpless today as I was the day her mom had died.

"I can clean out Chelsea's room," she continued, "and move in there. After today, she isn't going to come back."

My hands, kneading her shoulders, stilled. "Wait. Chelsea was at the house today?"

She scoffed in disgust. "Yep. Turns out the red sports car we saw last night belongs to her latest actor boyfriend. She supposedly stopped on their way to a movie they're filming in the mountains. The visit wasn't pretty and ended just like it had the last time she'd come home, with Dad asking her to leave and her storming out."

Something dark and unsettled washed over me. A fleeting thought I couldn't quite grasp.

"She left before you did?"

"Yeah. Before I could tell her about Dad's stroke or the trouble he's in with the house. Not that Chelsea would help him even if she had the money."

"You said you'd need to clean out her room if you moved in, but when I cleared the house today—" My mouth went dry at just the memory of that terrifying moment when I'd thought Maisey might be there. "Her room was completely empty. Nothing there but the furniture."

Maisey's mouth dropped open, and she forced herself out of my arms.

"Empty, empty? Like, no old clothes? No movie posters on the wall?"

"Not even an empty mascara tube."

I went to draw her back, and she swatted at my hands. I shoved them into my pockets to keep from reaching for her as she returned to her restless pacing.

"Why would Chelsea take everything now?" Maisey's brows furrowed together. "Anything she thought was of value, she would have taken with her a long time ago."

Unless she was going to set the place ablaze and wanted a few more mementos of her childhood. Wait. Did I really think Chelsea would set fire to their house? Or was the idea just a leftover of my wounded past, knowing my mother had done just that?

Subconsciously, Maisey twirled one long strand around her finger.

Every fiber in me hated that these new traumas were breaking open old wounds she'd done all the hard work to put behind her. Maisey deserved a future that left behind those pained moments. That gave her the forever after and the permanence she craved.

I certainly hadn't helped her along that path with my lie today.

But hell, it might actually end up helping us both. I wouldn't ever be able to give someone forever—not after what I'd lived through and not after what I'd done to Del—but I could help Maisey temporarily, and she could help me. What did they call it in romance books? A fake-engagement trope. It never worked in the books, but it could work for us.

I could keep my new and uncomfortable obsession with the way her hips swayed to myself. I could keep my dick in my pants. I wasn't some fictional character.

"You can't move into that house right now," I told her truthfully. "The inspector will have to clear it, and the water restoration people need to dry things out. I boarded up the back door before I left today, but I don't think the house will be livable for months. You and your dad can move in with me while the repairs are made."

Her feet froze so fast that she stumbled over them. "Wh-what?"

"Look. If you insist on helping your dad, you'll need a place to live free of charge. I have two extra bedrooms that aren't being used. I've painted them and refinished the floors, but that's as far as I've gotten."

She was shaking her head before I'd even finished.

"No. Absolutely not. We're not taking advantage of you like that."

Everything in me zeroed in on her response. "How is one friend helping another taking advantage?"

"Beckett, you could rent those rooms out and offset your own expenses."

"Please. You know I don't have a mortgage. Dad put me on the title, saying it was going to be mine when he kicked the bucket anyway. I've paid for the remodel as I had the money and time to do it, so I don't have any real debt."

She was still shaking her head, her entire body moving with the ferocity of it.

"Look. The truth is"—I swallowed hard—"if you moved in, you'd be doing me a favor."

She snorted in disbelief. "How do you figure that?"

I ran a hand through my hair, scratched the back of my neck, and then shoved my hands back into my pockets. "Well…things happened today at the station. Things I reacted to in ways I probably shouldn't have and had me saying things I had no right to say. But after some thought, it still makes a hell of a lot of sense."

Her brows furrowed.

I rocked on my heels. "Seems the chief isn't going to consider me as his replacement because he thinks I'm too single."

The confusion on her face grew more pronounced. "What in the world does that mean?"

"Means Nattingly, and the entire city council, wants a married man for the job." Suspicion flitted over her, but I plowed forward. "And then Delilah showed up, offering herself up as some sort of sacrifice, suggesting we should get married, as if it would help both our careers. And I sort of panicked. Sort of let my tongue wag before my brain caught up with it."

"Oh, Beckett…what did you do?" she breathed out, as if already starting to realize, as if knowing me for the majority of my life had given her the inside track to the way my brain worked, which it had.

I finally recovered my balls from where they'd been hiding and told her the truth. "I said I couldn't marry her because you and I were already engaged."

Her eyebrows hit her hairline. Panic flitted over her face, followed by something I thought might be fear, before she shut down again. Every single emotion disappeared, and I was left with the bland Maisey I wanted to banish.

"You're an idiot." There was no heat to the words. No passion or frustration or anger. And that sort of pissed me off because she *should* be angry with me.

"The last thing I am is an idiot," I said with a shrug. The only trouble I ever got into at school came from being bored, waiting for my classmates to catch up.

Maisey looked down and away, and I knew she regretted using the word idiot—a word she despised because of the way people had used it against her. But I proved just what a bastard I could be by using her regret to push my cause.

"Look. This is a two-way street here. I need a fake fiancée, and you need a place to live. You can save your rent money, put it all toward your dad's mortgage, and no one needs to know you aren't sleeping in my bed." I paused as that image slammed into me—her spread out across my navy sheets, dark hair spread over my pillows, naked skin glowing. I pushed it aside and kept going. "Plus, I can sweeten the deal by throwing in my manual labor. We can keep the repair costs down at your dad's by doing a lot of the work ourselves, just like I did with my house."

She pressed a hand into her stomach, but she didn't reject the idea again. Instead, I could tell she was thinking about it, weighing the pros and cons in that careful way Maisey was so good at doing.

"It's not like this is forever, Maise. We just keep up the engagement until I get the chief's job, and you get your dad back on his feet. It's a win-win."

"And what if Nattingly and the city council expect us to actually say *I do* before they give you the job?"

My hands turned sweaty, and my lungs filled with ash. I fought past it, shaking my head to give myself time. Once the worst had subsided, I said, "They'll need someone in the job far sooner than we could plan a wedding."

She rubbed her forehead. "This is a bad idea, Beckett."

She hadn't said no. If she'd been going to, she would have already. This was like when we'd been kids and she'd debated whether she should sneak out of the house to join me in the treehouse at night. She just needed a little nudge.

I closed the distance between us, tugged on a long strand of hair, and indulged myself in wrapping it around my fingers. She watched me slowly twist it, and I was rewarded with her breath turning choppy. This new chemistry wasn't one-sided. I relished knowing she was fighting the attraction too, even if I'd never let us act on it.

"Come on, my Maisey-girl, what's the worst that could happen?"

The answer popped into my head before she could respond. Sex. Sex and passion and things that might permanently break through the layer of scars that kept my heart from fully feeling anything, that might ruin the only real friendship I had.

No. I wouldn't risk her for sex.

You'll risk her for your job, though, a little voice whispered.

I shoved it aside. This wouldn't risk us. Wouldn't risk what we had.

If anything, this might bring us even closer. We could be there for each other as we'd once been when we'd lived next door as two broken kids.

This actually might be the best thing that had happened to either of us in a long time.

Chapter Nine
Maisey

CHANCES ARE
Performed by Lee Ann Womack

THREE YEARS AGO

HIM: You looked pretty darn cute when I left, passed out in your bed.

An hour later.

HIM: Are you not talking to me?

> *HER: I'm not sure what to say. I'm embarrassed. I don't even remember you putting me to bed.*

HIM: Nothing to be embarrassed about. We've all been there.

Another hour went by.

HIM: Maise, seriously. We've all gotten drunk and done stupid shit.

> *HER: Wait. Was there more? What exactly did I do? And there's no video evidence, is there?*

HIM: So I take it you want me to delete the video of you singing 'You Give Love A Bad Name'?

> *HER: I did NOT sing.*

HIM: Are you sure? Are you really, really sure? How much would you wager on it?

> *HER: If I did sing, which I seriously doubt,*

> *it was an alcohol-induced mistake. Let's just forget it ever happened.*

A few minutes passed.

> *HER: Beckett. I'm serious… Delete and forget. I'm begging you.*

HIM: Forget what? What am I forgetting? My mind is a blank.

> *HER: Dork.*

HIM: Nerd.

PRESENT DAY

With Beckett this close, with his hand wrapped in my hair, making me want things I knew better than to want, it was hard to banish the old teenage dream of Beckett finally realizing he couldn't live without me and getting down on a bended knee to ask me to be his forever.

But I'd learned the hard way that this ugly duckling was never going to be a swan. I wasn't the princess that the prince searched the kingdom for so he could keep her.

Even now, what Beckett was proposing wasn't because he actually wanted me—Maisey.

I'd just sworn to myself this morning I'd handle the disaster with Dad on my own. But for the first time in almost as long as I could remember, Beckett wasn't just offering to help me. He was asking for help in return. After years of not knowing how to pay him back, I had an opportunity to do something.

With Fallon, it was different. The financial scales might forever be tipped in her direction, but emotionally, I'd been there for her when some pretty horrific things had hit her life. Beckett, on the other hand, had needed very little from me because he'd had a fully functioning father who'd given him the shoulder he'd needed.

What Beckett was asking of me now was a simple thing that would have a huge impact on his future. I couldn't remember another time when he'd needed something this big and asked me to help him.

How could I say no?

But would I survive this particular request? Because if we did this, it wasn't going to end in a happily ever after like in my romance books. Beckett believed love always failed and used every broken relationship he came across as evidence. He had no desire to challenge his hypothesis by seeking out success stories. Even if, by some miracle, he changed his mind about love and marriage, he wouldn't want it with me. I was his friend. The sidekick. The anti-princess.

"You hate the idea so much you can't even consider it?" Beckett asked, and when I looked up, the plea in his eyes was nearly my undoing.

My pulse pounded so hard and so loud I was certain he could hear it. My heart and my conscience were warring with each other.

I could barely keep my barriers up with him now. I barely kept our friendship at the level it was destined to remain without ruining it with my desire for more. What would living in his house, completely surrounded by him, brushing up against him in the kitchen, flirting with him as we passed in the hall, do to me?

The plea in his eyes vanished, only to be replaced with a twinkle, and I realized I was in even more trouble. I couldn't resist his dimple on top of everything else.

"You afraid, my Maisey-girl?" he teased. "Afraid you won't be able to keep your hands off?"

I forced back the panic, looked pointedly at his fingers still wrapped in my hair, and tossed back, "If anyone can't keep their hands off, it's clearly you."

He let go, holding his hands up as he stepped back with a grin.

"Hands off from here on out."

I rolled my eyes, and he chuckled.

"You don't believe I can keep my hands to myself?" he taunted. "How about every time I touch you, I read one of your romance books, and every time you touch me, you owe me a meal?"

I frowned at him. "That sounds dangerously like a bet."

His smile grew impossibly wider, and I was a goner. "Not a bet. Not even a dare. Just two people promising we'll be on our best behavior with a penalty clause in place. I'll even keep the temptation down to a minimum—I promise not to walk around in my boxer briefs."

Just the thought hit me low and hard in my core, proving just how stupid it was to even consider the idea. I was proud when my voice sounded steady when I replied, "I need some time to think about it."

"Fair enough. But you know how Delilah works, and I can almost guarantee the news has already spread through town."

"You should have thought of that before you lied without consulting me first," I bit back. "Besides, no one is going to believe we're in love. I doubt Nattingly or the city council members are going to buy this engagement thing, even if you tell them you proposed."

Beckett frowned. "What's love got to do with it?"

My heart ached, this time for Beckett. For the damage his mother and Liza had done long before Delilah had pounded the last nail in the coffin.

Before I could respond, the radio on his chest squawked. Smoke had been spotted outside town. Beckett was already sprinting toward the captain's rig he'd driven to the hospital as he tossed back, "We'll finish the conversation later."

"Please be careful!" I yelled.

"Always," he promised before disappearing into the truck, hitting the lights, and tearing out of the lot.

While I wouldn't ever say I was grateful for a fire, I was grateful for the distraction. If Beckett had stayed any longer, he would have pushed, and I would have agreed without really weighing all the pros and cons.

Could I live with the real cost of this arrangement? To my pride, in letting my friend dig me out of a hole once again? To my heart and soul, who were already halfway in love with my friend? Would those costs be worth the chance to pay Beckett back for all he'd already done for me? Or would it eat away the last pieces of me so there was nothing left?

♫ ♫ ♫

I'd just sunk back into Titan's saddle, after executing a three-hundred-and-sixty-degree pirouette with my lasso in the air, when Fallon's voice rang out from the fence.

"Is there something you forgot to tell me, your supposed *best* friend?"

The dust our practice had stirred up mingled with sunshine as it crested over the hills as I led Titan over to the fence. Fallon climbed up onto the rail, ready for her day at the ranch in worn jeans, a sleeveless plaid button-down, a beat-up cowboy hat, and boots that had seen the better side of a decade.

Titan whinnied a greeting at her, and Fallon slid a hand over my horse's muzzle before shooting me a glare.

"Unless I did something in my sleep last night after you saw me at the hospital, I'm not sure I know what you mean."

She'd come by briefly to see Dad and me, but an emergency at the ranch with the upcoming Fourth of July festivities had drawn her away before I could even think of telling her about the rest of my day. And that was when understanding hit me.

My stomach fell just as she exclaimed, "You're engaged to Beckett!"

"Fallon—"

"You didn't even tell me you were dating. Neither of you even hinted at it the other night at Frank's. If anyone can understand how enormous it feels to finally get the one person you've always wanted to be yours, it's me. So why wouldn't you tell me?" she demanded.

Fallon had loved Parker from the time she was a kid, but a promise he'd made to their fathers had prevented him from starting anything with her. It wasn't until her life had been threatened that he'd finally realized what he had to lose. Once he'd woken up, he'd claimed her as his and never let go.

But the happily ever after Fallon had found wasn't ever

going to be mine.

"It's not like that," I told her softly.

"When Andie was at the Emporium last night, that's all anyone was talking about."

Well, hell, Delilah really had worked quickly.

My mouth went dry as panic tried to take over. Not because I was the center of a Swift Rivers rumor, but because of what it meant. I was stuck. The decision had been taken out of my hands. No way would I humiliate Beckett by denying what he'd told her.

But what Beckett hadn't realized yet was, to convince the city council our engagement was genuine, we would have to act like an actual couple. He'd teased about not touching, promised we'd keep our hands off, but exactly how would that work in public? How would we convince everyone we had real feelings for each other *and* keep our distance?

All the questions and worries that had kept me awake last night slammed back into me. I'd been trying to keep my feelings for Beckett at bay for so long that just the thought of pretending to be in love was enough to make me hyperventilate.

Knowing Fallon was the one person I could count on to keep my secret, I whispered, "It's not real."

"What isn't? Do you mean he didn't ask you? Or you said no? Or the rumor is false?" she demanded.

I inhaled deeply and then spilled everything that had gone down yesterday. When I was finished, she was quiet for a long time, looking out beyond the corral to the river rushing down to the lake sparkling in the sunrise.

Finally, she let out a long breath and said, "I don't want you to get hurt."

Just knowing that was her first thought made tears well. She wasn't saying anything I didn't already know. This was a bad idea. But if I was honest, the vicious bitch called Hope had wiggled inside my heart last night, whispering things I knew better than to allow.

I needed to shut Hope down to prove to myself, even more than Fallon, that I could do this and survive. "I'm not going into this with blinders on, Fallon. I know exactly what Beckett is and isn't capable of. I know he'll never want love and a permanent relationship. But the truth is, we both need something right now the other can offer."

"If it's money, you know—"

"I'm not taking money from you again," I said vehemently.

"Why not? I have more than I'll ever need in this lifetime. More than my kids will need. Hell, probably even more than my great-grandkids would need."

"No." I shook my head. "I'm not using you and taking money simply to make my life easier. The only reason I'm really considering this with Beckett is because I can finally help him with something after years of our relationship being one-sided, of him always shouldering my problems."

Her jaw tightened, and I knew I'd hurt her feelings, so I shifted Titan around so I could grab her hand. "As much as I don't want to admit Chelsea was right about anything, she *was* right when she said I've always let my friends swoop in and save the day. I'm not a kid anymore, and I refuse to be my dad, relying on others to dig me out of a hole. I hate that I'm relying on Beckett again, but at least, this time, I can help him in return."

"Chelsea wasn't right!" Fallon snapped. "Allowing your friends and family to help you doesn't make you some damsel needing saving. And it isn't like you were the only one who needed help. How many times were you there for me, Maise?" I tried to wave her off, and she plowed right on. "I wouldn't have made it after my stepdad died, or while I was dealing with Mom's addiction, or when I found out I was pregnant with Lila if you hadn't been there holding me up."

"That's different."

"You're right. It is different. Offering money…that's easy when I have loads of it to give. It's nothing. It doesn't require time and love and friendship. Offering yourself, truly being there for someone…that's the bigger sacrifice. Chelsea couldn't possibly understand that because she's never thought of anyone but herself. But you've always given of yourself freely. Your parents were lucky to have you on their side, just as Beckett and

I are lucky to call you our friend."

I wanted to believe what she said. I wanted to believe what I'd offered had been enough. That I was enough…

Sensing my discomfort, Fallon changed the subject to one we normally agreed upon.

"Speaking of that no-good narcissist, have you told Chelsea about your dad's problems? Because if she really got a movie contract, she might have the money to help."

I shook my head. "Even if she has the money, she wouldn't offer any of it for Dad or me. Not after spending an entire childhood bemoaning how I got everything and she got nothing."

I shuddered, thinking of how she'd thrown a vase through the kitchen window after she'd learned she hadn't been able to go to acting camp, while I'd been able to keep my classes at the riding school. That night, she'd locked me out of the house. I'd been in my headgear, terrified someone would see me in it. I'd slept on the porch and begged and cried the next morning for her to let me in. When Mom had found me distraught and confronted Chelsea, my sister had said it had been an accident, but it was one of the first times I'd wondered if Beckett was right about her.

Fallon sighed. "Fine, but if Beckett hurts you, I'll kick his ass."

Which was exactly why I'd never told Fallon about our childish kiss and how I'd ended up feeling humiliated and more broken than normal. Fallon would have gone after him, just like she'd gone after Carter for telling me I tasted like metal and rotten food when he'd kissed me after the homecoming dance.

It had been my own fault for saying yes to Carter when every instinct had been screaming at me to say no. He'd always been part of Chelsea's entourage, so I'd been shocked when he'd asked me. I'd told him I'd think about it, because I'd really been hoping Beckett would ask me. As soon as Chelsea had found out I'd put Carter off, she'd told me Beckett was taking Delilah and to stop jerking Carter around, so I'd reluctantly said yes and regretted it ever since.

"I need to finish up here with Titan and get going," I told

her. "The hospital said Dad was awake and much calmer this morning, but I want to talk to the doctor."

Not to mention I needed to stop by the bank and talk to the loan officer about the mortgage, call Dad's insurance agency to see if he was still covered, find a water damage restoration company to set up fans at the house, and pop by the firehouse to make sure Beckett really wanted to do this before giving notice on my apartment. It was going to be a really full day.

Fallon nodded at Titan. "You two looked good out there. You're going to knock the guests off their feet this year."

A tiny spark of happiness settled in my chest. I'd felt better on Titan's back today than I had yesterday, which was surprising, seeing as my problems had only grown since the day before.

"Thanks. Titan hasn't lost a step, but I'm still a little rusty." I patted my horse before remembering he really wasn't mine. I'd have to put buying him back on hold while I bailed Dad out, but it would happen.

Fallon swung over the fence and grabbed Titan's reins. "Let me rub him down for you." My shoulders stiffened, and when she saw my reaction, she burst out laughing. "For Pete's sake, I'm heading into the barn to check on the horses anyway. This isn't you *using* me or my *saving* you."

Behind the laughter, I heard the hurt, not just at my not having told her about Beckett, but because I'd rejected her offer of money. So, as a peace offering, I gave in.

I dismounted, spent a few more seconds giving Titan my love, along with a sugar cube I'd tucked in my pocket, and then let her lead him away.

Fallon had almost disappeared inside when I called her name, and when she looked back, I said, "Thanks for being such a good friend."

She just nodded.

Her words followed me the rest of the morning, battling with Chelsea's words from the day before, and Beckett's offer, and my own tormented feelings.

But by the time I jogged down the apartment steps after

showering and changing, I felt a bit more settled. I'd help Beckett out, and he'd help me, and in doing so Dad would have a place to land while we sorted his financials. For a few months, I could pretend to the town that everything I'd wanted had come true, and when it was over, I'd tuck my heart back into my chest and make believe nothing had changed.

Chapter Ten

Beckett

KEEP UP WITH A COWGIRL
Performed by David Adam Brynes

FOUR YEARS AGO

> HER: Thanks again for coming to my graduation and taking me to dinner. Having Kurt show up was a surprise. Make sure to thank him again for me.

HIM: You already thanked him so many times he's still blushing.

HIM: I couldn't be prouder of my Maisey-girl. Fallon and I are both proud of you. What was your dad's excuse for not showing up?

> HER: Rig broke down in New Mexico.

HIM: And Chelsea?

> HER: She had an audition in LA.

HIM: When she graduated, it was the middle of your finals, and you still drove six hours to attend, but she couldn't be bothered to show up for you?

> HER: Don't. I had a good day. I had the most important people with me. It's your turn next.

HIM: I'm not walking. I just need the paper stating I got my master's so I can move on to the next task on my list.

> HER: Celebrating your achievements is

important.

HIM: When I get my captain's bugles, we'll celebrate. I'll let you get me drunk and take advantage of me.

*HER: *** eyeroll and puke emojiis ****

*HIM: Darlin', I think something's wrong with the emojis on your phone. I think you meant to send *** drooling face, jalapeño, and fire emojis ****

PRESENT DAY

I was wrestling with Vader, who kept sticking his nose into the kitten's crate, making feeding her impossible, when Tejas's deep, flirty "Hey, Maisey" had me whipping around.

Maisey barely had time to say hello back before Vader abandoned me to go crashing into her. She laughed, the sound filling the air and loosening the knot that had been lodged in my chest since I'd left her at the hospital the night before.

"Well, hello to you too, boy," she said, brushing her hand over Vader's head.

I swore my dog quivered at her touch. Lucky bastard.

When her eyes lifted to mine, the beautiful picture she made ripped the air from my chest. Her hair fell in soft, tumbling waves over her shoulders, and all I could think about was how it had felt curled around my finger yesterday—soft and silky— filling me with visions of fisting it as we came apart together.

Today, it wasn't only her hair but another damn summer dress that did its best to wreck me. Blue and white with buttons tracing a line between her breasts, it taunted me to slowly undo each one. Or better yet, tear them open and feast on her until I sated this new, unrelenting, and reckless hunger.

The yearning I had for her these days felt so wrong. But how could I escape it when she looked like summer skies and weekend delights all rolled into a single, sweet package?

Maisey wasn't just beautiful. She was a gift to us mere

mortals.

A gift I could only sully.

I shoved the cat crate into Tejas's hands and strode over to her.

"Hey, darlin'. I wasn't expecting you."

A flicker crossed her face, something that felt like worry, maybe even a hint of fear, but it all disappeared behind a soft smile. It was the same one Maisey had given me from the moment I'd met her as a little girl. Full of affection and friendship. Although it made my body respond in ways I had to shut down, I still savored being on the receiving end of it.

"I just wanted to give you an update on…what we talked about yesterday," she said, eyes darting around to the rest of my crew lounging on the couches in front of the oversized television.

"Sure," I said casually, waving toward the hallway.

I let her go in front of me, ignoring the whispers I heard coming from behind me.

My focus was drawn to her hips and the way her short dress swayed around her bare thighs. Muscled thighs that would lock on to a man's waist and hold tight while—

I jerked my thoughts back to safer ground as I shut my office door behind us. Maisey turned toward me, twirling her keys on a long finger, and I realized she was nervous. Was it because she was going to accept my offer or because she was turning it down? My gut knotted.

"Are you sure you really want to do this?" she asked.

"Yes," I didn't even hesitate.

She inhaled, putting a hand to her chest as if trying to calm the racing of her heart. "Okay, I'll do it. Dad and I will move in with you—temporarily—and we can say we're engaged, but I won't go as far as to actually marry you. I draw the line there." She watched me carefully, shoulders tensing as if expecting me to push back.

I couldn't think about what would happen if Nattingly and the city council said we needed to actually be married before they gave me the job. We'd have to cross that bridge if and when we got to it. For now, this was enough. The pressure I'd been carrying around since talking to her yesterday—really, since hearing the chief on the phone—loosened even more.

"Thank you, Maise," I said softly.

She looked away, twirling the keys some more. "I just wanted to be sure before I talked to Randy about getting out of the lease on my studio. Then, I can tell the bank I'll be paying Dad's mortgage from here on out. I can use my savings to try to catch up on the amount that's due now. The hospital isn't going to release Dad until Thursday or Friday, but I want to have everything in order before then." She was rambling—another sign she was still a bundle of nerves.

I closed the distance, pulled her hand into mine, and she looked up at me with beautiful eyes that still held uncertainty in their depths.

"Stop," I told her.

"Stop what?" she asked, breath as choppy as it had been yesterday when I'd twirled her hair in my fingers.

"This is me, my Maisey-girl. Just me. Just two friends sharing a house and helping each other out. So what if the town puts a label on it? You and me"—I waved my hand between us—"know the real deal."

She swallowed hard and looked down before pulling her hand from mine.

"That's one."

I frowned at her in confusion.

"Hands to yourself, Fireball. That's what you promised. You owe me a romance book."

A laugh burst from deep inside. "Fine, but for the record, I want it known you *finally* accepted a bet."

It was her turn to frown. "Did not. You told me it was a promise."

"We can call it that," I said, leaning in closer, and she tried to back away but got caught by my desk. My lips coasted close to the shell of her ear as I said, "But we both know the truth."

I had the perverse pleasure of seeing her eyes flare before I stepped back so I wouldn't break my promise a second time.

She cleared her throat, shifted around me, and headed for the door.

"I'll let you know when we'll be moving in. We'll try not to get in your way too much."

"Neither of you will be in my way. My house is your house." I meant it from the bottom of my heart. I wanted Maisey and her things there. I wanted the house to feel like it was full of family again. Since moving Dad and his belongings out to the ranch, the house had felt decidedly empty. "If you can wait until Thursday, when my shift is over, I can help with the heavy lifting. But feel free to move whatever you want while I'm at the station."

I grabbed a ring from the hook by the door, pulled off my house key, and handed it to her.

Her throat bobbed as she took it. "How will you get in?"

"You can bring me the spare from the utility drawer in the kitchen."

She didn't say anything else but slipped out the door and headed down the hall. Vader was waiting for her with the kitten in his mouth again. He pranced over to her, showing the thing off and preening like a damn parent.

"What's this?" she laughed.

"Vader, the cat-savior-of-the-world, found another stray," I said with a sigh.

Maisey bent over to pet both animals. "Aw. What a sweetie."

Vader thumped his tail and pushed the kitten into her hands. Maisey took the little thing, brought it to her face, and rubbed her nose in the fur, and damned if I wasn't jealous of the cat now.

She turned to me, her expression opening in surprise. "Are you keeping this one?"

"No."

"Maybe if you keep one, Vader will stop bringing you more. Maybe he just wants a friend. Someone to care for," she said softly, and her words hit home in ways I couldn't quite describe.

My crew had moved from the couches to the table with lunch in front of them and were being unusually quiet, absorbing every word. Tejas made a choked noise at Maisey's idea, and Kasey didn't even bother to hide her laugh. The probie looked confused as normal, but it was Captain Mike Stone, standing at the head of the table, who actually responded.

"Yeah, Romeo. Maybe you should keep this one."

Stoney wore an SRFD baseball hat turned backward and had a Metallica T-shirt stretched across his chest. The outfit's youthfulness was at odds with his brown hair, which was turning gray at the sides.

"Stoney," I said with a chin nod in his direction. "What dragged you in today?"

He wasn't due for another three days, but there was a grimness to him, regardless of the tease he'd just dropped, that made me think he'd come to discuss the rumors about the fire chief position. While I could change my marital status, Stoney had no way to fix his lack of education in time to get the job. It had to be eating at him.

He could argue his experience surpassed my degrees and certificates, and it did. But he'd also made a few enemies on the city council last year, fighting the change to the ordinance on livestock within the city boundaries. It would be a toss-up which way the politicians would vote when it came down to him or me.

"I wanted to talk to you about the schedule," Stoney said, which we both knew was a lie.

Maisey bent over to put the kitten into the crate, and her dress rose in the back, teasing the curve of her ass and making my body go rigid. When I saw both Tejas and Leon shift to get a better look, I grabbed her by the waist and hauled her toward the exit. "I'm going to walk Maisey out. I'll be right back."

Maisey and I almost made it to the top of the stairs when a tinkling stopped us. When I looked back, wide grins were stretched across my crew's faces while they tapped their silverware against their water glasses.

"Congratulations, you two," Kasey said. "You've been awfully sly about it, but we all know you fit together like two peas in a pod."

My eyes jerked down to Maisey. It wasn't the delightful blush that crept over her face, one I wanted to put there for all the wrong reasons, but the wariness in her expression that I suspected would give our secret away. We had one chance to persuade everyone this was real. With Stoney here, I had even more reason to make sure the show we put on convinced them.

"Thanks," I said. "We wanted to keep it to ourselves for a while, but I guess Delilah couldn't keep her trap shut."

Stoney's face tightened with suspicion.

"Let's see the ring," he said.

"At the jeweler's, being sized," I answered glibly.

Maisey's hand slid into mine, and I squeezed it without looking down at her. I kept my eyes trained on Stoney.

"When's the wedding?" Leon asked while shoveling pasta into his mouth. That kid had a lot to learn about manners.

"We haven't set a date yet," Maisey said quietly, and Stoney frowned. "Fallon and I need to find an opening in the ranch's schedule, but we'll let you all know soon so you can save the date."

"Romero kept putting me off when I tried to set him up with my best friend's sister for the Firefighters Ball next week, but I guess he just didn't want to tell us he was bringing you," Leon said with a wink. "Astrid is going to be really disappointed."

"Maisey or not, I wasn't taking Astrid anywhere, probie," I grunted out.

I turned and headed for the stairs again, and this time, when the ping rang against glass, it was from a single knife. Looking over my shoulder once again, I found Stoney holding it.

"This isn't a wedding reception, asshole."

"Afraid to kiss the bride already, Romeo? You sure aren't living up to your nickname."

Damn him. Damn them all.

I reacted without thinking, sweeping Maisey into my arms, bending her backward, and planting my lips on hers.

It was supposed to be fast and light. Just enough to prove a point. But as soon as my mouth covered hers, every single spark, every single inch of chemistry that had been wafting through me for days now, burst into a fiery swell. Electricity shot through me from head to toe. Aching lust and pent-up need flooded my veins as the scent of her, that heady flowery smell that felt like coming home, surrounded me.

Instead of kissing her and backing off as I'd intended, I deepened the embrace, dragging my tongue along the seam of her mouth as if we didn't have an audience. I was rewarded with a little gasp that added fuel to the fire burning inside me— oxygen and dry wood being thrown on an already out-of-control inferno.

Her hands tightened on my shoulders, and her heartbeat slammed against mine. It cracked the hard shell I had hiding the pink, tender skin beneath the charred exterior. Like lava seeping through granite, it threatened an upcoming disaster. I was a volcano ready to blow, and when I did, it would be impossible to return to my previous state.

But at the moment, I didn't care. I only wanted to feed the fire. I wanted to feel her pressed up against me with nothing between us but skin. I wanted to listen to her gasps and whimpers and hear her chant my name in a whole new way, throaty and hoarse and full of desire.

A wolf whistle brought me back to reality.

To the loft in the fire station with my crew looking on.

I pulled back far enough to look down into her face.

Her blush had taken on a life of its own, curling over her from forehead to neck.

But the soft green of her eyes had turned as dark as a creek nearing the end of summer. Thick and slow and sensual.

And that was when the alarm sounded inside me.

I righted us both, twining our hands together to keep up appearances, before dragging us down the staircase. I hollered at my crew, "That's enough of a show for you losers. Finish your meal and get to work washing the wagon."

I was proud my voice sounded steady, even though inside my body was a tumultuous riot—desire and regret taking turns with doubt and fear.

We were past the engine and almost to the roll-up doors before she said, "I don't think that was you keeping your hands to yourself."

Usually, I'd bite back a tease, but I couldn't. Because at the moment, the last thing I wanted was to keep my hands to myself. I wanted more of the heat and lust Maisey promised beneath her gentle façade. I wanted the passion I'd always known existed inside her but had now experienced firsthand.

I cleared my throat but dropped my voice to a whisper as I looked over my shoulder to make sure Stoney hadn't followed us. "You were right. We'll have to convince people we're in love and not just getting married for the job. Otherwise, this won't work. At home, when the door closes, I promise to keep my hands to myself."

I'd have to find a way to do just that—for her sake as well as for my own. Because touching her in the privacy of my house, near a bed, would not end well for either of us.

Outside on the drive, I stopped and finally risked looking at her again. She'd pulled herself together. The blush had disappeared, but so had all the emotion. And because I really disliked it when she shut down, I did the opposite of what I'd just told her. I touched her, running a finger along a smooth cheek.

She grabbed my hand and pulled it away. "No one is here now. That's two romance books you owe me."

I glanced up to the second floor of the firehouse. No bodies appeared in the windows, but you never knew. Maisey's eyes briefly followed mine.

Quiet settled between us. Not quite awkward but more uncomfortable than it had been between us in a long time.

It was Maisey who broke the silence, asking, "The Firefighters Ball is next week?"

I nodded. "With the chief, the mayor, and the entire city council there, it would be the perfect opportunity for us to announce our engagement."

"You were planning on going stag like always, weren't you? How are you going to get a ticket?" she asked, swinging her keys again.

"I always buy two tickets. I just never use both." I fought the desire to touch her, shoving my hands into my pockets. "Do you think you can get it off?"

Her eyes darted around, looking everywhere but at me, before she finally said, "I'll figure it out with Meredith."

She started toward the curb, and I followed.

"You don't have to walk me to my car, Beckett."

"Appearances, Maise. We'll need to keep them up."

She didn't say anything else as we made our way down the street to where she'd parked her ancient pickup. It was old enough to be put out to pasture, and she'd been saving for a new one, and now every penny she'd set aside was going to save her dad's house instead.

It irritated me all over again. Lewis Campbell didn't deserve Maisey's help.

Maisey's sudden inhale—sharp and startled—snapped my attention back to her, eyes jerking to the place she was staring at.

A sheet of paper clung to her passenger window, the orange ink slashed across it like a warning flare. *You chose poorly. Fix it before someone gets hurt.*

It took too long for my brain to register it as a threat.

Too long for me to search the streets for a hint of whoever had placed the sign there.

We never received a lot of foot traffic this far down Main Street, as the tourists tended to stay closer to the shops and restaurants, but today the sidewalks were completely bare.

"What the hell?" I growled, turning back to Maisey.

She reached for the paper with a shaky hand, and I grabbed her wrist just in time to stop her. "Don't touch it."

"I. I don't understand. What does this even mean?" she asked, voice shaking.

Exactly my question. What wrong choice did it mean? Was this about me? Had I put her in the headlights by asking her to marry me under false pretenses? Who would be so pissed at us being engaged that they'd write a note like this?

Delilah? Sure, she'd been upset yesterday, but at the end of the day, we were friends. She wanted me to be happy, much like I wanted her to be happy, didn't she? It wasn't like I would have put a ring on her finger, even if I hadn't told her the lie about Maisey and me.

Stoney's sullen face flashed before me. Would he do something this stupid? Childish? He was ticked I had what I needed now to apply for the chief's position, but whatever I did or didn't do wouldn't make him a better fit for the job. The city council would likely have hired someone else, an outsider, before they'd hired him. Then, we'd both be stuck with someone we didn't know telling us how to run our house. With me in charge, he knew he'd still have a say. Still be part of a team. Didn't he?

All I knew was that whoever it was, they wouldn't do it again. I wouldn't let them screw with my Maisey-girl and try to scare her off. Screw that. They'd regret leaving this note, and I'd make damn sure they didn't leave another.

Chapter Eleven
Maisey

ALRIGHT
Performed by Lady A

SIX YEARS AGO

HIM: What is a romance book you would recommend to someone starting out?

HER: Who is it for?

HIM: Why does it matter who it's for?

HER: Who they are will determine whether I suggest a slow burn or a sweet read or something really steamy.

HIM: Never mind.

HER: That only makes me more curious about who it is.

HIM: Fine. It's me.

*HER: *** crying laughing emoji *** Why are you reading a romance book?*

HIM: I lost a bet about a prank.

HER: Wait. The King of Pranks lost a bet about one.

HIM: Don't rub my nose in it, my Maisey-girl. It's already painful enough.

PRESENT DAY

My vision turned spotty, and I realized I'd forgotten to breathe.

I inhaled slowly, forcing myself to count to four before letting it out. I repeated the action, all while staring at the orange words written on a piece of white construction paper. It looked like the signs the cheerleaders used to make for the high school football team. The ones Chelsea would have spread out around the living room while she and the other cheerleaders laughed and joked and gossiped.

Beckett stopped me just as I reached for the sign. His hands were warm, searing into my wrist, searing into me and reminding me of the heat that had existed in our life-altering kiss.

He'd bent me over movie-star style and kissed me. Not a gentle peck. Not a mere brush of lips. Instead, it had been the kind of kiss you gave in the dark. Full of longing and lust.

It had felt like returning home and being wrapped in love and acceptance.

It had felt like an inferno of desire had been released, blazing through our veins.

If his crew hadn't whistled, we might have ended up on the floor in a tangled twine of legs and lips and mouths. Or at least, I'd wanted us to end up there before I'd remembered our audience. Before I'd remembered the kiss was for show.

Beckett had put on a top-notch performance, but I had to remember that was all it was. An act. One I'd been struggling to play along with, just like I was struggling to pull together my emotions as I stared at the note on my car.

I pressed a hand to my stomach, reading the words on repeat.

Fix it before someone gets hurt.

Fix what? And did it mean emotionally hurt? Physically? Was this an actual threat?

"We need to bag it and take it to the sheriff."

Lost as I was in my own spiral, it took a minute for me to really register what Beckett had said. "What? Why?"

When I looked from the note to him, fury swept over his features. An angry flare I hadn't witnessed since our teen years.

"What do you mean, why? So we can see if there are fingerprints on it. I want to have a nice long talk with whoever left this and set them straight." Beckett's voice was dark and menacing. It sent goosebumps over my skin in all the right and wrong ways.

"It's just some stupid prank. I'm not wasting the sheriff's time with something like this," I said, reaching for the note once more, only to have him jerk me away again. I was up tight against him with my shoulder pressed against his chest and our hips jammed together.

It was too much touching…or maybe not enough.

"We are absolutely giving this to the sheriff," he insisted.

"This isn't any different than when the kids used to call me Corny the Deformed Corncob. Or Frankenstein Mouth. The best way to handle it is to ignore it." I hated that my voice shook a little.

"It's not the same at all. Whoever this is, threatened you."

I took a deep breath, glancing back at the sign. It could mean nothing, or it could mean everything. I frowned. The only choices I'd made today had been about moving out of my apartment and in with Beckett while pretending to be his fiancée. I could think of only one person who would despise that choice. Only one person who still felt like she had a claim on Beckett, even though he'd never really belonged to her.

I pulled away from him, ignoring everything he'd said and tearing the sign off the window as he grunted in disapproval.

"I'll talk to her," I said.

Inside, I was groaning. I didn't want to add "confront Delilah Nattingly" to my growing list of tasks.

"Her?" Beckett's jaw clenched tight. "So you think this is Del."

I rolled my eyes. "Of course it's Delilah."

I unlocked the truck, opened the passenger door, and threw the sign and my phone inside before turning to face him.

"I'll make a detour to city hall on my way to the bank," I

told him.

Worry flashed over his face, followed by anger and regret. "You have enough to do. I need to drop by the mayor's office with the budget numbers anyway. I'll talk to her. If this was her, she won't bother you again, Maisey. I promise."

The surety in his tone should have relieved me, but I knew better. Delilah hated me as much, if not more, than she hated my sister.

She and Chelsea had been bitter rivals from middle school on. In high school, Chelsea had taken it to a whole new level, spewing rumors about how Delilah was willing to spread her legs for anything on two—or four—legs just like her dad's mistresses. Chelsea had never let up once.

My sister's smear campaign, on top of everything happening in the press with Delilah's parents, had sent Delilah off the edge in her senior year, and it had been Beckett who'd ridden in like a white knight to save her. From that moment on, the crush she'd had on Beckett had become an obsession, and Delilah had always seen my friendship with him as the one thing in her way.

Finding out we were engaged would be just the thing to set her off.

But I also knew Delilah wouldn't be inclined to listen to me today any more than she'd listened a decade ago when I'd told her she needed to get out of Swift Rivers for a few years for her mental health. If there was anyone who had a hope of reaching her, it was Beckett. He was the one person she really wanted. The one person who'd been a friend to her more than anyone else.

"Fine," I said. "You talk to her."

I slammed the passenger door and went to move around the truck to the driver's side, but he grabbed hold of my hand one more time.

"I'm sorry, Maise."

When I looked up, he was studying my lips. This time, he wasn't apologizing for Delilah's note. He was apologizing for kissing me, like he had when I was twelve. I beat back the humiliation before it could hit fully.

I tugged my hand away, putting the truck between us before responding. "Nothing for you to be sorry about, Beckett. You don't owe me a romance novel for that kiss. We both knew it would take a lot to convince people we were a real couple. I'm not going to pass out from shock or expect more."

"That's not what I meant."

I didn't respond. I just jumped into the truck, celebrated when the engine started, and pulled away from the curb while Beckett watched from the sidewalk. He had his hands shoved into his pockets and a frown between his brows. Was the frown because he didn't believe me? Or because he did?

Because my heart absolutely didn't believe a single syllable of the lie I'd uttered.

I'd always wanted Beckett for real.

My sister's words from fourteen years ago, when I'd come out of the bathroom with my headgear on after Beckett's first kiss, rang in my head. *Don't do something stupider than normal and start to think that kiss was the real deal, Cornlette. You'll only end up with a twisted heart to match your twisted jaw.*

I just had to find a way to make sure my heart got the picture this time.

♫ ♫ ♫

While Beckett was at the station for the last three days of his shift, I spent my after-work hours moving most of my belongings to his house. I still had the larger furniture and the heavy boxes of books to move, as well as Dad's bedroom set and whatever else he wanted with him, but I needed Beckett's help for most of those things.

Spending time in Beckett's home and seeing all the beautiful renovations he'd done made walking into the burnt remains of my childhood home with Dad on Thursday even more painful.

Dad's eyes filled with tears as he took in the charred walls and the boarded-up door and window. His raw pain echoed mine, and I had to blink rapidly so I didn't break down in front of him.

"What did I do?" he whispered angrily.

At least he was fully aware right now. He wasn't calling me Marjorie and telling people I was coming home from school. While he'd been in the hospital, he'd had several more bouts that had sent him reeling into the past. The doctors told me it was a side effect of the transient ischemic attack, or mini-stroke, he'd had when he'd crashed his rig. The cognitive decline and vascular dementia should be temporary, but the knot on his head he'd earned the day of the fire, and the stress of the disaster itself, had likely exacerbated the effects.

While I wasn't sure what I'd do with Dad when I was at work if he continued to forget where he was, what he was doing, and what year it was, I knew it was important to keep him calm when we were together. So, even though my heart was bleeding at the damage to the house, just as much as his was, I looped my arm through his and tried to lighten the mood.

"This is the last time I ever let you try to cook anything again."

Shock traveled over his face. "I was cooking?"

Try as he may, Dad couldn't remember the fire.

"Guess so. You didn't have to burn the house down to get a meal, you know. I would have made one for you," I continued to tease.

He didn't respond, and I tugged on his arm to get him moving. We stepped around the fans the water restoration company had set up and headed toward the bedroom he and Mom had shared on the opposite side of the house from my old room.

I set down the boxes I'd brought and started assembling them. Dad wasn't going to be much help with his burned hand still wrapped, but I needed him to tell me what he wanted to take with him to Beckett's.

"We can obviously come back and pick up more things if you forget something you really want, but let's try to take what you'll need to be comfortable."

Dad stopped at the dresser, looking down at the frames scattered across it. His wedding photo was front and center with Mom in a fluffy, Cinderella-style dress and him in a tuxedo.

The other pictures were a collage of memories. One was of my parents at the hospital, holding a newborn Chelsea. Another was of the four of us around a Christmas tree when I was a toddler. And next to it was one of my sister and me squeezed together in the tire swing after Mom and Dad had first hung it.

The ache in my chest grew, not only because of the sorrow on Dad's face but at the poignant memories. Unsure how much more I could take, I stepped into his tiny walk-in closet, calling out, "Come tell me what clothes you want."

"Where's her jewelry box?" Dad demanded. His tone was brittle. Sharp.

I ducked my head back out. "What?"

Dad pointed at the antique vanity Mom had bought from a junkyard and repaired when it had seemed a lost cause. An ornately carved jewelry box had always sat atop it. I remembered tracing my fingers over the delicate butterflies and hummingbirds as a kid. It had been filled mostly with costume jewelry, as we hadn't had enough money for her to have very many expensive pieces. But Grandma's wedding set and Mom's engagement ring had been in there along with a set of real pearls.

Chelsea and I had always fought over the pearls whenever we'd played dress up, and she'd usually won. But occasionally, I'd played without her and draped them over myself, pretending to be a runway model.

"Did you move it?" I asked Dad.

He stood there, motionless, while I searched around the vanity, lifted the old, faded dust ruffle to look under the bed, and then moved back to the closet, hunting the years of accumulated items on the racks and shelves.

An ugly fear started to form in my head, thinking of the two large suitcases Chelsea and Gavin had taken with them, and the fact Beckett had said she'd cleared out her room. But not even Chelsea would do something so brazen and hurtful, would she?

"You can't just take things, Maisey." The anger rippling from Dad's voice surprised me as much as his words. "I may be losing my mind and my job and my home, but you can't just take what you want without asking."

He thought *I'd* taken it? Pain sliced through me. I came out of the closet again, and the dark look he sent me sent a chill up my spine.

I bit back my instant retort that would have been full of hurt, opting for patience I wasn't sure I'd hold on to for much longer. "I didn't take anything, Dad. I'd never take something from your house without your permission."

Had he taken it and sold its contents, attempting to cover some of the money he owed the bank, and just couldn't remember it? By some twist of illogical fate, he'd paid the house insurance five months ago, although it was due again in a month. It was a small blessing, meaning we'd get a check to cover some of the damages. But Beckett had been right, we'd need to do a lot of the repairs ourselves.

"Then where is it?" he challenged me.

Pain carved a fresh wound into my soul.

"I don't know, Dad. You tell me what happened to it. You're the one who's been keeping secrets." As soon as I said it, I regretted it, but I'd be damned if I'd sit there and have him accuse me of stealing from my own family.

"Don't take that tone with me, young lady," Dad hissed. "I'm still the father, and a father doesn't burden his kids with his troubles."

My patience snapped completely as I turned away from him and said under my breath, "Please. Like I wasn't the one to pay all the bills after Mom died?"

"Don't talk to me that way!" he yelled and then kicked one of the empty boxes. I barely had time to put my hands up and deflect it as it came flying at me.

My hands shook as I righted the box just as Beckett's deep voice asked, "What's going on here?"

I looked up to find him in the doorway, frowning. Everything turned fuzzy. Unreal. As if I'd stepped into an ugly dream.

My dad sat on the bed. He said vehemently, "I'm not leaving. This is my home. I'm staying here. I won't have more of her things stolen from me while I'm not here to watch over them."

I rubbed a hand over my face and then tugged at the end of my ponytail.

"You can't stay here, Dad. There won't be any electricity until they can fix the wiring in the kitchen."

"I don't need electricity."

"You can't stay on your own," I said as softly as I could. "Not right now."

"Who are you to tell me what I can and can't do? I'm the parent!" he roared.

I wanted to scream back. I wanted to tell him to start acting like it for the first time in nearly a decade and a half. I wanted to remind him of all the things he'd left me in charge of while he'd been out driving the country.

The horrible moment when I'd had to call and say Mom had passed in her sleep flashed before me, ripping through my heart and soul. I'd had to make the arrangements for her body to be picked up while he'd been hundreds of miles away. Kurt had done more for me in those few hours and days than my own father.

Therapy had helped me try to forgive, but I'd never forget, and I'd never be rid of the scars those moments left behind.

"You know what," I said, inhaling. "You're right. You're the parent. You're an adult. You can do whatever you want."

I brushed past Beckett and stormed out of the house. My body was trembling. Years of anger and frustration and sorrow jumbled together, vying for release, trying to burst through the surface.

Outside, I looked back at the house and hesitated for a few seconds. He wasn't himself. The doctors said the temporary dementia would make him volatile while his body healed.

I needed to have patience.

Then, the paper cut on my hand from where the box hit me throbbed, and my heart tore a bit more. I stalked over to my truck and slammed the door behind me. When I turned the engine over, it coughed pitifully, and dread held me in its grip for two seconds before the motor finally kicked in. I sent a thank you to the universe and then drove away, heading for my studio apartment and the few things I had left to do there.

I'd barely pulled into the apartment's parking lot before I started kicking myself.

Dad was losing everything. He couldn't remember what had happened the day of the fire and was terrified of what came next. Finding Mom's jewelry box gone on top of everything else was probably just the last straw. He'd lashed out, and I'd been the body in the wake. It hadn't been personal, but it had felt that way.

I mean, how could he think I'd steal from him?

I hadn't even realized I was crying until a tear hit my hand. I brushed my fingers over damp cheeks and hurried up to my apartment.

As I walked into the tiny studio I'd barely afforded on my own, sorrow filled me. I'd really loved having my own space for the first time in my life. I'd loved decorating it without having to ask for permission or wonder if my roommate would be okay with it. It had been a little oasis for me at the end of my shifts.

Dad wasn't the only one losing things.

More tears came, and I let them fall over the next hour while I worked. I dismantled the high-top dining table for two, dragged the mattress and box spring off the bed, and set my power tools to the stubborn screws on the wrought iron bed frame. I was hot and sweaty, but the tears had worked themselves out and left a numbness behind.

I couldn't do much else without help. It would take at least two people to navigate the queen mattress down the stairs, and it would take a body with way more muscles, or at least two of me, to haul my boxes of books down to the truck.

The books were my only splurge I'd allowed myself while putting aside for a new car and saving to buy back Titan. Being able to lose myself in the joy of those happily ever afters whenever my reality got to be too much was worth it.

A knock on my door brought me out of the bathroom with the last bit of toiletries I was throwing inside a basket. I looked through the peephole to find Beckett on the landing. I swung the door open and then left him standing there to head back to the bathroom.

"Don't say anything," I said over my shoulder. "I know I shouldn't have lost my cool."

"You actually think I'm here to call you out for that? If anything, I wish you'd lost your cool with your dad ages ago."

Why did that hurt so much? Why should I *have* to lose my cool with my father? Why couldn't we just have a relationship where loving each other was enough?

In the bathroom, I threw my flat iron and makeup bag into the basket. Beckett followed me, grabbing the doorframe with both hands. He scanned every inch of me, lingering on my face, which was a mess from the tears I'd shed, just like my hair and clothes were a mess from disassembling the furniture.

I returned his stare, taking in his tall length and the way his biceps flexed as he gripped the frame. His SRFD T-shirt rode up at his waist, exposing a slim line of tan skin and the waistband of his boxer briefs above his jeans. The silence that landed between us felt heavy and loaded. Full of want and desire—things I'd always felt but that I'd suddenly seen in Beckett's eyes this week too. A return flame that would do me in if I dwelled on it too long.

Doubt slammed into me. How was I going to live with him for months when just this, just him standing two feet away from me, looking at me in just that way, made my heart race and my thighs tremble?

I inhaled, counted to four, and then let it out.

No. I could do this. I'd done way harder things than spend a few weeks in Beckett's home.

I could help Dad and Beckett without losing myself.

Beckett cleared his throat, looking away. "I told your Dad it was against fire code for him to live in the house at the moment. I said he could be fined, and as a firefighter, I'd have to report it."

I scoffed. "And he believed you?"

Beckett shrugged, lips twitching. "I'm very convincing. But honestly, I think the idea of owing more money was what motivated him to start packing. We hauled a few boxes of his belongings to my house, and when Tejas dropped by, he helped me move the bedroom set and the TV your dad had in his room. I left the two of them reassembling everything at my place so I could come help you."

Tears threatened again, but I was able to get out, "Thanks."

He let go of the doorjamb and stepped into the bathroom. The small space seemed to shrink even more. Before I realized his intention, he'd pulled me into a tight hug. My face was smashed to his chest, with his scent washing over me. The warmth of Beckett's hand on my back was soothing, daring me to let down my defenses.

For two seconds, I let myself indulge in the comfort before I mumbled into his shirt. "You owe me another romance book."

He snorted and then said, "I guess I do."

He tugged on my ponytail, forcing my head up and scanning my face. His voice was deep and dark when he said, "You've been crying. I hate it when you cry."

"He thought I stole from him, Beckett. That I stole from my own father."

Beckett's brows shot up in surprise, and the pain of Dad's words tore through me all over again. After everything I'd done to try to hold our family together, how could he even consider the possibility?

"Why would he think that?" Beckett demanded.

I shrugged. "It's probably the meds making him irritable and the trauma his brain has been through with the stroke. But Mom's jewelry box *is* missing, and I'm the one who looks after the house while he's gone. I guess it makes sense he'd think it was me."

"Chelsea was just there," Beckett said.

I'd had the same thought before Dad's accusation had wiped it away. A piece of me didn't want to believe Chelsea was capable of taking Mom's things without asking Dad…or me… But another part of me realized it was exactly the sort of thing she'd do. She took what she wanted all the time now.

What would make this any different?

Chapter Twelve

Beckett

BURN MY SUMMER
Performed by Kelsey Hart

THREE DAYS AGO

HIM: I don't think it was Del who left the note on your truck. You should have seen how shocked and wounded she looked when I accused her of it.

> *HER: Which Delilah did you get? Business Delilah or Victim Delilah or Sexpot Delilah?*

HIM: I know what you're getting at, but she's always come clean with me before. I'm not sure it was her.

> *HER: Who else could it be? I've literally done nothing to piss anyone off but get fake-engaged to you.*

HIM: Stoney was really pissed that I might get the chief's job now. He tossed the measly eight years I've been working at the station in my face. He said all the classes and certificates didn't stack up to his twenty-five years of experience. And he's right.

> *HER: It wasn't Stoney. He would've just come for you, not me.*

HIM: I know you're right, but I don't think it's Del either.

> *HER: It doesn't matter. For all we know, it*

> *could have been left on the wrong truck.*
> *We're better off just forgetting about it.*

HIM: Maybe. Just promise me you'll be extra careful.

PRESENT DAY

The scene at her dad's had done a number on Maisey. The raw pain from her father's accusation left her looking bruised and worn. And while there was nothing I could do about what had gone down, I *could* lighten her load and her mood, even if it was only for a few hours. We'd finish moving her things to my house, and then I'd find a way to give her an escape.

I tweaked her hair one more time before stepping back. "Let's get the rest of your things to my place."

We worked in mostly silence, hauling the bed and the mattress down the stairs along with the other furniture she'd had in her studio before finishing up with the boxes. She'd moved most of her things on her own this week, and I hated that almost as much as I hated how her dad had made her cry.

Maisey had always tried to do as much as possible on her own. She hadn't wanted to be a burden, not even at fifteen, taking care of a dying mother. She'd felt guilty every time Fallon or I had done something to help. While she wasn't the desperately sad teenager she'd once been anymore—in fact, most days she was full of sass and confidence—the last few days had torn at the scars she'd healed. It was easy for wounds that deep to break open when targeted. I should know.

Some days, I wondered what it would take for both of us to cleanse our souls and start over.

When we finally locked up her apartment and drove back to my house, Tejas was still there, sitting on my leather couch with my dog at his side and the kitten curled up in his lap. My teammate was eating my chips, feeding them to my animals, all while watching a soccer match on my television that was just a hair too big for the space above the fireplace.

During the remodel, I'd kept as much of the Craftsman design as possible while knocking out a couple of walls to turn the unused dining room and living area into one big open space that flowed into the kitchen. I'd kept the original built-ins but moved them to frame the new energy-efficient windows and then decorated with dark woods, wicker, and copper fixtures to give it a fiery warmth. While I wasn't anywhere close to being a decorator, I'd liked the outcome, and I was even happier when Dad's jaw had dropped, and he'd gone on about it for weeks.

Just as Tejas went to feed Vader another chip, I grabbed it out of his hand. "Who said you could eat all my chips? And no more fried food for Vader and the cat, or I'll be cleaning up runny shit for days."

Vader whined, and Tejas smirked. "Providing a snack is the least you can do for the muscle I provided."

Maisey came in the door behind me, and my dog bounded from the couch to spin circles around her. She greeted him with pets and a smooch to the top of his head. Vader's tongue rolled to the side, and his eyes turned goofy. I swore the dog loved her more than he loved me.

"Hey, Tejas. Thanks for helping," she said. "Is my dad in his room?"

"He shooed me out so he could, quote, 'unpack in peace.' Vader and I took it to mean it was time for a well-earned break."

I'd bet Lewis had kicked Motor-mouth from the room more out of self-defense than because he didn't want the help.

"Well, now you can earn a beer by helping me get the furniture out of Maisey's truck," I told him.

It was a sign of what a good friend and crew member he was that he didn't hesitate.

I locked the kitten in my room while we hauled Maisey's things in. We stored the larger furniture she didn't need at her dad's house in Chelsea's room and carted the rest to my guest room. Despite Vader's best attempts to trip us as he ran back and forth between us, the three of us had her truck and my SUV almost completely unloaded in no time.

It wasn't until we were on the last load, grabbing her bookshelves, that I realized our mistake. The last thing we needed was Tejas wondering why Masiey wasn't moving into my room if we were a happily engaged couple. So, as I hauled one of the shelves toward me, I looked over at her and asked, "Are these going in *our* room or the guest room?"

She inhaled sharply and started to snap a reply before my eyes darted to Tejas, hoping she'd catch on. She bit her lip and said, "I thought I'd make a little reading nook in the guest room, so let's set them up there."

After we'd gotten the shelves situated, I patted Tejas on the back and all but tossed him down the hall, saying, "Drinks on me tonight. See you at Frank's around seven?"

"You trying to get rid of me?" he asked, his lips twisting into a knowing grin.

While I was trying to get rid of him, it wasn't for the reasons he thought. But I played along, shoving him hard enough for his shoulder to hit the wall. "Yeah, get the hell out so I can help my Maisey-girl unpack."

"Is that our new euphemism for sex?" He laughed. "Wouldn't *pack* be better than *unpack*?"

Maisey came out of the bedroom while his words still hung in the air, and it was obvious from the red that coated her face that she'd heard every word.

"Just get out of here. I'll see you at the bar later."

Tejas headed toward the front door and looked back to where Maisey stood next to me. His smile disappeared, expression turning somber as he said, "I'm really happy for you, man. Both of you. You two are couple goals. Hurts that I lost the bet, but I'll forgive you."

"What bet?" Maisey and I said simultaneously.

Tejas's humor reappeared. "How long it would take before Romeo here stopped fooling around with Delilah and fell for the real deal."

Maisey inhaled sharply, and I knew she was going to say something that would blow our cover, so I hauled her up against me, kissed the top of her head, and growled, "How many times did I tell you there was nothing between Del and me?"

Tejas raised his hands in defense. "You did. You did. Our

bad. Just glad to see you happy."

He didn't wait for us to respond, heading out of the house instead.

Maisey exhaled a shaky breath and moved away from me. "I hate lying almost as much as I hate the idea they all thought I was just waiting around for you and Delilah to be over."

I wasn't exactly fond of being the subject of their bet. But something in my chest tugged at Tejas's words, something at the back of my brain that was working overtime trying to put together pieces I couldn't quite grasp. Things that caused the smoke to fill my lungs until I let out a choked cough.

Maisey raised a brow. "You okay?"

I nodded. I wasn't sure I was. I felt like things were unraveling around me, taking a lifetime of beliefs with them. A lifetime of safeguards I'd carefully put in place.

When I didn't say anything else, she pulled on her ponytail and said, "Thanks for helping me move the big stuff. I'm going to go check on my dad and then start putting my bed together."

She moved down the hall toward the room her dad had taken.

"Maise," I called after her, my voice full of apology.

"It's all good, Beckett. I've said it before, and I'll say it again so you believe it…I know what I signed up for."

My chest ached, and I couldn't put my finger on all the reasons why. It had to be the lies we were telling. I was good at joking around, but I'd always tried to be honest. It was something my dad had pounded into me. A code we both believed.

Damn. I needed to talk to my dad before the rumor about Maisey and me hit his ears.

I'd call him later, but first I'd do what I'd planned. I'd get Maisey settled and then get her out of here for a few hours. With a renewed purpose, I strode out to the detached garage for my tools and was already putting her bed frame together by the time she came out of her dad's room.

"How is he?" I asked.

"He seemed embarrassed by his outburst and apologized,

and then he asked for help setting up the WiFi so he could stream his shows. But by the time I got it all hooked up, he was asleep on the bed."

My jaw clenched. At least he'd apologized before asking for more help. Lewis Campbell was a nice guy. You couldn't be in the room with him and actively dislike him, but I could despise the way he had never hesitated at using Maisey.

We assembled the bed and moved her dresser and bookshelves to where she wanted them, and I stepped back to assess what we'd done. The tiny room was crammed so full of furniture, there was hardly room to walk, but Maisey didn't seem to notice—or at least, she didn't complain.

Then again, it had never been Maisey's style to complain any more than she lied.

I wiped the sweat off my forehead with my shirt and shot a scowl at my dog. He'd claimed Maisey's bed as if it were his new favorite spot and was watching every move she made. I let my gaze follow my dog's. She was sweating too, ponytail askew, gray T-shirt damp. But it was the shadows under her eyes that really got me.

She needed an escape from the heaviness of the entire week, and we both needed to cool off. So, as she flipped open a switchblade and opened a box of shoes, I pulled it out of her reach.

"No more unpacking for today. It's time you let off a little steam."

Her eyes went to my mouth, and her voice was breathy when she asked, "What did you have in mind?"

My dick twitched, a reaction that had somehow become my new norm with her, after years of putting her in a zone carefully labeled "friend" and never detouring from it. If I didn't get a handle on these emotions soon, I was going to have a permanent hard-on with her living here.

"We're busting out of here."

"I've got a lot to do," she said, reaching for the box, and I just pushed it farther out of her reach.

"It'll all be here when you get back. Vader and I need to

cool off at the lake."

Vader went from relaxed to ready to pounce in a nanosecond. He barked his approval, thumping his tail so hard it sounded like a bongo.

Indecision warred over Maisey's face.

I tapped her on the nose with a finger. "Put a swimsuit on, my Maisey-girl, and meet me in the living room in ten minutes. If you're not changed and ready, I'll just toss you over my shoulder, haul you to my rig and dump you in the lake fully clothed."

She pushed my hand away. "That's book three you owe me, Fireball."

I heard the hesitation in her voice. The desire to escape was just hovering around the corner. But then her gaze darted to the wall dividing her room from her dad's, and she sighed. "I don't think I should leave him."

"We'll be back in a couple of hours. In plenty of time for dinner. That's less time than you'll be away at work on a normal day."

She bit her lip, worrying some more.

"I'm not letting you stop your life to care for him," I said. She'd already done that once with her mom. I would do just about anything to make sure she didn't do it again for a father who didn't even appreciate what she'd done. "If we have to hire someone to be here while you're gone, we will. But for today, you get to escape for a few hours, and he'll be just fine."

She huffed. "You're not the boss of me, Beckett. Don't act like we're *really* getting married, and you get to make those kinds of demands or those kinds of promises."

My newly obsessed brain jumped right to all the demands and promises I could give her while she writhed on my bed and begged me for relief. Desire hit me like gasoline reaching its flashpoint. Sharp and fast and brutal. What would it be like if I just let myself give in to it? What would it be like to have Maisey? To leap over the scars sealing my heart and take what I wanted?

I yanked myself back from the dangerous abyss. Denying

myself Maisey might just be the hardest thing I'd ever done in my life. Harder than fighting fires for five days straight in the deepest mountain terrain. Harder than carrying a hundred pounds of equipment up twenty flights in full turnout. Harder than watching Dad all but bleed open as another woman left him for bigger dreams.

But Maisey's friendship meant more to me than anything else on this Earth, and I wouldn't jeopardize it. Not even for the earth-shattering sex I was suddenly certain we'd have if we gave in to this lust.

"What'll it be, Maise? The easy way or the hard way?"

She rolled her eyes, and I grinned, dropping my shoulders as if I was getting ready to pick her up. She finally laughed, warding me off with a hand. But just that single laugh told me I'd done the right thing by pushing her.

"Fine. Fine. You get your way today. But only because I'm hot and tired and the lake sounds perfect."

I headed to the door. "Ten minutes, Maise. Ten minutes or else."

She threw a shoe at me, and I just batted it away with a chuckle.

♬ ♬ ♬

As we crested the hill and Crystal Lake came into view, the sunlight caught on the surface, turning it into a sheet of teal-blue glass. The mountains stood tall behind it, the forest pressing close on the far side, and just the view was enough to release some of the tension I'd felt over the last few days. And when Maisey sighed, it reassured me I'd done the right thing in pressing her to come.

The sandy beach on the Harrington Ranch was meant for resort guests, but Maisey and I had always had free rein. These days, I mostly came by to check on Dad or help out with odd jobs when he was short-staffed, so I couldn't remember the last time I'd been there just to relax. It might have been since last summer.

I parked my SUV near a row of golf carts used to shuttle guests back and forth to the hotel and grabbed our bags from the back. As we headed down the pebbled path to the beach, Vader strained at his leash, insulted I'd put it on him. I didn't blame him, but I also wouldn't risk some guest freaking out because he was roaming around untethered.

The resort was packed with the Fourth of July approaching, and we were late enough arriving that almost every lounge chair and blue-and-yellow striped umbrella was taken. Just as I was about to suggest we head in the opposite direction, out past the boat dock, a couple at the far end of the beach started collecting their belongings, and I jogged to grab their spot.

I looped Vader's leash over the handle of the lounge and adjusted the umbrella while Maisey started rubbing sunscreen over her skin. The scent brought back memories of summers we'd played together as kids, and she'd been doused in the stuff so her fair skin wouldn't burn. But once she yanked off her T-shirt, all thoughts of our childhood disappeared.

My mouth went dry at the sight of the magenta bikini top that left one shoulder completely bare. I'd barely been able to restart my heart when she unbuttoned her jean shorts and let them drop. My chest tightened right back up, my balls swelled, and I was sure I was going to do something incredibly embarrassing before she turned away from me and said, "Get my back, will you?"

An innocent request. Something I'd done dozens, if not hundreds, of times before, and yet I was suddenly afraid of touching her.

When I hadn't moved after several long seconds, she peeked over her shoulder at me. Nothing sexual about the turn of her head or the look she gave me, and yet it felt incredibly sensual anyway.

"Beckett?"

I cursed silently, grabbed the sunscreen, and pretended I was waxing the engine at the station rather than slathering her with cream. My hands slid under the strap, down along the smooth expanse of her shoulder blades, and I swore she shivered and inhaled. It didn't help. I had to lighten things up before I did something stupid.

"Just so we're clear, that was *you* asking *me* to touch you. I don't owe you another romance book for helping a friend."

She chuckled, and as I reached around her to hand the bottle back, she turned at the same time, and it brought our mouths dangerously close. The smell of her, the water lily scent that existed below the sunscreen, filled my lungs.

"Thanks," she said softly, looking from my mouth to my eyes and back.

She stepped away, and both relief and remorse shifted through me.

"Last one to the dogwood tree has to buy the nachos," I said and then grabbed Vader's leash and strode toward the lake.

I was surprised when a flash of vivid pink and pale skin sped past me.

Maisey was in the water, with a little squeal at the iciness, before I'd even dipped a toe in. She swam almost parallel to the shore, heading for the rope that divided the swimming area from the rest of the lake. Just past the buoys was a secret little cove, surrounded on three sides with oaks and pines and a single Pacific dogwood tree. Too narrow for Jet Skis and boats to enter, the inlet was the perfect hideaway we'd discovered in our younger years and used to escape the crowd of guests once the resort had opened.

A laugh escaped me as I watched Maisey race through the water. How had I forgotten how competitive she could be? It was a bit of Fallon that had rubbed off on her, or maybe it was simply the Maisey who would have bloomed if life hadn't shit on her one too many times.

I hit the water, using long strokes and strong kicks to chase after her while my dog used superhuman speed to pass her right up. I didn't catch her until she'd already ducked under the ropes, slid past the buoy, and swam into the tiny cove.

As I drew up next to her, I looped an arm around her waist, halting her before she could win. She kicked and struggled, trying to reach the single dogwood where Vader waited, shaking his entire body on the rocks beside it.

The harder she fought to escape, the tighter my grip got. She was smiling and laughing as she turned to face me, pushing on my shoulders and causing her slim body to rub against me in all the right and wrong ways.

"Let go, you big cheater," she laughed.

"Says the woman who started before the count." I grinned at her.

The green of her eyes was so pale in the sunlight that it nearly vanished into the whites. Her lips gleamed. Her hair sparkled. She was breathtaking. One-hundred-percent Maisey, stripped to her bare essence. Very few people saw her like this anymore. She usually hid behind makeup and perfectly styled hair, years of old insecurities ensuring she took her time getting ready each day. But this was the Maisey I'd first called my friend, and I couldn't look away.

The amusement on her face slowly faded the longer I stared.

She licked her lips, and my body responded. With her pressed against me, it was hopeless to disguise the reaction, and when she inhaled sharply, I knew she'd felt it.

Her throat bobbed, and the tension between us grew, a charge waiting for the right moment to ignite. I longed to kiss her. To take whatever she was willing to give.

Then reality hit me in the back of the head like a slap. I'd promised I'd keep my hands to myself if she took this leap with me, and here I was, breaking that promise for at least the fourth time already.

I moved my hands so they circled her waist, and her eyes darkened. Her chest heaved as if she'd run a mile. So damn sexy. Inviting.

But I had to prove to myself, as much as to her, that I could ignore whatever this was that had flamed between us. So, I planted my feet in the sand and rocks and tossed her backward in the direction we'd come. She laughed and screamed at the same time, right before she hit the water with a huge splash.

I didn't wait.

I hauled ass toward the dogwood, hoping to leave the scorching heat of desire in my wake.

Chapter Thirteen
Maisey

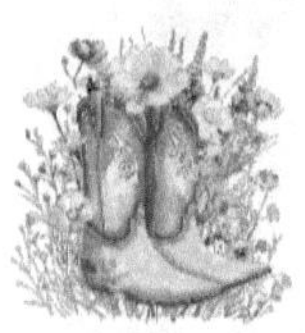

RUIN THE FRIENDSHIP
Performed by Taylor Swift

FOURTEEN YEARS AGO

>*HER: I'm down at the river with the bait. Where are you?*

HIM: I'm not gonna make it.

>*HER: Oh. Okay. I'll just let the worms go, then. What's wrong?*

HIM: Liza left.

>*HER: I didn't know she was traveling again. When will she be back?*

HIM: She won't be back. She left us for good.

>*HER: What are you talking about? She's marrying your dad. They've got the date set and everything.*

HIM: She wanted to postpone it. Wanted to go build another damn school first. They argued. She left. And he told her if she walked out, not to bother coming back. She left anyway.

>*HER: Where are you? I'm coming over.*

HIM: Don't come. I'm not good company.

>*HER: Are you in the treehouse? I'll be there in five minutes.*

PRESENT DAY

Beckett Romero was a cheater. I repeated this to myself as I sputtered my way to the surface. I'd forgotten he could and would use any unfair advantage to win in a race. He didn't even feel bad about it.

He was a no-good cheater. Too bad he was also a sexy-assin cheater.

I cursed to myself and cut through the water after him. His shoulders and back glistened in the sunshine as water streamed off him with each stroke. He had a swimmer's body. All lean muscle with those wide, wide shoulders. Too attractive for his own good.

After throwing me behind him, he easily made it to the dogwood tree in our private little cove first. He would have likely beaten me even if he hadn't cheated. My two-second head start hadn't been enough for me to beat Fireball in a head-to-head race.

Vader raced along the shore, barking at us, trying to get us to join him on land, but Beckett was still in the water, watching me as I swam the last few feet to join him. Satisfaction lit his face. I used both hands to send a wave of water over him, but it barely doused him. He smiled at my pathetic attempt, that sinfully adorable dimple of his popping out.

"Is that the best you've got, darlin'?" he chuckled.

I used a Fallon ploy that she'd taught me ages ago and flipped onto my back, propelling my feet through the water to send a bigger splash in his direction. I kept kicking and kicking, even as Vader barked at me from the shore, and Beckett issued a warning.

Two seconds later, I was dragged under by an ankle before he let go. I got a noseful of lake water and came up gasping. Beckett laughed, completely pleased with himself. So sure. I narrowed the distance and tried, hopelessly, to push him under. He didn't even budge. While I couldn't stand with my head above water in most of this cove, Beckett could, and he had his feet planted in the silt and soil.

His arm banded my waist as I struggled to dunk him,

drawing me closer, until my bikini-clad body was tucked up against his bare chest. We had far too much skin rubbing. He'd wanted us to cool off, but all this did was kindle the aching need I always felt when we were this close. Feelings I'd had since I'd been far too young to understand what the sudden woosh in my nether regions really meant.

"You owe me a meal. I do believe you touched me first," he teased.

"Only after you grabbed me and threw me in the air, I think we'll call this one a draw," I said, shoving his shoulder again.

Beckett continued to laugh at my attempt to get away. "It's like fighting off a gnat."

Vader barked again, wagging his tail furiously before finally diving into the water as if he was afraid of missing out on all the fun.

"You're such an egomaniac." I smacked Beckett's chest again.

Giving up, I stopped moving, letting our bodies settle against each other. Our lips nearly brushed, and his smile slipped. A sharp pulse of electricity wound through the space between us, making my skin tingle and my body hum. The heat felt almost visible, rising in waves and thickening the air.

Beckett's focus stayed rooted on me. Something warm and curious flickered across his face as I inched our mouths closer until, at the last minute, I shifted sideways and bit his shoulder.

His reaction was instantaneous. A surprised grunt that had him loosening his hands.

I held my breath and sank below the surface.

My mind was full of payback, and I acted without fully thinking it through. I reached for his swim shorts and tugged them down, watching as they slipped over his hips and down to his knees.

For two seconds, the sight of him, naked under the water, made me wonder at both my bravery and my stupidity. Made me wonder if I'd just made a colossal mistake. Because he was long and hard and beautiful, even in the cool lake. Enticing. My body ached to grab hold, just to hear him moan, to say my name in a breathy voice full of longing and desire.

I was two seconds away from doing just that when I finally pulled myself together, flipped over like the mermaid I used to pretend to be, and raced for the rocky shoreline on the opposite side of the cove. I kept below the surface until my lungs burned. I broke out only to inhale another deep breath before diving under again.

When I reached the boulders that circled the cove, the lake was still at my waist, and I had to use all my muscles to pull myself up and out.

From behind me, I heard Beckett cussing and splashing, and it allowed the humor and lightness to seep back into me. I'd taken him by surprise far more than I'd surprised myself.

When I'd clambered to safety atop the rocks, I turned to find him rising out of the water. The rippling waves danced around his hips, hiding his bottom half as Vader paddled around him with a stick he'd found in his mouth.

I grinned at Beckett, knowing I looked like a loon but proud that I'd finally gotten one over on him. But then, the expression on his face tore the breath from my body.

Lust. Desire. Pure need.

Damn, did I want that to be mine.

He hooked his finger, demanding I come back into the water. "Come here, you little pantser."

I laughed, shaking my head. Water went flying from my drenched hair. I was sure I looked like a wet rat with the strands plastered to my face, emphasizing all my flaws and scars, but I didn't care. How could I, when the tension flying between us was so delightful? When it felt like Beckett had finally acknowledged the desire as much as I had. There was joy to be found in that simple notion. Joy and a niggle of Hope that would surely leave me scorched.

"You playing chicken, my Maisey-girl? Never knew you to be a chicken."

He was wrong. Oh, so wrong. I'd been a chicken so many times in my life, but he and Fallon had always chosen to see the moments when I was pretending to be brave as the real me.

Beckett's hair glimmered in the sunshine, his dark strands lit by fiery highlights, and those dark-chocolate eyes remained centered wholly and delightfully on me. He took a couple of steps, water pouring off him as he came closer and accentuating every cut and groove. The swim trunks he'd pulled back up were now clinging to him, showing off rather than hiding his impressive package. A package that was still as hard as it had been when my body had been tucked up against it.

"You look a bit uncomfortable there, Fireball. I think you'd better step back into the water and…cool off."

A wicked mischievousness curled his lips, making me want to wipe it away with my mouth pressed against his.

"Just remember, you started this, darlin'. One good prank deserves another."

My chest fluttered and swooped. The firefighters at Beckett's station were famous for pulling pranks on one another, and once prank season started, it went on for months before anyone called a truce. Beckett was the reigning King of Pranks. The top dog. The ultimate champ.

And now that I was living with him, he'd have easy access to me.

"Harmless. What I did was utterly harmless," I tried to backpedal, but it only caused his teeth to flash and a spark to enter his eyes. "No big deal. You weren't even embarrassed by it. No one saw anything." I waved toward the trees hiding us from the crowded beach.

"But now you've seen far more of me than I've seen of you," he said. "It's like that episode of *Friends*. The one where everyone is trying to see each other in the shower, and they keep getting the wrong person until it spins out of control. Except, it's just you and me in the house."

"And my dad. Are you going to rip the shower curtain back and see my dad in all his glory?" I couldn't even think it without my gag reflex kicking in.

"Small risk for a chance at payback," he said, dragging his gaze down my body, and even though my bathing suit covered all the necessary spots, I suddenly felt very, very bare.

My thighs trembled, and my throat nearly closed. How

many times in my life had I envisioned being naked with Beckett's eyes on me? How many times had I read a book and seen him as the hero and me as the heroine and lived out my fantasies through their actions?

Too many to count. Too many to be healthy.

That was when reality slid home, as if I'd been slapped. What had I been thinking? We were just friends. That was all Beckett would ever want, regardless of how he was looking at me now. Even if he'd started to see me as someone desirable, someone he wanted to get sweaty and naked with, it wouldn't end with a *real* ring on my finger.

And I wanted more than heated looks and a sinful night spent twined in his sheets. I dreamed of a happily ever after. I wasn't ridiculous enough to think life was like my romance books, but I did deserve someone who actually wanted to love me—who wanted love at all—and Beckett held it off with a superpower-like strength.

I looked down, breaking the hold his gaze had on me. "I lost the race, even though you cheated, so I'll go get the nachos. You want a lemonade or a beer?"

For a moment, I didn't think he'd answer, but when I looked back up, all playfulness had been wiped away. It was several long, tension-filled heartbeats before he finally responded. "Just a water, please."

Then, he turned, diving back into the water with his dog chasing after him. They swam toward the dogwood again, Beckett's long arms breaking through the water with the same ease he seemed to do any physical activity. I watched for a few more seconds and then turned away.

I found the old path through the rocks and trees that led back to the beach and picked my way over to our lounge chairs. I slid into my T-shirt and shorts, grabbed my wallet, and headed for the snack bar, all the while cursing myself for letting our lighthearted fun get to me. For letting that bitch Hope dangle a carrot I'd almost swallowed.

When I came back with the food, Beckett had returned from the cove and was drying off.

I placed the ginormous plate of carne asada nachos and two

water bottles on the table between the chairs, determined to act casually. To act as if nothing out of the ordinary had occurred in our secret spot.

"Your phone has been vibrating nonstop," he said.

I instantly panicked, thinking of Dad left alone. I dug frantically in my bag, hoping nothing else had happened to him. Guilt hit me in the chest. I shouldn't have left him.

I finally found my phone at the bottom and swiped it open to see a series of messages from Meredith, verifying I'd be back at work on Sunday. Relief that it wasn't Dad was followed by unease.

I didn't have a choice but to go back to work. I needed my paycheck, but I also couldn't afford to have someone come and stay with Dad while I was gone. On the other hand, I certainly couldn't afford to have Dad burn Beckett's house down in a moment of forgetfulness.

"What is it?" Beckett asked, coming to stand next to me and tucking a single wet strand of my hair gently behind my ear.

Maybe Chelsea was right about me after all. Maybe I was greedy and selfish, because all I wanted was to have the lightness Beckett and I had shared in the water back. I'd do just about anything to have the delightful tension torturing me rather than thoughts of how to, once again, take care of my father.

When I still hadn't responded, he prompted me with a gentle, "Maise?"

"It was just Meredith, confirming I'll be back at work on Sunday."

"Okay? Why did that freak you out?"

He knew me too well after years of friendship for me to even try to deny it. "I'm terrified Dad is going to lose his mind again and start a fire at your house by leaving something on the stove."

Beckett scratched the back of his neck and wouldn't look at me. Knowing him as well as I did, the longer he remained silent, the more I was sure he was holding back some awful truth because he thought hearing it would hurt me.

I pressed a hand to my stomach and said, "Just say whatever

you're thinking."

"I don't think your dad forgot something on the stove, Maise."

"What? What do you mean?"

"Ron called me today." He hesitated once more, looking away and back.

I pushed harder into my stomach, hoping to tame the sickening roll. "What did the fire marshal have to say?"

"After the fire was out, I found an empty Sterno can in the kitchen. When I told Ron, he took some samples from the remains of the stove and counters. He got the mass spec results today, and it was, in fact, Sterno that had been spread all over the kitchen."

"Sterno?" I frowned. "Like the stuff we used to heat the ancient fondue pot?"

Beckett nodded.

I inhaled sharply. "You think Dad did this on purpose? That he started the fire?"

"It's likely someone did," he said softly.

My legs gave out, and I landed on the chaise behind me.

The ringing in my ears dimmed the noise of the beach as all sorts of possibilities stormed through me. Dad had looked devastated as he talked about the stroke and losing his job and potentially losing the house.

Had he tried to kill himself?

The ache inside me grew to a blinding pain.

I pushed the thought away, clinging to another possibility—a lesser evil, but still not good. My voice was barely audible when I said, "Do you think he was doing it for the money?"

"I don't know what he was thinking, Maise. If the entire house had been lost, the insurance payout would have gone to the bank to cover the mortgage, right? As it stands now, you'll get a bit of money from the claim, but you still have to pay the mortgage. I don't see him coming out of this ahead, no matter what happened."

Another horrible thought filtered in. "Do you think Dad is faking his memory issues so he won't get in trouble?"

Beckett's response was slow in coming, thoughtful. "No. He was really out of it when we got there, Maise. It wasn't an act. And even at the hospital, he thought it was years ago, right?"

I rubbed my hands over my arms. "I can't afford more time off. If I take a family leave to care for him, I won't get paid. But I also can't afford to hire someone to stay with him."

Beckett sat on the lounge across from me, both of us lost in our own thoughts. No matter how I flipped it, I couldn't see a good reason for Dad to have had the Sterno out. I wasn't even sure he knew what it was for, let alone how to use it. I couldn't remember any of us using it in the eleven years since Mom had died. It was yet another item that should have been tossed a decade ago.

Beckett drew me out of my dark thoughts. "Stoney has been griping about his son needing a summer job. With Mikey's swim practices and meets, it's been nearly impossible for him to find anything that will accommodate his schedule. I bet we could pay him to stay at the house."

My throat closed more. "With what money? Everything extra I have is going to the mortgage. The bank was happy to take my savings but then said I'd still have to double up the payments for three months to finish catching up."

"I can pay Mikey," Beckett said.

I shook my head, and he leaned over to capture my hands. "Please. Let me do this."

I closed my eyes so I didn't have to see the plea in his eyes. He wanted to help me again. Sweep in and come to the rescue once more. Gratitude filled me, like it always did when my friends helped, but I had Chelsea's voice pounding in my head these days too.

Would I become just another Campbell adult who couldn't stand on their own? Who constantly needed others to step in and fix their messes?

At least this time, Beckett was getting something out of the situation, but pretending to be his fiancée was nothing compared to what he was doing for us. Could I live with myself if I let him do more? Did I really have any other options?

"Maisey, sometimes the brave thing to do is to accept help when it's offered. You want to prove you're really not chicken, then let me do this." When I still didn't respond, he added on, "It's not like I'm paying hundreds of dollars an hour for a healthcare worker. This is a teenager. We're basically paying him to babysit, and he'll eat my food, watch my television, and play video games while he's at it."

I rubbed at my chest, the ache there growing until it might consume me.

I couldn't come up with a better solution. Not today.

When I opened my eyes, I let out a resigned sigh and even managed a twisted, fake grin. "Don't tell my dad it's babysitting. He'll have a conniption and move back out."

"We'll figure out something to tell him."

I nodded. Beckett looked over at the food neither of us was hungry for anymore. He picked up the plate. "Let me get this wrapped to go. I'll order something for your dad while I'm up there, and we can head home."

I nodded because I couldn't speak. Too many words and too many emotions were locked in my throat. Not just at what he'd offered and what he was doing for me, but because of that single word he'd uttered—home.

But Beckett's house wasn't mine. We weren't going to get a happily ever after. Not now. Not ever. If my heart didn't accept that soon, it wasn't going to be just my dad in trouble. I'd be so torn up there'd be nothing left of me for anyone to rescue.

Chapter Fourteen
Beckett

LOVE THIS PAIN
Performed by Lady A

EIGHT YEARS AGO

> *HER: Why are guys so lame?*

HIM: I'll try not to take offense. What's up?

> *HER: If all you plan is one night with someone, just be upfront about it.*

HIM: Whose dick do I need to rip off?

> *HER: No one of importance. What I mean is, don't make it seem like you're into someone, like you want to start a relationship, when all you really want is a few hours of sex.*

HIM: Maise... Are you okay?

> *HER: I'm fine. Really. It's just...disappointing. The entire thing was disappointing. The sex was disappointing. He was disappointing. I guess I was probably disappointing too, otherwise he would have wanted to see me again, right?*

HIM: Fuck this guy. You are NOT a disappointment. You're a goddamn angel.

> *HER: No one wants to sleep with an angel, Beckett. Sweet and innocent is boring. You don't go for the quiet girl in the room. You go for the sexy dynamo you think will tie you*

to the bed.

HIM: Hate to break it to you, darlin', but I don't ever want to be tied to a bed.

> *HER: No? I guess I can see that about you. You'd want all the control.*

HIM: Sex shouldn't be about power and control. It should be about giving each other equal pleasure.

> *HER: But there's pleasure in giving up control, right? Feeling safe enough to let go.*

HIM: You've been reading too many romance books. You should always feel safe when you're having sex. If you don't, you shouldn't be doing it.

PRESENT DAY

As I stalked toward the snack bar with the untouched plate of nachos, I was virtually kicking myself in the ass.

Maisey had smiled and laughed, just as I'd intended when I'd left the house. The worry had slipped off her shoulders for a few minutes, and she'd even, briefly, tossed aside her normal inhibitions with that little stunt in the cove. But I'd pushed the taunt a step too far and caused her to run.

But the day could still have been saved. I could have returned to our lounge chairs and made a joke. Instead, I'd brought up what Ron had found out about the fire and stolen any chance of laughter from her. The truth was, she'd needed to know, but I could have allowed her a few more moments of levity before dropping the hammer.

At the snack bar, I requested the staff put the nachos in a to-go container and ordered two sets of sliders to take with us. I was waiting for the food when a hand clapped me on the shoulder.

I turned to find my dad with his cowboy hat tipped back and his salt-and-pepper brows raised. "Thought that was your rig I saw fly by the barn earlier."

"Hey, old man," I said, giving him a hug with a hard pat on the back before releasing him.

"Don't you 'hey, old man' me, shithead."

"What did I do now?" I laughed, but before I'd even finished the question, I knew.

"You got engaged, without giving me a heads up beforehand that you were going to ask Maisey or even thinking to tell me after she said yes."

I glanced out toward the water to the lounge chair where Maisey was waiting for me, glad she wasn't nearby to overhear this conversation. I didn't need Dad scaring her off, especially when she needed this as much as I did now.

"Is she here with you now?" Dad demanded, looking in the same direction as me. "Heard you already moved in together."

I ran a hand through my hair, debating whether to tell him the truth. Dad and I had always been straight with each other. Always. But I knew his take on love and marriage, knew he believed in the institution, even after his wife tried to burn down our home with me in it, and his fiancée left us because she'd loved her work more than she did us. Dad would still think it was some sort of blasphemy to enter into an agreement for marriage in the way Maisey and I had.

"We wouldn't have moved in together yet, but you might have also heard about her dad's place catching fire. They're both living with me while the repairs are made," I said, giving him a partial answer.

Dad took a slow, calming breath, fixing me with a steely glower. "Beckett. That girl has had stars in her eyes looking at you since she was knee high to a grasshopper. You can't mess around with her like this. If you tell me you love her and want a future with her, I'll be happy for both of you. But we just had a conversation the other day about grandkids that nearly sent you running for the hills, and now you tell me you're getting married?"

He was right. When he'd brought up kids, I hadn't told him I was dating Maisey or thinking about marrying her. Instead, I'd panicked, as I always did, at the thought of being tied to someone.

I also wasn't an idiot. There'd been times as a teenager when I'd known Maisey felt something more for me, the same way Del did. But I'd sworn I'd never be the reason another woman nearly died. And since Maisey returned to Swift Rivers, she hadn't shown a hint of wanting me that way.

We were friends. Nothing more. She'd even played wingwoman while I found a tourist to take home, never so much as flinching. Because Maisey understood my limitations. She'd seen the wreckage up close, way back when I was eight and my mom had traded me for a payout.

Dad had agreed to not pursue an investigation into the fire if she gave up custody. And she'd taken the money from their divorce and run east. He'd packed us into the truck and driven west, as if putting miles between us could erase the connection, and the damage, my mother had done. But it hadn't. And when Liza left, Maisey saw that destruction too. I'd sworn I'd never be my dad. I'd never keep offering up a heart that only knew how to bleed.

Still…if anyone could fit into my life, it was Maisey.

I remembered what Kasey had said at the station, about Maisey and me just fitting, and what Tejas had said about us being couple goals. Maybe what we had was better than love's false promises. Maybe marrying Maisey was exactly what I needed in my life.

Even as the thought settled, I was shaking my head at the ridiculousness of it. Maisey should have the undying love she wanted. I could give her friendship. I could give her sex—really damn good sex—but not a happily ever after.

"What are you shaking your head for?" Dad asked.

I dragged a hand through my wet hair. I couldn't give Maisey forever, but we could offer each other a temporary solution to our temporary problems and maybe even a temporary sating of the lust that dangled in the air between us these days. A fix for the ache.

Dad wouldn't approve of that any more than he'd approve of me proposing to Maisey.

So I simply gave him a half-truth, saying, "Neither of us is going into this with our eyes closed. Maisey and I both agreed this was what we wanted."

Dad let out an exasperated breath, proving he wasn't an idiot either because he read between the lines and came up with some, if not all, of what I wasn't telling him. "This is some dumbass arrangement, then." When I still didn't answer, he kept going. "Is this about the fire chief job?"

"This is about Maisey and me and what we both need right now." It was as close to admitting the truth as I could come.

"Damn it, Beck. You both deserve more than this. You deserve a love so all-consuming you can't think of anything but ending your day and getting back to that person. A love that has you offering up your right hand if it'll mean the other person doesn't suffer a single inconvenience. A passion you see as a gift and not as a burden. I hate that bearing witness to my failures with love scarred you, closing you off to the possibilities just because my attempts at it didn't turn out right."

When I scoffed and started to say something, he cut me off. "I don't regret your mother, because our time together gave me you, and you're the best thing in my life. I don't regret Liza, because she showed me I still had love to give. But if you do this with Maisey half-assed, you will regret it. You'll hurt her and lose a piece of yourself you'll never get back."

Before I could respond, Maisey joined us. She had both our bags slung over her shoulders and my dog's leash in her hand.

Vador yipped excitedly at my father, and Dad bent to give the wet mutt a whole-body rub.

Maisey darted a look from me to my father and back, as if sensing the tension in the air.

She smiled weakly. "Hi, Kurt."

Dad rose and hugged Maisey, glaring at me over her head. "Hey, sweet thing. I hear you've had quite the week."

When he let her go, she looked at me with wide eyes, as if asking what I'd told him.

"The rumor mill got to Dad before I could tell him about us."

"I'm sorry you had to hear about it that way," she told him, touching his arm.

He stared at her for a long moment. "All I want is for you and my boy to be happy. If you love each other and are willing to sacrifice and meet each other halfway, you'll make it work."

He'd emphasized the love part, and Maisey shifted uncomfortably.

My order was called, and I hesitated, not wanting to leave them alone while I went to get it, but when they called the number a second time, I stalked off.

When I came back, Maisey looked even more serious than she had been before. Now, I wanted to kick my dad's ass, in addition to mine. But I'd been the one to start us on this path, not Dad.

Maisey had more than earned a fairy-tale kind of love.

And she'd get it, just not with me.

Why did that notion make my stomach turn sour?

Dad hugged us both goodbye and sauntered off to one of the ranch rigs.

Maisey and I followed him to the parking lot. When I tried to strap Vader to his safety belt in the back seat, he whined, sensing the strain in the air.

"Let him ride up front with me," Maisey said.

I shook my head. "No. He knows his place. It's safer back here."

As Maisey took our things and climbed in the front, I snapped Vader in and whispered, "We both know our place, bud. We just got to be reminded of it sometimes."

I ran my hands over his head and tweaked his ear before shutting the door.

As I drove home, Maisey remained silent and thoughtful, and my mind and body continued to war with each other. The trip to the lake had been a complete and utter failure. It had only stoked this new desire I felt for Maisey and had ended with her carrying a heavier burden than when we'd arrived. If that wasn't proof I wasn't built for relationships, nothing was.

♫ ♫ ♫

At home, I refocused on my earlier objective of lightening Maisey's mood. While she reheated the takeout and I fed the animals, I taunted Vader about the kitten.

"The way you've been collecting younglings, I should have named you Yoda or Obi-Wan instead of Vader. But I will go all Anakin on you if you bring another cat home."

Her dad snorted, and my dog grinned, but Maisey remained serious.

"What's the cat's name?" her dad asked.

"It will not have a name as long as it is in my care. You name an animal, you keep an animal. This cat will be going to a family as soon as I can find one."

Vader's ears drooped, the kitten turned its back on me, and when Maisey finally looked at me, the expression she wore was as wounded as the animals'.

Shit. I didn't need a cat. I didn't have time for a cat.

When we sat down to eat, the silence from the ride home returned, and Lewis's look bounced between us as a frown took over his face.

Maisey hardly ate, tugging her hair and giving away that she was struggling with her thoughts.

Even after being drenched in the lake and drying in the heat, her hair still looked soft and silky. My hands itched to lose themselves in it. In her.

If you'd told me a month ago that it would be nearly impossible for me to have Maisey here and keep my hands off, I would have laughed you out of town. But here I was, not even a day into this new arrangement, and all I could think about was touching her. Claiming her. Listening to her moan my name as we both came apart.

What would it be like to come home from a shift and be able to lose myself completely in her? The appeal of it had my lungs tightening until I could barely breathe.

But would it really be so bad if we temporarily gave in to the chemistry churning between us? Could we take our friendship and add the benefit part without either of us losing a bit of ourselves? Without it ending in a marriage that would only serve to break her…or me…or both of us?

But if we slept together and Maisey ended up wanting more, my childhood wounds would eventually resurface. What would happen when she reached for me and found only wood where my heart should be?

Delilah's bloodless face swam before my eyes from one of the worst nights of my life.

No, it was better to forget the lust, leave it completely out of our friendship.

It was easier said than done though. I'd been trying to put these new thoughts of Maisey behind me for a week. And with her in and out of every room of my house with me for two days before she went back to work, I'd be continually tempted. I'd have to fight every second to keep my hands off her small, delightful curves and my mouth off those sweet lips.

I shook my head. What I needed was a goddamn project to keep my ridiculous hands busy. I needed hard labor that would drain me of all energy so my dick was too tired to crave more, at least until I returned to the station in four days, where I'd get a respite.

The next big project at my house was supposed to be the backyard, but I could start on her dad's place instead. The sooner we finished there, the sooner she'd move out, and we could return to the easy friendship we'd had for years without me destroying it by giving in to my stupid-ass libido.

I cleared my throat, drawing Maisey and her dad's attention. "We'll need an inspection and permits before we demolish the damaged kitchen, but I'm going to start tearing off the ruined porch tomorrow."

Her dad's jaw clenched. "It can wait until my hand is better, so I can help."

Maisey sighed, and just that little exhale hit me low in the groin. How had it gotten this bad so quickly? Too bad, with the entire town knowing we were engaged, I couldn't head to the bar and find some tourist to screw senseless just to take the edge off.

"We're going to need Beckett's help, Dad, so we should work around his shifts. It makes sense to start while we're both off. Our schedules won't always overlap like this."

Lewis stared at Maisey for a long moment, and when he spoke, it was choked with emotion. "You're so much like her that, at times, I can almost see her standing there."

My chest constricted as Maisey's face paled, and her fist tightened on her fork until her knuckles turned white.

"Once your mother got an inkling to do something, it took hellfire to stop her. Remember the time she reroofed the house while I was gone?" Lewis's eyes remained glossy and lost in the past.

"Chelsea was livid because she ruined her manicure."

Lewis's reply was quiet and pained. "You were too young to be on the roof. It should have been me. I let you all down so many times simply by not being here."

"That's not true," Maisey said, throat bobbing. Except, it was. Lewis should have been the one to find his wife when she died, not Maisey.

Lewis's response surprised me. "It is true. But I'm going to do my best to be here now. So if you two want to work on the porch tomorrow, I'll be there, doing what I can one-handed." He rose from the table and put his plate in the dishwasher. "With that plan in mind, I guess I'd better get some rest."

He came over and kissed Maisey on the top of the head before walking down the hall.

Maisey stood and started clearing the table. I joined her, loading the dishwasher while she boxed up the remaining food.

"You okay?" I asked.

"Sure."

"Maisey—"

She shook her head, put the last of the food in the fridge, and then pressed a hand to her stomach. "Can we not do this right now? I don't think I can handle one more emotional discussion today. I'm tapped out. All I want to do is unpack a few more boxes and collapse in bed with a book."

She was avoiding me, not just because of the conversation that had just happened with Lewis, but because of whatever my dad had said to her at the lake. But the truth was, I needed the space as much as she did. I needed to get my head and body back in alignment before I did something stupid and tossed all my beliefs and all my baggage to the side and tried to claim her as mine.

So when she walked down the hall, and my dog and the kitten followed her, I didn't say a word to stop any of them. I just headed in the opposite direction, hoping a good night's sleep would somehow fix the turmoil the day had wrought.

Chapter Fifteen
Maisey

CHEMISTRY
Performed by Kelly Clarkson

TWELVE YEARS AGO

HIM: Was your mom mad that you got in past curfew?

> *HER: She didn't even know. It was Chelsea who met me at the back door.*

HIM: Next time, I'll set an alarm. That way, if Shakespeare bores us to sleep again, you won't be late.

Moments passed.

HIM: Maise?

More moments slipped by.

HIM: You okay?

> *HER: Why do you still read with me? I mean, I'm so grateful you helped me when I was little. I'd never be the reader I am now without you. But there's no reason to read with me anymore.*

HIM: I can't like hanging with my friend, doing something we both enjoy?

> *HER: What sixteen-year-old boy really wants to spend his Friday night reading Shakespeare in a treehouse with the kid next door?*

HIM: Did Chelsea say something? Is this her getting in your head? I like reading books. You like reading books. What does it matter where we do it? You know better than to listen to her.

> *HER: She's just worried about me. That's what big sisters do.*

HIM: The only person Chelsea is ever worried about is herself.

PRESENT DAY

I couldn't decide if I was a cowardly chicken or a woman hiding in self-preservation. All I knew was that I'd been dodging Beckett since dinner last night. The little episode in the cove and Kurt's words had sent me into a tailspin.

Like a reel on repeat, I kept seeing Kurt's worry as he'd said, "You love Beckett, and my son loves you, but he has issues he hasn't worked through yet. I'm afraid if you two do this now, it'll end badly for both of you. It'll prove his point about relationships rather than heal them."

And when I'd started to reply, he'd cut me off, saying gently, "Don't get me wrong, sweetheart, the two of you belong together. I've known it since you were little kids and couldn't be separated. I couldn't be happier to have you as my daughter-in-law. But I don't want either of you to get hurt because you haven't taken care of your own house before merging them. That was my problem with Liza. I hadn't fixed the damage left behind by Camila, and it sent her scurrying away."

Beckett had returned from the snack bar before I could respond, which was for the best. Because I wouldn't have been able to tell Kurt the truth—that this was all temporary. That while Beckett and I loved each other, he'd never wanted me like a man truly wants a woman. Not as a girlfriend. Not as a wife. Not as the mother of his kids.

The heat in the looks Beckett sent me lately was new, but I wasn't naïve enough to believe it meant he'd suddenly decided he loved me. If anything, he might be considering a friends-with-benefit situation, but that would be as bad of an idea as a real relationship would be. Because I didn't need much more than a nudge to fall completely and utterly *in* love with him. And if I did, when this arrangement ended, I'd never recover.

Truth was, Kurt was right. Beckett and I carried too much baggage to make anything work between us.

The situation in college with the frat boy who'd taken my virginity had forced me into therapy. Believing he'd actually wanted me, only to find out he'd slept with the plainest girl he could find all for initiation points, had nearly shattered what was left of my soul. But it had also made me see how desperate I'd been to be loved. To be the center of someone's world.

So I'd sought help. And I'd done the hard work to put the worst of my childhood wounds behind me. But they'd been cracked open this week by Chelsea's visit and Dad's situation.

It was a struggle to keep my eyes wide open and my heart sealed shut. But the deal I'd made with Beckett wasn't going to end in forever any more than the time with the loser frat boy had.

With my emotions still raw this morning, I hadn't been any more prepared to face Beckett than I had been last night, so I'd stayed away as long as possible. I'd kept to my room until Dad was ready to go next door with me, simply so I had a buffer.

When Dad came into my room in jeans and a T-shirt that still smelled like smoke, my guilt leaped to the surface. I should have stayed home yesterday and done some laundry instead of galivanting to the lake and stirring pots I knew better than to stir.

"Let's start a load of laundry before we go next door," I told Dad. "Everything you own smells like burned plastic."

He sniffed his shirt and grimaced.

"I don't need you to do my laundry, Maisey. I'll start it when we get back. Right now, I want to get out there before Beckett does all the work himself. I see he already had a dumpster delivered. Make sure he knows I'll pay for it."

I followed him out the front door, wondering exactly what money he thought he'd use to pay for anything when his checking account barely had a few dollars left.

We skirted around the bright-red dumpster in Dad's driveway and headed into the backyard, where Beckett was at work with a chainsaw, cutting apart the destroyed deck.

He wore safety goggles, work boots, jeans, and a T-shirt that was already clinging to his back in the early morning heat. He had his baseball hat turned backward so the brim would be out of his way, and his biceps flexed as he cut through a board, the muscles on his back rippling with effort. He was sexy as sin, and all I could do was stare. Every warning bell I'd told myself to listen to disappeared as heat shot straight to my core.

Thankfully, before Beckett caught me drooling, Vader distracted me by galloping up from the river with a stick in his mouth and his tail wagging. He dropped his prize at my feet and shook, the water spraying all over me.

I laughed. "What do you got there?"

He barked and nudged the stick with his nose. I picked it up and threw it as far as I could, which wasn't far. It ended near the old chicken coop. The coop was in worse shape than the house itself, all but collapsing in on itself after nearly eleven years of being ignored.

Beckett turned off the saw, pulled his goggles down below his chin, and said, "You start throwing that stick for him, and you'll spend all day at it."

He tossed a blackened board into a pile he already had going.

Dad grabbed it with his good hand, balancing it over his shoulder and heading for the front yard and the dumpster. I watched him, worried. His apology last night had simultaneously soothed old hurts and torn them back open. Just knowing he felt bad about the way he'd left us to handle life without him was a salve. But it didn't mean I wanted him to sacrifice his health to prove he wasn't doing it again.

Vader came bounding back, proudly presenting me with the same stick. Beckett intercepted, taking the stick and throwing it way past the coop and the tree swing.

"That's it, dog. We're done. Go chase squirrels," he said.

Vader took off down the slope leading to the river.

"And don't bring back another cat!"

The dog barked, but it sounded like a laugh.

When I went to grab one of the piled-up boards, Beckett halted me. "You got gloves?"

I shook my head.

"I figured. I put a couple extra pairs over there."

He waved his hand to a folding table where he'd set up an orange water cooler, a stack of cups, and some other tools. Beckett had been hard at work this morning while I'd been hiding in my room.

Another round of guilt hit me.

"Thank you," I choked out. When he started to walk away, I put a hand on his arm, saying, "Beckett…about yesterday."

He shook his head. "We were both out of sorts. Let's just leave it."

The knot returned to my throat. My life felt like I was mid-pirouette on Titan's back, and if I took my eyes off the horizon for one second, I'd fall flat on my ass. I wasn't sure I could pull any of this off—helping Dad or Beckett—without losing myself in the process.

But at least the manual labor would keep me from obsessing over it.

Beckett went back to the saw, and I grabbed a couple of gloves and met Dad as he came back around the house, handing him a pair. He took them with a thanks, but then struggled to get one over his bandaged hand. When he winced, I took it from him to help.

"You really shouldn't be doing this," I said quietly. "You're still recovering."

Dad was somber, steel in his tone as he said, "If you're here, then I'm here."

I blinked back the tears that threatened and whispered, "Okay."

We spent the morning tearing apart the burned porch, sorting what little could be saved and tossing the rest. Vader kept sprinting between the river and the house, proudly delivering one soggy, pathetic "gift" after another—a filthy tennis ball, an empty soda can, even an old fishing pole. Each new offering made Beckett swear under his breath, though the corners of his mouth twitched like he almost wanted to laugh.

By the time we were down to the joists, the sun was straight overhead, and the heat was almost punishing. Even with water breaks, Dad had gone pale and shiny with sweat, and my shoulders ached.

"I think you two are done for the day," Beckett said, frowning as my dad wiped his forehead and leaned heavily against the side of the house.

"Let me see your hand," I murmured, tugging off his glove. The skin was torn and bleeding. He'd been trying so hard not to use it, but I'd seen him slipping, lifting boards when he thought I wasn't looking. "You should call it quits, Dad. We can't risk an infection."

"You going to stop too?" he asked.

And I hesitated, not wanting to leave Beckett alone, cleaning up after my family.

"You know what I could use?" Beckett said, trying for lightness. "Pizza. Jack's meat lovers. Why don't you two go grab it while I finish the last couple of boards?"

"You're right. We need fuel," I said, forcing a smile. "But Dad gets vegetarian with light cheese so we can start to unclog those blocked veins of his. I'll call it in so it'll be ready for us to pick up once we clean up."

"I'll order it," Dad insisted. "You two are fixing my mess. The least I can do is buy lunch. My phone's at Beckett's. I'll go grab it."

"Why don't you stay there and shower. That way I can rebandage your hand before I clean up." Dad looked like he might object, and I pushed with a tease. "Can't go into Jack's smelling like the trash Vader's been bringing up from the river."

Beckett stepped in to help, just like he always did. The kidding in his voice was far more successful than mine. "Please, for the love of God, take Vader with you before he brings an entire dump's worth of garbage up."

I glanced gratefully at Beckett when Dad's lips twitched. He tossed the gloves onto the table and whistled for Vader. The dog bounded up from the river with yet another mangled pinecone—proud, oblivious, happy in a way that made me jealous.

"Let's go get a treat, boy," Dad told him. Vader's ears shot up. He dropped the pinecone and tore out of the yard toward Beckett's place. My father trailed behind him with a tired determination that made my throat sting.

"Your dad's pride is hurting him more than his hand," Beckett said. "You continuing to baby him is only going to make him feel worse."

Even though I knew he was right, I still couldn't stop myself from snapping back, "Don't tell me how to handle my dad."

I turned back to the partially dismantled porch and picked up one of the drills Beckett had been using to undo the screws on the joists. I attacked the next set of screws with a vengeance, ignoring Beckett when he came to stand behind me.

"If you keep taking your frustration out on that screw, you're going to strip it," he said, raising his voice over the noise of the drill.

"I've got it."

The next thing I knew, his arms were around me, and he was yanking the drill from my hand. The motion tossed me off balance, and I slammed back into his chest. He stabilized us by widening his legs on either side of my hips.

I ignored the ever-present flare at his touch and hissed, "Back off, unless you want to owe me another romance book."

Instead of stepping away, Beckett took my hand, placed it on the drill trigger, and then moved our hands together toward the next screw. "You have to be a bit gentler. Patient. You can't go at it all fierce and determined, my Maisey-girl. Sometimes, slow and steady really does the trick."

It shouldn't have been suggestive—we were unscrewing a bolt, for heaven's sake—but it was. With his hands on me, his body surrounding mine, and words that weren't sensual yet held a promise of what would happen if I let Beckett take his time with me, my body lit up.

I turned my head to look at him and found his lips were a mere inch from mine. Warm and full. Tempting and tantalizing. My gaze slowly drifted upward to his eyes. The chocolate had turned dark and molten—a lava cake ready to be consumed. His breath hitched, but he didn't move. Neither of us did.

The drill stopped.

In the silence left behind, birdsong filled the air, joined with a few pitiful croaks from the frogs down by the river. A car engine revved before heading off. A phone rang in the distance.

"You have a bit of…" Beckett had removed his gloves, and now he ran a bare finger along my cheek before settling it on my lips. "You have the sexiest lips I've ever seen."

My heart slammed into my ribcage at the words. Harsh. Fierce. Aching.

"Catching a taste the other day was like stealing moments with a goddess." His voice was so deep, so full of lust and want and need that I'd have to be dead not to discover a return craving surging in me.

"You've got our roles reversed, Fireball," I said, proud when my voice didn't reveal the depth of my longing. "If anyone is going to be a deity in this scenario, it's you."

His lips quirked upward, an amused light sparking in his eyes.

"You're right. You're not a goddess." I refused to let his words hurt. He hadn't meant them the way my childhood would have me believe. Beckett had been the first person in my life to insist I was beautiful. "You're more like a saint."

I cringed at the word, Chelsea calling me Saint Maisey ringing in my ears. By the time she'd started using it instead of Cornlette, I'd learned enough about my sister to realize it was a disparaging nickname and not a sweet one.

"I don't want to be a saint or a goddess, Beckett. I'd trade any and all claims to those titles for a single night where I could be anything *but* a saint. To experience, for at least once in my life, the kind of life-altering passion and sin that prevents any thought, any plans, any worries from sinking in."

I inhaled sharply. My words were the opposite of what I'd said to myself yesterday. I'd said I wanted more than a night of sin. But what if this was all I was able to get from him? What if Beckett could give me the passion that had been missing in my real life…for one single night.

The rumble that grew from the depths of Beckett only lit the already simmering fires. Only fueled my desire to have him wrapped around me, over me, in me.

"Do you know how much of my soul I'd offer up to be the person who handed it to you? To be the person who gave you not just one night but a multitude of nights of sin and sex?"

My eyes fluttered closed. I couldn't stand looking at him when he said such beautiful things. Things that spiked all my secret dreams and wishes. It hurt too much.

His finger slid across my mouth. Slow. Sensual.

"Ask me, Maisey. Ask me to give it to you." It was a beg. A dangerous, delightful plea.

If I asked, if I let us both give in to the enormity of the chemistry that spun between us, I'd give too much of myself to him. More than he already owned. Because one night would never be enough, and I would have traded it for the last piece of my heart that still belonged to me. I'd hand it over and have nothing left.

My phone trilled in the side pocket of my yoga pants. Loud and insistent. It was my generic ringtone, so it wasn't anyone I knew. But it could be the insurance company or the water damage restoration company, arranging to pick up the fans they had drying out the house.

Regardless of who it was, they'd ruined a beautiful, tantalizing moment.

Or saved me from another regret.

When I opened my eyes, Beckett was still focused one-hundred-percent on me. The plea he'd issued remained in his heated look, demanding an answer. One I couldn't give.

When my phone stopped ringing, it buzzed with a text message.

Finally, Beckett dropped his arms and stepped back, and I

had to use what remained of the porch to stop myself from falling over.

His throat bobbed, gaze dropping to my mouth and back, but his voice was stable, no hint of the beg in sight when he spoke. "You should get that, and then why don't you go clean up while I finish this last section?"

I couldn't answer, but I did manage to step away from him and the porch as I pulled my phone out and unlocked it.

At first, I thought it was spam.

UNKNOWN #: I can't believe you!

I almost didn't respond, but I was suddenly tired of stepping away from every challenge and every uncertain situation. Why was I so afraid to take what I wanted? So what if it was only one night. Beckett would never completely disappear on me. Things might be awkward between us for a while, but he wouldn't cut me from his life completely. And I'd have a beautiful memory to hold onto when I was alone in the dark.

ME: Who is this?

UNKNOWN #: Chelsea. My phone died, but we're filming today, so I can't get a new one until tonight or tomorrow.

Leave it to Chelsea to drop her filming into the conversation as soon as it began.

ME: What do you want?

UNKNOWN #: Were you ever going to tell me about Dad? Or the fire at the house?

How had she heard? When Chelsea left Swift Rivers the day after graduation, she hadn't just left Dad and me—she'd left everyone. She'd broken up with Randy, dropped all her friends, and marched into the next phase of her life, determined to shed every ounce of baggage before stepping into her future. But if she'd heard about Dad, she must still be talking to someone.

ME: You made it clear you wanted nothing to do with us when you left.

UNKNOWN #: I was just blowing off steam at

Dad. We're still sisters. He's still my father. I have a right to know what's happening. Like the fact he had a stroke and is losing his mind and lost his job. Are you really going to pick up the pieces for him yet again?

> *ME: First, how did you even hear about any of this? And second, if you mean, am I helping to ensure he has the healthcare he needs and that he has a place to stay while we repair the house? Then yes, I'm picking up those pieces.*

I'd never tell her about the mortgage and the fact he'd almost lost the house altogether. She'd never understand me coughing up my savings to help him.

> *UNKNOWN #: Is this why you got engaged to Beckett? Is he giving you money? Either way, this sounds like another stupid Cornlette mistake. I don't want to see you get hurt again.*

I didn't respond. I wouldn't let Chelsea get to me. Instead, I tried to puzzle out who was feeding her information about me and Dad.

> *UNKNOWN #: Beckett is broken. All you'll ever be is his sidekick. You're setting yourself up to get hurt even worse than when he kissed you and you mistook pity for something real. It's like you got stuck at age twelve, hiding out in Rivers and using Beckett as cover—the same way you used to hide behind your hair.*

Her words were cruel, and yet they also had that edge of concern she always dropped. Enough truth for me to wonder if she really did care and was looking out for me, or if it was just gaslighting at its best.

> *ME: Just because I'm not like you, trading one boyfriend for another to help advance my career, doesn't mean I'm hiding.*

> *UNKNOWN #: Everything I've done was to get myself out of that town. And now, I'm reaping the*

rewards with my acting career blooming and a boyfriend on his way to stardom. We wrote a screenplay together, and his company, Lost Acres Productions, is producing it. With us as the leads, we'll sweep every award in the business. I have big plans, Cornlette. You wouldn't know a big idea if it hit you in the ass.

I didn't bother to respond. I'd never change Chelsea's opinions of this town or me or the life I'd chosen.

I was surprised when she texted again, and her question made my chest ache.

UNKNOWN #: So is he dying?

She still cared. She might try to pretend she didn't, but underneath her starlette façade, Chelsea still loved us.

ME: No. He burnt his hand and had a stroke, which caused some temporary dementia. He's not dying.

But her response ripped away my momentary belief in her.

UNKNOWN #: I bet you nurse him for years until he takes his last breath, just like you did Mom. Make it easier on yourself and just walk away. Leave him to whatever fate has in store. It's what he deserves.

UNKNOWN #: And look at it this way, when he croaks, your half of the life insurance and house will give you a chance to get out of Rivers.

Anger, grief, and overwhelming sadness filled me as I read her words. The force of my emotions was so strong my hands shook, and I almost dropped the phone. Even Chelsea couldn't possibly be that heartless. She couldn't mean just to leave Dad…to what? Die? She didn't really want him dead, did she?

"Maisey?" I whipped my head up to see Beckett watching me, brows furrowed in concern. He dropped the drill and strode toward me. "What is it?"

I shook my head. I didn't have words, couldn't answer if I'd wanted to.

He pulled my phone from my hand, scanning the conversation.

"What the hell?"

My sister hadn't always been cold and cruel. My earliest memories of her were full of laughter and love. I remembered us as little kids, heads bent, coloring together in the kitchen while Mom made cookies. When a pop song came on that we all liked, the three of us used wooden spoons as microphones and did our best karaoke rendition of it, dance moves and all.

I had dozens of good memories just like that one. Times full of love and joy.

Looking back, I could see that things with my sister had changed once my parents had started spending money on my dental work. Had it just been about the money? Or had she felt slighted? Like she had less of our parents' time and attention and love simply because they'd been caring for me?

When Mom got sick, Chelsea had all but disappeared. She'd spent days at a time at her friends' houses or, though our parents didn't know it, at her much older boyfriend's. She'd left me to care for our mom alone. It had been mere months between Mom's diagnosis and her death, and I'd never regret the moments I'd spent with her. I'd have done just about anything to have had a few more months, a handful of more memories.

Memories I wanted now with our father too. So, I'd never walk away. I'd do whatever it took to help the dad I loved, failings and all. Knowing he felt remorse for what had happened in our childhood only proved how important this time together was. It would give us a chance to heal. To fill the cracks life had smashed into us.

I grabbed my phone from Beckett and shoved it into my pocket. "She doesn't mean it."

It was an automatic response I'd spent years offering.

But if anyone knew it wasn't true, it was the man standing in front of me.

I turned and headed out of the yard with him on my heels. He wasn't going to leave this alone. He was going to demand I respond. And it pissed me off, because I'd much rather respond to his plea about sex and passion than a question about my sister.

It wasn't until we were on the steps of his porch that I realized I wasn't going to have a chance to answer any of it.

Chapter Sixteen

Beckett

MERCY
Performed by Shawn Mendes

ELEVEN YEARS AGO

> *HER: Are you okay?*

HIM: I can't stop seeing the blood.

> *HER: You saved her life.*

HIM: I knew better than to take her to the dance, Maise. Even though I told her we were just going as friends. I knew better...

> *HER: This isn't on you. You've always been honest with her. The rumors about Delilah that Chelsea started just so she could win a stupid homecoming crown are more to blame than you are for being a good friend.*

HIM: When the sheriff showed up, at first, he thought I'd hurt her.

> *HER: WTF? No! No way anyone could ever think you'd do something like that.*

HIM: I was covered in her blood, Maise.

HIM: God. It's all I can see.

> *HER: Meet me at the treehouse.*

HIM: It's one in the morning.

> *HER: So what. If you don't show up, I'll just come to your room. Your back door is never*

locked.

HIM: Bring something to read. Something without *blood and gore.*

HER: The Princess Diaries?

*HIM: *** puke emoji *** Romance?*

HER: A comedic coming-of-age story with a cat who makes me snort-laugh.

HIM: Fine. This one time, and one time only.

HER: If I were the type of person to bet, I might actually suggest one because I think if you gave romance a chance, you'd be hooked.

PRESENT DAY

𝒜s 𝒩aisey left the yard, ℐ stalked after her. I was cursing myself for exposing the cracks in my resolve to her almost as much as I was cursing her sister for being the bitch she'd always been. Neither of us was worthy of Maisey.

I was an asshole for even considering having sex with her when it couldn't be more than that. But the moment Maisey had uttered the words about giving anything to experience passion and sin for one night, I'd yearned to be the one to give it to her.

But she should have more than just one night, or even a handful of nights, of passion. She should have it every night for the rest of her life.

I could give it to her. I could give her forever if I'd only let myself believe in it.

Even as the thought took root, the smoke that was nothing more than a figment of my imagination took hold. I was smart enough to realize I was still trapped in my childhood bedroom with fire burning outside my door. My body had been saved, but my heart had been charred to a crisp.

And I'd never do to Maisey what I'd done to Del.

The guilt from that horrible night still ate at me.

Del had been on edge with all the cruel rumors, and I'd thought giving her one night of fun at the dance would help. I'd told her I was only taking her to homecoming as a friend, that it couldn't be more. I'd even told her I was going to keep an eye on Maisey, who was still reeling from her mother's death and hadn't heard what Carter was saying about her behind her back. I'd been unable to tell Maisey the truth about Carter, afraid it would break her heart, and instead, I'd driven the last splintering wedge into Del's.

When Delilah had texted me the day after the dance, I'd ignored it at first, frustrated she hadn't listened, annoyed she'd tried to kiss me when I'd dropped her off at home. I didn't understand why she couldn't just be happy with my friendship.

But her next text had shot worry through me. It wasn't so much an ultimatum as a final goodbye. And still, I'd thought it was a ploy. Not a real cry for help.

By the time I'd convinced myself to check on her, it had almost been too late.

She'd been lying under the bleachers, pale and lifeless, covered in blood I'd had trouble staunching.

All the while I'd held my shirt to her wrists, all the while I'd waited for help to arrive, the truth had repeated through my mind. Delilah had almost bled out because I'd been unable to give her my love. I was as responsible for her scarred wrists as the blade she'd used.

And since that day, that truth had never left my side.

No way in hell would I repeat that history with Maisey.

Regret and self-reproach coated my tongue with bitterness as I followed Maisey up the porch steps.

I was yanked out of my spiral by the sound of my easygoing dog growling inside the house. I hadn't even processed the frantic edge in his bark before Maisey's startled gasp pulled my eyes to the orange paint dripping down my front door.

Poor choice. End it now or else.

The note forced the anger that had been simmering in me over Chelsea's texts, my weak resolve, and the entire situation to boil over.

Maisey had been threatened. Again.

And the asshole had damaged my house to deliver their message.

I whipped around, scanning the empty street much like I had on Monday when the note had been on her car, and just like then, there was no one around. The road was as quiet as ever.

But someone had been there long enough to slop paint all over the fucking place.

There was a slim chance one of the neighbors had seen something, but we were pretty isolated at this end of the cul-de-sac. The Helmers' place was the closest, and even it was across and down a bit. Plus, who knew if the renters were even there today?

I cursed myself for not installing a doorbell camera, but I'd never felt like I needed one. Swift Rivers had always felt like a safe community. I might not let my female friends wander around at night by themselves, especially after drinking, but I hadn't ever been afraid of being robbed or violated.

Because that was what this was. A violation. Not only of my home but of Maisey's peace of mind.

"Fuck," I hissed.

I grabbed the doorknob, and my hand froze. We'd left it unlocked. That shouldn't have mattered—we were only next door—but it had given whomever this was free rein of the house.

Thrusting open the door, I barely had time to grab my snapping and snarling dog before Maisey bolted into the house, straight for the guest bedrooms.

"Wait!" I shouted, but she didn't slow down.

I slammed the door behind us, dragged Vader inside, feeling his claws dig into the floor, his wild energy thrumming through me. The air hung heavy, charged with a sharp edge.

The asshole probably wasn't here—no one would dare face a near-rabid Vader—but the thought that someone could be, someone targeting Maisey, sent ice into my veins. My pulse hammered in my ears, every breath a ragged inhale.

"Stop, damnit!" I commanded, every second stretching too

long as I fought to catch up.

She tore down the hall as if she hadn't heard me, calling for her father with the same fear and desperation in her voice that I felt. "Dad?!"

Lewis poked his head out of the guest bath, brows raised. "Yeah?"

The relief that sped across her face at the sight of him seeped through me.

"Are you okay?" she asked.

He raised his burned hand. "Just trying to figure out how to wrap it."

"Stay here," I ordered, all but shoving them both into the bathroom and yanking the door shut.

As I crossed the hall, Vader was right on my heels, hackles still raised, and that caused mine to do the same. He stayed right at my side as I entered Maisey's room. I barely had time to take in the empty boxes she'd flattened and leaned up against a bookshelf before I was storming back out.

My rage grew with each room I cleared.

I hadn't kept her safe. After the first note, I'd sworn no one would threaten her again, and yet I'd done nothing to stop it. I'd confronted Delilah, but when she'd denied it, I'd let old guilt push me into backing off. Since then, I hadn't lifted another finger to figure it out. And now, whoever this was had left another note on my goddamn door.

When I was certain no one was in the house, I headed back to the great room. Vader leaned up against me, and I crouched down, giving him a good rub. "Good dog, Vader. Good dog."

His fur was finally laying flat, and his tail thumped.

"You keep watch like that, and I'll forever forgive you for bringing up stinky trash from the river."

He looked toward the crate, where I could hear the kitten scrabbling with its claws to get out.

"Maybe not more cats, Vader. I have to draw the line somewhere."

He let out a bark that was all relaxed playfulness, just as Maisey emerged from the hall with the switchblade she'd used to cut open boxes in her hand.

Any relief I'd found disappeared. I gritted my teeth in frustration. "I told you to wait with your dad."

"And I was supposed to let you face whomever this was on your own? Let you get hurt while I sat like some defenseless princess in the bathroom?" She shook her head. "No way, Beckett."

I hadn't done a good job of protecting her anyway. I'd let someone close enough to scare her again. To scare us both.

"Did your dad hear anything?"

"He said no," she replied. She tossed the blade onto a side table, wrapped her arms around herself, and stared at the closed door.

I pulled my phone out, dialing the sheriff's office.

"I don't understand, Beckett," Maisey said quietly, pain in every word. "Why would someone hate us being together so much? What have I done that would make someone try to destroy our relationship before we even have a chance to be together?"

My nails bit into my palms. If this was Delilah, I wouldn't let unresolved guilt stop me from holding her responsible. I wouldn't let her destroy Maisey to get my attention. I'd hand her over to the sheriff in a heartbeat.

As I hadn't called the emergency line, it took a minute for Suzanne at the front desk to pick up. When I explained about the vandalism, she put me on hold then came back to say Deputy Cleaver was on his way.

Which was just fucking great. It was bad enough fury was still raging through me with the speed of a brushfire, but now I'd have to deal with Josh Cleaver flirting with Maisey. Nothing about my mood was going to get better. I had to find a way to work these intense feelings out of me before I did damage to something…or someone.

"Stay," I told Vader when he attempted to follow me out of the house. "Protect."

I stormed out to the garage, brought back paint remover, sandpaper, primer, and the leftover paint from when I'd redone the door to begin with. After Cleaver did his thing, I'd work all afternoon and into the night if I had to, but there would be no sign of this nastiness by the time tomorrow came.

I'd just returned to the house when Cleaver drove up in his official vehicle. The man was a year younger than me and had gotten the unfortunate nickname of Beaver in school, not only because he looked just like the kid from the old 1950s show, but because he'd had an unfortunate overbite back then. It was how he and Maisey had become friends. They'd both spent an inordinate amount of time in the orthodontist's office together.

I wasn't sure Maisey had ever realized how infatuated he'd been with her back in school, but then again, Maisey never expected anyone to see her as beautiful and desirable. And Carter Smythe and the asshole frat boy had only added to her distorted self-image.

Worse was the realization that I'd done nothing to help. Nothing to ensure she saw herself as desirable and wanted. I'd been too busy keeping our relationship carefully in the friend zone so I wouldn't hurt her the way I'd hurt Delilah. I'd let Maisey assume she'd never be enough for me, when really it was me who wasn't enough for her.

As Cleaver stepped onto my front porch, my foul mood was at nearly epic proportions and had me snapping, "What took you so long?"

His eyes narrowed at my tone, but he remained calm, saying, "Afternoon, Beckett." He tipped his hat at Maisey as she came out of the house, quickly shutting the door before Vader could follow her. "Maisey."

"Thanks for coming," she said softly, easing up next to me.

"I'm going to take some pictures. Sandy is on her way with an evidence kit to get some fingerprints. We'll need to take elimination prints from the two of you too."

"My fingerprints and Maisey's are already on file because of our jobs," I bit out.

He nodded. "Sure. Sure. Anyone else here in the last few days?"

"My dad is here," Maisey responded. "And Tejas was here yesterday, helping us move in."

Cleaver's lips tightened. "Guess the rumor is true, then." He looked at Maisey's ringless hand, disappointment all but radiating from him. "You two really are getting hitched?"

It was much more than just playing a part that had me hooking my arm around Maisey's waist and pulling her tight up against me as I said, "Yep."

She briefly stiffened before relaxing and leaning into me.

Cleaver looked like he might actually cry before he turned back to the door. He took a dozen pictures and then stepped off the porch, saying he was going to walk the perimeter.

I should have done the same thing. I'd cleared the house but hadn't thought about whoever this was lingering outside, safely away from my dog's teeth. They could have been watching and waiting this whole time.

A chill ran up my spine, and my anger turned into a backdraft, just waiting for more oxygen to burst forth and destroy everything in its wake.

When Cleaver returned, he scratched his clean-shaven jaw and said, "I don't see any unusual activity anywhere else around the house. No footprints by windows or broken windows. Suzanne mentioned something about another note. Do you still have it?"

Maisey shook her head. "But I took a picture."

"Send it over to me, so we'll at least have it for the file."

"Do you still have the same number?" she asked.

Cleaver nodded, disappointment flashing once more, which only caused my ridiculous jealousy to flare again. How could I not want anyone else to have Maisey, when I knew I'd never be able to give her the happily ever after she wanted? I knew it wasn't healthy, for me or Maisey, and yet I couldn't seem to control it.

The deputy's phone buzzed, and he looked down at the image she'd sent him. "Similar wording. Any idea who's behind it?"

He looked up from his phone at the two of us. Maisey shot me a knowing look that seared my chest with regret.

"The only person who's ever been upset about

my…relationship with Beckett has been Delilah," she said softly.

"Waiting for someone you care about to return your feelings can certainly make you do stupid things. Can make you wait years for the right moment to appear," Cleaver responded, eyes full of hearts that only made the wild and feral jealousy beating in my veins grow stronger.

Maisey missed his innuendo, but I returned the glare Cleaver sent my way.

Maisey's dad joined us on the porch. His face was grim as he took in the vandalism. When he glanced my way, I saw concern layered with a hint of the anger rolling in me. But he didn't drop any of the accusations he could have—that I'd put her in danger or that I'd done little to protect her.

Instead, he looked at Maisey and said, "The pizzas are ready. Why don't we head over to Jack's to pick them up while Josh and Beckett handle this?"

"Let me just get my purse," Maisey said.

She slipped inside the house and picked up her bag from the side table by the door. Cleaver studied it as she came out.

"Was your purse right there all along?" When she nodded, he asked, "Are you missing any cash or credit cards?"

She pulled out her wallet, thumbed through it, and then shook her head.

"Not a robbery, then," Cleaver said.

"I don't think a robber would have left a fucking note."

"Beckett," Maisey scolded softly.

I gritted my teeth. She was right. I shouldn't take out my pissy attitude on the deputy. I fought to rein in my turbulent emotions, trying my best to push them down to a slow simmer.

But then, as Maisey and her dad headed down the steps, she looked back at Cleaver and said, "Call me if you need anything else."

That's all it took for everything to leap back up to a boil. I hated the idea of him calling her as much as I hated the way he watched her walk all the way to the truck.

As Maisey's pickup disappeared down the street, Sandy

pulled up to the curb.

"Look," I ground out. "I don't want to believe this is Del. When I talked to her after the first note, she vehemently denied it."

"I'll have a chat with her and see what comes of it."

He eased to the side as Sandy mounted the steps with an oversized evidence kit almost as large as she was. She whistled in surprise at the orange paint and then got to work without a word.

Cleaver tipped his head, inviting me farther out onto the porch.

"The first note was on Maisey's car, right?" he asked. "But the second is here at your house. As I hadn't heard she'd moved in here, I'm wondering if the vandal knew either. Is there a chance these notes are directed at you and not her?"

I crossed my arms over my chest, considering the idea before shaking my head. "If it was directed at me, why not leave the first note on my car at the station?"

In the silence that followed, my irritation grew. If this *was* about me, I'd be damned if I could understand why. The only choice either Maisey or I had made recently was about the engagement, and I said as much to him.

"You're applying for the fire chief position, aren't you?"

I barely stopped myself from rolling my eyes. "Nattingly hasn't officially retired, so as of right now, the job isn't available."

"But you will?"

"Yes."

Cleaver scratched his chin. "Well, we'll canvas the neighborhood and see if anyone saw anything unusual. I think the Helmers' place has a doorbell camera, but that's pretty far away to have caught anything."

His attention settled on Lewis's house. From here, you couldn't see the residuals of the fire, but he stared at it for far too long before asking, "Anything related to what happened next door?"

It was like a fist hit me in the solar plexus. The fire had been suspicious, but it had happened before we'd agreed to our fake engagement. There'd been no reason for me to think the choice the notes were talking about had been about anything else.

"Talk to Ron. He's got some evidence he's working through. But I can't see how it would relate to Maisey and me." I waved at the door. "The notes seem very personal, and the fire happened before I'd asked her to marry me."

He gave a curt nod. "I'll follow up with him. I'd like you and Maisey to put together a list of any and all decisions you've made in the past few weeks, no matter how small, and who they might have impacted."

Cleaver started for the steps but then turned back and landed me with the deadliest look I'd ever seen on the man. "Anyone hurts Maisey more, and I'll be busting heads."

I scowled back at him. "You do your job, and she won't be hurt at all."

"I'm not just talking about the door, Romero."

We glowered at each other for a moment.

"Take your pissing contest somewhere else and let me work in peace," Sandy huffed.

I bit my tongue, stepped around her, and headed inside.

I needed a cold shower. I needed to calm down before I did something stupid.

At the station, on the job, I was usually the coolest one of the bunch. I went into the flames with a clear head and complete concentration. But right now, my emotions churned with such ferocity that I wasn't sure how to quiet them.

I was angry at whoever was threatening us. Jealous of Cleaver for simply looking at Maisey. Frustrated by my inability to stop the insatiable desire I had to touch her. Strangled by childhood wounds and images of blood-coated wrists that held me in their grips and prevented me from reaching for more.

Prevented me from claiming the person I wanted most.

Prevented me from claiming Maisey for real.

These last thoughts scared the hell out of me far more than words painted on my door ever could.

Chapter Seventeen

Maisey

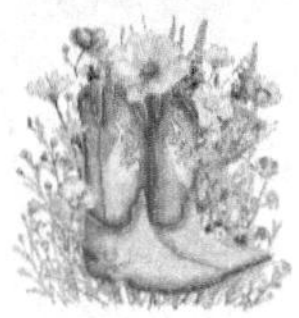

I HATE LOVE

Performed by Kelly Clarkson with Steve Martin

SIX YEARS AGO

HIM: I read the book you recommended and met all the obligations of my stupid bet, so thanks for that. But I have a question.

> *HER: You're welcome. And shoot.*

HIM: What's with this forced-proximity thing? I mean, you either want someone or you don't. If you and I were living together, we wouldn't suddenly go goofy in the head, or groin, and decide we couldn't keep our hands off.

> *HER: I'll try not to be offended.*

HIM: You know that's not what I meant. You're sexy as hell. I'm just saying, friends are friends. Lovers are lovers. End of story.

> *HER: Let's pretend for a minute that you aren't you. That you don't have a dead heart. Let's pretend you had a friend who you actually believed was sexy as hell, but you made a stupid decision to place them in the friend zone years ago and regretted it. And now, you're in the same hotel room, and you catch her in nothing but a towel. Are you telling me you wouldn't make a move?*

HIM: Dead heart aside? No. That's a violation of

*the sacred trust of friends. How could you ever go
back to being friends after that?*

> *HER: You're missing the point, Fireball.
> Neither of them really WANTS to be JUST
> friends. They want MORE. They want trust
> AND love AND lust AND forever.*

*HIM: Then why not just go for that in the first
place? Why pretend to be friends?*

> *HER: I give up.*

*HIM: This is why more men don't read romance.
None of it is logical.*

> *HER: You're missing the point yet again. It's
> the fantasy that romance readers crave, not
> logic. We want to savor the endorphin rush
> of a grand gesture and the heat of a happily
> ever after, not drink a cold cup of reason.*

PRESENT DAY

My pulse was still racing as I drove with Dad to the Italian restaurant in town. The sexual tension that had drifted between Beckett and me had all but evaporated, as had the disgust I'd felt at my sister. In its place, fear had taken root. When I'd seen the note on Beckett's door, for a few awful seconds, I'd thought something horrible had happened to Dad…all because of me.

The fierceness of Beckett's emotions hadn't helped. The anger that had vibrated off him and wafted through me had been all-consuming. A Beckett I rarely saw. I'd seen him laughing and teasing to diffuse a situation, and strong and assertive to protect someone hundreds of times. But I wasn't sure I'd ever seen him angry enough to do physical damage.

Unfortunately, Josh had shown up just in time for Beckett to direct his aggression at him. Leaving the two men together probably hadn't been smart, but I'd been relieved when Dad had suggested going to pick up the pizzas.

I'd played chicken yet again and escaped. But if I hadn't, my own emotions might have exploded.

Dad's voice drew me from my thoughts. "I'm sure the sign wasn't on the door when I came in." I heard the uncertainty in his voice, and my heart twisted in concern. "But the way my mind has been playing tricks lately..."

Worry for my father finally allowed me to push back the spiral of darker emotions.

"It'll get better, Dad. The dementia is just temporary. Once you've had a chance to heal, everything will be back to normal. I'm thrilled you're trying to stop smoking. I know it's hard, but it's a huge step toward improving your overall health. Now, we just need to work on those arteries of yours."

His lips flattened into a straight line as he took in the nicotine patch on his arm. "Not sure it'll stick. Never been able to give it up before, but being off the road where the boredom triggers me will help." After a few more seconds, he changed the subject. "What's the deal with the note?"

I didn't want to add to his burdens by making him worry about me, so I shrugged it off. "Just kids being stupid."

He shot me a look I hadn't seen in a really long time—a fatherly one that said he knew I was lying. "*Poor choice. End it now or else* are pretty strange words for a prank. Seems to me, if it were kids, they'd write something stupid like *You suck*. So tell me, do I need to worry about this? Is Beckett involved in something? Or you? Or is this about your engagement?"

Surprise registered, and Dad's brow went up just as one side of his lips did.

"I'll try not to be hurt that you didn't tell me yourself. But that Tejas kid couldn't stop jabbering about it yesterday."

I swallowed hard, not wanting to lie to him, so I told him a half-truth. "The town gossips have done a good job spreading it quicker than we could. Don't feel too bad. Kurt heard about it the same way."

I parked the truck, and Dad waited for me on the sidewalk before we headed down the street toward Jack's.

"You didn't have to put your stuff in that tiny room, you

know. We're all adults. I'm not going to keel over if you come out of Beckett's room in the morning."

I flushed, the heat spreading from my cheeks all the way up to my hairline. "Dad—"

He chuckled, and the sound eased the pressure in my heart a little because my dad had a really great laugh. It wasn't loud or booming, but it was infectious. I found my lips turning up.

"He's a good man. That's all a father wants for his girls. Someone who loves and respects them but can also protect and provide for them." I inhaled sharply, and he waved me off. "Don't get all up in your craw. I know you can provide for yourself." He opened the restaurant door and waved me inside. "As it is, you're providing for your screwed-up dad too, but knowing Beckett *can* provide for you, that he'll look out for you if the worst happens…that's a good thing."

I couldn't stand lying to him this much. I couldn't stand him thinking Beckett and I were going to get all the way to a white wedding. So, instead, I simply gave him another half-truth. "Honestly, Dad, I'm not sure if it's going to work."

"Did you have an argument? Or are you letting someone scare you off at the first sign of trouble? If you want a marriage to work, you've got to struggle like hell to keep it together."

When I didn't respond, he kept going. "Fighting is easy to fix when you're a couple. Actually, most of the time, an argument is just a prelude to the best kind of make-up sex. Sometimes I'd pick a fight with your mom just because I knew we'd end the night tangled together."

I choked, and he laughed. "TMI, Dad. Way too much information. There are some things a daughter doesn't *ever* want to hear about her parents."

But I thought back to all their quiet arguments growing up, and how they'd made my stomach knot. Had some of those fights been Dad's way of engaging in a little foreplay? It made me want to gag, and yet, I could see him doing it, pushing Mom just to get a reaction out of her.

"Maisey!"

I turned my head at my name to find Meredith hustling toward me from a table in the corner.

"I'll go get the pizzas while you talk," Dad said, patting me on the shoulder and heading for the counter.

"Hey," I said as my boss stopped next to me.

"Your dad looks better. You're still planning to be at work on Sunday, right?"

"I'll be there."

Relief flooded her face.

"We need all the help we can get these days. And about the L&D position—" My heart leaped, but before she could finish, she caught sight of her granddaughter standing on a table. "Nellie, get down!" she hollered and hustled away.

Hope and I battled it out as I wondered what she'd been about to say. Were they giving me the job or not? I guessed I would find out when I returned to work. For now, I had other things to worry about.

As I turned to join my father, I ran straight into Carter. He steadied me with his hands on my arms, and revulsion at the touch had me jerking from his hold.

The overpowering musk of his cologne made my head spin, and I tried to back away farther, but the booth behind me prevented me from getting far.

"Did you talk to Lewis about selling the house?" he asked. He looked toward my father and back before he rubbed his knuckles along his bright-red nose.

"I talked to the bank instead," I told him. "Dad isn't selling."

It was when Carter's glassy eyes narrowed in on me that I realized he was high. The redness around his nostrils suggested coke, but other drugs could cause similar symptoms, especially if he were crashing down.

"How'd you swing that?" he demanded. "He was months behind."

"Not that it's any of your business, but I had some savings."

"Chelsea told me it would be a piece of cake to get your dad to sell. Said the place is falling down around him anyway."

My stomach bunched up. "You're in touch with Chelsea?"

His wild-eyed gaze darted around the restaurant and back.

"Sure. Saw her in LA not long ago. Told her about the development I had planned for Meadow Lane."

"What development?" My pulse sped up as an ugly suspicion started to form.

"We've got people flocking to Swift Rivers who need houses. I figure I can squeeze about thirty homes on ten acres at the end of the lane and another forty or fifty townhomes on the remaining five. Big money."

My mind whirled with the numbers he threw out. I inhaled a shaky breath. "Fifteen acres? You'd need more than Dad's land. You'd need Beckett's and the Helmers' place too."

"Already put in a bid on the Helmers' lot." He spun his watch around his wrist. "The deal's cooking."

"Even if Dad wanted to sell, Beckett would never give up his home."

Carter's brow raised. "You've got a way with both of them. You could convince them to sell if you wanted to. I can cut you in for a share—"

"You again," Dad said as he approached with two pizza boxes balanced in his good hand.

Carter glanced from me to my dad and back. "I gotta head out. Just think about what I said."

He strode for the door, leaving the overwhelming scent of his cologne behind him.

"That boy has always been no good," Dad said. "Didn't like him when he hung out with Chelsea, and I sure as hell didn't like finding out he'd taken you to homecoming."

Surprise kept me from responding as we made our way out to my truck. Dad had been gone so much I hadn't even realized he'd known about the dance.

"What did the weasel want?" Dad asked once I'd pulled onto the street, heading back home.

"He wanted to know if you'd given any more thought to selling the house."

"I did think about it. The house has never been the same without your mother in it. She took such good care of it, and I've let it deteriorate. She'd be disappointed in me." His voice turned thick and scratchy. "But then there'd be nothing left for you when I die."

My stomach cramped at his words.

"You're not dying!" I said vehemently. "And I don't want anything from you. Not the house. Not money."

He reached over and patted my arm as I drove. "I may not be dying today, sweetheart, but I am going to die. I should have stopped smoking a lifetime ago." He looked out the window, drifting for a moment to a faraway place. "Maybe if I had, she wouldn't have…" He shook his head. Grief and regret spread across his face.

The amount of pain he showed took my breath away, leaving me unable to respond yet again.

"Anyway," he continued, "since the fire, I've been thinking about it some more. Maybe I should sell the place so you don't waste any more of your money on it and me. I could use whatever's left from the sale to move into one of those new-fangled retirement homes. You know the ones where there's a nursing staff if you need it. I don't want you having to care for me in the end like you did her…"

His voice cracked, and the pressure in my chest grew.

"Dad—"

He talked over me, "That's not negotiable, Maisey. I failed you back then. I won't fail you again."

My vision blurred, and I had to blink violently to hold back the tears as I pulled in behind Beckett's SUV.

Turning off the engine, I glanced over at my childhood home and wondered if maybe it would be better for him to sell. If he moved into a retirement community, he'd have other adults around for company, and depending on the type of community, he might not have to cook or clean. If his dementia worsened or he had another stroke, there'd be professionals available to assist him.

But it meant letting go of the last of Mom's memories. Could either of us really do that?

As we got out of the pickup, I pushed over the lump in my throat to say, "It might be a good idea, but you don't have to make that decision today. And we definitely should finish the repairs, otherwise you'll never get the full market value for it."

"That little weasel offered me top dollar as is. But if I sell our home, it won't be to someone who's going to tear it down and put a dozen more on the land your mother loved."

At least on that, we agreed.

When we got to Beckett's front porch, he was already at work on the door. He'd wiped some of the paint away with paint remover and was sanding it with a ferocity that spoke to his state of mind. It didn't seem like any of his anger and frustration had eased in the time we'd been away.

"Pizza's here," I said.

"I'm not really hungry. I want to take care of this first. At least get a coat of paint on it."

He looked up from his work to take me and my dad in, and as if sensing the heaviness that lingered around us, his brows drew together. "Everything good here?"

Dad considered Beckett for a moment. "You tell me? Are you really taking care of my girl? Because I don't see a ring on her finger, even though the entire town is yapping about your engagement." Dad looked at the front door. "And to make matters worse, you've got someone taking aim at you."

Beckett's brows lifted, and it took him a beat too long before he came up with an adequate response. "I wanted Maisey to pick out her own ring."

He'd told Stoney it was getting sized, which had just been to shut the man up, but we were going to keep getting the question. If mom's jewelry box hadn't disappeared, I could have used her ring.

Dad shook his head as if in disgust. "I thought you were better with the ladies than this, Beckett. No matter what they tell you, a woman doesn't want to pick out her own ring. It's more romantic knowing you picked one out while thinking of her."

When neither Beckett nor I responded, Dad's expression changed, an amused twinkle appearing in his eyes.

"I'm gonna take this pizza inside while the two of you

discuss that and whatever else is brewing here.”

Once he'd stepped past Beckett into the house, Dad turned and winked at me before heading toward the kitchen with a whistle that sounded a lot like Chicago's "Hard To Say I'm Sorry."

It made me want to both laugh and cry, knowing Dad was giving us space to make up after a nonexistent argument. I hated not being honest with him about what was going on between Beckett and me. But even if we'd been in a real relationship, I wasn't sure I'd be able to *make up* the way Dad had insinuated, not knowing my father was on the opposite side of the house and assuming we were doing just that.

Beckett put the sander down and looked up at me from where he was kneeling. "I'll get you a ring."

I lowered my voice so my dad wouldn't hear and said, "It's stupid to spend money on one. Just let everyone think the same thing you told Stoney, that it's at the jewelers."

"For months?"

Months. I kept forgetting I was in this for months. Not just a day or two or a week. It would take months for the chief to retire and the city council to hire a replacement.

I'd be living with Beckett for months.

That did horrible things to my pulse. To my stomach. To my core.

How was I going to survive this when I'd nearly offered myself to Beckett twice in a matter of two days? When I'd nearly accepted his plea in the backyard, simply because I wanted to know what it was like to be consumed by him?

As if his thoughts had also journeyed to the same place, Beckett's eyes turned molten, and the electricity leaped to life between us, zinging through the air like lightning waiting to spark.

His jaw tightened, and he picked the sander back up. "I'll get you a ring," he grunted out. "But right now, I need to fix this damn door."

I pressed a hand to my stomach, guilt flickering in over the desire. The first note had clearly been left for me, which meant the second likely had been as well. Someone had ruined his beautiful door to leave me a nasty message. "I can help. I don't know what to do, but you could tell me."

"Thanks, but fixing it will let me work out some of my…anger before it blows."

He wouldn't look at me, and the knots in my stomach grew more knots. Pretty soon, there'd be a whole family of knots living in there.

But I also knew, from the way Beckett had hesitated over the words, what he needed to work out wasn't just anger.

Because I understood those feelings, I let him get back to work while I did exactly what I'd wanted to do this morning— I avoided Beckett for the rest of the day.

Chapter Eighteen
Maisey

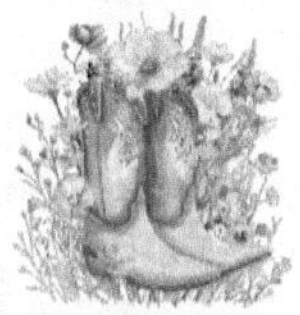

LOVE YOU TONIGHT
Performed by Ella Langley

PRESENT DAY

> *HIM: Shall I grab lunch for us on my way back from the station?*

Minutes passed.

> *HIM: Maisey?*

More time passed.

> *HIM: Damnit, where are you?*

When I dragged myself out of bed the next morning, it was to a text message from Beckett saying he was going to work out at the station before checking in with Ron on the investigation. He'd left Vader behind, telling me to be on alert if his dog started freaking out like he had yesterday.

While Beckett was gone, Dad and I had gone next door and finished the rest of the porch, with Vader bringing up more garbage from the river the entire time. Then, we'd walked through the house with the water damage restoration folks and an insurance adjuster.

We'd both come back to Beckett's feeling exhausted and fighting our discouragement.

It was going to take a lot more time and money to fix the house than either of us had thought. I'd figure it out…somehow. I just had to think about it. See what else I could shuffle around.

We'd been through worse.

What I held back from Dad was my worry the fire would be determined to be gross negligence, or purposeful, and that we'd never see a penny of the insurance. If that happened, we might be out of luck. We might have to sell it as-is for a lot less than it was really worth.

While Dad took the first turn in the shower, I searched the house for the kitten who'd knocked over her crate again. Vader found her first, barking from Beckett's bedroom.

I hesitated before entering the new suite he'd added on to the house. It was as much to get the cat as it was a perverse need to see where he slept that had me stepping inside. The room was full of the same neutrals and dark woods he'd decorated the rest of the house with, but the king-sized bed where the kitten lay curled surprised me.

With its gray padded headboard, the bed felt strangely soft and feminine in a space I'd expected to be purely masculine. It was sexy and sensual, inspiring images of bodies tangled together on it in the heat of passion. And just knowing I was actually thinking a *bed* was sexy nearly sent me running from the room.

The cat sat up, mewling sweetly as Vader nosed her. She was the cutest little thing, begging for love. It tugged at my heart. No one but Vader had really given her much attention since Beckett had brought her home. I certainly hadn't given her much thought with everything else that had been going on.

"You're quite the little escape artist," I said, petting her between the ears while Vader licked my hand.

I'd always wanted a cat, but a lot of apartments didn't allow them, so I'd resisted the urge up until now. This little gray-and-white furball had a tiny white, mask-like stripe around her vibrant green eyes and a pink, shiny nose. While I continued to pet her, she rested a paw on my hand, and I was a goner.

"How about you come stay in my room?" I picked her up, and Vader wagged his tail as if he was happy to see me holding her. "What should we name her, Vader?"

He woofed as we made our way out of Beckett's room and down the hall.

"I'm not naming her Woof." I considered her. "Maybe Dorothy, the world-famous escape artist, or Dorothy from *The Wizard of Oz*, because she blew into our lives."

Vader barked, the cat rubbed its head against my chin, and my heart warmed. "Okay. Dorothy it is."

The cat explored my room, batting at the cardboard boxes, while Vader watched over her. When I came back from helping Dad with his bandages, the two animals had curled up together, tails entwined, on the foot of my bed, just as they had the night before. Since the dog adored Beckett with a heart-eyed fervor, I'd been surprised when he'd stayed with me. But looking at them now, I realized it was much more about the kitten than me.

It was clear the two animals had bonded. I wouldn't be able to keep Dorothy because Vader had already claimed her. I took a picture to send to Beckett, determined to convince him to keep her.

I grabbed some clean clothes and headed to the shower, but once I'd scrubbed off the sweat and smell of burned wood, I realized I'd forgotten my bra. I wrapped a towel around my middle, peeked out into the hall, and then scurried across to my room.

Vader thumped his tail on my return and then put his nose back in the kitten's fur.

I'd just dropped the towel when the door of my room was flung open with so much force it banged against the wall with a loud crack.

I screamed and turned, hands to my breasts, heart leaping into my throat.

Beckett stood in the doorway, face dark and frustrated.

"Where the hell have you been?" he demanded.

"Get out!" I hollered, scrambling for the towel.

When I stood back up and tried, with shaky hands, to wrap it around me again, it was to find Beckett's gaze locked on my barely covered chest. His Adam's apple worked overtime, and it took far longer than it should have for his eyes to make their way back up to my face. The longer our eyes clashed, the more the spark between us flared into something dangerous. Into the same intense longing that had all but consumed us yesterday. That had left me achy and him begging to show me what he could do to me.

Instead of leaving the room, as I'd requested, Beckett took a step toward me, and my belly wooshed. A low, tantalizing thrill danced through me, and I knew if he touched me, I'd be a lost cause. I'd let down the feeble wall I still had left. I'd let him do whatever he wanted, and damn the consequences to our lives…our friendship.

I had one chance…one chance to push this back into the right territory. To right the ship before it sailed. I forced my voice to be light, forced a tease into it I felt far from, as I asked, "Are you happy now? You've got your tit for tat. I saw you. You saw me. We're even. Now get out."

He didn't. He stepped even closer, and I moved backward only to run into a bookshelf.

"Beckett." I shook my head and put one hand out as if to ward him off while the other still grasped the towel.

"You didn't answer my texts, and then I walk in the door, and there's no Vader, no you, no Lewis. Do you know what that did to me? After yesterday?" he growled.

A tremble coursed through me as he removed the last few inches that separated us, stopping so close his shoes could kiss my toes.

"We were next door, working and meeting with the adjuster, and then we came back and got cleaned up. I left my phone here, charging, because I fell asleep reading last night, and it didn't get charged." I was rambling. I knew I was, but I couldn't seem to stop it. "Vader has been with us all day, and then we had to find the kitten because she'd escaped again. She's just lonely though. I think Vader is too. See the way they're curled up together…"

Beckett's head swiveled slowly over to the animals, who were still twined but watching us with interest. Then, he turned back to me. "No. I'm not keeping the cat. It wouldn't be fair when Vader and I are at the station for days at a time."

"She can stay with me. Once we fix up Dad's place, I'll likely stay with him, so I don't need to worry about an apartment. It'll be fine."

He put a finger on my lips, and my voice faded away. The look he gave me was dark and sinful. I wanted to dive in and get lost in it for hours.

"You're babbling. You only do that when you're nervous. Why are you nervous, darlin'?"

It seemed almost impossible to breathe. Shifting his hand, he glided a thumb sensually over my jaw. When he hesitated over the almost invisible scar, I was finally able to push him away.

"I think that's five now. Five romance books you owe me." My voice was still a bit shaky as I was unable to break away from the simmering look sparking in his brown depths.

How could this ever be wrong? The pulse of want that was so strong it was almost its own entity. How could that ever be anything but right?

"It was a draw at the lake," he said, voice low and deep. "So, I think this makes four."

He leaned forward, not quite far enough for our bodies to touch, but his mouth inched closer to mine. My almost nonexistent breath evaporated completely. Every fiber of my being ached for him to kiss me. To have those beautiful lips land firmly on mine.

I'd once told Fallon I'd never had an earth-shattering, life-altering kiss, but I suddenly realized I had now. When Beckett had dipped me over and planted one on me at the fire station, it had changed everything I'd known and thought about kisses. My life would forever be a series of befores and afters from here on, and I wanted more of what he'd given me. It was why I'd subconsciously taunted him at the lake, and in the backyard, and…

His hand fell away from my cheek, and disappointment, hot and furious, welled through me, even as I tried to convince myself it was for the best. My walls were too shaky. Too torn. I'd never survive another kiss from him, only to have to go back to being just friends.

With his eyes still holding mine, he leaned even closer, reaching his arm past me so it grazed my ear and had my nipples hardening and goosebumps bursting out along my skin. As if he saw it or sensed it, Beckett's lips quirked upward.

And then he was moving back, a book from the shelf behind me in his hand.

"Will this one do to start?" he asked.

My grip on the towel tightened. I fought to recover. Fought to stabilize my senses.

It took far too long for me to focus on the book he held—a steamy, historical romance.

I cleared my throat. "If you want to read about rakes and ladies, sure."

His smirk grew into a full-on grin. "Forced-proximity trope, right? You like that one."

My throat seemed to close, and I had to force out my words. "I do."

He glanced down at the towel and the swell of my breasts above it before fastening me with a heated stare. If possible, his voice got even deeper as he said, "I think I'm finally getting how tempting it can be."

As he stepped farther away, my breath escaped, and my stomach unclenched.

"You might appreciate a romantic-suspense novel more than that," I said.

"I've got three more after this, right? You can recommend one. For now, let's see"—he read the back—"how the Duke of Thornton manages with Miss Danvers."

The more space he put between us and the more he teased, the more it allowed me to regain my wits. "Fine. But don't judge all romance by one historical, even if it is a really great one."

"You forget, Maise, I've already read a couple of romance books."

I scoffed. "You didn't really read *The Marriage Solution* when you lost that bet, did you?"

His dimple popped. "Someday, you can quiz me on it and find out." At the door, he turned back and looked at my nearly naked body. "I feel like I should get extra points for not touching you right now. It took an inhuman amount of effort."

I wished I had something to toss at him. Instead, I said, "I'm going to the Emporium for fajita fixings. Can I get you anything?"

His brow raised, and a little growl escaped him, tantalizing me all over again.

"Get your mind out of the gutter, Fireball."

"You're lucky I can think at all, darlin', after what I saw under that towel."

My pulse rocketed again. My mouth turned dry, and for two seconds, I couldn't remember why we were denying ourselves what our bodies clearly wanted.

All humor faded from Beckett's face, and he was the one who finally looked away. "I promised Tejas drinks the other night and then forgot to meet up with him. He insists I now owe him dinner *and* drinks for leaving him hanging." He hesitated. "So don't plan on me for dinner. I'll likely be late."

I looked down at my toes, noticing the polish was chipped.

"You don't owe me any explanations, Beckett. We're not actually in a relationship. Go do whatever it is you need to do."

When he was silent for far too long, I risked looking at him. Not even a hint of his smile remained. His lips were flat. His expression grave. "I'm not going out to try to get laid, Maisey. The entire town thinks we're getting married, and I'll damn well show you the respect you deserve while that's the case—show us both the respect we deserve. I may not have ever seen myself as married, but I'd never cheat on my spouse if I were."

It shouldn't hurt, because it was exactly what he'd said—respectful—and yet, for some reason, it did. It was because, stupidly, in my secret heart of hearts, I wished it wasn't pretend.

"Well, at least be a good wingman, then, and help Tejas get laid."

"Tejas doesn't need the assist, but if Leon shows up, that kid needs all the help he can get." He looked at his dog. "You staying here?"

The dog thumped his tail without budging.

"Vader and Dorothy have bonded," I told him.

Beckett groaned. "You actually named her? I told you not

to name her."

I laughed. "Vader deserves companionship."

Our eyes met again, a flare of longing zipping back across the room.

"Good luck getting him to clean the litter box," Beckett teased.

Then, he walked out the door with my romance book in his hand and his humor and smile restored.

♪ ♪ ♪

I'd finished cleaning the dinner dishes, and Dad and I were into our second round of King's Corners, when Vader sat up and barked two seconds before a fist pounded on the front door.

My body froze before I heard Fallon's voice demanding to be let in. I swung the door open to find my friend waving a bottle of margarita mix and a bakery box while Andie stood right behind her with a bottle of tequila.

My brows raised. "What's this?"

"Celebration," Fallon said, eyes drifting toward Andie and back. "Andie wanted to celebrate with you and make some plans for the wedding. We need to get the date on the ranch's event calendar before we book up."

My tension, which had slowly ebbed away during our uneventful evening, crept back up. I couldn't tell Andie the truth. I liked her, would even say we'd become good friends since the three of us had started a book club together last fall, but this secret had to remain just that, at least until Beckett got the chief's job.

Dad looked up as the three of us entered the kitchen. "Fallon! Good to see you!"

He got up to hug her, and Fallon squeezed him back. "How's the hand?"

"Better than my brain. It's all whacked up these days," Dad said with a self-deprecating laugh.

"We're interrupting a game," Andie's voice held an apology. "What were you playing?"

"King's Corners," Dad responded. "You play?"

"I'm a bit addicted to cards, but I haven't played that game before."

Andie sat down across from him, and while Dad was explaining how to play, Fallon and I moved off to make the margaritas. When the blender was going, she whispered, "Sorry, I didn't know how to get out of it without blowing your cover."

"It's fine. We'll just consider it a girls' night." I shrugged.

"She's already got plans forming and several dates in mind," Fallon told me with a little grimace.

"As long as she doesn't spend any money or ask me to hand over a deposit, she can do whatever she wants."

When we got back to the table, Dad had set up a new game for the four of us.

Only Andie and I had tequila in our margaritas—Dad was still recovering, and Fallon claimed she needed to drive—but by the time we'd been at the game for a few hours, it was clear that, even tipsy, Andie was a ruthless player. Dad was tickled, acting like a proud teacher every time she went out with a bang.

When his laughter filled the kitchen, the tension and heartache of the last few days eased away once again, and I was suddenly very grateful my friends had shown up.

After Andie trounced us several more times, Dad called it quits.

"That's it for me. I've created a monster." He winked at Andie. "I need some rest, and the three of you have girl things to discuss."

He kissed me on the cheek, hugged Fallon, and patted Andie on the shoulder before heading down the hall.

When Andie shuffled the deck one-handed and started to deal another round, Fallon groaned. "No more! I had no clue you were such a card shark."

The humor on Andie's face faded, and a faraway look came over her. "I haven't played in a really long time." She purposefully changed the subject. "So, what time of year were you thinking of for the wedding?"

I swallowed the rest of my margarita. I'd need more alcohol

to get through this discussion. When I went to retrieve the pitcher, the room spun a bit, and a warning screamed through me. I was dangerously close to drunk, meaning I was too far away from the clear head I needed while staying with Beckett, but I ignored caution and poured myself another glass.

After all, I'd earned this drunk with the week I'd had.

"I'm not ready to set a date, Andie. This"—I waved my hand around the house—"is already more than I can handle at the moment."

Andie straightened her perfect bun. She looked like she was ready to walk into a business meeting with her silk tank and pressed slacks. Even her shoes were business-worthy little peep-toed heels. I wasn't sure I'd ever seen Andie in jeans and a T-shirt.

"I want to make sure your wedding is perfect. Everything you dreamed," she insisted. "And next year, our weekends are nearly full, and the year after that is booking up fast."

I took another sip of the margarita, disregarding the way my heart panged at the idea of having a dream wedding with Beckett. "We don't need a big venue. It's not like either Beckett or I have a huge family that'll show up. We could hold the wedding here in the backyard if we needed to." Beckett just had him and his dad. No grandparents, aunts, uncles, or cousins had ever come around. And my parents had both been only children. My grandparents on both sides had all passed when I was little, well before my mom had died.

"You do have family," Andie insisted, startling me. "Just think about the crew at the fire station and the hospital staff. You add in their plus-ones and Fallon's family, and you're going to need a bigger space than the backyard."

It hit me hard how right she was. Beckett and I had made families for ourselves. I wasn't sure the hospital staff were people I could count on, but Fallon and her family absolutely were.

But thinking about putting together a big wedding, even just to keep up the pretense, made my head hurt. Maybe the way Fallon and Parker had done it, eloping in Vegas and then throwing a celebration months later, was the better way to go.

Way less pressure.

"Just put me down for whatever date is available and let me know." Andie's mouth dropped open, and I asked, "What?"

"I was sure you were going to keep putting me off. I was sure you weren't really engaged."

"What? Why?"

"Most of the town is talking about it. While everyone knew you two were friends—good friends, maybe even friends-with-benefits kind of friends—you've never been openly affectionate. No one's caught you kissing. And now, with the mumblings about the chief retiring and the city council wanting a married man in the position, everyone has been wondering if that's why you two decided to get hitched." As if realizing what she'd just spilled out, Andie blushed. "I'm sorry." She looked down at the empty margarita glass. "I shouldn't have drunk so much. It makes me say things I'd normally filter."

My cheeks flushed at the idea of people talking about Beckett and me being friends with benefits and nothing more. I was pretty sure Delilah was the source of the gossip, but if Andie had heard the rumor, it meant the entire town had heard the same thing. It meant Beckett and I would have to do a lot more to convince Nattingly and the city council that our relationship was real.

The entire idea of it made the alcohol I'd drunk churn uncomfortably.

"That's just Delilah being nasty," I said. "Just like the notes she's been leaving us."

That caught Fallon's attention. "What notes?"

I pressed my hand to my stomach, realizing my slip. I didn't really want to tell my friends about the notes, but at least it would switch the subject from weddings and love, so I caught them up on what had happened.

"This is serious, Maise," Fallon said. "What did Delilah have to say for herself when Josh talked to her?"

I frowned. "I don't know. We haven't heard from him today."

Fallon's brows raised, and she smirked. "How upset was

Josh when he found out you're getting married to Beckett?"

"What do you mean?" I asked, and my friend rolled her eyes.

"You know he's had a crush on you for most of our lives. Since you moved back to Rivers, he's been pining away, hoping you'd finally say yes to a date."

I waved a dismissive hand at her. "I mean, sure, in high school, Josh asked me out, but that was just because we were friends. It wouldn't have been a date-date. Truth is, it would have been smarter for me to go to homecoming with him rather than Carter 'The Jerkwad' Smythe. But that was years ago. Josh doesn't like me that way. I've been home for three years, and he hasn't asked me out."

But an inkling of doubt winged in. Had I been so busy avoiding whatever this was with Beckett that I hadn't even noticed Josh was interested in more than friendship? If I continued down this pretend path with Beckett, if we convinced the town we were actually engaged, and then we ended the fake relationship, would that somehow make me a pariah in the Swift Rivers dating world? Would I lose not only Beckett but also any chance of a happily ever after?

"It would have been hard for him to ask you out with Beckett always hovering around you," Andie said.

Surprise shifted through me. "What do you mean?"

"I mean, look at Sweeney. That guy has made no bones about being attracted to you, and Beckett shuts it down every single time."

"Sweeney?" I squeaked.

"I told you," Fallon said, exchanging a look with Andie. "Maisey is completely in the dark when it comes to guys liking her. She has no clue how beautiful she is. How beautiful she's *always* been, regardless of the issues she had with her jaw."

A flush crept over me again. I needed to change the subject again—fast.

As if he'd heard my silent call for help, the front door opened, and Beckett strode in, halting the conversation and causing my heart to leap at the sight of him.

Maybe it was the alcohol, or maybe it was Andie's words about the town doubting our relationship, but I found myself rushing over to him on unsteady feet. Before I'd really thought it through, I'd looped my arms behind his neck and pressed my lips to his.

For two seconds, I felt his hesitation before his arms surrounded me, one hand settling on my lower back and pushing me into him so we were perfectly aligned. My lips tingled, my body flamed, and I knew I'd made a mistake, but I didn't care.

For two seconds, he was mine, and I was his, and the entire town of Swift Rivers was wrong. When we were tucked together like this, we were far more than friends. We were one heart, one soul, rejoining after being separated for far too long.

We were the forever after I'd always wanted us to be.

Chapter Nineteen
Beckett

I WANT TO BE THE ONE
Performed by Lonestar

SIX YEARS AGO

HIM: Tell me why someone saying, "I'm not looking for anything serious," seems like a challenge.

> *HER: Tell me why people say, "I really like you," when they really mean, "I want to fuck your brains out and then slink away before the sun rises."*

HIM: Any guy who walks away from you is an idiot.

> *HER: And those words are what give the ladies hope you'll actually come around to wanting something more.*

HIM: But not you?

> *HER: Nope. I've known that dead muscle in your chest for far too long.*

HIM: Ouch.

> *HER: Please. Dead muscles can't be offended.*

PRESENT DAY

The entire walk home from the bar, I'd had three competing thoughts circling in my mind on vicious repeat. First was Tejas's warning about how the town was taking bets that Maisey and I weren't really a couple. Second was how to keep my hands off her while she was in my house, tempting me every second of every day. But the third was the most destructive thought of them all.

That one had been in my head since seeing the towel drop in her room, since seeing rosy tips and small, firm breasts. That thought had me wondering why we couldn't do the entire friends-with-benefits thing. Why couldn't we assuage this scorching need and still remain friends?

For all we knew, giving in might be exactly what we both needed. Maybe it would kick the desire in the ass so we could concentrate once again on being just friends.

Doubts whispered in behind it, because what if touching Maisey only made me hunger for more? What if having her made it even more impossible to see other men looking at her? What if our hearts and souls decided they needed forever? Worse, what if hers did and mine didn't?

That was usually when my lungs seized. That was usually when the ash of my past stole my breath. But tonight, the grip didn't seem quite so vicious. I was still able to inhale the cool, pine-scented air.

So, what did it mean?

Every single thought went sailing the moment I walked in the door, and Maisey ran into my arms and kissed me. Was still kissing me. And not a simple peck. The kiss she gave was fierce and claiming. The kind of kiss that said we were truly a couple who'd missed each other in the few hours we'd been apart.

And the truth was, I had missed her. The entire time I'd sat listening to Tejas bemoaning the Swift Rivers's dating pool, my mind had been on her. On what she was wearing, and what she was doing, and if she was reading a book that would have her aching with need that I could easily offer to sate.

I'd wanted to be home, kissing her just like this, drowning myself in her sweetness, getting lost in the heat that had burst into existence between us. I wanted to let the inferno loose until it consumed us, consequences be damned.

So I was ecstatic she'd taken the first step.

Until a laugh from the kitchen drew us apart.

Our gazes remained locked as Vader leaped and danced around us in a circle. I never took my eyes from Maisey as I reached down to pet the top of my dog's head, trying to calm him. My attempt was as ineffective on him as my conscience was at calming the hunger crawling through me.

Until Fallon taunted, "I guess that ought to put an end to any doubts you had, Andie," and Maisey blushed.

Then it wasn't calm but disappointment that took over as realization hit. She'd kissed me to prove to others that we were real. That we weren't just an agreement put together to satisfy the city officials.

It was the same problem I'd been grappling with on the way home. But maybe the actual problem was in not making this real—or real enough.

We could twine our bodies and our lives a bit more, couldn't we? I was still breathing clear air tonight. That had to mean something, didn't it?

I took a deep breath, as if to prove I could, and then wove my fingers with hers. Maisey stiffened ever so slightly before she gripped me back, and we made our way into the kitchen.

"I just spent three hours telling Tejas the same thing I'll tell both of you." I took turns fixing her friends with solemn looks. "Maisey and I are real. Get used to it because this isn't a flight of fancy or some ridiculous romance book with a fake-engagement plot."

Maisey made a weird noise I ignored. Instead, I tugged her into my side, kissed the top of her head, and then stared down her friends once more. "Any more questions?"

Andie laughed. "No. I think that pretty much takes care of it."

She got up, steadied herself on the table, and it was then I noticed the margarita glasses and the ingredients spread out along the counter next to the blender. They'd been drinking.

Maybe Maisey's rush of affection at the door was as much alcohol-induced as it was to ward off the doubters.

That hint of disappointment I'd felt grew larger. I'd wanted the way Maisey had greeted me with a kiss to be real. I'd wanted her enthusiasm and her embrace and her devotion to be mine.

But could I give her enough in return to satisfy her? To keep her heart whole? To ensure she didn't end up lying in a pool of blood?

"And, with that, I think it's time for us to head home," Fallon said.

"You been drinking too?" I asked, and she shook her head. She seemed sober enough to me, but her lips were quirked upward, as if she was trying not to laugh.

She and Andie gathered their phones and bags and headed for the door. Maisey dragged herself away from me to follow them. They all hugged goodbye, and Andie said, "I'll send you the dates we have available first thing in the morning, and you can pick the one you like best."

Then, they disappeared down the porch steps and into the night. Maisey shut the door, locked it, and turned to lean up against it while looking at me across the expanse of the great room.

"Sorry," she breathed out.

Damn, did she look delightful. She was in nothing more than yoga pants and a tank that clung to the delightful curves I'd gotten a full view of earlier.

Before I could really think it through, I was crooking a finger and saying, "You'll have to come closer for me to hear you, darlin'."

The thready beat of my heart echoed through other parts of me, overpowering any other thoughts but the one that whispered I should finally relieve my desperate need for her.

Maisey wobbled as she slowly tottered her way across the room to me. When she got close enough, she made a detour, rounding the table to start picking up glasses and plates.

"Sorry," she repeated. "I didn't know they were coming. And Andie was insistent on talking about the wedding, and then she said everyone was talking about how we weren't really—"

I stopped her rambling by stepping into her path and pressing a finger to her lips. The contact sparked like it had earlier, heat licking up my arm. With that soft mouth against my skin, I felt seared and yet somehow more alive than I'd ever felt before.

"You don't have to apologize to me, Maise. Not for having your friends here or greeting me at the door with a kiss." My pulse raced. "Truth is, coming home to you that way… I liked it. I wanted it. I wanted more."

I trailed off, unable to finish as my breath disappeared as usual, but I was amazed when, after a few seconds, the tension in my lungs eased, and the air cleared.

"I think we should reconsider our position," I told her.

"Are you drunk?" she asked, sweet lips moving against my fingertip.

I wanted to laugh as she'd expected, wanted to shift back to the taunts we were so accustomed to handing each other. But I couldn't. Not when the longing I had for her, the absolute necessity to taste her before I lost the chance for good, was this large. It was too big to be denied any longer.

I withdrew my hand from her lips, and I wanted to believe it was disappointment that crossed her face. Instead of backing off, I grasped a single, silky strand of her hair that had escaped her ponytail and wrapped it slowly around my finger.

"I had one beer at Frank's, so no, I'm not drunk. Are you?"

"Drunk is a really strong word. I would say, I have a good buzz going."

My entire body yearned to give her a different kind of high. One that had her panting and chanting and calling my name.

Her stare bored into mine. "It would be a shame to waste this kind of buzz, don't you think?"

The electricity notched up between us, zipping and zapping, scouring my soul.

When I didn't respond, when I couldn't because I was fighting with everything I had to hold back and not sweep her into my arms, stalk with her to my room, and toss her on the bed, she closed down.

"Or maybe I *am* really drunk. Just ignore me."

She started to move away, and I couldn't let her do that. Couldn't let her feel like I was rejecting her. Couldn't let her think she wasn't enough when she was so much more than that. So, I caught her around the waist and hauled her to me. She let out a quiet shriek I ignored, turning to set her on the island before stepping between her legs so she couldn't escape.

My entire body went hard at the position and the accompanying flare of desire in her eyes. When she licked her lips in nervous anticipation, a rumble escaped my chest.

"You want a real buzz, my Maisey-girl?" I asked.

Her eyes widened, but she didn't respond.

"I can give you the best buzz of your life. Right here, right now."

She gulped, darting a look down the hall to where her father was tucked away in my guest room. And I proved once again I was a bastard, because it didn't matter to me that he was there. All I could think about was putting my hands on Maisey and seeing her flush at my touch. I wanted her soft and trembling, undone by my fingers, my mouth—by me.

I wanted to lose myself in her, even knowing that doing so was fraught with pitfalls I'd carefully avoided since I was a teenager.

Her eyes closed as I trailed my finger over her cheek, down her throat, and along the swell of a breast peeking out of the tank. Goosebumps broke out over her skin, and her nipples pebbled just as they had earlier in her room. It had taken all my strength to walk away from her then. I simply let myself revel in it now, indulging myself by brushing a hand over a hard little tip. She gasped, hands going to my wrists as if to push me away, but she didn't.

"Look at me, Maisey," I demanded.

Her lids popped open. The soft sage of her eyes had turned to deep forest green.

"Tell me you want more. Let me touch you," I demanded. I searched her face for an answer as she searched mine in return.

She didn't move away, but she didn't respond either. "Do you want what I can give you tonight?"

She gave me a nod. A hardly perceptible move.

"Say it."

"I want you to touch me." Her voice was unsteady. Breathy. Delightful.

I didn't have to be told twice. I slid my hands under the hem of her tank, coasting slowly over her warm stomach and upward until I was brushing those beautifully hard pebbles. My chest tightened. My own anticipation grew, but I couldn't and wouldn't take her fully the way I really wanted to tonight. Not after she'd been drinking. If and when we went all the way down this path, she'd be completely sober. Drunk only on me.

I stroked and twisted and flicked, and her lids slammed shut again.

"Nuh-uh," I said. "You want this. You watch."

She dragged her eyes back open.

I skimmed my palms downward, coasting under the waistband of her yoga pants, exploring the sexy curve at her belly button and the wide breadth of her hip bones. She shivered again, lids fluttering shut and then back open. I dragged her forward until her butt hit the edge of the counter, and the position forced her to lock her legs around my waist.

My breath caught. And I had to take a second to steady myself, to gather the wisps of control that remained. I hungered for her mouth. I wanted my tongue thrusting inside her at the same tempo as my fingers, but I wasn't sure I trusted myself to stop if I lost myself in her completely.

If she were sober, it would have been different. But until she was, until we'd already put new ground rules in place about this new game we were playing at, this would have to do.

So, I satisfied myself by doing what I'd fantasized about all week. I curled my hand farther into her yoga pants, past the tiny excuse for underwear she wore, and gently stroked the warmth at her core.

I was rewarded with the absolute wrong emotion crossing her face.

Not lust. Not desire.

Panic. Pure panic.

She put both hands on my chest and pushed as hard as she could.

I took three steps back, tucked my hands into my pockets, and waited while confusion and disappointment swept through me in equal measures. And below it all was a stab of pain. A stab of rejection. A stab of fear that I'd already destroyed something beautiful.

"I. No. We can't." She shook her head.

"Why not?"

She jumped off the counter and moved farther away. "Friends. We're friends. We can't complicate things that way. Friends are friends. Lovers are lovers. *You* were the one to tell me that. And you were right. We can't be both."

I hated I'd told her that. Hated more that I'd thought it was the truth at the time.

I hadn't been ready for more with her then. I wasn't sure I was ready for it now either, but I wanted her. I wanted her in my house, greeting me with a kiss when I walked in from the station. I wanted her in my bed, telling me about her day. I wanted her spread across my sheets with me feasting on her.

But just because I'd taken that leap in my head to something more than what we'd been before, didn't mean she had. With nothing better to say, I told her the only truth I could. "I was wrong."

Shock flitted over her face, and she rubbed her forehead.

"I can't…" She shook her head again. "I can't do this with you, Beckett. I need you in my life too much to risk losing our friendship by doing something stupid like mixing it with sex."

"Believe me, there'd be nothing stupid about what we'd do. But tell me why it would risk me being in your life if we did?"

"You know why!"

"No, I really don't."

"Because friends and sex never end well! Do you think I could have you…have you like that and then watch while you flirted with another woman? While you left Frank's with someone else at your side? It would destroy me.”

“And you’re assuming that’s what would happen. That I could have you, taste you, claim you as mine, and then be able to move on to some other woman?”

The truth of my words astonished her as much as me. What was I expecting? Asking? What did I really want? Whispers of dark fumes swirled through me, trying to fill my lungs, trying to hold me in their grip a bit longer. But I fucking wanted out. I wanted out of the bedroom I’d been trapped in for twenty years. I wanted to forget bloody wrists. I wanted to escape it all and lose myself in her sweetness, in the utter goodness that was Maisey.

It hit me that this wasn’t really a new desire. It wasn’t a new wish. I’d just buried it. I’d denied it for too long simply because I believed I was broken. Because I believed the abandonment of my youth had left me brittle and hard so all I would ever be able to do was slice people open. But I was more than my past. More than my wounds. Just like Maisey was more than the scars her childhood had left on her.

I wanted to tell her every single screwed-up thought in my head about us and all the possibilities I suddenly saw before me. I wanted to offer her my dead heart and see if she could bring it to life and keep it that way, simply by remaining at my side.

She grabbed her ponytail and tugged and then finally let out a shaky breath she’d been holding. “I’m so confused right now, Beckett, and I don’t think it has anything to do with the tequila I drank.”

She was right. I was bungling everything because I was confused too.

I didn’t know how to make a relationship work, not a friends-with-benefits arrangement, or the more complicated scenario that was jogging around in my brain. What I did know was I needed to sort through my baggage if we were going to have a chance at something else. It wasn’t fair to ask Maisey to bring my heart back to life. I had to do it on my own first. I had to figure out how to break free so I could hand her a healthy, pink heart that could beat with love rather than cold wood destined to ruin everything.

Those thoughts had me stepping away from Maisey, even though I really wanted to wrap her in my arms and soothe us both. Instead of folding her in an embrace, I tried to reassure her with the simple truth.

"I'm confused too, Maise. I suddenly want things I've never wanted before. So maybe you were right to stop us from going further tonight. But I don't want to close the door on the possibility of something else."

She rubbed her hands over her eyes, smudging the makeup ever so slightly. I loved her this way. Not perfect. Not carefully made up. I relished knowing I was one of very few people she allowed to see her like this.

"I don't know if I'm drunk and dreaming or if you've left and walked back in the door as some other version of Beckett. You want time and space? Fine, take it. I need some too."

"Fair enough."

She turned and started down the hall.

And I let her go. I didn't push because I was struggling with the enormity of my thoughts and emotions, trying to make sense of how my world had flipped in minutes, hours, days.

As Maisey disappeared into her room, Vader's nails scrabbled on the wood in his attempt to follow her.

"Where do you think you're going?" He looked back at me, gave me that curled-lip look that always seemed like a grin, and then continued trotting after my girl. "Traitor. Traitor Vader is your new name," I called after him.

But he didn't come back, because he wasn't stupid. He knew lying next to Maisey, sharing her bed, and waking up at her side would be a little piece of heaven. A heaven I'd denied myself for far too long.

I scrubbed my hand down my face. What had happened to me? I'd gotten fake-engaged and moved her into my home, and the proximity had done me in. I chuckled to myself. I was a goddamn romance novel.

When I dragged my hands away, the mess in the kitchen came into focus. Served me right to be stuck cleaning it after scaring her away. After causing her to duck and run with a simple touch.

But the truth was, it hadn't been my touch that had sent her scurrying away. It was the way I'd reversed course on her after twenty years of telling her I'd never want anything more than sex.

The entire time I cleaned up, my brain whirled with new possibilities, and my heart continued to crack through the shell I'd placed around it.

The fire was out. I'd left it smoldering for far too long. But the haze was finally clearing, letting fresh new air into my lungs. I was amazed the wreckage left behind wasn't as bad as it could have been. That there was still soft, tender skin left.

But could that freshly exposed heart give me an entirely new outlook on life? On relationships?

Could I start something with Maisey that wouldn't end with her or me slashed to pieces?

For the first time in my life, I was desperate to find out.

Chapter Twenty

Maisey

FAVORITE KIND OF HIGH
Performed by Kelly Clarkson

TWO YEARS AGO

HIM: Fallon had the baby?

> *HER: Yes! Lila is perfect. I know people say babies are just little blobs who don't look like anyone, but I swear she's all Fallon.*

HIM: I don't envy Parker raising another Fallon.

> *HER: He's already wrapped around Lila's pinky, just like he's wrapped around Fallon's.*

HIM: I wish them luck.

> *HER: I can hear the sarcasm in those words from miles away.*

HIM: Name one relationship, one you know personally, that's survived this world unscathed?

> *HER: Rafe and Sadie.*

HIM: They've barely been together.

> *HER: Ten years.*

HIM: Well, it's about time for the fireworks, then.

> *HER: True love exists, Fireball.*

HIM: If it exists, you deserve to find it, darlin'. Just make sure it stays the hell away from me.

PRESENT DAY

By the time I finally dragged myself out of bed to get ready for work the next day and made it into the kitchen, I found Beckett making an omelet.

My head was pounding, an incessant throb that pulsed behind my eyes, and it wasn't just because I was slightly hungover. It was because of what I'd done last night—what we'd almost done last night—and because of the hint of a promise Beckett had laid down.

I'd always thought Hope was a deadly bitch. She could send you soaring, hinting at unparalleled joy, only to flip the switch and taunt you with the agony of defeat.

I wasn't sure I'd survive the hope of having Beckett and then having it torn away. I wasn't sure what would be left of me if we slipped into something more but never quite reached the happily ever after I truly craved.

But then again, maybe I'd made the entire encounter up in my tequila-filled brain.

As if to contradict my unspoken thoughts, Beckett intercepted me on my way to the refrigerator for my lunch bag. Knife in one hand, a dripping tomato in the other, he still managed to lean in and press a kiss to the top of my head.

"Morning, my Maisey-girl."

And the nickname he'd always called me took on an entirely new meaning this morning, as if he actually believed the "my" as much as I did.

My breath evaporated, and I forced myself to step away from him before I made matters worse by doing something stupid.

"You're dripping."

He glanced down at the tomato and walked it back to the island. He set it down, wiped his hands, and then met me near the back door, where I was assembling all the items I needed for work. He took my bag from my hand, grabbed my elbows, and tugged me to him.

My heart skipped a beat or two too many, leaving me a bit breathless.

"Just so we're clear," he said, "last night wasn't a drunken hallucination or an alien taking over my body. I meant everything I said."

"I'm not sure I understood what you said."

Amusement twinkled in his eyes. "I know. I was surprisingly unclear for me. I want us to be more than friends, Maisey. I don't know what that means fully. I just know I like it when I come home and you kiss me."

He leaned in and kissed my forehead. The sweetness of it didn't make it any less sexy. My body flamed at the touch, and maybe knowing there was a possibility of us taking it further, of finally giving in to the chemistry flaring between us, was what made it burn hotter than ever before.

"We both know, after living together for just a couple of days, that it's going to be impossible to keep our hands off each other. So how about we stop pretending we don't want each other and just let things happen," he suggested.

I scoffed. "You're the one who bet you could keep your hands to yourself and have repeatedly lost."

He smirked. "Thought it wasn't a bet. Thought you didn't bet." My emotions bounced around. Hope. Terror. Lust. "Are you afraid, my Maisey-girl? Afraid to take what you want—"

I fisted his T-shirt, rose on my toes, and placed my lips on his, reveling in the fact I could do so. Reveling in the knowledge that he actually wanted this as much as I did. While it was a closed-mouth kiss, not intended to kindle desire, it was firm and fierce. I let all my hopes and fears linger there for a few seconds before letting him go.

If this ended badly, I'd deal with it then. I'd survived worse and made myself whole again.

The simple truth was I wanted this more than I wanted to be whole. What I'd said yesterday to him in my dad's yard was true. I'd give anything for a night full of passion and sin, so now I'd back those words up with action. I'd risk the damage to my heart and soul if it meant enjoying every last moment we made together.

His eyes were locked on my mouth as I lowered to my heels.

"You've always been a helluva kisser." His voice was gruff and a little shaky. Pleasure coasted through me as I realized I'd done that to him. I'd made him as unsteady as I was. But then the joy disappeared when he said, "Not once, since our very first kiss, have I ever found someone who could light me up the way you do."

"You mean the kiss where my braces made you bleed? Getting a mouthful of metal was hardly sexy," I said scornfully.

Anger filled his expression, taking me by surprise. "Don't do that. Don't you dare *ever* lessen what we've experienced together with stupid words other losers tossed at you. Assholes who didn't know what they had when they had the privilege of touching you."

It was hurt as much as irritation that had me snapping back, "So, you didn't tell Chelsea no one would want to kiss a mouth tasting like metal?"

"Fuck no!" His eyes flared. "Is that what she told you? Is that what you've thought all these years? That I was no better than Carter fucking Smythe? Or that asshole frat boy you gave your virginity to?"

My heart slammed hard against my rib cage, looking down and away from the fury on his face. His hand landed on my chin, forcing my head up and fixing me with a fierce stare.

"Your sister was pissed I'd kissed you when I'd turned her down repeatedly after Delilah and I broke up. That day, she threatened to tell your parents I was doing a lot more than kissing you, so I kept my hands to myself afterward."

He took a huge breath and then kept going. "But it's also true that what I felt at fourteen, kissing you... I didn't know what to do with the enormity of it. Liza had barely left my dad, and I was terrified I'd end up like him. I told myself, and you, we were just friends because I let fear solidify my heart.

"I'm sorry. I'm sorry Chelsea hurt you with her words, and I hurt you with my actions—or lack of them. I'm not that kid anymore, Maisey. While I can't promise I won't hurt you ever again, can't promise I won't let you down, I can promise I'll do everything in my power not to."

I didn't know how to reply. I didn't know if I could. So, instead, I slid my arms around his waist, pressed my face to his chest, and just held on while the bitch Hope taunted me to try to heal the childhood wounds that had locked us both in the past, enough to try to keep him.

♫ ♫ ♫

I'd worked my regular shift plus two hours of overtime for Meredith by the time I walked in the door at nine o'clock. Dad was nowhere to be seen, but Beckett was watching television in the living room. He was in workout shorts and a T-shirt, lounging on the couch, with Vader at his feet and Dorothy on his chest. He smiled as I walked in. A lazy grin full of temptation that had my body igniting.

He muted the TV and asked, "How was work?"

"We're still short-staffed, and that summer cold has taken out more of us, so everyone is working extra hours to cover the gaps, but at least it was fairly quiet." His eyebrows went up, and I laughed. "Don't worry, I didn't jinx us to chaos by saying it while on duty."

He chuckled and patted the spot on the couch next to him.

I dropped my bag on the armchair and joined him. I petted Vader before running my fingers over Dorothy, all without touching Beckett. For the first time in a long time, I felt awkward next to him, as if I didn't know what to do with my limbs.

Sensing it, Beckett picked up the cat, set her on his opposite side, and then hooked me around the waist, tugged me close, and kissed me. Not the sweet kiss on my forehead from this morning or even the fierce, closed-lipped one I'd given him in return. This was a knock-down, drag-out, life-altering one. He licked the seam of my mouth, and I opened for him, my tongue gliding against his, the velvety touch sparking the desire that always simmered beneath the surface when he was near.

Fisting my hair, he dragged my head back, caressing my

jaw and neck with determined lips. His teeth slid along my earlobe before sucking it into his mouth, and heat pooled low in my belly, an almost violent need demanding to be sated. It was a bit of heaven being in his arms. Being kissed by him. Touched. Wanted.

My hands slid under his T-shirt, sliding over the tantalizing ridges of his eight-pack, but he caught my wrists, drawing them away. My brows rose in confusion. Had he changed his mind? Then, why had he kissed me?

"Last night in the kitchen was a mistake," he said.

Damn that bitch Hope. My heart fell to my chest. As if sensing my thoughts, he grabbed my chin and placed another heated kiss on my lips.

"I haven't changed my mind. I want you, Maisey. More than I want air to breathe, but it was also good that you stopped us last night. It wasn't right to take you there in the kitchen where your dad could have walked in. That wasn't respectful to you or him. So I won't do what I want right now either, while we're in the middle of the living room. Believe me, I'd love nothing more than to tear those butterfly scrubs off and scramble your brain until the only word that escapes those perfect lips is my name. Until we can do that, until we have a room and a night to ourselves, we'll have to keep it PG-rated."

My heart thudded. He was right. I would have been embarrassed if my dad had walked in on us last night or today. It was also sweet and charming that he'd even considered it.

Instead of responding, I just curled into him and turned to watch the muted television.

"Maise?"

My pulse leaped at the rawness of his tone, and I looked up at him, chin resting on his chest. "Yeah?"

"I really fucking like you coming home to me."

My heart squeezed, and my eyes watered.

We sat there for a few more minutes, with our limbs twined, hearts beating almost to the same rhythm, and wants and worries filling the silence. But for the first time in longer than I could remember, I felt like I'd truly come home. I felt safe and wanted. Like I might just be enough for this one person.

Then, I stopped my thoughts before they got too carried away.

Being on shift today had allowed me the time and space away from him that I'd needed. I reminded myself that what was happening with Beckett wasn't him saying he was in love with me. He'd simply said he wanted more, which meant sex. He wanted to turn our friendship into not necessarily a friends-with-benefits arrangement, but something a bit more than friendship and a bit less than love and marriage. And he'd promised to try not to hurt me. It was up to me to guard my heart.

I had to remember his limitations. Just wanting some sort of relationship, wanting something more was a massive leap for Beckett. And I'd signed up for whatever he could offer this morning when I'd shut him up with a kiss.

I'd chosen passion and sin over love and forever after.

So instead of fretting and worrying and trying to change what I'd agreed to, I let myself enjoy the feelings of home and connection that being locked in his arms brought me. My eyes drifted closed as peace filled me. Days of very little sleep and high stress were all catching up with me. I felt my body loosen, dreams tugging at me, only to be pulled back to the surface by Beckett's soft tone.

"Before you conk out completely," Beckett murmured, tucking a lock of hair behind my ear. "I wanted to tell you Cleaver called today."

That pulled me completely out of the hazy warmth of sleep. "Yeah? What did he say?"

"He talked to Delilah." His voice held that clipped edge he only used when something was off. "She was pissed—like ready-to-burn-the-station-down pissed—that we tried to pin this on her." His arm around my waist tightened. "She told Cleaver she wasn't even in town Friday. Said she took the day off and went with Carter to Visalia. And when Cleaver asked Carter, he backed her story."

I frowned. "But...?"

"But she refused to give him any receipts from the trip, and

Cleaver doesn't have enough to get a warrant or a court order to force it." He exhaled sharply, frustration vibrating through the room. "Sandy didn't find any unexpected fingerprints on the door or anywhere else on the house. No one on the block saw anything. And whoever is renting the Helmers' place never answered the door."

He raked his free hand through his hair. "Which means we're right back where we started."

A new and familiar weight of dread settled on my chest. "Did you give any more thought to the list he wanted us to make?" I asked quietly. "About any decisions we've made lately that could've pissed someone off?"

"I can't think of anything I've done that would cause this." Then he paused. "What about you?"

I hesitated then said, "I told Meredith I wanted to be permanently assigned to Labor and Delivery with Lisa leaving and if she didn't put me up for it, I'd have to consider moving to a different hospital. She told me today, once she hires someone for the floater pool, they'll transfer me."

Beckett shifted, eyes widening. "You did? I'm so damn proud of you, Maise."

I flushed at his compliment and then arched a brow at him. "What's on your list?"

"Stoney is obviously not thrilled about what's going on with the chief's position. And I told Carter to fuck off when he made me an offer for the house."

I blinked. "So Carter actually made you an offer too?"

His brows lifted. "Too?"

"Before the fire, he told my dad he'd give him top dollar, even though the house is a mess."

"What did your dad say? Is he considering it?"

"He's thinking about selling, but not to Carter." I shook my head. "He doesn't want anyone tearing down the house for some stupid development."

A silence settled between us, filled with opposing emotions. There was comfort in lying together, holding each other, with possibilities thrumming through us, but also the impotent frustration at our inability to figure out who was threatening us…me.

"We both agreed the notes aren't from Stoney," I said. "He'd just come at you straight. And I can't imagine Carter thinking past his next high long enough to write a note, especially not in orange poster paint."

"He's using?" Beckett's brows pulled tight.

"He had every sign of it when I saw him at Jack's."

"I'll pass that knowledge on to Cleaver," Beckett said. "But yeah, I agree about Stoney." He shifted again, his voice gentling. "Speaking of, I talked to him about having Mikey help us out with your dad."

My chest tightened, gratitude and guilt twisting together. Not just because I couldn't afford to hire anyone, but because I didn't know how to tell my father we were having someone watch him without crushing what pride he still had.

Reading me as he always did, Beckett offered a solution without me saying a word. "Mikey wants to get his EMT certificate and a Fire Science degree after he graduates next year. We'll tell your dad I traded access to my textbooks and notes for him watching the kitten."

"Thank you," I whispered.

"It's not perfect. Mikey has got his swim schedule. But between the three of us, we can make sure your dad is only alone for a couple of hours at a time."

"If I know your schedules, I can see what I can do at the hospital to switch things around," I said.

I needed to go to bed if I wanted any chance of surviving another long day in the ER. But leaving this sweet moment, this shared warmth and companionship, felt impossible. Beckett had said he liked me coming home to him, and the simple truth was, I liked it too.

Seeing him curled up with Vader and Dorothy, waiting for me, had hit me square in the chest.

I was just deciding how to pull myself away from his intoxicating embrace in order to head to bed when a piercing crack split the night. I jerked away from Beckett, and Vader shot to his feet with a snarl, charging for the door. A second, equally loud blow reverberated through the night and sent Beckett rushing to the windows.

I was right behind him as he flipped the wooden shutters open. With no streetlights on this end of the cul-de-sac, it was nearly impossible to see anything beyond the reflection of the living room lights.

The sharp, unnatural clang of metal hitting glass rang out a third time, followed by a sickening shattering sound. My stomach rolled, fear pulling every muscle in my body tight.

Beckett slid his feet into a pair of sneakers and yanked open the door, barely catching Vader's collar as the dog growled and attempted to leap out the door.

I reached for Beckett, trying to hold him back. "Beckett! Don't go out there."

He looked down at me, face full of fury. "Stay here. If this is our friend leaving another gift, I'm going to end it right now."

He stepped out on the porch, shutting the door and locking a distraught Vader inside with me. I ran to my bag and dug through it until I found the pen-sized Taser Parker's dad had given me when I'd gone off to college.

With the stun gun in hand, I opened the door to race after Beckett, and Vader slid past me before I could catch him. His bark was fierce as he headed straight for Beckett, who stood on the sidewalk, hands fisted, scanning the street.

When I'd arrived home from my shift, the night had been full of sounds, owls and insects, and the soft rush of the river behind our homes. Now, the dark was nearly silent beyond Vader's warning rumbles. A darkness hung in the air that sent a shiver up my spine.

Beckett caught Vader's collar, and the two of them stormed in the direction of my truck parked in front of Dad's. As I joined them and saw my destroyed windshield, I felt the color bleed from my face. It had taken a lot of fury and muscle to do this much damage.

A porch light went on at the Helmers', and movement in their front yard caught my eye. A figure dressed in dark clothes slinked across the lawn, heading in the direction of Main Street.

Vader howled, breaking away from Beckett and shooting off like a pistol.

Beckett was right behind him.

Alerted to the chase by the bark, the person in the hoodie burst into a full-out sprint.

I did my best to follow them, but my much shorter legs couldn't keep up with Beckett's long ones in a high-speed foot pursuit.

By the time I caught up, Beckett was on Main Street, and I was out of breath. He was standing under a streetlight, once again gripping Vader's collar. Both of their chests were heaving, but it was Beckett's expression, full of anger and remorse, that did me in.

"I lost him," he bit out angrily. "I fucking lost him. One moment he was there, and then, poof, he was gone."

I looked toward the throng of people standing around outside One-Eyed Frank's. It appeared to be a group of tourists, saying goodbye, with some of them already heading toward the parking lot. My eyes caught on a bench near the bar's entrance and a small black mound sitting atop it. I crossed over to it and saw it was a discarded hoodie. Plain. No logo that I could tell, but I wasn't about to touch it.

Beckett and Vader joined me.

"Whoever this was used the crowd as cover," I said, shaking my head in confusion and fear. "This all seems ridiculously dramatic, Beckett. Like we've landed in the middle of some crime show."

He used one arm to pull me to him, placing a soft kiss on my temple. "The person was tall. Not as tall as me, but taller than you. And lean. I never caught a look at their face or hair with that hoodie pulled up and hanging past their ass, but we have more to tell Cleaver than we did before."

I pulled my phone from the pocket of my scrubs and searched for the non-emergency number to the sheriff's office. As I dialed, I asked, "Who could hate me this much?"

A lump formed in my throat. I tried to be a good person. I tried to help people. I filled in as much as I could at the hospital.

I was never cruel if I could help it, not even when Delilah and Chelsea pushed me to my limits.

Unease accompanied another shiver up my spine as I thought of the dark-clad figure who'd smashed my windshield. It hadn't seemed like Delilah, and yet, it could have been her. She was taller than me and shorter than Beckett. But like Beckett had said, it had been hard to distinguish anything about the person in an oversized hoodie.

What I'd told Beckett at the house still rang true. The whole thing felt immature, ridiculously childish. Someone trapped in their teen years…or an actual teenager. And I didn't personally know a single teenager.

But the pattern of escalation made it impossible to ignore. A taped note on a car was nothing compared to a shattered windshield. And the timing—God, the timing—felt deliberate. The closer Beckett and I drifted toward turning our fake engagement into something real, the more unhinged this person's reaction became.

Except, how could they possibly know?

Aside from that one kiss at the firehouse, Beckett and I hadn't really been seen together in public.

My mind flicked to our tangled bodies in the lake, the almost-kiss in Dad's backyard.

I shook my head hard. No one should have seen those. No one could have, unless…

A cold shiver coasted up my spine.

Unless someone had been watching us.

Watching me.

Acid churned through my stomach.

I might be willing to risk my heart for a few stolen, breathtaking moments with Beckett, but would I risk my life?

Beckett's life?

My dad's?

The thought landed like a fist—sudden, brutal, and terrifyingly real.

Chapter Twenty-one
Beckett

CRAZY 'BOUT YOU
Performed by Kelsey Hart

FOUR YEARS AGO

> *HER: Tight dress with no cleavage, or loose and flirty with a deep V?*

HIM: I have all sorts of images in my head now that aren't going to help me with the training I'm doing in fifteen minutes. So thanks for that.

> *HER: *** crying laughing emoji *** Just answer the question.*

HIM: What is this for? And who are you going with?

> *HER: Holiday party at the hospital. And no one.*

HIM: Might I suggest a boxy sweater and baggy pants?

> *HER: Oh, yes. Why didn't I think of that? Maybe because I'd LIKE to end the evening with a date? Or the hope of a date.*

HIM: Bad idea, Maise. If you fall for someone in Bakersfield, you'll never move home to Rivers. Remember your endgame. Wait until you're home to fall in love.

> *HER: Puh-lease. Like there are any single guys in Swift Rivers who are date-worthy.*

HIM: *Ouch. Just ouch.*

> HER: **** rolling eyes emoji *** Have you changed your mind about relationships? Have you suddenly decided you're up for love and forever after?*

HIM: **** person screaming in horror gif *** Believe me, this is not one of your romance novels. I'll be single till the day I die.*

PRESENT DAY

Once Maisey called the dispatcher, I stood guard over the sweatshirt and tried to let the fury rolling through me subside. It was the same rage as I'd experienced with each of the notes but amplified with a horrible sense of foreboding. Whoever this was, they'd escalated each time, and I was terrified the next time someone would be hurt. That it would be Maisey who paid the price…

My heart hammered against my rib cage. I couldn't let Maisey be hurt.

But what could I do to stop it?

As we were waiting for Cleaver to show up, Delilah appeared, coming from the tiny parking area in the back of Frank's. My jaw tightened as I scanned her. It was Sunday, so she wasn't wearing her business uniform, but I was surprised to see she wasn't in a skimpy dress or shorts either. She was wearing black jeans, low-heeled cowboy boots, and a sleeveless blue top that made her eyes pop.

What new version of Delilah was this? What new role was she playing?

When she got close, she started to smile and say hello, but I cut her off with a snarl. "Was this you?"

Her lips tightened as she looked from me to Maisey and back. "This again? What did I supposedly do now?"

I closed the distance between us, towering over her. "Stop with the games, Del. Stop before something bad happens."

Hurt danced across her face. Hurt that usually had me feeling like shit and backing off. "You actually think I'm wasting my time terrorizing poor little Maisey?"

I grunted out a sound of displeasure, and Maisey grabbed my arm, holding me back from doing something stupid, like shaking the truth out of Delilah. The wounded look on Del's face disappeared into a scornful smirk.

"Whatever's going on, I'd say the Campbell girls earned it."

Her careless, hard remark only increased my fury. Maisey had never done one thing to Delilah. She'd been nice to her, had even tried to counter Chelsea's rumors, but Del had never once seen it that way. Guilty by association. I leaned my face toward her, dark with a promise I meant. "I swear, Del, if this is you—"

"You'll what?" she tossed back just as Maisey said, "Beckett, stop."

"Hey, what's going on here?" Carter strolled up in jeans and a lavender button-down shirt with the sleeves rolled to his elbows. His eyes darted between us, and he rubbed his nose with the back of his knuckles. "Do I need to call the sheriff? This looks pretty intense, Romero."

Vader had relaxed enough that I'd let go of his collar, but now he gave a low rumble of warning and stood in front of me, protecting Maisey and me.

"It's against the city ordinances to have your dog down here without a leash," Carter said, looking at my dog and spinning his expensive watch around on his wrist.

Cleaver's sheriff vehicle rolled up to the curb with the lights going but no siren. He hustled out of the driver's seat and over to where we'd gathered in front of the bench.

Carter lifted his chin in greeting. "Perfect timing, Cuz. You need to cite Romero here for his unleashed dog. Maybe intimidation. He was going at Del good before I stopped him."

I scoffed. As if he could stop me from doing anything. Even if he wasn't high on whatever, he'd never be able to prevent me from cleaning the ground with his face.

Cleaver stepped into the middle of us, blocking Vader from Delilah and his cousin and shooting a warning at me. "How about we all calm down."

A deep rumble in Vader's throat had Cleaver frowning at him.

"Put your dog in the back of my rig, Beckett." His voice was calm but deadly serious, and when I didn't budge, he sighed. "Now, or I will have to cite you."

"Beckett," Maisey pleaded.

I reached down and grabbed Vader's collar. My dog wasn't happy about leaving, dragging his feet enough that I had to pick him up, open the back passenger door, and shove him inside. "Stay."

While I was taking care of Vader, I heard Maisey start to explain to Cleaver that we thought the sweatshirt on the bench had been left behind by the person who'd been leaving us notes.

I jogged back, crossed my arms, and looked at Del. "Awfully convenient you showed up a few seconds later."

Her face flushed. "I'm sick of you blaming Maisey's problems on me."

"I'm sick of my fiancée being terrorized," I snapped back. Then, I turned to Carter. "What were you doing here tonight?"

Carter looked over at Cleaver. "Seriously? I don't need to deal with this shithead. If you don't get him out of my face, Cuz, I'm filing a complaint."

"For what?" I bit out. "For demanding to know where you were when Maisey's windshield was smashed all to hell?"

Delilah inhaled sharply, and Carter's brows lifted in surprise. Either they were both better actors than I thought they were, or they hadn't known.

"Romero. If you don't calm down, I'm going to lock you in the back of my vehicle with your dog." Cleaver's tone was a calm attempt to defuse the situation.

Maisey twined her fingers with mine, and that simple, gentle touch brought me back to her. When I looked down, unshed tears glimmered as her eyes darted around at the crowd we'd gathered.

Damn. I'd made a scene, and Maisey hated being the center of attention. The only time she didn't mind was when she was on her horse, bending and twirling as if the two were one.

When I looked back up at Cleaver, his lips were drawn in a straight line, but his voice was still cool and unruffled in a way that made me respect him more than I ever had before. "We can clear some of this up right now, Delilah, if you could just tell us where you were a few minutes ago."

She crossed her arms over her chest. "At home. Getting ready to come down to Frank's for a drink."

"Alone?" Cleaver asked.

"Yes, I was by myself. Mom and Dad were home, and their lights were on when I drove by the main house, but I can't be sure if they saw me pull out of the drive or not."

She didn't really have an alibi if she'd been alone in the pool-house-turned-apartment where she lived behind her parents' house. But unless she'd changed shoes, there was no way the person I'd chased to Main Street had been wearing those fancy-ass cowboy boots. They would have made more noise than the shoes the person in the hoodie had.

I glanced over at Carter's shoes. He was wearing men's dress shoes that I doubted would have been silent either. And what would he get out of smashing Maisey's windshield and leaving threatening notes? The only thing Carter wanted was our land.

"Where were you?" I challenged anyway.

Carter's eyebrow raised, and he dragged his knuckle across his nose again. If he were all doped up, I could certainly see him thinking, stupidly, that attacking Maisey might make her dad and me assume the area was no longer safe, but we'd never sell because of it. And why wouldn't he just come at us instead of her?

"I don't have to tell you shit," Carter said then shot a glare at his cousin. "But I'll tell you anyway so we can *clear this up.* I was at the office, waiting for a client. I'm sure there's footage of me leaving if you feel you need to pull it, Cuz."

"Are we free to go now?" Delilah asked, shifting closer to Carter and slipping her arm through his.

Cleaver nodded, and Delilah shot me and Maisey another dirty look as they headed for Frank's.

As they walked away, I heard Del say quietly to Carter, "Thought you weren't coming." And his equally quiet response, "Client was a no-show."

As they disappeared inside the bar, I tried to recall the crowd that had emerged from Frank's as I'd burst onto Main Street at a full run. Had the person I'd chased joined them as they'd walked out the door? The entire group had moved farther down the street, disappearing around the corner of the building toward the small public parking lot at the back after Maisey had caught up. It was the same direction Delilah had come from.

But she'd seemed legitimately surprised by what had happened to Maisey's truck and hurt we were accusing her. She'd been defensive, as she always was, when it came to the Campbells, and yet she was the only person I knew who would be this unhappy with our engagement.

Nothing made sense. The rage I'd felt at seeing Maisey's windshield shattered had eased some, but in its place, a frustrated impotence grew. My inability to do something about what was happening felt a lot like being stuck in a bedroom with flames outside my door.

I turned to Cleaver. "Speaking of cameras, does Frank's have any outside?"

Cleaver scratched his chin. "I'm not sure, but I'll ask. I know they have cameras inside and out the back door. We've used them before when a fight broke out."

Sandy pulled up and got out of her van, looking like she'd been yanked from bed. Her eyes were puffy, and her salt-and-pepper hair was a mess, but her crime-scene jumper was buttoned to her chin, and she snapped on a pair of gloves as she neared us. Cleaver got her caught up, and she took her kit over to the bench, taking pictures.

"Join me at Beckett's place when you're done here," Cleaver told her, and she just waved a hand in his direction. He turned to Maisey and me. "Get in. I'll take you back."

I opened the front passenger door of the sheriff's rig for Maisey, sliding a hand down her arm in reassurance as she got in. Her hands were shaking as she reached for the seat belt, and that tightened my chest right back up. She was afraid, and I was man enough to admit I was too. But my fear wasn't for me.

I climbed into the back with Vader, feeling like the criminal Cleaver usually placed there. In attempting to get what I wanted, I'd brought danger to Maisey's door.

But if this wasn't Del, I wasn't sure who else to look at next. Carter, possibly.

The list of people who'd want to hurt Maisey was infinitesimally small because she was exactly what Chelsea had always called her—a saint. Or as damn near one as anyone I'd ever met.

But thinking of Chelsea reminded me of her text messages to Maisey the other day. The cold and calculating cruelty that had shaken Maisey. But Chelsea was nowhere near Swift Rivers. And what would she get out of terrorizing her sister, other than the perverse pleasure she'd always gotten? I couldn't see a win for Chelsea out of this. It could only lead to bad press if news got out that an up-and-coming actress was bullying her little sister.

No, we were infuriatingly back to square one.

♫ ♫ ♫

It was after midnight by the time Cleaver and Sandy left, and I was able to lock the door behind them. Maisey stood with her arms wrapped around her waist and that same wide-eyed, haunted look she'd had on the street outside Frank's.

I tugged her to me, and it took a moment, but her shoulders relaxed, and she hugged me back.

"You can drop me off at the station tomorrow morning and take my car to work," I told her.

"I can walk," she said.

"No." It was a fiercely uttered command that had her stiffening. "No way you're walking around on your own right now, especially if you'll be off late. I can use the rig at the station for whatever I need during my shift."

"What if your car gets vandalized too?" she asked, pulling

back to look up at me.

The idea of her being here alone with only Vader and her injured father while someone came at my SUV or the house or her made my stomach roll. Cleaver had promised he and the other deputies would drive by regularly, but that wasn't going to prevent someone from waiting until they'd turned the corner before they struck.

What if whoever this was broke into the house? Vader would go nuts, but what if they injured my dog to get to her? What if it hadn't been her dad who'd spread the Sterno over his kitchen? What if all of this had nothing to do with Maisey and me at all?

"Maisey, do you think this could have something to do with your dad?"

Confusion drew her brows together. "Dad?"

"The fire at the house started before all this. And it's been your car targeted, which might be someone using you to send him a message. Whoever it is would assume you'd tell him about it, and my door was painted after he moved in."

"I can't imagine anyone coming after Dad."

"Maybe someone he interacted with for his job?" I asked. "Did he ever drive for someone shady?"

"You're asking if he was working for criminals? Delivering what? Drugs or guns?" Her eyes turned stormy. "Absolutely not. I mean, the company Dad works—worked—for handled all the actual clients, but if Dad knew they were moving anything illegal, he wouldn't have stayed with them."

She was likely right. I might not have the highest opinion of Lewis after what he'd done to Maisey, but I'd always considered him a straight arrow.

"Besides, we both said this feels immature. I can't imagine drug dealers writing a stupid note or smashing a windshield," Maisey added.

I couldn't disagree. But nothing else really made sense either. Not even landing back with Delilah as the perpetrator. Sure, her personality fluctuated dramatically day to day. You might get work Delilah when she was at the mayor's office, or flirty Delilah at the bar, but the truth was, I still considered her more friend than foe. And when Del was actually pissed at you, she usually came straight at you with a nasty barb and, occasionally, bared claws.

My head hurt from all the possibilities. Possibilities we wouldn't be able to resolve tonight.

We needed a few hours of rest to clear our heads. But I also couldn't stand the thought of Maisey going to the guest room and tossing and turning by herself. So, I pulled her hand into mine and tugged her down the hall—not in the direction of her room, but in the direction of mine.

Her feet slowed, dragging a bit. "What are you doing?"

"I won't get any sleep if you're alone in another room. I'll just lie there, worrying about you."

She huffed. "Starting tomorrow, you're going to be at the firehouse for four days, Beckett."

My chest tightened all over again. "Don't remind me."

When we stepped inside my room, Vader pushed past us to join the cat, who was sleeping in a tight ball on the foot of my bed. He licked the kitten before curling up beside it. His natural prey instincts should have told him to chase the cat, but instead, he was a complete pushover. A goner. It was pretty sappy, but the truth was, I was as much a goner for Maisey as my dog was for a cat.

Those thoughts and the word sappy squeezed my lungs instinctively. An old habit. But I reminded myself it was just a reflex, born of years of allowing my past to rule me.

But if I wanted more with Maisey, I had to retrain my body.

I had to change what I believed about relationships and expose my heart. Take a risk. Because if I didn't, and I continued to pursue whatever this was, I'd only end up hurting both of us.

Maisey dropped my hand and tugged her ponytail. "Look. I don't think this is a good idea."

It probably wasn't. Not when I hadn't figured out how to undo years of bad habits. Not after a night filled with rage and frustration and fear.

"I won't promise to keep my hands to myself." Her mouth popped open at my comment, and it made me smile for the first time since we'd heard the smashing of her windshield. "But I will tell you I have no intention of making love to you tonight. Not with ugly emotions still clinging to us and you dead on your feet after a fourteen-hour shift and a chase down Main Street. When I touch you, it's going to be when we're both firing on all cylinders, have hours to explore each other, and aren't fighting off panic."

She bit her lip. "I need to wash up. Get my pajamas."

"You can use my bathroom. And I'll grab you a T-shirt."

She finally let out a laugh, light and soft and utterly Maisey. "Beckett, all of my things are literally down the hall."

"Humor me, my Maisey-girl. I'm feeling the need to keep you in my sights."

It wasn't just about her safety, although that was the most important part. It was also because if I let her out of my sight, I might retreat. I might let the dead parts of my heart take back over.

I opened my closet, pulled a folded Swift Rivers Fire Department tee from my shelf, and handed it to her. "I'll even let you use the bathroom first," I told her with a wink.

She didn't argue. She just grabbed the shirt and disappeared behind the door.

When I'd designed the bathroom suite, I'd put in two vanities and a shower with dual heads, even though I never brought women here. I'd convinced myself that it was for the resale value of the house, except everyone knew I'd never sell this place. Had I always, subconsciously, expected Maisey to be the one to use it with me?

Was this really why I'd always stepped between her and Cleaver or Sweeney, or any of the other men who'd looked at her with desire all but pouring from them? Not because I didn't think they were worthy of her, but because, somewhere deep inside, I'd been trying to keep her for myself?

I was assaulted by dozens of memories. Happy moments we'd spent tucked together in my treehouse as kids. Frustrating ones when I'd found out she'd put herself out there, and some douche had taken advantage of her. The disappointment I'd felt knowing she was going to the homecoming dance with Carter. Joy when I'd heard she was moving back to Swift Rivers.

The simple truth from last night hit me all over again. I'd always wanted her and simply denied it. Denied us both. I had to stop this ugly cycle. I had to keep her, or I had to fully let her go so she could find the happily ever after she wanted.

She came out of the bathroom with her cheeks pink and her hair swirling around her breasts, and the beauty of her sliced through me.

And I knew the truth. I could never let her go. I could never handle seeing some other man touching her. Just the thought of it hurt far worse than the lack of oxygen to my lungs ever had.

I wanted to take my T-shirt, that looked damn good on her, toss it to the floor, and show her exactly how she should expect a man to touch her. To give her the passion and sin she said she craved. But I'd meant what I said about not making love to her tonight, even before I'd rewritten our entire lives in a few short breaths.

So instead of wrapping my arms around her and kissing her until she had no breath left, I retreated to the bathroom in an attempt to pull myself together.

When I came out of the bathroom, Maisey had turned off the light, and it took a few seconds for my eyes to adjust. She was in my king-sized bed, but she'd landed as far over on the right side as she could get without rolling off. And just that simple act, the absolute adorableness that was Maisey, eased the chaos, allowed the swirl in my brain to stop.

As I climbed in on the opposite side, she went stiff as a board, and I simply reached out and pulled her toward the center, spooning her so her back was to my front, and my legs tangled with hers.

The overwhelming rightness of it washed over me like a balm.

Regardless of what had or hadn't happened before, Maisey belonged here with me now.

I kissed her temple and uttered a guttural, "Sleep good, Maise."

She squirmed, shifting in my arms as if trying to put some distance between us, and said, "I don't know how I'm going to sleep like this. You're like…a thousand degrees."

It brought a lightness to my heart I needed and allowed me to respond with a tease. "It isn't just me, darlin'. It's what happens when we're together. I'm gasoline, and you're a lit match, so quit wiggling before we set the whole place on fire."

She let out a little snort but then seemed to snuggle closer. It didn't take long for her breath to even out and sleep to take her. It didn't come so easily for me.

I was still awake, with my nose buried in her hair, reliving more of our past through an altered lens. It wasn't smoke that haunted me now, but blood. The brutal attack on Maisey's windshield had ended with Delilah in front of me. And she was a good reminder of the damage relationships could cause another human being—that I had caused another human being.

All my life, I'd believed love was followed by pain. That relationships did more to destroy than build you up. But I couldn't start something with Maisey, believing we were going to end up ruining each other.

She deserved the happily ever after her books demanded.

I promised I'd take the time to figure out just how to give her one. To give us both one.

And that was my last thought before sleep finally found me as well.

♫ ♫ ♫

When my alarm went off at five in the morning, my bed was empty.

Maisey wasn't due at the hospital for another couple of hours, so I should have been the first one up. Instead, she'd vanished, slipping out of my room without waking me. I hadn't even gotten a chance to kiss her good morning. After falling asleep with ideas of happily ever afters wrapped around me, everything about that irritated me.

On top of that, my dog had deserted me too, continuing his new "Vader the Traitor" ways. Then again, it was probably for the best if he stuck close to her. I liked the thought of him being there if anyone came after Maisey while I was gone.

The idea of not being there when she needed me sent a cold wave of panic down my spine. I dragged myself out of bed, threw on my workout gear, grabbed my go-bag, and made my way toward the kitchen.

Where all the panic dissolved in something far more appealing.

She was at the stove, making breakfast in a satiny-blue robe she'd thrown on over my T-shirt. A robe that screamed at me to take it off. She looked perfectly tousled—a morning wet dream. And even with her dad sitting at the island, reading something on a tablet, I was unable to stop my body from reacting to the sight of her dressed like this, in my kitchen, after a night in my bed, looking like she belonged.

With her dad there as an audience, I wasn't able to say or do the things I really wanted, but I could still make her pay for sneaking away this morning before I'd even gotten a kiss.

I pulled my phone out of my pocket and sent her a text with a smile tugging at my lips. When her phone didn't even buzz, I realized she must have left it charging somewhere. Disappointed again, I had to live with the comforting thought that I knew exactly what she'd look like once she read my message. She'd be pink from head to toe.

With that image plastered in my head, I sauntered into the kitchen. "Morning."

She jumped and whirled around with a spatula in hand. Her dad took in her reaction, jaw clenching as he glanced at me. "Maisey told me about the excitement last night. I'm shocked I didn't hear any of it. I'm usually a light sleeper."

"I thought about calling off today, but things are on edge at the station right now."

While it was true, unease *had* settled over our house as the teams waited for Nattingly's announcement and a new chief to be selected, I wasn't sure it was a good enough reason to leave Maisey while things were escalating here.

As if reading my thoughts, Lewis's face grew grim. "We'll be okay."

I wanted to believe him, but he'd admitted he hadn't heard anything last night. Not my dog snarling or the shattering glass. Would he really be awake and able to help if someone came for her?

This time, when my lungs tightened, it had nothing to do with relationships. It was the same panic I'd felt when I woke, returning with the force of a hammer. But then I reminded myself Maisey wasn't even going to be home most of the week either. The majority of the time, she'd be at the hospital, and she'd have lots of people around her. She'd be safe there.

"I'm leaving Vader here."

Hearing his name, the traitor came sprinting down the hall from Maisey's room with the cat chasing his tail. I bent down and gave him a full-body rub, all while trying to put a lid on my emotions. The kitten jumped all over me as I pet my dog, chewing on my fingers as if they were a new toy.

"Do you want breakfast?" Maisey asked.

"Not before I work out. I'll just grab something at the station afterward."

"Oh, crap," she said, looking down, as if suddenly realizing she wasn't dressed. "I was supposed to drive you to work."

It eased the alarm and tension in my heart once again, and I chuckled just as her dad snorted.

"I needed to get a run in anyway. I haven't put in enough miles this week," I told her. "The fob for my SUV is in the drawer by the front door."

She watched as I slung my bag across my body. "I can drop your stuff off on my way to the hospital later."

"Maisey." She looked up from the duffel to my face. "I haul a hundred pounds up and down stairs and mountains regularly, both for training and while fighting fires. I think I can handle hauling my bag for a mile or two."

Her stare drifted down my body in a way that had me hoping she was thinking of all the same things I'd been thinking about—tearing off clothes and feasting on warm skin.

She shook her head, as if clearing her thoughts, and said, "Thanks for letting me use your car. I'm hoping to have the windshield replaced on my truck in a day or two."

"No hurry."

I couldn't leave the house without touching her one more time, without taking a bit of sweetness with me to help me remember all the things I wanted to make come true for her. So, I made my way over to the stove and backed her up against the counter. Her eyes widened, darting over my shoulder to where her dad sat. I simply lifted her chin and covered her mouth with mine.

I didn't take it far, not with the audience we had. I didn't thrust my tongue between those delightful lips and say good morning the way I would have if she'd still been in my bed when I woke, but I also didn't deliver just a peck.

It wasn't until her dad cleared his throat that I eased back. But I was inordinately pleased with the flush that coated her cheeks and even more satisfied knowing that blush would grow darker once she read the messages I'd left her.

I winked and said, "Check your texts."

When Vader tried to join me at the back door, I ordered him to stay, and he looked like I'd shot him in the chest. I rubbed his ears and said, "Protect. Vader, stay. Protect."

He sat on his haunches and looked back at Maisey, her dad, and the kitten attempting to crawl up a stool, and I was certain he nodded at me.

Regardless of the darkness hovering around us, I was smiling as I walked out the door. Because having Maisey in my bed last night, seeing her in the kitchen in that sexy silk robe, and leaving with the taste of her etched on my lips, had made this one of the best mornings I could remember having in years. And I was determined to have another thousand mornings just like this, a forever after full of them.

Chapter Twenty-two
Maisey

SAVE YOUR LOVE
Performed by Great White

PRESENT DAY

> *HIM: What a shitty way to wake up.*
>
> *HIM: I had plans for our morning, darlin'.*
>
> *HIM: But now I have new plans. The next time we spend the night together, I want you in nothing but that blue robe. I want nothing on below it but warm skin so, when I push it open, all I see are those pretty pink nipples. I want to feast on them for a long while before I slide my finger inside you and watch your eyes go from sage to forest green. I want to hear you pant and beg and scream my name.*

Thirty minutes later…

> > *HER: Holy bejesus, Beckett! I read that text while sitting next to my dad at breakfast! What would I have done if he'd glanced over and seen something?!*
> >
> > *HER: You can't say things like that, not without warning me first so I can hide my phone.*
> >
> > *HER: Maybe you're taking this friends-with-benefits thing a bit too far.*

Two hours later….

HIM: Hey, Maise?

HER: Yeah?

HIM: Warning...

HER: ...

HIM: I also want you to wear that robe while you're sitting on my kitchen counter. I want to spread you open, drop to my knees, and make a meal of you. I want to give you the buzz I promised the other night.

HER: I'm at work!

HIM: It might be cruel, but I like knowing you're aching for me just as much as I'm aching for you. Four days at the station have never seemed so interminable.

HIM: And let's be clear—we've never simply been friends, and this is a hell of a lot more than friends with benefits.

The sexy texts Beckett sent the first day of his shift were just the start of a steady stream of them that tortured me for four days.

They were tantalizing. Addictive. Excruciating.

Even after I'd told him to warn me before sending any more, he never really did. He'd simply text the word "warning" followed two seconds later by something so steamy it made me blush harder than any romance novel ever had. Maybe it was because I'd always known those weren't real. They were fake things fictional people said to each other. But knowing Beckett's hands had typed those words made my body feel like it might combust.

To get even, I slipped into his room one morning wearing nothing but the blue robe he'd first mentioned and snapped a selfie on his bed. Nothing explicit—just a hint of cleavage, a bare thigh—but enough to make my pulse race as I hit send. I was half thrilled, half terrified. It felt reckless, with a bit of that sinfulness I'd told Beckett I wanted to experience. Still, the thought of the pictures somehow getting out in the world made my stomach twist. Then again, if they did get out, they weren't racy enough to ruin me. Maybe enough for names to be whispered in my direction, but I'd been called names before and survived it.

Besides, I really liked this—the new way we'd found to taunt and tease. The back-and-forth exchange felt like an extended round of foreplay, which made waiting for Beckett to finish his shift—waiting for what he'd promised—seem to last for years rather than days. Not even extra practice sessions with Titan or long hours at work helped ease the ache.

The only thing that pulled me from the endless wait was dealing with Dad's chaos. His memory failed several times during the week. The first time, he called me Marjorie and asked when Chelsea and I were getting home from school. And one time, when I'd been at work, he turned on Mikey, demanding to know why he was being held at Kurt's like a prisoner. He stormed next door, and when I'd hurried home and found him, he'd been staring, horrified, at the fire damage. By the time he came back to himself, we were all shaken.

After that, I clung to every lucid moment he had, treasuring every card game and every laugh, as if they might be his last. So when I came home one night and he showed me a list of retirement communities, my heart lurched. None of them were in Swift Rivers, and even the closest felt too far. I wasn't ready to lose seconds with my dad, let alone miles.

The never-ending week meant that by Thursday, after working two extra shifts so I could have the weekend off for the Firefighter Ball and the Fourth of July show, I was running on fumes. When I walked through the front door, I was ready to bury my head in my pillow and sleep for twelve hours straight.

Laughter greeted me—a girlish giggle that had my brows raising. When I walked into the kitchen, I found a teenage girl sitting with Mikey and Dad at the table. They weren't playing Dad's favorite, King's Corners, but poker, and there was a pile of real cash sitting between them.

"What's all this?" I asked, unable to keep the worry from

my tone.

Mikey looked up with a grin that looked just like Stoney's. "Mr. Campbell is teaching Letty and me how to play poker without any tells."

The pleasure on Dad's face eased the concern that had gripped me.

"I think I've been taken in by another card shark. This one and Andie should start a club," Dad said with a wave at the girl. "Letty's blank face is better than your sister's, which is saying something because Chelsea is a damn good actress."

My pulse leaped. Dad didn't often talk about Chelsea—and certainly not to compliment her. I hadn't realized he'd ever seen my sister act. He'd always been on the road, and while Mom had filmed my sister's plays and my horse shows for him, I'd never seen him watching them. But the way he'd praised her so matter-of-factly made it clear he *had* seen her. That knowledge made me sad for all of us, but mainly for Chelsea, because she'd been the one most wounded by his apparent disinterest.

I came to stand next to Dad, elbow resting on his shoulder, and watched as they finished the hand. Letty won the pot, shoving a fist in the air in triumph.

"That's it. I'm done. You've taken all my cash," Dad chuckled.

The four of us set the kitchen to rights, and then the teens gathered their belongings.

"Why don't you head out to the car," I told them. "I'll be right there."

"We can walk home," Mikey offered.

I shook my head. "No way. It's late. I'll drop you both off."

The disappointment on the teen's face was comical. I was clearly thwarting his plans for the trip home. I watched them leave before turning to my father with my lips twitching.

"I can't believe you taught them how to gamble."

Dad shrugged. "I had to pay him somehow. Kid has been babysitting me all week."

All humor vanished. "What?" I shook my head. "No."

Dad raised a brow. "After all these years, don't start lying to me now. It sucks knowing I need someone watching over me, but we both know it's the truth." He suddenly looked older and more tired than he had since coming home from the hospital. "I set fire to the house, Maisey. We're lucky the fire marshal's report was as inconclusive as it was, or the insurance wouldn't have paid a dime."

It *had* been a relief when Ron's report had noted the Sterno's presence but left out any hint of the fire being set on purpose. I gave Dad a side hug, squeezing him tight because I didn't know what else to say.

"Hurts even more than losing my job did to know I need watching," he said quietly. "But if I did something while we're staying here"—he looked around the house—"I'd never forgive myself. Better to live with a bit of wounded pride than much bigger regrets."

Tears welled, and he patted my shoulder.

"Don't be sad. It's just life. We'll get through it. Now, go take those kids home before they start making out in your back seat."

I snorted. "You're far wiser about the actions of teenagers than I ever expected."

"Just because I didn't have to worry about you, doesn't mean I wasn't aware of what Chelsea got up to. Your mother and I went a few rounds about it, but neither of us knew exactly how to put an end to her antics. Truth is, if we had, it might have forced her to run away before she'd finished school."

He said it with regret, as if he wished he hadn't told Chelsea to leave. I hadn't blamed him for drawing the line at the time, but I also hadn't known it had hurt him as much as it obviously had. Worse, Chelsea would never know what it had cost him.

As horrible as the situation with Dad's finances, the fire, and his stroke had been, it had also given us something good. It had given us this time together, not as a child and a parent or as a caregiver and a patient, but as two adults who cared about each other.

The lump in my throat returned, and I was unable to respond. Instead, I grabbed my bag and Beckett's key fob and headed out to the SUV.

Much to my amusement, as soon as they heard the back door slam, the teens jumped apart from where they'd been leaning against Beckett's car with Letty in Mikey's arms. He held the passenger door open for her, and she climbed in with a bashful smile so different than the one she'd given my father after winning the last hand.

I dropped Letty off first, and Mikey walked her to the door, gave her a quick peck, and then came back to me with a similar bashful look.

When I pulled into his drive and he stepped out, I said, "Thanks for all your help this week, Mikey. I'm truly grateful. I hope you have a good weekend. I'll see you on Tuesday?"

He ducked his head back in, eyes startled. "Beckett asked if I'd spend the night tomorrow. He said you were going to the Firefighters Ball and would be staying overnight."

While I hadn't forgotten about the ball or the fact I'd agreed to stay with Beckett at the hotel, I hadn't thought about Dad either. Hadn't thought about needing someone to stay with him overnight when it should have been my priority. Instead, the sensual texts from Beckett had been practically all I could think about.

Then, the realization that both Dad and Mikey would know exactly what it meant that Beckett and I were staying together hit me, and I flushed bright red. Sex wasn't embarrassing or shameful, but that didn't mean I wanted my father and a teenager to know I was planning on having it.

After clearing my throat, I said, "Right. Thank you for staying with Dad again."

As soon as he'd shut the door and headed up the steps, another realization struck. I had a much bigger problem than anyone knowing I'd be sleeping with my supposed fiancé. As I turned the SUV around and drove back toward the house, I called Fallon.

"Hey, Maise," she greeted.

"I don't have a dress."

Silence beat between us for a second before she said, "What?"

"I don't have a dress for the Firefighters Ball. And it's *tomorrow*. And I have nothing but summer dresses that are absolutely not appropriate. And I need new underwear. Something sexy because Beckett made plans for us to stay the night at the hotel."

Fallon laughed. "What are you really panicking over? Not having something to wear or the fact Beckett will be taking the dress off?"

"Both!" I exhaled shakily.

When I'd been at the ranch, practicing, this week and told Fallon about how things had progressed with Beckett, she'd been surprised. But she also hadn't been as certain as I was that it would end badly. She seemed convinced everything would end up just like in my romance novels.

"I'm scheduled to take a group of beginners out on a ride tomorrow," she said. "But I'll see if Chuck can take it for me. I'll come pick you up, and we'll go shopping for a dress *and* for the lingerie to go with it."

Relief bled through me.

I pulled into Beckett's driveway and shut off the engine, switching her call from the car's speaker to the phone's before opening the door.

"Thanks for agreeing to go with—"

I barely registered a sound coming from behind me before my head exploded in agony. The blow drove me to my hands and knees, a cry tearing out of me as pain spiraled through my skull. My phone skittered across the gravel and disappeared beneath the SUV.

My ears rang. My head spun. From somewhere distant, I heard Fallon screaming my name, tangled with Vader's frantic barking.

Instinct surged—move, fight, do something. I forced myself onto my knees, but another hit slammed between my shoulder blades.

My chin hit the gravel, white lights burst in my eyes, and my vision swam.

Through the blur, I made out a pair of shiny, steel-toed work boots stopping in front of me. A gloved hand fisted in my shirt, ripping it, and true panic surged, stealing what remained of my breath. Ugly fears and uglier possibilities crashed over me. I commanded my hands to move. To punch. To claw. To slap. But my body refused to obey.

Instead, darkness whirled, and oblivion took me.

Chapter Twenty-three
Beckett

WITHOUT YOU IN IT
Performed by Kelsey Hart

TEN YEARS AGO

HIM: I'm going to strangle Carter.

> *HER: You can't strangle him for telling the truth. I just need to be done with boys until the braces are gone and the surgery is behind me. It's fine.*

HIM: That's bullshit.

> *HER: Why? It's not like it's going to be the end of the world if I don't date in high school. And maybe you're right, Beckett. Maybe all relationships are doomed. Maybe people are always destined to hurt the ones they say they love.*

HIM: It's okay for me to think like that, but not you. I won't let my Maisey-girl's dreams be ripped away. You WILL have your forever after.

PRESENT DAY

I wasn't supposed to use the lights on the captain's truck for personal reasons. But screw that. I had the lights and siren blaring as I sped from the firehouse toward home.

Something had happened.

She'd been attacked.

My stomach lurched, and rage filled me.

I should have fucking called off. I shouldn't have left her alone.

The call from Fallon had terrified me. I hadn't even been able to fully listen to what she was saying after she'd told me Maisey had been assaulted in my yard. I'd hung up, grabbed the keys, and headed out, with my crew demanding to know what had happened.

I'd been such an idiot for so long. Holding her at arm's length. Blaming my heart and my childhood wounds. Even now, even realizing I wanted her, wanted something more, something permanent, I'd held back, telling myself I needed time to figure my shit out.

But really, it had been the last dregs of fear that had stopped me from taking what was mine.

Fear of ending up like my dad, fear of getting burned, figuratively or literally. Fear of wanting everything and ending up with nothing.

But Maisey, my sweet, gorgeous, kindhearted friend, would never set my house on fire with me in it or take off for South America, abandoning our family.

Instead, she'd always considered me worthy of her time, her effort, her touch.

She was certainly worthy of *my* time and effort and adoration. She deserved for someone to put her up on a pedestal, fall to their knees and give her the pleasure and love she desired.

I'd promised myself I'd give us both a happily ever after, and now, it might be too late.

Fuck. Fuck that. It wasn't too late.

Please, I begged to the universe, to any higher power that might truly be out there. *Please, let Maisey be okay. I'll do anything. Anything to get another chance to give her everything she's ever dreamed.*

When I screeched around the corner onto our street, it was to find the sheriff's SUV and an ambulance parked in front of my house. Spotlights were set up in the driveway, and people were crawling all over my yard.

I slammed the brakes and barely waited for the wheels to stop before I flung myself out of the truck and ran toward the ambulance. Lewis stood at the back, staring inside, looking decidedly frail, my dog's leash in his hand. Worry furrowed his brows, and fear slashed through me all over again.

My mind filled with a million horrible images. Bloody ones.

Ones I'd lived in vivid color.

As I rounded the ambulance door, my eyes immediately landed on Maisey, sitting on the edge of the box rather than on a gurney. Her eyelids were closed, her ponytail askew, and her chin bloodied. Seeing her upright and cognizant enough to be holding an ice pack to the back of her head unclenched my heart, until the deathly pallor of her face and the dirt on the front of her scrubs registered.

Goddamnit…she'd been on the ground…

All breath left my body as more nightmare images spun through me. Ones that had bile singeing my throat.

What exactly had he done to her?

"Maisey." My voice was hoarse. Raw. Full of regret.

At the sound of her name, her eyes popped open. Unshed tears welled, spilling down her cheeks. Bugsy was picking at Maisey's free hand with tweezers, but I pushed her aside and tugged Maisey into my arms. A sob escaped her. She fisted the back of my uniform shirt, clinging to me.

Vader shoved between us, pressing his body into our legs.

I looked over Maisey's head at Lewis and demanded, "What the hell happened?"

To his credit, her dad looked angrier than I'd ever seen him.

"She came back from taking Mikey and Letty home, and someone hit her on the back of the head as she got out of the car."

In my arms, Maisey shifted. I could actively feel her pulling herself back together, forcing the tears to stop and straightening her shoulders, all so she could appear calm and strong and brave. And she was those things, but she didn't have to be. She could let go here, with me, and I'd catch her.

Another vehicle squealed to a halt on the street behind us. Two car doors slammed, and Fallon and Parker rushed over. Fallon's expression held the same fury the rest of us were feeling.

Once Maisey saw her friend, she started to step away from me, and I hated it. I didn't want to let her go. Not until I'd gotten the entire story. Not until I was sure that a knock to her head was the worst thing that had happened. But Fallon gave me no choice, yanking Maisey to her and squeezing tight.

Maisey hugged her back, burying her face in Fallon's shoulder.

Ridiculous jealousy bloomed, but I couldn't help wanting to be the one caring for Maisey.

Parker's hands were in his pockets as he rocked back on his heels. "What happened?"

"That's exactly what I want to know," I snapped, looking at Lewis and then Bugsy.

It was Cleaver who answered, leaving his search to join us at the back of the ambulance.

"Someone hit her twice." He held up a crowbar with gloved hands that looked just like the one I'd left in Lewis's backyard while working on the porch. "Don't know if Fallon's voice on the phone or Lewis letting Vader out the door scared them into leaving it behind, but they did. They also left this."

He handed me a clear bag. Inside was another note. As my fury grew, the words blurred, and I had to force myself to focus to read it.

Last warning. Stay away, or you'll both end up dead.

Fucking hell.

Fallon ripped the bag away, read the note, paled, and then gave it to her husband with a hand that shook. Parker's face darkened before he gave the note back to Cleaver.

"This has gone far enough," I growled at the deputy sheriff. "Do something about this, or I will."

Cleaver frowned. "If you have actual proof of who did this, hand it over, Romero, and I'll happily arrest them." I grunted an objection he ignored. "If you think I'd let anyone hurt Maisey and get away with it unpunished, then you don't know me at all."

"Maybe I don't know you. Maybe none of us do. Maybe you're the one pissed she's here, living with me, getting married to me, and trying to scare her off." I didn't think it. I knew he was jealous and unhappy about her being mine, but I didn't think he'd actually hurt her to get her to leave me, and yet rage still had me spewing things I couldn't seem to stop.

Cleaver reacted, stepping toward me with anger radiating off him. "Screw you."

"Stop!" Maisey's quiet voice, raised in frustration, had me swallowing my retort. She looked from me to Cleaver and back.

Bugsy cleared her throat. "Can we all just take it down a notch? Maisey, sit down so I can finish cleaning those scrapes, or I'm going to insist you go to the hospital."

The full force of my gaze landed back on the woman I loved.

Loved.

I loved her. Wildly. Completely. Ferally.

Proving once and for all, my heart wasn't a dead block of petrified wood.

I didn't just love her. It was so much more than that. It was as if she were the reason I breathed. The reason I existed at all. I'd been put here to be of service to her. I'd done a decent job of it as kids, distracting her from her sister and the stupid headgear. I'd even been there when her mom died, but I'd utterly failed once we'd reached adulthood.

No more.

I narrowed my gaze on Bugsy.

"She's absolutely going to the hospital."

"I agree," her dad said.

Maisey shook her head and winced. "No. I'm really not. There's no need to take up a bed in the ER for someone to tell me what I already know. I have some bumps and scrapes. Nothing more."

One look at my face had her gentling her response, soothing

me, when she should be the one receiving comfort. "Seriously, Beckett. I doubt I even have a concussion, so there's no reason to freak out over nothing."

The EMT put her hand on Maisey's elbow and guided her back to the ambulance. "Let me finish cleaning the pebbles out of these scrapes at least." As she worked, Bugsy said, "Beckett and Maisey both know what to look for if she does have a concussion. Her eyes are clear and steady. That knot will hurt like a bitch, but I think it's fine for her to stay here if she wants."

"No one should be staying here," Parker stated dryly.

I had twelve hours left on my shift, but I'd call Stoney and have him cover for me. I wasn't leaving Maisey. Not now. I wasn't sure I'd ever be able to leave her again.

And that did cause a moment of alarm. A twinge in my chest. I loved my job. Maisey loved hers. We wouldn't be able to be tied at the hip for the rest of our lives. But those were all things to think of later. After we'd figured out who was doing this and stopped them from hurting her worse than they had tonight.

"Parker is right," Fallon said. "You should all come to the resort and stay with us for a few days."

Maisey shook her head and paled once again. She was hurting and trying to hide it. Big fucking surprise. She didn't want to be any trouble. Didn't want anyone to have to take care of her.

"Fallon, it's the Fourth of July weekend," she said softly. "The ranch is packed. You don't have room for three more guests."

"We can put the kids together, so someone can stay with us, and Mom and Teddy have a guest room. They won't mind someone staying there," Fallon insisted.

"I booked two nights at the Carlyle for the Firefighters Ball," I said. "Maisey and I will be there for the next two nights."

Maisey looked from me to her dad, concern practically dripping from her.

"Would you stay with Lauren and Teddy for a few nights,

Dad? I'll feel better if I know you're somewhere safe while Beckett and I are gone."

"This isn't about me, Maisey," Lewis said. His voice was hoarse, broken with the same raw emotions I was battling. "You're the one they keep coming after." The furrow in his brows deepened. "I just don't understand why."

When everyone in the group's attention turned to Maisey, she flushed. "I wish I understood it myself."

"I'm hoping to get some prints off the crowbar or the note this time," Cleaver broke in. "And I'll follow up on the boots you described, Maisey."

Confusion bled in. What exactly had she seen? "Wait… You saw him?"

"No," she said. "They struck me from behind, but I saw their boots when they stepped close enough to shove the note in my shirt…" she trailed off. My insides clenched. They'd touched her. They'd put their hands on her skin.

As if sensing the direction my thoughts had gone and the rage and fear that swamped me, Maisey grabbed my hand with her free one and squeezed it. Comforting *me* yet again. "Nothing happened, Beckett. They just left the note."

It didn't bring the relief it should have because it wasn't *nothing*. They'd hit her. They'd knocked her out. And even if they hadn't done something more tonight, they could have while she'd been lying on the ground unprotected.

Cleaver cleared his throat. "No one sells those boots locally. But anyone could have bought a pair online. I'll do my best to track them down, just don't get your hopes up on it leading us anywhere."

"What type of boot?" I demanded.

Cleaver's eyes fell to my feet. "From what Maisey described, it seems like the boots you guys wear with your Class B's."

What the hell? Was this one of my team? Stoney? Someone else at the firehouse whom I hadn't even started to suspect? New pain squeezed my lungs tight—new fear and new regrets.

If I were the reason she was being targeted, should I walk

away? After just promising the universe I'd do anything to make all her dreams come true if she was all right? After finally realizing she was my entire world? I wasn't sure I could do it. And that might just make me a worse bastard than I'd ever considered myself to be.

The silence that had settled turned heavy and weighted. It was Fallon who broke it by putting her hand on Lewis's arm and asking, "Can I help you pack a bag?"

Maisey's dad looked from Maisey to me. "You're not going to let her out of your sight?"

"Not even for a second."

He nodded, moved in to kiss Maisey on the temple, and then went with Fallon into the house.

Sandy called to Cleaver, and he strode off into the spotlights. As Bugsy began wrapping gauze around Maisey's hand, Parker jerked his head toward the street and the Harrington Ranch rig they'd shown up in. I followed him.

"What can I do to help?" he asked.

When Fallon had been in danger three years ago, Parker had walked away from his SEAL career to protect her. I was a firefighter. I didn't have the same set of skills as a Special Forces operative, but I'd protect Maisey with every last breath I had. But I didn't have to do it alone.

"Someone has been watching her. It can't just be knowing her schedule, because no one could've known she'd come by the firehouse the day she got the first note. Hell, even I didn't know she was coming."

"Do you remember my old teammate Cranky? He's coming for the holiday with some of the guys. They're arriving tomorrow. Between Sweeney, my old team, and the ranch's security, we can arrange twenty-four-hour surveillance. We'll catch this asshole."

The pressure in my chest eased. "I'd appreciate the help."

"I'd like one of the guys to stay here." He nodded toward my house. "Maybe at Mr. Campbell's as well."

"I'm fine with doing whatever it takes to catch this asshole." I looked down the darkened street. "The Helmers rent their place out through one of those online vacation rental services. It's highly unlikely, but if they don't happen to have someone booked, we could stick someone there too."

Parker's focus shifted down the block. "It would be good to have all three houses covered. I'll talk to Sheriff Wylee and see what we can do." He looked back at the ambulance where Bugsy was finishing up with Maisey. "You staying here tonight?"

Unease filled me at the thought, but I doubted whoever had done this would be back tonight. They'd wait to see if Maisey heeded their warning. I said as much to Parker, adding on, "It'll be just for a few hours, so she'll get some rest. Then we'll head to the Carlyle in the morning."

"I'll send one of the ranch's security to sit out front until you leave," he said as Fallon and Lewis emerged from the house. They each had a duffel thrown over their shoulders. Maisey's father looked faded. Weary.

Once again, I wondered if this had anything to do with him. I didn't see how, but I also couldn't see anyone hating Maisey enough to attack her like this, certainly not over some misplaced desire for me.

I didn't realize I'd spoken my thoughts aloud until Parker responded, sending a shiver up my spine. "You can't use logic to understand or explain the actions of people like this, Beckett. If someone is unhinged enough, nothing they do or say will make sense to anyone but them."

It had certainly been true of the assholes who'd come for Fallon. And it had certainly been true of my mother, who'd had zero compunction about leaving me, even after she'd realized I was in the house she'd set on fire.

The authorities hadn't been able to prove Mom had even been at the house, but I'd seen her leave. Everyone had thought it had been my smoke-filled hallucination because she'd had an alibi. The guy she'd been cheating on Dad with had sworn she was with him. Dad was the only one who'd really believed what I'd seen that day.

Maisey joined Fallon and Lewis as they threw his things in the back of the Harrington rig with Vader right on their heels.

"I can't take my dog with me to the Carlyle."

"He can come with us," Fallon said.

"We've got a kitten too," I said with a sigh.

Parker's lips twitched. "Theo and Lila will be thrilled to have a cat over."

"Let me grab her and their things."

When I came back out of the house with the cat in the crate and a duffel full of their food and toys, Maisey was hugging her dad. Vader's look, when I loaded him and Dorothy into the back of the vehicle, was worse than the one he'd given me the day I'd left for my shift. It was enough to make my newly pinked heart bleed a bit more.

I rubbed his ears. "You're a good boy, Vader. A good boy. This is just for a few nights. We'll all be back together soon. Back together and home where we all belong."

I shut the door and then pulled Maisey to me.

We watched as the car drove away, with Lewis and Vader both watching us out the windows with matching sorrowful expressions.

Careful of the bandages on her hand, I twined my fingers with Maisey's and tugged her toward the house.

"You need more ice for that bump as well as some Tylenol. But most of all, you need rest."

At the top of the porch, she dragged us to a stop, watching as Cleaver and his team still scoured the drive. She stepped into me, resting her forehead on my chest and giving me a fierce hug. With her face muffled, I barely heard the words as she said, "I just want this to be over."

The lump in my throat grew, and I hugged her to me, hoping beyond hope that between the sheriff's department and Parker's team, we could make her wish come true.

BE THAT FOR YOU
Performed by Lady A

THREE YEARS AGO

HIM: Why is it folks think just because a person is wearing a uniform, it means they want to be hit on?

> *HER: This is new. You're actually complaining about being hit on?*

HIM: Sometimes, a guy just wants to have a beer and relax.

HIM: Think putting a fake wedding ring on my finger would be a deterrent?

> *HER: For some, they'd only see that as an additional challenge.*

HIM: Annnndddd, this is yet another reason why I don't believe in HEAs.

> *HER: Okay. Who is this really? You're using "HEA" and complaining about being hit on. This is NOT Beckett. Is this Stoney? Kasey? Did one of you steal his phone?*

*HIM: *** laughing emoji *** Funny, Maise. Funny.*

> *HER: If it's really you, then you have to be sick. I'll swing by and check your temperature.*

HIM: My door is always open for you to…check my temperature.

*HER: *** puking emoji *** And now I'm sick.*

PRESENT DAY

My emotions felt balanced on a razor's edge, ready to fall precariously in one of two directions. On one side, panic and fear, and on the other, a hollow numbness. I chose door number two, if only to get me through the night. I wanted to forget everything about those few moments when I'd felt powerless and afraid. When the hand had slid—

No. I refused to go there. The worst hadn't happened to me. I had a bump and some scrapes, and my composure was shaken. But otherwise, I was fine.

When we were finally able to escape the chaos outside and the door had closed on the nightmare I'd lived through, Beckett insisted I stay in his bed again. It wasn't a hardship. The mattress was like a cloud, and with Beckett next to me, holding me, I knew I'd feel safe.

I wanted to shower. I wanted to wash off the grit of the ground as well as the knowledge that someone had touched me without my permission, but reapplying ointment to my scrapes and rewrapping my hands would require energy I didn't have. So instead, I stripped my clothes, put on another of Beckett's T-shirts, and crawled into bed while Beckett grabbed me water, ice, and pain medicine.

After he was satisfied I'd been sufficiently cared for, he tossed his uniform aside and joined me. It was another testament to how exhausted I was that I didn't drool over his nearly naked body or freak out at him drawing me up into his chest like he had last time we'd been in his bed together.

Beckett squeezed me to him so tight I thought our bones would meld. His voice was full of grief and recrimination as he said, "I'm sorry, Maisey. So damn sorry."

Surprise shifted through the fatigue and numbness that had taken over, and I turned in his arms so I could meet his gaze.

"This isn't your fault."

"I wasn't here…" Tears filled his eyes that he blinked back.

His tears nearly broke me. I was barely holding myself together, barely holding the numbness around me like a cloak. I needed that for a few more hours, but I wouldn't—couldn't— let him take responsibility for something that was absolutely not his fault.

I ran my fingers along his jawline. He had to have started the day clean-shaven, but now the stubble coated his chin and cheeks. I was a sucker for a good layer of scruff. It was sexy and tantalizing. I wished I wasn't too tired to take advantage of it.

Instead, I did what I could to comfort him. "Don't do that, Beckett. The only person responsible for this is the person who attacked me. Not you. Not me. Not the fact we've told everyone we're engaged."

He kissed me. Tenderly. Sweetly.

The flame flickered to life between us, but it was dimmed because of the detachment I'd draped myself in, and I hated that maybe even more than I hated the fact that someone had come for me again.

I turned my cheek, resting it on the hard expanse of his chest, and my eyelids immediately drooped, the aftershock of the adrenaline rush dragging me under.

His chin rested on the top of my head, and his arms tightened around me again. He murmured something…something my subconscious told me I wanted to hear, but I couldn't pull myself back from the abyss enough for it to truly sink in. I was gone. Lost in the darkness.

Until the early morning, when a nightmare finally bled through the cocoon he'd wrapped me in. In the dream, when I hit the ground, my clothes were torn from me. Someone was touching me. Reality mixed with the fear of what could have happened…

I jerked awake. Heart racing. Palms clammy.

"Shh. I'm here. I'm here, Maisey. You're safe."

I looked up into Beckett's warm gaze, and my body instantly relaxed. I was safe. Here with him. I'd always been safe with him. I blinked away tears that welled.

As Beckett gently brushed my hair away from my cheeks, I scoured his face. He looked as tired as I still felt. Eyes shadowed. Light dimmed.

That shook the numbness away. Screw whoever this was. I refused to let them take our joy. Refused to let them take the pleasure of these moments we were making together and turn them into a tragedy. They wouldn't get the best of me...or Beckett.

We'd both survived worse.

"Did you sleep at all?" I asked.

"A few minutes here and there."

I registered the bright sunlight shifting through the wooden shutters on his windows. Crap. It was far later than I'd expected. I was going to be late. I sat up, demanding, "What time is it?"

He tried to pull me back to him, but I batted his hands away. My head spun as I turned too quickly, trying to catch a glimpse of the clock. Nine o'clock! I'd barely have time to get ready. "Fallon is going to be here in thirty minutes."

"What? Why is Fallon coming?" Beckett's voice was rough and raw.

"We're going dress shopping for the ball."

"Yeah. No. That's not happening." He sat up, brushing a hand through his thick waves.

"What? Why? Do you not want to go to the ball anymore?"

He gritted his teeth, clearly debating the answer.

"Beckett, the entire reason we started this pretend engagement was so you could convince the city council and the chief that you were ready to replace him. Showing up at the Firefighters Ball is a requirement for anyone who wants the job. You *have* to go tonight. *We* have to go. It's the first time anyone will really see us together."

"Everyone will understand. You were *attacked* last night."

As if the nightmare I'd just woken out of hadn't already

reminded me. I swallowed hard, playing with my hair in that nervous habit I'd forced myself to outgrow. I pushed the messy strands behind my ear, baring my face on purpose.

I didn't need to hide. And I wouldn't allow whoever had attacked me to ruin Beckett's chances at the chief position any more than I was going to let them ruin the time we were sharing together.

"If we don't go, then we're letting whoever did this win," I said. To hell with that.

I threw the covers back and stood, careful to keep my balance even though my head was pounding as if a woodpecker was drilling into it, and my shoulder ached like a bitch. If Beckett saw I was hurting, it would only give him more reason not to go tonight.

But I wanted this. Not just for him, but for me. I wanted to show up on his arm in a fancy dress and prove to the town Beckett was mine. Even more, I wanted what came after. I needed what he'd promised me in his texts all week. The tangled skin. The sinful, feral claiming. I wasn't going to skip it because of one asshole who thought they could scare me into giving up everything I'd always dreamed of having—giving up Beckett.

When he still hadn't responded, when he still sat there with a stubborn set to his chin and expression broody and dark, I knew I'd have to do something drastic to break him out of it. So I raised a brow and said, "So you're all talk and no action."

"What?" His eyes narrowed.

Even though it hurt my scraped hands, I crawled on all fours across the mattress toward him.

"You made promises, Fireball. Four days of them. About just what you were going to do to me in and out of my blue robe, and I want every single thing you promised you'd do. We both expected that to start tonight, after the ball. And I have plans for the dress I'm buying today. Plans of watching you beg me to take it off."

Heat flickered across his face as he watched me approach. I straddled him. His gaze immediately dropped to my mouth while his hands landed on my hips.

"Maisey." It was a warning. A plea to stop.

I ignored it. Instead, I leaned in and took his lips with mine, lingering there for a moment, indulging in the simple joy of touching him. Then, I licked along the seam, demanding entrance. He groaned, and I thrust my tongue inside, dancing along the velvety warmth that greeted me.

I'd meant the kiss to be a tease, a slow dare I then planned on walking away from. But the instant we were joined, everything in the world faded but us. Nothing existed but our mingled breaths and twined bodies and the insatiable need radiating between us.

His hand went to the back of my neck, pushing us closer. My breasts pressed tightly against the hard muscles of his chest. My body flickered with sparks only Beckett had ever caused. No man had ever made me feel this way. Alive. Desired. Full of want.

Enough. Enough to please. Enough to keep.

Our kiss deepened, mouths and teeth and tongues battling for control.

I bit his bottom lip and was rewarded with those brown eyes turning to molten chocolate.

The layers of sheets and pajamas suddenly felt like way too much.

I wanted him. I wanted his hands on my bare skin, between my legs, on every inch of my body. I wanted him inside me, calling my name.

I wanted what the romance novels promised and so few people really got.

I could have that with him.

I *would* have it with him.

But I wanted it tonight, after I'd had the chance to wear a beautiful dress with my hair done and makeup on. I wanted to be the princess I'd once thought I could never be, with the charming prince claiming me as his in front of the entire town.

I wanted to beat that bitch *Hope* into submission when she realized I'd won.

I ripped my mouth from his, slipped off his lap and onto the floor.

His eyes were so dark it was like looking into the night sky from the top of a mountain. No streetlights. Nothing but stars across a satiny expanse.

He reached for me, and I danced back out of reach with a sly smile.

"You want to finish that, Fireball?"

His lips twitched, and his hand went to the hard-on straining beneath the sheets. "You can clearly see I do."

He stroked himself. Once, twice. My nipples pebbled, and my core clenched.

"Come back to bed, darlin'. I'll prove my actions are far better than my words."

Maybe tonight could be a follow-up to this morning. Maybe I could have both.

He saw his lure was working, and he smugly patted the mattress next to him.

I shook my head, and the pain spiked.

No. I wanted the day to feel better. Wanted more hours placed between what had happened and our moment together, so I could concentrate on just Beckett and me and the way we made each other feel in the dark of the night.

"Nope. I have shopping to do," I said, turning toward the door so I could head to my bedroom and the bathroom I'd been sharing with Dad. "Are you wearing your Class A uniform tonight, or did you rent a tuxedo?"

"Class A's."

My hand was on the doorknob, and then, suddenly, it wasn't. Beckett dragged me away from the door and back against him, his hard-on pressed into me, and his bare chest warm against my back. When his mouth landed on my shoulder exposed by his oversized T-shirt, and the tease of teeth and tongue danced over my skin, I nearly moaned.

"Where do you think you're going, Maisey?" he asked, voice husky and low.

"To shower."

"I promised your father I wasn't letting you out of my sight.

I meant it."

"I'm not showering with you."

He didn't respond. He simply swept me off my feet, bridal style, and carried me toward his bathroom.

"Beckett, put me down."

He ignored me, holding me pressed up against him while he reached into the shower and turned on the water.

"Takes a minute to warm up," he said.

I struggled, and he finally let me slide out of his arms. Every inch of me shivered with delight as our bodies rubbed against each other. His gaze worked its way down me, the smirk on his face letting me know he understood exactly what he was doing to me. It was pure retaliation for how I'd straddled him and then left him in the bed.

My heart was pounding furiously, longing and lust making it almost impossible to talk. But I was eventually able to croak out, "I don't think Dad meant I couldn't shower on my own."

"Doesn't matter what he meant. Only matters what I promised."

I huffed out a laugh. "I need my shampoo and conditioner. It's the only kind that works on my hair, so it doesn't look like a wet dog."

"Maybe I should help. Your hands are pretty banged up. Wouldn't want the shampoo to sting them."

"I'll manage. You don't get to shower *with* me until you've delivered on all your promises."

"I will be delivering," he said, stepping closer, heat sparking, and grin widening. "I can provide the first installment right now. I promise this isn't a limited-quantity deal. In fact, once I've touched you, tasted you, and watched you climax, I'm never going to want to stop."

His words flared hope of the forever I knew he wasn't necessarily promising. I put my hand out, pushing against his chest to keep the distance between us.

"No can do, Beckett. I want the fairy-tale moment. The gorgeous dress and the handsome prince and the sinful night you said you'd give me."

He grabbed my hand, placing a soft kiss atop the gauze wrapping my palm.

"You're right. You absolutely should have all of that, my Maisey-girl." At the door of the bathroom, he turned back and said, "Better get in before I change my mind."

My heart hammered against my chest. I took a fortifying breath. "Bring me my shampoo!"

He waved a hand and left.

But I hadn't really thought this through, because once I was in the shower, naked as a blue jay, he returned with the bottles in hand. He stopped outside the glass door, slowly taking in every inch of my nakedness, eyes stroking me as if they were his hands. My thighs quivered, my core ached, and I had to put a hand out on the shower wall to steady myself.

"I deserve a goddamn medal," he said, voice husky and raw.

"Yeah?"

"The sacrifice it's taking to walk away from you right now…" He set the bottles down outside the shower, inhaled, and then shook his head with his eyes closed. "Yeah. A fucking medal isn't even enough."

He'd turned away and started for the door when I called his name. His focus returned to me, and I gave him my very best saucy smirk. "You deliver tonight, and we'll see about getting you a medal."

A smile broke over his face, the large one that always did things to my insides. He was whistling as he left the room.

I kept that happiness with me as I unwrapped the gauze and cleaned my wounds, vowing to myself I'd keep the joy and lose the fear. I'd concentrate on what he'd promised me, even if it was only for a night or two…or a dozen. Even if, eventually, I ended up with a broken heart as Beckett pulled away. For now, I'd concentrate on the present. Not the past or the future. And I'd forget completely whoever was gunning for me for a few hours.

After I got out with a towel wrapped around me, Beckett took his turn in the shower, and I stayed to admire the image he made, taking in every groove and the impressive length of him that I'd barely caught a glimpse of at the lake. His smug look grew, brows raised in question as his hand trailed down his chest and lower. When he got to the rising length, I turned tail and ran. Not because I was embarrassed, although my cheeks were a healthy red, but because I was afraid I wouldn't stick to what I'd said about wanting to wait until tonight, until we'd had a magical evening together.

I defied his orders to stay in sight and finished getting ready in the bathroom Dad and I had been sharing. The scrapes on my hands were still sore and raw, but they'd be okay without bandages. The cut on my chin, however, needed more ointment. After I covered it with a Band-Aid, the sight in the mirror hit me hard. I'd spent years fixing my jaw and teeth, and one simple bandage tried to throw me back to my girlhood. To the insecure child who'd thought she was ugly.

I ground my teeth together. I wasn't going to let some jerkwad attacking me in the dark undo all the hard work I'd done to feel better about myself. I applied my makeup with a steady hand to draw attention to my eyes instead of my chin. Then, I layered on the hair products so I'd have a base to work with later.

By the time I came out of the guest bedroom after packing a bag, I expected to find Fallon had already arrived. But when I walked into the kitchen, Beckett was alone at the island, with two to-go cups of coffee waiting and irritation on his face.

"What part of 'not out of my sight' did you not understand?" he groused.

"Seriously? I had all my stuff in the other bathroom. Don't take the protective-hero stuff too far, Fireball. It's attractive, but only to a point."

He smirked. "Are you sure, because in that Brynne Asher book, *Souls*, I'm pretty sure the heroine was down for every command."

My mouth fell open, shock hitting me dead center. "Wait. When did you read that book?"

He shrugged.

Disbelief had my voice squeaking as I asked, "Have you been reading romance books ever since you lost that prank?

Have you been reading them for *years*?"

"What can I say? You should have made that bet way back when, about me liking them if I tried them."

The surprise that whirled through me was almost enough to make my head spin. "I can't believe you! So, when you promised not to touch me and said you'd read a romance book for every time you did, you weren't offering up anything you weren't already doing!"

His smile broke free, wide and unfettered. "It definitely wasn't the deterrent it should have been."

"You're a cheater!"

He laughed.

"A no good, big fat—"

My words were lost in a kiss, a slow and sensual one, full of a promise that took my breath away.

When he lifted his head, I dragged his mouth back to mine and continued the kiss with new fervor. Maybe simply because I could. Maybe to prove to that fleeting feeling, Hope, he was mine and she couldn't take him away. Maybe simply because it felt too good not to.

He was chuckling as he lifted his head the second time. "Come on, my Maisey-girl. We have a dress and a ring to buy."

He shoved the coffee at me and picked up his key fob.

"A ring?" I all but gasped out.

"I told you I was buying you a ring. I figure, if you show up without one tonight, people are really going to question the truth of us."

And just like that, I landed back in reality.

This time with Beckett had an expiration date. We were playing house. Playing at friends with benefits. Playing at something more. So he could get a job, and my dad and I had a place to live.

And just like that, Hope won, easily stabbing me in the gut as she wiped away every stupid dream I'd started to believe might come true.

Chapter Twenty-five
Beckett

LIFE WITH YOU
Performed by Kelsey Hart

FOUR YEARS AGO

HIM: I don't get it.

HER: What?

HIM: I'm watching Neil get married, and I can't for the life of me understand why anyone would spend tens of thousands of dollars on a few hours, when you can say I do in front of a judge and then spend the money building your future—if you even have a future, because we all know there's more than a fifty-percent chance someone is going to cheat, and they'll be getting a divorce before they hit their ten-year anniversary.

HER: Do you even have a romantic bone in your body, Fireball?

HIM: I haven't had a single complaint from anyone I've kissed.

HER: Sex isn't romance. You'd know that if you read one of my books.

PRESENT DAY

As I watched Maisey's face, the laughter and tease

and even the heat from our kiss disappeared behind her blank wall. I'd mentioned the ring, and she'd gone cold.

My vulnerable heart, so recently exposed, took a hit. Did she not want this? Did she not want me? Had I somehow cleared my way through the smoke only to find my house really was on fire?

No. Screw that. Maisey had feelings for me. I'd even go as far as to say she loved me. Not as a friend, but as something more. It was part of the reason I'd worked so hard to keep us in the friend zone. I hadn't wanted to mislead her. Hadn't wanted her to end up like Delilah with blood coating her wrists.

But maybe I'd pushed her away for so long that she'd gotten as good as I had at denying us. Denying the feelings that had always been there. Because that was the simple truth—I'd always loved her. Fate was laughing at me. My disbelief in soulmates was having a good chuckle.

We were fated soulmates, but we were also so much more.

I needed to tell her. I knew it was important for her to hear the words so she'd understand exactly how far of a leap I'd taken, but would she believe it? Would she believe it after the years where I'd scorned love and happily ever afters?

Words were cheap. If I'd learned anything from reading romance novels, it was just that. The hero had to *show* his heroine what he meant. A grand gesture.

I could do that. I could give her that tonight and turn an evening that would have already been special into something truly magical.

Maisey moved away from me, glancing at the clock with a frown. "Let me just text Fallon. I don't know why she's not here yet."

"I told her not to come. That I was taking you."

She gave me that look—the one that said I'd overstepped—but it only made me smirk. "I know, I know. I'm taking the protective-hero thing too far again. But the truth is, I'm not ready to let you out of my sight. Last night, when I got the call you'd been attacked…"

I couldn't finish. I tugged her hand into mine, squeezing it, while I took several long, slow breaths. Finally, I choked out, "Keeping you close today is more for me than you."

Maybe the stupid-ass tears that had welled had done the trick, because she simply gave in.

And a few hours later, when she began apologizing for taking so long picking out a dress, all I could do was remind her that I'd signed up for the trip. Still, a flicker of anxiety was starting to creep in, because by the time lunchtime came around, she'd barely managed to find a dress and a pair of shoes—an outfit she hadn't even allowed me to see or let me pay for—and we hadn't even begun looking for the most important thing on the list, the ring.

When she suggested we stop for a bite at one of the mall's restaurants, I insisted we didn't have time for a sit-down meal. Even though the food court felt like the wrong place to take the woman you loved on the day you bought her an engagement ring, we were pressed for time if she still wanted to hit up the lingerie store before we went to the jeweler's.

But once we were in the lingerie shop, all thoughts of hurrying flew right out the window. As I watched her pick through lace bras and barely-there thongs, I remembered her words from this morning and knew she was right. I was going to beg her to take off whatever dress she bought simply to see her in that sheer excuse of a bra and panty set she'd picked up.

While she was in the dressing room, I texted her, telling her exactly what I wanted to do to her in and out of the underwear she was trying on, and she came out with a delightful pink coating her cheeks.

"You're a menace," she said.

"Darlin', it's your own fault. You can't bring me to a place like this and expect me *not* to have those kinds of thoughts."

"You're the one who demanded to come along."

I stroked her cheek while we waited in line. "Can we go to the jewelry store now?"

She studied me for a long moment, and something in her look caused the ugly worry I'd had this morning to return.

"What's wrong?" I demanded.

"I just…don't want you to buy a ring for something that…"

She faded off. I grabbed her chin, forced her to look at me, and held her gaze with a steely one.

"This isn't temporary." For a second, she looked panicked before she shut down again, showing me that blank expression I wanted to remove permanently. "I told you I wanted to explore whatever this was between us, but that wasn't exactly true, my Maisey-girl. I want more with you than I've ever wanted before. Than I ever thought I *could* want."

Before she could respond, the clerk called, "Next," and we had to move up to the register.

I cursed the timing. But I promised myself that, after tonight, she'd never doubt us again.

Maisey paid, and I grabbed the bag, adding it to the pile I was already carting.

"I can carry some of those, you know," she said.

"You can, but you won't. You're already doing too much today. You should be resting after the hit you took yesterday." She grimaced, and I kicked myself for bringing it up, hurrying to cover it up with a wink and a taunt. "It's going to be a long night, and I wouldn't want you to fall asleep before it's over."

Her brows rose, lips quirking. "If I fall asleep, you won't get that medal you want."

A chuckle escaped me.

And finally, with an enormous sense of relief, I was able to guide her toward the jewelry store I'd picked out. While she'd been trying on dresses, I'd researched for the best stores in the area, intending to leave the mall behind and take her to an upscale shop. But I'd been surprised to find a mom-and-pop store with an almost perfect rating right there in the shopping center.

"Where are we going?" she asked as we passed several chain jewelry stores.

"Someplace better."

Tucked in a corner, the shop had a stained-glass sign and the atmosphere of a museum. It was hushed, almost church-like. The carpeting was deep and luxurious, the wallpaper had a satin sheen, and the display cases were all antiques with wood waxed to a shine.

The rightness of the place only added to the feelings I'd felt since last night. Maisey and I were forever. We weren't fake or pretend or going to end. We could actually do this thing called love and survive it—together.

A bald man with a white goatee greeted us. His suit and bow tie were almost as old as he was, yet they fit the sophistication of the store.

"Good afternoon, lovebirds. Let me guess, you're here for a ring?" His eyes twinkled.

Maisey let out a little laugh. "Are we that obvious?"

"True love always is."

Maisey tugged at her hair, but his words reassured me.

He waved us over to a display case filled with rings. Maisey and I looked inside, and my stomach clenched. Not because I was buying her a ring, or even because I had no idea of the price of them, but because, at first glance, nothing seemed as right as I'd hoped.

"Nina!" the man called toward the back, and a moment later, a young woman our age, in a black dress and heels, joined him.

"Yes, Papa?"

He waved at Maisey. "Size this young lady's ring finger and see what she thinks of our collection while this gentleman—" He waited for me to supply my name, which I did, and he continued, "While Beckett and I head over here to chat."

The young woman brought out a measuring device and took Maisey's hand in hers. They were talking about sizes and ring styles as I followed the man over to a corner case.

"Is there a price we need to consider?" the man asked, pulling a pair of glasses from his front pocket and sliding them on.

"She can have whatever she wants," I said, meaning it. I had savings, but I also wasn't an overly wealthy man by any means. "I can't afford for it to be the price of a house, but I want her to have something special. Something deserving of her."

He nodded, turning away from the counter to a case behind it. He brought out a covered tray and set it in front of me, with the jewelry underneath hidden.

"Have you ever heard of the *toi et moi* style ring?" he asked.

I shook my head. "Honestly, I never thought I'd be buying one at all."

He nodded knowingly. "Love is even more beautiful when it hits you in the chest like that. I knew as soon as you walked in, the two of you were perfect for each other."

I laughed. "You're already going to make a sale, so you don't need to butter me up."

He winked. "I can see how you'd think that, but I always speak the truth. And your truth radiated from you, which brings me back to *toi et moi*. It means 'you and me' in French. In my opinion, it is one of the most romantic ring designs because it reflects the unity of two people becoming one. It embodies the bond between you, symbolizing two separate entities being made into one by love."

He pulled a ring from under the velvet. It was simple and yet not. One side was a platinum band that ended in a pear-shaped white diamond. That first stone nestled against a similarly shaped yellow one, attached to a gold band. The two different bands twisted into a graceful swoop at the back. While the ring was truly beautiful, it was his words, even more than the ring itself, that sold me because Maisey and I were one.

"That's it," I said, taking a huge, smoke-free breath and reveling in it. "That's the perfect ring."

His face brightened. "I've been saving this for a special couple." He glanced over to where Maisey and his assistant were still chatting happily. "Let me just make sure I've got the sizing right and get you a box."

I took out my wallet and slid the credit card over the counter. I had no idea how much it was going to cost me. I didn't even know if my credit limit would be enough, but it didn't matter. That was Maisey's ring.

He took it, discreetly pocketing it before stepping over to

the women. He said something quietly to his assistant, she nodded, and then he disappeared into the back room.

I joined Maisey, sliding my arm around her waist and rejoicing in my ability to do just that, wondering why it had taken me so long to get here. Why I'd let fear and the past and other people stop me from being with the one woman who'd always shown me unconditional love.

"I'm being difficult." Maisey's voice held a tone of remorse as she tipped her head back against my shoulder.

"No, you're not. Picking out something you're going to wear every day should take time. And if we don't find what you want now, we'll figure out something to tell everyone tonight." We wouldn't have to. I had the ring and a tentative plan I'd formed this morning. But I also didn't want her to worry.

"What do you think of this one?" Maisey asked, holding up a simple solitaire on white gold. It was probably the least expensive ring in the case.

"No."

She looked up at me with a laugh. "No? Just no?"

"Just no. Try again."

"Fine. How about this one?" she asked, picking up a ring with a square-cut emerald and two small diamonds on either side of it. It was completely different from the first one, but it was equally bland. It was nothing special. Nothing that screamed of a bond between two people, and I was even more sure I'd made the right choice.

"No."

"You're going to be even harder to please than me." She laughed again, nervously tugging at her hair.

The jeweler came out of the back and tilted his head, waving me over to the side. I reluctantly let Maisey go to join him. He slid my credit card back as discreetly as he'd accepted it, followed by a sage-green velvet box that was nearly the same color as Maisey's eyes.

"Thank you," I said, my voice full of all the emotions I'd been so desperate to hide for years as I slyly added the box to the single shopping bag in the bunch that was mine. "She's going to be upset about not having something on her hand right now."

"Ah. Let me handle it," the man said, striding back over to Maisey. He put a hand over the rings on display. "These are not right for you." Maisey startled, darting a worried glance at me. "I have a shipment coming in. If you come back on Sunday, I will show you the perfect ring."

I saw her hesitation, and I twined our hands.

"Sunday, my Maisey-girl. I'd rather wait and give you the perfect ring than rush and have something on your hand for the next sixty years that neither of us likes."

Her mouth popped open. "What?"

"You're right. Sixty years means we'll only be in our eighties. Make it a hundred years."

She let out a small giggle. "You're ridiculous."

I gathered all the bags and then grabbed her hand again. I met the jeweler's eyes, mouthed thank you, and he winked.

As we stepped outside the store, she turned a worried face to me. "What are we going to do now? You're the one who insisted we needed a ring to prove to everyone this was real. What if they don't believe us?"

"They will," I said confidently. My plan would ensure it. More, I hoped it would convince Maisey this wasn't fake for me. That I truly wanted her to marry me.

I almost did a victory dance right there in the mall when that thought didn't choke me or bring back images of wrists covered in blood. Instead, it made me think of all the times I'd had Maisey tucked up against me. All the times I'd already kissed her. And better yet, all the future kisses we had yet to experience.

But my happy thoughts were interrupted by a sharp laugh and a voice that caused the hair on my neck to rise, saying, "You've got to be kidding me."

Chapter Twenty-six
Maisey

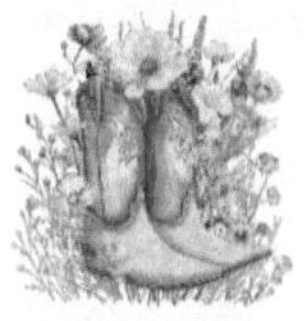

HONEY
Performed by Taylor Swift

THREE YEARS AGO

> *HER: Have you ever used handcuffs?*

HIM: Excuse me?

> *HER: You know. While having sex, have you ever used handcuffs?*

HIM: No. Please tell me you're not considering letting some asswipe tie you up.

> *HER: Not yet. Some guy would have to remain interested in me long enough for me to really trust him, and I've never been a keeper, you know?*

HIM: Screw that. I hate when you talk like that. No guy has been worthy of you.

> *HER: Yeah, yeah. I wasn't saying that so you'd toss a pity compliment my way. I'm just curious whether I'd ever have the courage to give up that much control, and if it really heightens the experience.*

HIM: It wasn't a damn pity compliment! It was the truth. But because I know you're uncomfortable with the entire notion of actually being a beautiful, desirable woman, I'll answer your question instead of fighting with you. In my opinion, if you need to play games to get off, then you're doing it wrong.

> *HER: Millions of people would disagree with you.*

> *HIM: Millions of people also end up destroying each other.*

PRESENT DAY

As if the entire conversation with Beckett hadn't already done a number on my taxed emotions, hearing Chelsea's laugh and snide voice skated a knife down my spine. Vicious and cruel. I watched as she flounced over to me with Gavin trailing behind her.

"Did you actually buy her a ring? How far are you really taking this farce, Beckett?"

A rumble escaped Beckett's chest. A warning, low and guttural that sounded almost as feral as Vader's had when I'd come to last night on the ground with Dad at my side.

"What are you doing here?" I demanded before Beckett could respond.

My sister waved a hand in Gavin's direction. He held an assortment of bags, much like Beckett did. "Not that I need to explain myself, but we had a few essentials to grab on our day off before we return for the next round of filming. I see you're back to wearing bandages on your face. Whoever paid for this cosmetic surgery should ask for their money back."

"That's enough," Beckett insisted as my hand went to the Band-Aid I had on my chin. It wasn't that I'd been able to forget about it. Every time I'd looked in a dressing room mirror today, I'd seen it, but I'd done my best to fight the memories just like I'd promised myself I would.

Gavin's brow raised as he scanned me and then Beckett before asking in a scathing tone, "*This* is the guy you've been talking about?"

Chelsea flushed, shaking her head at Gavin before glaring

at Beckett. "Our parents are no longer able to stop you from messing with Maisey, so it falls on me, as her big sister, to step in. Do you know what's going to happen when you break it off? She'll be the laughingstock of Swift Rivers all over again. This time, worse than she ever was when they made fun of her deformed jaw."

Her words did exactly what they'd always done. They picked at my insecurities and fears—ones that were already trying to drag me under with the bandage on my face today. But she wasn't wrong, at least about Beckett. When this "more" he and I were playing around with ended, I'd be left devastated. Alone. More broken than I'd ever been.

And yet, I desperately wanted to prove she was, once again, wrong. Not just about me, but about Beckett. About *us*.

This didn't have to be temporary. It didn't need to have an expiration date. We could turn this *more* Beckett talked about into forever. I just had to fight for what I wanted as I'd once had to fight for my self-worth.

I had to fight for the man I loved. The man I was head-over-heels, passionately, endlessly in love with. Had always been in love with. I'd just hidden it because I'd thought he didn't want it. Didn't want me. It had been pure self-preservation that had me denying it.

But the way Beckett was acting, the things he'd said not just today but last night, made me believe I didn't need to worry. That I didn't need to hide the love I felt anymore.

While I was catching my breath from this spiral of revelations, Beckett responded, snapping out in my defense. "Let's be honest, Chelsea. You aren't trying to protect Maisey. In actuality, you'd get off on it if I broke her heart. You're jealous because she's always had the things you wanted and couldn't have. Real friends. Love. A fucking soul."

Chelsea laughed again. It was the kind of laugh that scratched down your spine like nails on a blackboard. "As if *I* would ever want or need anything *Maisey* has. She'll be forgotten as soon as she's dead and buried, even by those she blindly serves, whereas no one will forget *my* name. I'm going to be remembered for generations."

How was it possible for her to still slice me to pieces while supposedly looking out for me? How had I not learned before now to put her words in a box and toss them over a cliff? But I would. Right now, I'd take a stand. I had to.

I started to respond, but Beckett beat me to it. "Yeah, you'll be remembered all right. As a soulless, cold-blooded carnivore who ate people's hearts for the hell of it."

"The villains always have the more intriguing roles. I'll gladly sign up to play one whenever a part like that is offered," she tossed back. But he'd gotten to her. I could tell because she tugged at her necklace the way I usually tugged at my hair.

Every last remaining thread of hurt and humiliation disappeared as my vision locked on the pearls. Fury emerged instead. I'd suspected she'd taken Mom's box but had forgotten about it with the chaos of the last week.

I closed the distance and grabbed her wrist. "What the heck, Chelsea? You took Mom's pearls?"

Chelsea ripped her hand away from mine, backing up closer to Gavin. "They were always supposed to be mine."

"Mom never said that! And even if that were true, it didn't give you the right to take her entire jewelry box. Dad was distraught! He accused *me* of stealing it."

She laughed again. "Oh, that's perfect. Saint Maisey accused of stealing. I bet that burned."

"You need to give it back. All of it."

She raised a brow. "No, I don't. I really don't. You got your cut. You're wearing it on your face! This is mine. And besides, most of the jewelry was worthless. I barely got anything for it."

She'd sold Mom's things! That ripped through me with even more violence than her words. I hated that Chelsea had found yet another way to wound me. But I promised myself it would be the last time.

Beckett's hand settled low on my spine, instantly comforting me.

Even if I was wrong about Beckett and what he'd been showing me over the last few days, even if I couldn't convince him that we weren't just *more* but *everything*, what I experienced with him now would always be better than anything Chelsea had ever felt in her entire life. She was exactly what Beckett had said—a soulless, cold-hearted caricature of a human being. I didn't think she'd always been that way. I wanted to believe the love I'd felt as a little girl was real, but she'd let bitterness turn her into this shell of a human.

"Go ahead and play the villain, Chelsea. It's certainly a role that fits you. But you know what? The villains rarely get top billing, do they? Means you'll forever be second-class. A 'B' actor, scratching and climbing but never reaching the top." For the first time, maybe in my entire life, my words hit her. She flushed, rage coating her face before she wiped it away.

"I think this has gone far enough," Gavin said, taking Chelsea's arm. "You don't need this, babe. You need to clear your mind for what comes next."

She shook him off and pointed a finger at me. "When you have nothing left…no home, no money, no fake fiancé…don't come crawling to me for help. I won't have a tissue to spare, and I certainly won't give you a dime of my hard-earned money. Not one single dime."

She spun on her heel and started to walk away.

I called after her, "Hey, Chelsea?" She looked back over her shoulder, and I said, "The only favor I want from you is for you to delete my number."

She stormed off, and Gavin looked at me with something that might have been sorrow. "She strikes out when she's stressed. You don't get the pressure she's under, we're all under."

"Then she must have been stressed for the last twenty-eight years, because what you saw just now has always been the real Chelsea," Beckett bit back.

Gavin brushed a hand through his hair and then hustled after her.

Beckett dropped our bags and pulled me to him, wrapping his arms around me, soothing me, protecting me as he always had. Because what we had was more than what I'd ever had with my sister. More than what I'd had with any other soul.

And that damn well meant something. Just like the spark

that bloomed when we touched meant something. We'd spent so many years of our lives letting our childhoods convince us that we couldn't have anything real, solid, permanent, that we'd wasted time we could have had together. No more. From here on out, I'd convince him we were worth fighting for.

"I'm sorry. Don't let her ruin the rest of our day." His voice was low, and the rumble of it vibrated through me, providing yet another reassurance.

Ten years ago, a year ago—hell, maybe even a month ago—Chelsea's words would have ruined my day. They would have clung to me and followed me into my dreams and rattled all my worst thoughts awake.

But strangely enough, today, it didn't feel like Chelsea had ruined anything. It actually felt like a weight had been lifted from my shoulders. As if removing the noxious burden of our relationship had brought into clear focus the relationship that really mattered—the one with Beckett.

People talked about how cutting toxic people from their lives had changed everything for them, and I'd thought too many people were too quick to cut ties when they should try to work out their problems. I'd thought you needed to give people the opportunity to change and grow and make amends. Now, I also saw there was a line you had to draw. A time and place to say, "No more." I hadn't expected crossing that line and making such a radical decision with my sister would bring such lightness and relief.

"You know, she's wrong," Beckett said softly. "She's always been wrong."

He ran a finger along my cheek. He'd done it multiple times over the last few days. It was a new, affectionate touch I found myself craving more of.

"I do know. Chelsea will never have the success she seeks because she doesn't understand human emotions well enough to portray them in a way viewers will believe. Her acting will always be missing something."

"I agree, but that wasn't what I meant. I meant she was wrong about you. No one ever thought you were ugly. Not before the face masks and surgery…and certainly not after. It isn't just Cleaver who fell for you growing up. You've always been beautiful, and not just on the outside. You've always had an inner light that radiated out of you like a beacon, calling us mere mortals home."

My heart skipped several beats, and tears swarmed. But they weren't sad tears. They weren't even for my decimated relationship with my sister. They were for the Maisey of my childhood who'd always thought she was the ugliest person in the room. They were because I'd let those wounds keep me from the most wonderful thing in my life—they'd kept me from claiming Beckett.

♫ ♫ ♫

The Carlyle was the only five-star resort near Fallon's, and it was the complete opposite of the ranch. The one-room suite Beckett had reserved was modern, sleek, and alive with light. Black and white and steel blended with Japanese prints and vivid green plants, a far cry from the Victorian-meets-Art-Nouveau charm of the Harrington Ranch.

We'd barely checked in and unloaded my shopping bags and our luggage into the suite when Chief Nattingly called. He wanted Beckett to attend a meeting with fire department brass from multiple counties being held before the evening's festivities.

Beckett hesitated, torn between his duty and staying at my side.

I insisted he go. Nattingly requesting him proved he considered Beckett first in line to replace him. Beckett needed to do this if he intended to get the chief's job—and I needed a few minutes to think and plan.

After our encounter with my sister, my mind was spinning, not in the way Chelsea had hoped, but in a direction of all the possibilities that were before me. I had to find a way to ensure Beckett saw the truth of us as much as I did. To prove to him that I'd never abandon him, just as he'd never do anything to destroy me.

That we could be one of the rare exceptions, love would never fail us.

Reluctantly, Beckett decided to go to the meeting after I agreed not to leave the room without him. He kissed me softly, and it felt like a promise. Not just for tonight, when we'd finally lose ourselves in each other, but for everything that came after, and my heart leapt with not hope, but pure belief.

When he pulled back, he looked like he wanted to say something more, something important, but instead, he went and changed into his Class A's while I showered. He was gone when I came out, but he'd left another text, demanding I call him when I was ready, and he'd come and get me. It sent a warm curl of pleasure through me. As much as I liked protective Beckett, just like the heroines I read liked their overprotective heroes, it was time to take control of my own story.

I wanted Beckett. Not just tonight. Forever.

And I was determined to make that happen.

I took off the shower cap, careful of the tender knot on the back of my head, and twisted my hair into a loose bun that framed my face with curls. When the pain spiked, I was forced to sit for a second, but I refused to take anything stronger than ibuprofen. I wanted to be clearheaded tonight. I wanted every second scored into my memory.

Once the throbbing eased, I removed the bandage on my chin and used practiced strokes of makeup to all but erase the cut and bruising. Plums and grays drew out my green eyes, a deep berry colored my lips, and a dusting of shimmer finished the look.

Then I slipped off the hotel robe, catching my reflection in the mirror. The sheer pink lingerie did nothing to hide my body, and knowing Beckett had seen me buy it, that he'd known exactly what I'd be wearing under my dress tonight, sent a thrill through me.

This was my Cinderella moment—the one little-girl Maisey had dreamed of, the one romance-novel-loving Maisey had always longed for. Tonight, I'd go to the ball with the most handsome man there, and later, we'd devour each other the way I'd always wanted to be devoured.

These moments were all that mattered. The ones we made together. And after, I'd convince him that we could have a lifetime of moments just like these. A hundred years of moments, just like he'd teased in the jewelry store.

I pulled the mulberry mermaid gown I bought off the hanger. I'd chosen it after trying on dozens of dresses, because it was both daring and elegant. The front hem skimmed my knees while the back brushed the floor. The heart-shaped satin bodice offered a teasing glimpse of cleavage, shrouded by a chiffon overlay that swept across my chest and down to my wrists. The back dipped low, the sheer fabric softening every hint of exposed skin and hiding the bruising on my back. It was sultry and sophisticated. Perfect.

I zipped up and slipped into sparkling stilettos that would murder my feet by the end of the night but would be absolutely worth it. Then, I did a gleeful little spin in the mirror.

The woman staring back was a far cry from the twelve-year-old Beckett had first kissed. I wasn't an ugly duckling. I'd never been one. More importantly, I'd slowly proven to myself I wasn't broken.

The truth was, if Beckett and I had gotten together back in high school, we probably wouldn't have lasted. Not because we didn't love each other, but because we hadn't yet learned to love ourselves. We'd needed to heal first, to make peace with the scars we carried so they wouldn't bleed into our future. We may have fit together back then, but there would have been gaps between the puzzle pieces.

Now, I truly believed what we were could be sealed tightly and enduringly together. No gaps. No missing links.

I would never leave him. He'd never hurt me.

Tonight could be the beginning of forever.

I was smiling, content—happy, even—as I left the bathroom and picked up the little clutch I'd left on the dresser. I slid my lipstick, ID, hotel room key, and credit card inside before heading for the hotel room door while dialing his number.

It took several rings before he picked up, and I was startled to find him a little breathless.

"Hey, you okay?" I asked.

"It's already loud in here. I was terrified I wouldn't hear your call."

"I'm just leaving the hotel room."

"No. Wait for me. I'll come get you."

The worry in his tone dimmed my joy, bringing back all the reasons why he was concerned. My attacker was still unknown and still out there waiting for me to heed their last warning. And I was doing the exact opposite of what they'd demanded. I was moving closer to what I wanted.

Nerves rattled through me, and I looked both ways down the corridor as I opened the door. It was silent. Not a soul in sight. And the elevator was literally right across from our suite. I let the door shut and hurried the three steps it took to push the down button.

"I'm already at the elevators. Meet me by the staircase," I told him. He grunted his disapproval as I stepped into the car.

I'd barely put my phone in my bag before the doors were opening again. The elevator had stopped a floor above the lobby, and a gentleman stepped in. Unease skittered through me once more, and rather than stay inside with someone I didn't know, I brushed past him onto the mezzanine.

I hurried toward the grand staircase made of glass and steel, and the noise from the lobby hit me—music and chatter. When I glanced over the rail, I saw men and women in tuxedos, Class A's, or evening gowns, mingling, laughing, already enjoying the night. The chandelier above them was a phenomenon of intricately woven geometric shapes and vibrant colors that cast rainbow hues over them.

I took the first step, hand on the rail, searching the crowd for Beckett. When I found him, he had his profile to me with his eyes fixed on the elevator banks.

I wasn't sure how it was possible, but he looked even more handsome than usual. His hair was slicked back, accentuating the sharp angle of his jawline and the curve of his brow. The straight cut of his Class A's stretched perfectly across his broad shoulders. The two gold stripes on his sleeve and bugles on his collar indicated his rank. He also had a series of ribbons and medals on his jacket that he'd earned in his service with the department, a telltale sign of not only his bravery but also his dedication to the job.

He looked exactly like a prince in a fairy tale. *My* prince.

Because he was absolutely, one-hundred-percent mine.

That sent a delightful thrill through me.

No one could take this from me now, especially not the adoration and awe that came over his face as he turned and caught sight of me. This moment was worth everything I'd been through to reach it. All of the events in my past had to have happened for me to land here—with all my dreams coming true.

My happiness spread across my face as I slowly and carefully made my way down to him. By the time I reached the second-to-last step, Beckett was already reaching for me. He placed both hands on my waist, lifted me, spun me around, and then set me down in front of him.

His smile matched mine. Large and full and handsome. Dimple on full display.

"You're stunning, my Maisey-girl. Except, stunning is actually a useless word for what you are. I've never in my life seen anyone or anything as magnificent as you."

My breath disappeared, tears threatened, but I refused to cry, not even out of happiness tonight. I brushed my hands over his shoulders before meeting his gaze. The love that bloomed full and strong in my heart beat so fiercely against my ribcage I was sure he could hear it. See it. Feel it.

Because that was the simple truth.

I loved Beckett. With every fiber of me. With every thought and hope and dream.

"At the mall," I said, "you told me I had an inner light, but Beckett, you're the one who really and truly guides people out of the dark. If you hadn't entered my life, I would have always felt stupid and ugly. You helped me see my own worth. Everything I have and am now is because you saw the real me and allowed me to see it too."

He groaned. "I want to kiss you. I want to kiss you and do all the things I promised all week. It might kill me a bit to wait hours to take this dress off you."

I leaned in and gently put my lips on his. It felt like a gift— the ability to do so as much as the rightness of it. Those happy tears threatened once more. I pulled back, swiping my finger over his mouth to brush away the very faint hint of lipstick I'd left behind.

"That wasn't enough, darlin'. Not *nearly* enough. But it'll have to do for now." He took my hand, placing it on his arm, and asked, "You ready?"

I nodded, and he guided me forward. As we walked through the ballroom doors, my heart galloped as fast and furious as it did when I rode Titan through the fields at the ranch. It seemed as if every person in the room swiveled to look in our direction, and I was not imagining the whisper that rushed through the crowd.

Heads bent as people muttered behind hands and champagne glasses, and I wished I could stick up my middle finger and shout, "Screw all you doubters!" Instead, I smiled my largest, most adoring smile up at the man next to me, and he smiled down with the same look I'd seen as I'd descended the staircase. Awe and love.

I didn't need to hear the words. Beckett loved me as much as I loved him. He'd already shown me in a million little ways over our lifetime together.

And that would never change, no matter how many people in this room were placing bets on just how long we'd last.

Chapter Twenty-seven
Beckett

I CAN LOVE YOU LIKE THAT
Performed by John Michael Montgomery

ONE YEAR AGO

HIM: Dinner and drinks?

> *HER: Careful who you text that to. Some people might consider that a date.*

HIM: You deserve a date, my Maisey-girl. Too bad there aren't better options for you in Swift Rivers.

> *HER: The dating pool is more pitiful than I remembered. Maybe I should have stayed in Bakersfield. I was working in L&D, like I'd always wanted, and I had guys asking me out. I haven't had a single date since I came home.*

HIM: You couldn't stay away. You missed me too much.

> *HER: That ego of yours is ginormous. I missed ALL my friends and family and my horse.*

HIM: Admit it. I'm your favorite.

> *HER: Puh-lease. Titan ranks higher than you.*

HIM: Wanna bet?

PRESENT DAY

It was a cruel kind of torture, knowing I had hours to go before I could take Maisey upstairs and divest her of that dress. The gown was a masterpiece of temptation, hugging her like it was made for sin, showing off just enough to ruin a man's concentration, all while hiding enough to drive him wild. It was graceful, elegant, almost demure, and still the sexiest thing I'd ever seen.

I wasn't an idiot. I knew the stares that followed us as we made our way through the ballroom were ninety percent about her, about the utter perfection that was Maisey, while the remaining ten percent were waiting to see which of the rumors about us were true. Were we real? Were we fake?

I couldn't wait to set them all straight.

I was lucky to be the one escorting her tonight, and I promised myself I'd never forget that. She was a gift, and I'd nearly let her slip through my fingers. From here, we would succeed or fail simply based on what we put into this relationship, and I was determined to do whatever it took to keep her happy for the rest of our lives.

As we neared the DJ's booth next to the tables piled with auction items, Chief Nattingly intercepted us with Delilah on his arm. His blue uniform was snug over his rounding belly, but everything else about him was fastidious, from his neatly clipped dark hair with its hints of gray to his manicured nails. His eyes matched his daughter's, a bright blue that stood out against his uniform.

Delilah wore a red dress, glittering with so many sequins it was almost blinding. It kissed the floor in an elegant swoop but was cut low at the bodice and back so that it left little to the imagination. While it was elegant, it leaned more toward the sex-kitten look she wore when out on the town than her business persona.

Some people would consider her glamorous. But, to me, she didn't come close to Maisey's beauty. Delilah was missing the inner shine, the glow of goodness that radiated from my girl. Add in my recent doubts about her and the attacks on Maisey, and any friendship or empathy I'd once had disappeared.

I scoured her face for any hint she was behind what was happening to us as she took Maisey in, but all I saw was typical Delilah—a smile that didn't always reach her eyes and an act that ensured people overlooked how smart she really was.

The chief gave Maisey a small smile, "You look lovely, Maisey." Then he glanced down at Delilah and patted her hand. "But I think I have the prettiest girl on my arm tonight."

Del gave him a smile she reserved for her daddy. Sweet and tolerant. "You have to say that because you're my dad."

"It doesn't make it not true. Right, Beckett?"

I inhaled sharply. Did he actually expect me to say Delilah was prettier than Maisey? Prettier than not only my date but my fiancée? Screw that. Even if it were true, which it absolutely was not, I would never hurt the person I loved like that.

I ground my teeth together before doing my best to ease the situation while still speaking the truth. "Delilah always looks beautiful, but we'll have to disagree on who's the luckiest man tonight, because my Maisey-girl will always be at the top of my charts."

Maisey squeezed my arm, and when I looked down at her, I saw gratitude and love wash over her face.

"Delilah, why don't you take Maisey to get a drink—my treat—while I talk with Beckett?"

"It's an open bar, Dad," Delilah said with a little laugh. "But we women can take the hint. Right, Maisey?"

She looped her hand around Maisey's free arm and tugged her away from me.

Panic slid through me. An alarm that was reflected on Maisey's face for a brief second before she hid it. But then I reminded myself, even if it was Delilah who'd attacked Maisey last night, she could do nothing to her here, in a sea of people.

"Don't go far," I told Maisey. "I need to dance with my fiancée."

She understood the warning.

"The bar is right there." She pointed to the far corner where a line of firefighters had gathered, many with glasses already in hand. "Come get me when you're done."

I watched as the two women attempted to make their way through the crowd to the bar but were stopped every few feet as people greeted them. Delilah's expression was pleasant, smooth, and professional, the flirty airhead tucked away. But it was Maisey's smile that held people's attention because of its charming authenticity.

I wondered if Delilah realized she paled in comparison to Maisey as she'd once paled in comparison to Chelsea. Worry scoured through me. Was Del really behind this? Was there any way to force her hand and prove it? The more the attacks had escalated, the less and less it felt like Delilah, but I couldn't be sure. I'd never be sure until we caught the person red-handed.

"We haven't had a chance to talk one on one since you heard I was retiring," Nattingly said, drawing me back to him.

"You're retiring?" I said it as if it were a question, but we both knew it wasn't.

"Don't be ridiculous, son. We both know you've heard about it, just as you heard the unofficial condition the city council has placed on the job description. I made sure you heard they wanted a married man to take my place. Except, I had a different vision in my head for how you'd solve the problem."

It infuriated me all over again, just as it had that first day at the station when I'd heard him talking on the phone. I'd known what he wanted, and I'd panicked, trying to find a way out, but what he didn't know was, in finding a way not to play the game by his rules, I'd finally broken free of the prison I'd locked myself in. I'd finally taken what was always supposed to be mine.

His gaze followed the two women like mine did. They'd almost made it to the bar.

"The city council is going to choose the next fire chief based on my recommendation," he said, drawing my focus back to him. "I'd like to give that recommendation to the man who makes Delilah's dreams come true. This little show you and Maisey are putting on isn't going to get you what you want."

It wasn't blackmail, but it was close. Too bad for him I'd already made my choice. I wouldn't give Maisey up for a damn job. I could get another position as a firefighter. It wouldn't be as convenient, nor would it be in the town I loved and wanted to serve, but it would ensure I kept the most important thing in my life. It would allow me to keep Maisey.

"I hate to break it to you, Chief, but this isn't a show. This is me finally claiming the woman who's always been mine and her claiming me back. Nothing less and nothing more. If loving and marrying Maisey means I don't get the position I'm more than qualified for as you retire, so be it."

Surprise drifted over his face.

"Don't be hasty, Beckett. We can all still get what we want here."

"You're wrong. If I gave up Maisey for a job, neither she nor I would have what we want."

He huffed out a laugh. "Everyone in town knows this engagement is just for show. I backed you into a corner, and you swerved. It can still be fixed the right way."

I stared at him for a few seconds, letting anger eat away at my insides, but then it hit me. If he made me choose, and I didn't get the job, it would prove to Maisey, once and for all, that I was with her *not* because it helped me get my dream job or because she and her dad had needed a place to land, but because there was nothing I wanted more on this Earth than her. Nothing.

It would be the ultimate grand gesture. I hoped I wouldn't have to give up the job I wanted, but I would. Readily. Easily. No questions asked.

For now, I'd give her the gesture I'd already planned.

Instead of responding to the chief's comment, I whirled around to the DJ booth. Leaning in, I asked, "Excuse me. Can I borrow a mic for a moment?"

The guy raised a brow, shuffled around, and came up with a microphone. He stopped the music, and at first, the chatter in the room seemed amplified.

"What are you doing?" Chief Nattingly demanded.

I ignored him, shouldering my way to stand in the middle of the dance floor and whistling to get everyone's attention.

"Sorry to interrupt your night, folks," I said. The room grew quieter but wasn't silent yet. "This will just take a moment, and then we'll move on to dinner and dancing and your generous bidding on the items in our auction for the fallen firefighter's family fund."

As I continued across the dance floor, people parted for me with ease. As I neared Maisey, the room became so quiet you could almost hear a waterdrop land.

"There's been a misunderstanding in the rumors circling town lately. While Chief Nattingly has confirmed he's ready to retire, the timing of it has very little to do with the changes I've decided to make in my life."

I finally reached Maisey's side. She looked panicked, eyes darting around the room and then back to me. She bit her lower lip and tugged at a curl artfully framing her cheeks. The only thing I regretted about this was knowing she'd be nervous. But she would have her romance-novel-worthy moment, damnit.

"Twenty years ago, I fell out of a tree and landed in my new neighbor's backyard. When I finally caught my breath, it was to find an angel standing over me with concern on her face. She held out her hand to help me up, and even though I was just an eight-year-old kid, lightning struck me as I took it. That single spark traveled its way to my heart, planting itself there, where it has lived ever since. A spark that she has always owned."

"What are you doing?" my girl whispered, a flush coating her cheeks.

I smiled at her, reaching into my pocket and pulling out the green box I'd hidden earlier. Her mouth parted in surprise.

"I'm not going to lie," I said into the mic. "I've spent many of the years since that first meeting letting the rightness of what I felt that day scare me into pretending I didn't want to be anything more than your friend. But not long ago, I had the discomfort of watching another guy flirt with you and realized what a screwed-up idiot I'd been. I realized how many years I'd already wasted by denying the truth the universe had set before me the day you'd first held your hand out for me."

I bent down on one knee, opened the box up, and said, "I hope you can forgive me, Maisey. I hope you'll let me start making amends right now. So, I'm asking you, once again, to marry me, and I'm doing it here and now, where everyone in this town can finally see the same truth I do—that we belong together. Marry me, my Maisey-girl, and make me the luckiest, happiest man on this planet. Say yes, and prove to everyone this isn't a scam or a farce or a damn lie. The only lie was the one I told myself when I said I wanted to be single. But the truth is, I've never been single. Not from the moment you held out your hand all those years ago."

She pressed a hand to her stomach, and tears threatened to overflow. Then, she cupped my face and leaned down to kiss me. It wasn't a sweet, innocent kiss. It was passion and promise twined. Far too heated for a ballroom with hundreds of people watching, but neither of us cared.

When a throat cleared nearby, I chuckled and drew back just enough to say into the mic, "Is that a yes? I feel like you need to say yes so everyone is very clear on what we're doing here."

"Yes, Beckett. Yes. I'll marry you."

Even though I'd already known what her answer would be, even though I'd had no doubt she'd say yes, joy still filled my heart at her response.

A roar of applause and cheers rang up around the room. Over Maisey's shoulders, Delilah's face crumpled. Tears. Fury. A flush of embarrassment. She whirled around and pushed her way through the crowd. A spike of alarm pierced through my happiness. If it was Delilah who'd been coming for Maisey, our little scene hadn't helped, but maybe it would force her out into the open. Maybe she'd come for me this time instead of my girl.

Maisey grabbed my hand, helping me up off the ground. As people began crowding in to congratulate us, I ignored them. Instead, I drew her close and moved us into the middle of the dance floor. I looked over at the DJ and spoke into the mic one more time, "I think we need a song, maestro."

The air filled with the strands of a love song. I shoved the mic at the nearest body, wrapped my arms around Maisey's waist, and tucked her close to me. Then, I drew the ring from the box, took her left hand, and slid it into place. The *toi et moi* ring looked perfect there. It looked just like the symbol it was—two becoming one.

"You got a ring," she whispered in awe, staring at her hand resting on my chest as we swayed to the music.

"Do you like it?"

"It's exactly what I was looking for without even knowing it."

I kissed her gently, tucked her even closer, and lost myself in the scent of her, the beat of her heart, and the beauty that came from being joined. Knowing I had to wait a few more hours before I could fully revel in her, truly twine myself to her body and soul, was irritating, but that annoyance was soothed by the knowledge I'd finally done something right when it came to Maisey. I'd claimed her for the whole town to see, and she'd claimed me back.

When the song was over, we had no choice but to deal with the congratulations people had waited to give. It continued through dinner and right on through the speeches, the auction, and the dancing that came afterward.

It was well past midnight, well past the hour when Cinderella's coach should have turned back into a pumpkin, by the time I was finally able to drag her out of the ballroom for good. We were halfway to the elevator bank when someone called our names. I let out a pained sigh, and Maisey let out a soft laugh, but we turned simultaneously to face the mayor.

She was approaching seventy but had the vivacity of someone much younger. The shimmering black dress she wore draped elegantly over her full curves, the dark color accentuating her white, short cap of hair. She was smiling as she approached, making the wrinkles on her face more evident, but her gray eyes were serious.

"Mayor Nattingly," I greeted.

She looked from me to Maisey and back. "You both looked so happy tonight. Congratulations."

"Thank you," Maisey replied, fingers tightening on mine.

"I just wanted to say, contrary to what my husband might have told you, the city council is *not* looking to make a decision about his replacement solely based on *his* recommendation. Nor are we necessarily looking for someone who's married. While we want whoever we hire to live in Swift Rivers, we are all painfully aware marriage doesn't necessarily prove someone has the honor and integrity to do the job, does it?"

Sadness lit her face. While there hadn't been a whisper of the chief cheating on the mayor lately, her husband's infidelities had been the center of the town's gossip for years. While I'd always known that I hadn't been the *only* reason Delilah had slit her wrists, I'd thought I'd been the catalyst. Now, I could see that, while I might have been the last straw, the pile under me had been the driving force. It was time to relinquish the responsibility I'd felt. I had to so I could make my dreams with Maisey come true.

"I know what they both wanted," the mayor continued when neither Maisey nor I had responded to her. "It takes a whole lot of gumption to defy both my husband *and* daughter. It takes the kind of bravery I very much think someone in a leadership position in our community needs."

Gratitude filled me for her honesty and strength. It proved she'd earned her decades-long post as mayor of Swift Rivers.

"It's not that I don't like Delilah, Mayor. It's just I found my forever after first."

The mayor waved her hand. "You don't owe me, or anyone else, a justification, Beckett. While I won't deny wanting to see my Delilah settled down with a family of her own, I want her to find it with someone who adores her. Who sees her as the center of their whole world in much the way you see our Maisey."

Mayor Nattingly looked at Maisey with real affection, and it eased some of the tension in my heart. "I'm thrilled to see you both so happy after everything your families have gone through. Sometimes, it takes trauma and disappointments to realize exactly what we have. Good luck to both of you."

She started to walk away and then looked back at me. "And Beckett, make sure you apply for the job no matter what my husband tries to tell you."

She walked away, humming a tune that sounded a lot like "Better Than Revenge."

Chapter Twenty-eight
Maisey

YOU'RE STILL THE ONE
Performed by Shania Twain

TWO AND A HALF YEARS AGO

> *HER: Sex is disappointing.*

HIM: I nearly choked on my hamburger. Give a guy some warning, will you?

HIM: And sex isn't the problem. It's the idiots you've let take you home.

> *HER: Maybe. Or maybe my romance novels have set up a false expectation. I always hated it when people said that, but perhaps it's true.*

HIM: I'd offer up a bet to prove your romance novels are right, and it's just the guys who are wrong, but I know you wouldn't take me up on it.

> *HER: I'm nearly desperate enough to let you choose a guy for me AND place a bet.*

Minutes passed.

> *HER: Did I lose you?*

HIM: I'm trying to restart my heart at the idea of you actually taking a bet.

> *HER: I said I was ALMOST desperate enough.*

HIM: Darlin', that's the problem. If a guy is doing

it right, you absolutely will be desperate. Desperate, panting, and shouting his name.

PRESENT DAY

*B*eckett and *I* were quiet on the elevator ride up to the suite. Every time I moved my left hand, the diamonds he'd given me sparkled in the lights. It was the perfect ring.

The fact he'd given it to me while making a grand gesture in front of an entire ballroom of people gave me more hope that I was right about him. About us. Maybe we were both ready to accept that what we had was not temporary. Had never been temporary.

The sweet moment he'd given me was a gift almost as important as the ring itself. It was exactly the kind of scene my heart lurched happily at in romance books. And the look on his face as he'd dropped to one knee? It had been full of real love. Endless love.

The truth is, I've never been single. Not from the moment you held out your hand all those years ago.

My heart flipped all over again at those sweet, perfect, book-worthy words.

Yes, he'd done it after talking to the chief and before hearing from the mayor that he didn't have to slip a ring on my finger to get the job he wanted. But I had to believe it didn't change anything. The fake engagement had done exactly what it always did in my books. It had forced us to see what we already had and couldn't afford to lose.

And I wouldn't lose him.

On our floor, he guided me across the corridor to the suite door, opened it for us, and then surprised me by sweeping me off my feet before crossing the threshold. I let out a squeal of laughter. As the door clicked shut behind us, I met his gaze and was stunned all over again by the pure love I saw there.

It smoothed away any remnants of doubt and worry that had tried to stick around.

As he carried me into the bedroom, I tossed my clutch to the nearest available surface and slid my hands into his thick hair, messing it up. He huffed out a laugh. "What was that for?"

"You looked incredibly handsome, all smooth and slicked back, but that isn't the Beckett I fell for..." I swallowed, holding back the *I love you* I wanted to give. It would come. At the right time, it would come out. "I fell for a boy who always had strands of hair sticking up, taught me how to read, and told me I looked like an avenging angel."

"I didn't lie when I said you looked like one," he said. "It was your eyes that hit me first. That impossible color." He set me down slowly, allowing my body to slide tantalizingly along his. "And tonight, this fucking dress made your eyes glow as if they were the pearly gates themselves. As if they were a neon sign, flashing welcome."

I ran my hand down his uniform, slowly reaching for the first button and undoing it.

I was rewarded with his breath turning choppy.

"On a scale of one to ten," I said, pure pleasure lifting my lips. "How desperate are you to get me out of my dress?"

His eyes turned molten.

"I'd break the damn scale, darlin'."

Joy winged through me, the intensity of it so large it could almost take shape. I barely had time to revel in it before his mouth was on mine. Hot. Needy. Sparking into a full-blown blaze in a mere heartbeat.

His hands slid up my arms before tracing the whisper of chiffon across my back. Then he drew me closer, until every curve of me fit against every solid line of him. It felt inevitable, the way our lips met, molding together as though they'd been made for this—for us. Separate pieces finally forming a whole.

He licked into me, tasting like chocolate and cherries and the smoky hint of whiskey. Or maybe that was simply him, a delicious blend of fire and life that left behind the cleansing scent of ash and pure want in its wake.

Our tongues wove together, plummeting into secret depths until hunger rippled like a hurricane through me. I needed to feel his skin, his heat, the pulse of his body against mine. His teeth caught my bottom lip, his fingers threading into my hair to tilt my head back. A flicker of pain sparked where the injury lingered, but it vanished beneath the pleasure of being claimed, consumed, undone.

I fumbled with his remaining buttons, urgency turning my fingers clumsy. His jacket fell to the floor with a muted thud. When he reached for the zipper of my dress, I caught his hand and pushed it away, not wanting the moment to be broken yet by the cold dread that often hit me when a man's hands touched me. I wanted his urgency to infect me. I wanted to end up as he'd once told me I should when having sex—I wanted to end panting and aching for the simple graze of a finger.

"You first," I gasped. "I need to touch you. I need to feel your skin. I need to know this is real."

He stepped away and impatiently undid the buttons on his dress shirt while simultaneously stepping out of his shoes. When his cuffs took longer to undo than he wanted, he tugged viciously, and a button popped off, pinging and hitting the dresser.

I couldn't hold in the laugh.

"Is my impatience funny to you, darlin'? Seems to me, you're the one demanding skin as if it's your latest drug," he taunted. His voice was raw. The need in it skated over me, thrilling me down to the core.

"Not funny as much as"—I stepped back again as he tried to close the distance—"delightful."

His eyes darkened, and he let the shirt fall away from his shoulders, leaving a white T-shirt sculpted to his chest.

"I see. You like torturing me." I swore flames sparked in his eyes. "Just remember, Maise, payback's a bitch. I may be desperate. I may beg you to take that dress off, but I guarantee you'll be the one begging once I've got you flat on your back on the bed."

My mouth went dry, and I bit my lip.

He reached behind him, tugging at the tee and dragging it over his head, leaving his chest exposed. He was carved in the most beautiful way, not only by rigorous workouts but a life of service. He bore the marks of it. Scars from cuts and burns he'd earned fighting fires.

My body ached. To touch. To taste. To feel every single brush of skin before losing all sensation as we came apart together. But I wasn't going to let him have all the fun tonight. If he was going to torment me, I was going to torment him right back.

"Why does it have to be me flat on *my* back?" I demanded, arching a brow.

I stepped out of my shoes and removed the clip from my hair, shaking it out and running my hands through it so it would fall around my shoulders.

He groaned, dropping the belt he'd yanked off. I could see a hint of the sharp V at his waist, a trail of hair above the band of his briefs, and before I knew it, I was the one who'd closed the distance. I set my hands at the curves of his hips, sliding my palms along his waist and popping the button on his pants open before placing wet, needy kisses along his chest.

He drew my face to his, cupped my cheeks, and took my mouth with furious devotion, as if there was a storm inside him that matched the one in me. I'd relinquish my soul to get lost in the eye. To get lost in the glide of lips and teeth and hands. To feel perfectly and utterly used and adored like the people in my novels.

Our kiss turned brutal, savage in its intensity.

And when he reached for my zipper this time, I couldn't stop him if I'd wanted to. My knees shook. My fingers trembled. I wanted the dress gone. I wanted nothing left between us.

I gripped his pants, dragged them down as he tugged at my dress. Once the clothes fell away, once the gown was a crumpled pile of mulberry on the ground, Beckett stepped back, just as I had done with him, and took in every curve and valley of my body.

Usually, being in nothing but a sheer pink lingerie set would have had me covering myself self-consciously. But I didn't need to do that with Beckett. Not only because he'd seen me in bikinis growing up and naked several times now at his house, but because I didn't feel vulnerable and exposed with him. I felt as if this was just one more homecoming. A place I belonged.

Before I could protest, he'd picked me up, tossed me on the bed, and covered me with his body. His mouth landed on one hard nipple, laving it through the fabric. A soft bite had me crying out, arching off the bed. Strong hands pushed me back down, slowly and sensually exploring me.

My eyes closed as the sensations overwhelmed me.

Love. Hope. No… Not hope… Triumph.

He was mine. I was his.

The need that had brewed but remained hidden for far too many years burst to the surface. Flurries of want tugged through me as he did exactly what he'd said in his text at the lingerie store. He consumed me, tasting every inch, and once the fabric was as wet and hot as my insides, he simply tore it from my body.

Fully naked and overcome with passion, I writhed under his ministrations.

As his fingers pirouetted over my stomach, my body quaked. When his tongue slid over my hip, along my thigh, and, without warning, pressed into my heat, I cried out. I gasped as the want racing through me flashed to a peak. But before I could take the final plunge over the edge, he pulled back, chin resting on my thigh. I hissed in displeasure, and his deep laugh filled the room, vibrating through me.

"Open your eyes, Maisey. Open your eyes, and tell me this is what you want—me taking you with my mouth before I take you with my body."

I obeyed, my eyes settling on the lava burning in his.

"Say it, darlin'."

"I want you. Inside me, over me, consuming me."

"Then don't you dare close those beautiful greens. Watch as I finally get to do what I've wanted to for an entire week—a fucking lifetime—and give you the best high of your life."

Then, he proceeded to do just that. My hand twisted in his hair, and I chanted his name at the crest, sighing his name as I went over the wall. The nip he placed on my tight bud as I started to come down sent me over again. I'd never experienced such intense pleasure as what rolled through every muscle, every nerve with him. It shook me from the inside out, leaving me breathless.

I'd barely filled my lungs before he'd shifted to take my mouth with his and proceeded to rip the air away again. I happily handed it over, easily prepared to give every ounce of oxygen I possessed if it meant feeling the flames he incited licking along my skin once more.

My nails trailed along his back, and my legs banded his waist.

"Take me over the edge again, Beckett. Take all of me so I can feel all of you." He pulled away instead of doing what I said, and I moaned. "Where are you going?"

He rolled off the bed. "Condom. Goddamn condom is somewhere in my bag."

I grabbed his wrist and yanked. The unexpected movement had him falling back onto the bed. He barely had time to stop himself from landing fully on me with a chuckle.

"I'm on birth control," I told him. "And I'm clean. Have you been tested?"

It took a moment for him to register what I was saying, what I was offering. But this was the man I was going to spend the rest of my life with. I didn't want even the thinnest layer between us. I didn't want anything between us ever again.

"I've been tested." His voice dropped another notch. "And I haven't been with anyone…not for months."

I wrapped my legs around his waist again, and the full weight of him settled on me, chests and hips and cores aligning. His stare bored into me. "You're sure?"

My hand found the hard length of him, shifting so it landed right at my entrance.

"Show me the pleasure I've been missing, Beckett."

He plunged, and I gasped. I was so very, very full. Not just in body, but in mind and heart and soul. The homecoming was real and true and lasting. It was why none of the other times with any other guy had felt right, because this was the only place I belonged. And those thoughts only spiked the desire quivering through me. The flame that needed to be quenched. My hips slammed into him, and instead of speeding up, instead of driving and thrusting, he stilled.

My eyes found his again.

"Damn it, darlin'," he cussed. "I'm not going fast. I'm taking my time. I'm going to savor every shift and slide and sip."

He'd said he wanted me to beg, and I did just that as he proceeded to drive me nearly mad. His fevered hands and talented mouth dragged out the impending wave inch by inch. My need spiked to new heights. My breathing grew ragged. Every vein was taut and ready to crest, and yet he still dangled and danced and parlayed.

When I grabbed his hips and tried to increase the pace of our thrusts, he snagged my wrists and held them above my head with a growl. "Not yet. Not yet."

"Beckett," I pled.

"Yes, baby?" he asked, his lips lifting smugly.

I moaned and writhed and dug my heels into his backside.

"I'm so close…so close…" I shook my head, tugging at my arms. His mouth sank to mine, tongue plunging as our bodies moved. Slow. Sensual. I needed fast and furious. I needed the release that made my vision blur.

"I think the word you're looking for is please."

The level of need inside me had never been this enormous. Never been so large it was its own entity, ready to tear through my body.

"Please. Please, Beckett. Please."

He let go of my hands, his pace picked up, and a determined glint shone in his eyes. My nails embedded themselves into his shoulders. He chanted words of encouragement as he took me higher and higher and higher. The pleasure dangled just there, just beyond the next thrust. I needed more. More of his weight, more of the pressure. Just more. I didn't know what it was until he nipped at my earlobe, his breath coasting over me as he whispered, "I love you."

And that was all it took. I was gone. Flying. Soaring. Thundering over the edge in a way that had me sobbing out an inarticulate sound that was half his name and half a returned statement of love. Shuddering and shivering with a satisfaction that turned my world upside down for several long heartbeats.

I was still shaking, still sailing, as his pace turned frantic, as Beckett finally let go of the control he'd been using and slammed into me. And finally, it was my turn to chant words of encouragement and whisper *I love yous* that had him bursting over the top and shouting my name as if it was a vow and a pledge and supplication all tied together.

It took several more long moments for the slow rocking of our bodies to finally stop.

For my vision to clear and the room to come back into focus.

For my smile to meet his. And again, I found love and adoration and awe waiting for me.

Found the home that had always been nearby but had finally, truly become mine.

Chapter Twenty-nine

Beckett

OUT GO THE LIGHTS
Performed by Lonestar

TWO AND A HALF YEARS AGO

HIM: The reception was nice, and Fallon seems happy. I'm glad.

> *HER: I can hear the doubt in your voice all the way here.*

HIM: Where is here?

> *HER: I'm in a hotel room at the ranch.*

HIM: Feel like hanging out? Or do you have company? Did one of Parker's teammates actually close the deal they were attempting to bring home all night?

> *HER: Ha. You're funny. No. I'm alone.*

HIM: You shouldn't be.

> *HER: According to you, I always choose the wrong guy, so I've decided to abstain until I find the right one.*

HIM: And none of the SEALs were it?

> *HER: SEALs have a reputation for one-night stands. I'm ready for a guy who knows I'm worth keeping.*

HIM: You're worth far more than just keeping, Maise. You're worth complete worship. Any guy

*lucky enough to catch you better be ready to bring
down the moon and stars and serve them to you on
a silver platter.*

PRESENT DAY

I wasn't sure I had a pulse anymore. For a brief moment, I was annoyed I hadn't been able to drag it out longer. That I hadn't taken her up and over the edge of release at least one more time before I'd let go. But the moment Maisey had erupted, the moment she'd gone limp, giving me not only her body but her mind and her soul, I'd lost any semblance of control that had remained. I'd been spellbound by the gift that was her.

How had I been so stupid as to have denied us this for so long?

I silently vowed that this, this feeling we had when joined together, would be my primary driving force for the rest of my life.

I'd do the job I'd been trained to do. I'd enjoy the job and give it my all, but it would never be more important than Maisey. Never more important than what we were when we were together.

I rolled to my side so I could hold her tighter without crushing her.

"I'll have to find you an appropriate medal," she laughed, placing a kiss on my chest. "You definitely delivered as advertised."

"You rushed me," I grunted out. "That wasn't award-deserving, darlin'."

"Rushed? That was hardly rushed." She shook her head, her face alight with happiness. And that look, full of satisfaction and love, made me hard all over again. Feeling it pressed against her stomach, her breath hitched in that way that only ignited me more.

"This time"—I rolled so I was on my back, and she was on

top—"we'll start here, and I will taste every single nip and corner of you. I will hear you chant my name at least two more times before we finish."

She sat up, straddling me, and I shifted so she couldn't take me in yet. My hands moved, squeezing, twisting, and soothing, and I watched with satisfaction as that blush covered every single inch of her perfect skin, and her pale eyes turned a dark forest green once more. She whimpered in pleasure.

"If you're successful in your mission, Fireball, I'll build a monument to you in town."

I picked her up and centered her core over my mouth. "Challenge accepted, my Maisey-girl. Challenge accepted."

And I spent the next few hours showing her just how successful I could be.

♫ ♫ ♫

An incessant buzzing jerked me awake. I wasn't on duty, but if an all-hands situation came across the wire, I'd be called in anyway. My heart sank at the idea of leaving the hotel room. Leaving her.

With Maisey spooned up against me, her back to my front, I had no desire to move. No desire to know what disaster had struck that required me to answer a call and leave the woman I'd just sworn I'd never be without again.

A second buzzing joined the first. Both our phones were vibrating from wherever we'd left them.

Shit.

I slowly unknotted my arms and legs from hers, rolling off the bed.

I searched the floor for my pants and the phone tucked in the pocket. I glanced back at her as I yanked it out. She'd sat up, and the spun silk of her hair spread around her face and chest. Her eyelids were heavy and sated. All I wanted to do was throw my phone away, crawl back onto the bed, and take her all over again.

"Is that my phone too?" she asked.

I nodded, glancing down at a string of text messages. What

I saw had ice hitting my veins.

The calls hadn't all been from dispatch at the firehouse. Most of them were from Fallon.

Maisey was halfway to me, naked and beautiful, when my gaze lifted from the phone to find hers.

She pressed a hand to her stomach in alarm. "What? What is it?"

I hated that I was going to be the one to not only burst the bubble of love and happiness we'd found but to send her into a spiral of worry and fear.

"It's your dad. He's missing."

She wobbled. I took one stride and caught her before she hit the floor. For two seconds, I made soothing noises, and then she was pushing away, out of my arms, and running to pull her phone from the clutch she'd tossed aside last night.

She'd already dialed as I scrambled into jeans and a T-shirt and began shoving all our items into the luggage.

"Fallon! What happened?" she demanded.

I handed her the first items of clothing I found as Fallon's voice, full of remorse, came back over the speaker. "I'm not sure, Maisey. Mom said when she went by her guest room this morning, the door was already open. She thought Lewis was in the kitchen, but he wasn't."

"He doesn't have a car with him. Where could he go?" Maisey's voice cracked, and my heart did right along with it. Her fear and anguish scored the tender pink muscle more than my own would have.

I rubbed my chest.

Maisey dumped her bathroom items into her luggage, and we were out the door in a frenzied rush as we listened to Fallon.

"Teddy went down to the resort right away, thinking maybe Lewis had gone to the barn. But no one there had seen him. Mom called us after that, and we mobilized the staff. Parker has called in search and rescue, and everyone is assembling at the castle now."

More of the messages on my phone were a slew of those alerts. SRFD wasn't the first call for search and rescue, but if the terrain was rough, or more bodies were needed, we were pulled in.

"You have him on your Find Family app, right?" Fallon asked.

"Yes. You're right. I didn't even think." Maisey swiped through the screens on her phone. "I don't understand. He's not there. His phone isn't showing."

Confusion bled in with her worry. My hand slid up her back, trying to comfort her, but she shrugged away from it as the elevator doors opened in the lobby.

"We're leaving," she told Fallon. "We're heading to the parking lot. But it'll take us an hour at least…" A sob escaped before she locked her emotions down. "We're on our way."

"I'm sorry, Maisey. I'm sorry to call you at all when I know last night was—" She cut herself off. "He might turn up before you even get here."

"I hope… God, I hope he does."

As they hung up, I handed off our room keys to the receptionist, and we ran for the revolving doors.

It was early yet, but the sun should have been out, baking the earth in the heat of summer. Instead, dark clouds greeted us. The pavement was wet, and the air was heavy with the scent of rain. A storm had blown in last night, and we hadn't even noticed. We'd been too lost in the storm of our own making.

As we sprinted toward my SUV, lightning cracked in the distance, and a few seconds later, thunder boomed. Maisey startled, and I longed to soothe her, but instead, I reached past her to open the passenger door, and she dove in.

I flung our bags in the back and raced around to the driver's side.

We were on the road, my foot heavy on the gas pedal, before she spoke again.

"He's out in the rain…"

"We'll find him, Maisey. I'm sure he just took a walk."

She scoffed. "Dad doesn't do nature willingly. That was all my mom. He only worked the farm at all to make her happy. And after she died, we'd needed the money, so he'd sold it all, but it was also because he couldn't imagine doing it without her."

My heart twisted for her and for Lewis. He'd lost the love of his life, and I now understood what that meant. I couldn't respond over the pain that just the idea shot through me.

Her voice was rough and raw when she said, "If his memory is playing tricks again, he'll be confused and disoriented by all the changes at the ranch."

The ball in my stomach felt weighted with all the unhappy possibilities. The cliffs and rivers and caves on the Harrington property were dangerous to someone not in their right mind. Hell, they could be dangerous to someone simply not paying full attention to their surroundings.

Add in the storm, and things could get messy quickly.

When we were only a few minutes away from Swift Rivers, Fallon called again with another update. The staff hadn't found him yet, but the canine unit Sheriff Wylee had requested had picked up a trail. It headed up into the hills instead of down to the ranch.

A horrible thought slithered through me as we drove through the steady downpour. Was this something worse than her dad having wandered off after another mental break? Was this whoever had been coming for Maisey, for us, coming for him?

My mouth went dry, remembering again the Sterno spread around Lewis's kitchen. Maybe the attacks really had started there rather than with the note on Maisey's truck. But I kept the idea to myself. Maisey didn't need me to add more worries to the ones she already carried.

By the time we pulled up to the barn beyond the castle, Maisey was wrung so tight I thought she might shatter at a mere touch. I'd barely put the car in park before she was out and running toward the barn.

"Maisey!" I called out to her, but she didn't stop.

I had to run flat-out to catch up with her. Usually, ranch hands and guests would have filled the space by this time of the morning, especially with the Fourth of July festivities looming tomorrow. Instead, the barn was eerily empty. The storm and the search had cleared it out.

Maisey opened a stall door as a crack of lightning filled the windows, turning the barn into a silver-toned mirage. The white light was immediately followed by another boom that shook the beams above us.

"What are you doing?" I demanded, grabbing her arm in an attempt to slow her down.

She jerked away and approached her horse, making soothing noises. Fallon may own Titan, but he'd always been Maisey's. Maisey trusted the animal in a way she didn't trust many humans. She had a bond with him from years of doing complicated tricks together, and that bond meant the American Paint easily picked up on her emotions, snorting and pounding a hoof.

"The fastest way to catch up to the canine crew is on horseback," she told me.

She was right, but I didn't want her going out in a lightning storm with rain pouring down. I especially didn't want her going without me, not with the doubts that had beat themselves into me on the drive still swarming in my brain.

She clicked at Titan and drew him out of the stall. Even though she was rushed, I knew she wouldn't skip the important steps to ensure her horse was safe, so I grabbed her saddle from the racks while she brushed Titan from the withers down and cleaned off the blanket. Once the saddle was on and she was cinching the girths, I worked him into the bridle. I'd barely secured it in place by the time she swung herself up.

I stepped in to check and cinch the strap myself and said, "Hold on while I saddle up Henry the Eighth."

She shook her head, kneeing her horse to get him moving. "You can catch up. You know where I'm going."

"Maisey," I warned, grabbing hold of the bridle and halting Titan. He snorted unhappily, shifting at the tension. "No. You aren't going by yourself."

"Let go. I'm not waiting," she said, and when I didn't step away, unshed tears swam. "It's already been over an hour since Fallon called us, Beckett. Nearly three hours since Lauren found his room empty. He's been out there… He might be hurt.

At the very least, confused and scared."

"And this might all be another attempt to strike at you by your attacker," I growled.

She paled and lifted a trembling hand to push back her wet hair. Just the race into the barn had soaked us both. Her blue T-shirt was already damp and clinging to her. She wasn't dressed to be out in the rain.

"We'll go. Together. But we need jackets. Hats. Flashlights," I told her. "I need a horse."

She inhaled sharply. "Fine, you go find us supplies. I'll saddle Henry."

I waited for her to slip down out of the saddle before I took off for the back door of the hotel. Someone on staff would have what we needed.

It took me longer than I'd wanted to gather the items, and when I made it back to the barn, my stomach plummeted. She'd saddled Henry the Eighth and looped his bridle over the hitching post, but there was no sign of Maisey or Titan.

I stuffed my arms into a jacket that was too small, jammed a baseball hat on my head, shoved the items I'd obtained for her in a saddle bag, and mounted the horse. As we headed out of the barn, I whipped out my phone and hit her number.

It rang once. Twice.

Fear grew.

Finally, she picked up. "Goddamn it, Maisey."

"Fallon called. The trail died at the fire road. They can't get a scent. It's like he just vanished. I couldn't wait any longer."

If Lewis's scent had disappeared, did it mean someone had picked him up? Had he gotten into a vehicle? The dirt fire road was well-maintained. As part of my job, I drove it regularly, ensuring the fire department had easy access to the property. There was a bar gate at the entrance—a loose attempt to keep out trespassers—but a host of emergency services and ranch employees had the code to unlock it. Worse, the gate was easy enough to drive around if you had a quad or dirt bike.

"You're on your way there?" I demanded.

"Yes."

"Once you get there, don't go anywhere else without me or Fallon or Parker."

"I gotta go. I'm coming up to the river."

She hung up, and I let out a storm of swear words that had Henry shifting uneasily.

The rain had slowed slightly, but it was still a steady drizzle, and she was out in it. No jacket. No hat. The wind had picked up, not the icy teens and twenties we got in the winter but still chilly. Still much colder than early July should have been.

The mountains were wreathed in low clouds as I spurred Henry across the field. Lightning struck the earth in a majestic display, sparking fears of fires, despite the rain. Henry shied at the sight and the thunderclap that followed it, but I steered him back toward the hills. The trees dripped, and rivulets of water raced toward the three rivers splitting the property.

The fields and slopes were slippery, which meant the cliffs rising above the pines and mist would be treacherous. I had to believe Maisey wouldn't go that far on her own. That she wouldn't leave the fire road without one of us with her, but I couldn't help the cold dread that lit my veins, knowing she'd do anything for her dad. For any of the people she loved. Hell, she'd be out here even if it were her shitty sister who was missing.

The safer route to the fire road was to head for the bridge crossing the northernmost river farther upstream, but Maisey hadn't done that. Hoof marks showed exactly where she'd led Titan across a shallow area in the river that preceded the drop to the lake. Henry and I picked our way across while impatience warred with safety.

The relentless need to get to her, to make sure she wasn't out there facing an unknown danger alone, drove me to urge the horse faster as we climbed onto the opposite bank. Fear hung on me heavier than the mist on the mountains. Something wasn't right. Something I couldn't name. I dug my heels into Henry's sides, sprinting with him up the slope to the road that wound into the mountains.

Relief loosened the knot in my chest as the fire road came into view, and I saw the blue-and-red swirling lights of a sheriff's truck along with a small crowd of horses and bodies.

Faces glanced my way as Henry's hooves thundered toward them. Vader saw me, barked, and came sprinting. Henry didn't react, even as my dog dashed around him in circles.

As I neared the gathering, my relief vanished. No Maisey.

I pulled on the reins, drawing Henry up between my father and Fallon. Water dripped from their horses, cowboy hats, and waterproof jackets.

"Where's Maisey?" Fallon and I asked at the same time.

Shock widened Fallon's eyes. My heart pounded against my ribcage. Fear. Irritation.

"Fuck. She said she was coming here." I twisted in the saddle, looking back the way I'd come. "I followed her path. The hoofprints were easy enough to spot…" I trailed off. Fuck, I hadn't followed any prints after crossing the river. Any marks Titan would have left had been lost in the thick piles of pine needles and leaves scattered along the forest floor on this side of the river.

When I said as much to both of them, Dad flicked the reins on the large roan he was riding. "I'll head back to the river, see what I can find."

I pulled my phone out, blocking it from the slow, steady rain as best I could while Fallon did the same. Maisey didn't pick up for either of us.

The wrongness of the entire day loomed over me larger than the storm. She was alone. Goddamn it, she was alone.

Vader's whines jerked my eyes to my dog. He was desperate for my attention and wound up from the tension in the air. Fighting the panic that tried to close my throat, I reached down from the saddle and distractedly rubbed his head.

"Hold on," Fallon said. "I can locate her using the Find Family app."

"You shared your locations." Some of the pressure that had clogged my lungs eased.

Why hadn't I demanded she share her location with me too?

I'd been too busy getting her a ring and declaring to the whole town I loved her to think of what she really needed—

protection.

"We shared them in college so we could find each other in case we went on a date and…" she trailed off. "What is she doing up at the fire tower?"

The old firewatch hadn't been used since the late 1990s. Initially built by the Civilian Conservation Corps in the early 1930s, the windmill-style lookout sat atop a cliff in a particularly rough area of Fallon's property, abandoned by the forestry service. I wasn't sure when anyone had last been up there, as the path was difficult—a thin line with the cliff on one side and large boulders on the other. It would be slick and wet in the storm, making any fall treacherous.

As alarm and fear morphed inside me to a breaking point, I tried to bat it back. Maisey had grown up playing on this land with Fallon. She knew her way around. Knew the dangers.

"Maybe her dad finally called her?" I said. "Maybe he somehow found his way up there?"

I doubted it myself, even as Fallon shook her head.

"No. After Maisey couldn't locate Lewis using the app, Mom went back to her house and found his phone. It was just sitting on the railing of the back porch, turned off."

"Does Maisey know?"

Fallon shook her head, scrubbing her thumb with her fingers. "I didn't want to worry her more than she already was."

I pulled the reins, starting Henry across the fire road and up the steep incline on the other side as Fallon called out behind me to wait. I didn't. I couldn't. The apprehension that had clung to me since we'd arrived on the ranch pushed me to move. To leave. To go find her, kiss her, and then yell at her for going off on her own.

Vader barked, running alongside Henry. "Find Maisey, bud," I told him. "Maisey."

He sniffed the air and took off up the slope toward the cliffs and the abandoned watch. Vader wasn't a trained tracker. He wasn't even trained as an official firehouse dog. He was more mascot than service animal, but he was going in the same direction Fallon had pinged on her phone, and that allowed a teeny bit of hope to leak in.

Fallon and Parker thundered up behind me, and all three horses shied as another bolt of light hit the ground not far from us, right as thunder rolled through the air. It took a moment to encourage the horses to move toward the storm instead of away.

"It's too steep and rocky to take the horses all the way," Fallon said. "We'll have to leave them at the base of the cliff."

We pushed our way through the trees. Branches slapped at us like wet knives. Cold and sharp.

By the time the old lookout peeked above the treeline, I was shivering as rain dripped down my back. All I could think was that Maisey was out there in a pair of yoga pants and a thin T-shirt. She'd at least had sneakers on her feet, but she'd be freezing by now.

As we entered a small clearing near the overgrown path leading up to the fire tower, Vader barked back at us from where he was circling Titan. Maisey's horse neighed a nervous greeting. She'd left him there, untied, because you didn't tether a horse in the forest. If they were attacked by a cougar or other wild animal, they needed the freedom to run.

"Maisey!" I shouted. The sound rebounded through the rain and clouds.

Fallon and Parker repeated my call.

Vader's nose hit the ground near Titan's hooves and then sprinted through the brush toward the rocky incline before I could stop him.

I slid down from the saddle and headed after my dog at a dead run.

Chapter Thirty
Maisey

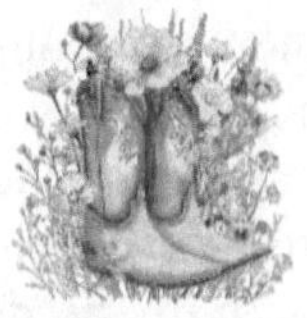

LET YOUR TEARS FALL
Performed by Kelly Clarkson

ELEVEN YEARS AGO

> *HER: I don't know how to thank your dad for helping me sort through all the bills.*

HIM: He was happy to help. But he was also frustrated your dad hadn't taken care of it himself.

> *HER: Sometimes, I'm not sure it even occurs to Dad there are bills to pay.*

HIM: It's not like he married your mom right out of high school. He was an adult with bills to pay long before he met her.

> *HER: But he's so…lost right now, Beckett.*

HIM: And you're not? You're fucking fifteen. And why isn't Chelsea helping? She's going to be moving out next year when she goes to school. She should be more prepared than you to handle this shit.

> *HER: You're more upset than I am.*

HIM: Someone needs to be upset on your behalf.

> *HER: It won't change anything. It'll only give you heartburn. Believe me. I know.*

PRESENT DAY

I shivered in the relentless rain. The downpour wasn't pelting me like daggers any longer, but it was still a steady stream. What had happened to summer? The heavy humidity that had been in the air for over a week had finally and truly broken, leaving behind a raging thunderstorm. It didn't have the iciness of our winter storms, but it was still cool—biting, even—as it whipped through my drenched clothing.

Lightning cracked, landing just above me on the mountaintop and causing me to nearly jump out of my skin.

This was stupid.

I had no weapon. No protection.

Beckett would be furious.

But the text had been very clear—*come alone to the old fire tower, retrieve your father, and then leave town for good.*

Another tremor ran up my spine, not only because of the wet and cold but because someone hated me this much. Wanted me gone so badly they'd risk my father's life. Risk mine.

I moved slowly through the trees, using the trunks as cover as I strained to see through the clouds drifting low over the path that led up to the abandoned lookout. Was the person who'd done this there? Waiting for me? The tower hadn't been used since before I'd been born. Aerial cameras and drones had long since replaced the human watch. For as long as I could remember, it had seemed like nothing more than an abandoned lighthouse sitting amongst the forest.

As kids, Fallon and I had ventured up to it once or twice, but like the caves where bandits had lived in the eighteen hundreds, the danger of it had kept us from risking it often. We'd gone just enough to satisfy childhood curiosities.

My phone vibrated once again. The slew of texts that had come in from Beckett and Fallon made my chest ache. They'd be angry I'd come on my own. But I couldn't risk Dad's life by not following the orders given to me. And hopefully, Fallon would remember she could find me on the Find Family app. Hopefully, they'd bring help while I still did what this unknown enemy wanted and came by myself.

The new text that buzzed wasn't from either of the people who loved me.

It was from the same person my phone had labeled "Spam Risk." Something tickled at the back of my mind about the number. It was familiar somehow, but I couldn't quite put it together. Certainly not while worried about my dad, and how he'd gotten up here, and wondering how I was going to face this person without winding up dead.

UNKNOWN CALLER: There's a chance he can be saved. If you take too long, it'll be on you, not me.

My stomach rolled, terror and grief blending. I didn't want to lose my dad, and I certainly wouldn't be able to live with myself if I were the reason he died.

I searched the ground for a weapon. A sharp rock. A heavy branch. Anything.

I finally found a limb that had recently cracked and fallen to the forest floor. Heavy with the scent of sap and pine, its flesh was still bright and white, but the edge was sharp. Not nearly sharp enough to penetrate skin, but it might hurt, and it was at least something I could swing. Something that would keep me at an arm's length from an attacker.

The path was even narrower than I remembered. Water ran in a tiny stream along it. I accidentally kicked a loose pebble, and it shot over the ledge, bouncing down the abyss to the canyon below. I swallowed hard and pressed myself against the boulders on the other side. If I remembered, the path emerged right at the base of the watchtower, and I'd be exposed to whoever was waiting there.

My stomach rolled once more. This really was stupid. Stupid to come alone.

Then I thought of Fallon. Three years ago, she'd been kidnapped and hidden in the caves on the ranch, but she'd found a way to fight back, and it gave Parker and his team time to find her. I could do the same thing. I could fight for my dad and myself while giving the people searching for us time to catch up.

I slid my phone into the wet pocket of my yoga pants, gripped the stick with both hands, and moved as fast as I dared around the last bend. The watchtower came into full view. The base, made out of axe-carved planks and rough-hewn stones, was surrounded by an eerie mist. A rickety wooden staircase jutted out of the clouds, leading up the back to the one-room cabin at the top. The stairs were usually chained off with a warning sign, but now, it dangled loose, bouncing in the wind.

As far as I could see, no one was waiting for me. I called quietly for my father but received no answer.

My heart raced, and my palms were damp from the strange mingling of sweat and rain. My blood pounded in my ears, making it hard to hear anything as I made my way toward the stairs.

I kept my back to the building much as I'd done with the boulders, picking my way up the rotted treads. The cabin had originally been painted a vibrant white, but the planks were now a mutilated combination of gray, black, and decay. The glass that had once provided an unobstructed, 360-degree view of the valley below had long since been broken and boarded up, making it impossible to see inside the single room. Impossible to see what waited for me in the dark.

The door swung open, creaking in the wind. The creepiness of the deserted tower crawled through me, sending chills and a warning I couldn't heed. Not if I was going to get to Dad. I eased onto the wooden walk surrounding the cabin and pushed open the door with a shaky hand before sliding into the interior and slamming my back into the wall. I blinked furiously, forcing my eyes to adjust to the shadowed interior.

No one came at me. Nothing moved. No sound of rustling clothes or pounding feet.

Maybe they didn't know I'd arrived? Should I risk my phone light? Risk calling for my father?

My mouth was so dry I could barely croak out, "Dad?"

My voice echoed in the silence. Raw and scratchy. Quivering with fear.

The air outside sparked with electricity as a bolt of lightning lit up the sky right outside the watch—white and hot. Thunder followed, so loud and strong the building trembled and moaned as if the entire decomposing frame might crumble down with us inside it.

Panic joined the terror thrumming through my veins.

I had to find Dad and get us both out of here.

Reluctantly, I let go of the branch with one hand so I could pull my phone out and turn on the flashlight. I fumbled with it before shining it into the darkened room. I swung the single beam around, taking in a pile of broken furniture that stood in the middle like a pyre waiting to be lit, before my eyes landed on a shadowy shape on the floor. A body. A crumpled heap of flesh and bone.

I ran, quietly shouting his name. The knot in my chest grew. My throat closed. He was there. Dirty and wet and with his eyes closed. But he was there. I dropped the stick and placed the phone closer to his face. He was so pale.

"Dad! Dad! It's Maisey," I said as I rolled him onto his back. The white flicker of the flashlight app turned him into a ghost. My heart thundered as I felt for a pulse, letting out a garbled noise of pain and denial when I couldn't feel one at first. But then I saw his chest rise, ever so slightly, and I pressed my fingers harder. Tears threatened when I finally found a weak and thready beat. It was dangerously slow, but he was alive.

"Took you long enough."

The words had me leaping to my feet and whirling toward the sound, straining to see whoever had spoken from the far side of the room. Laughter filled the air, but it was mechanical. Hollow. Some kind of device was modifying their voice, making it robotic. Harsh and evil. More so than if I'd been able to recognize it.

My entire body shook, and my breath came out in choppy gasps as I strained to see through the shadows. With the pile of furniture blocking my view, it was nearly impossible to catch a glimpse of them.

"Who are you? Why are you doing this to us?" I demanded as I slowly bent to pick up the stick I'd dropped and then eased around the pyre.

"Is that a stick? Really? That's pretty pathetic."

Anger bloomed and had me doing another stupid thing in a long list of them I'd done recently as I stepped closer to the voice instead of away.

"How do you feel, Maisey? Knowing you were too late to save him?"

I bit back my instant retort that Dad wasn't dead. That they hadn't succeeded in killing him. Because maybe it was smarter to let them think they'd won. Maybe they'd back off then.

I hadn't picked up my phone from the floor, and the light grew dimmer as I moved farther into the depths. The gross laughter filled the air again. Even mechanical and false, it sounded spiteful. They were rejoicing in my fear and anguish.

I strained my eyes, trying to find the attacker, and found a phone instead. It was propped up on the old window ledge, facing the door and my father's body. As I approached, my distorted image filled the screen, a strange black-and-green shape like the ones you saw on the ghost shows when they filmed at night.

I stalked over and picked the phone up, voice quivering with anger as I said, "I will find out who you are."

A cackle emerged. "I highly doubt it. But even if you do, I'll just take care of you the same way I took care of him. Now, be the good girl you've always been, and do what you're told. Leave town. Forget everything about Swift Rivers and your friends and family. Don't ever come back, and you'll keep them all safe. Otherwise, who knows who might be next? Maybe Beckett? Or Fallon? How about that cute little girl of hers? How about if I start another fire, this time burning this entire, rich-as-hell ranch to the ground?"

I couldn't help the pained gasp that escaped.

The evil laughter returned. "Your choice… Make the right one this time."

The image went blank as the person hung up.

I wanted to cry. Wanted to grab the phone and toss it to the floor and break it into pieces.

But I wouldn't mess with the evidence. I'd already done too much simply by touching it.

More importantly, Dad needed me.

I tossed the phone back where I'd found it and rushed back to my father. I searched for any visible injuries and found none. No blood or marks appeared on his face or neck. His hands and arms had scratches, as if he'd been dragged along the ground, but there was nothing else.

I inhaled sharply, fighting the tears. I had to get him out of here. I picked up my phone, swiping for 9-1-1 just as I heard a bark followed by someone shouting my name.

Beckett!

Relief had my legs quivering.

"Up here! We're up here! He needs an ambulance!" My throat screamed as I raised my voice, hoping he'd hear.

Vader found me first, barking and whining as I tried to keep him away from my father, but Beckett was right behind him. He stormed in, the flashlight in his hand twisting the light and bouncing it around eerily.

"Fuck! She's here!" he called out.

He fell to his knees at my side and wrapped his arms around me. He held me so tight my breath, which was already coming in strange pants, almost disappeared. Vader tried to squeeze between us, and when he couldn't, he licked both of our faces.

"I'm okay," I said, but my voice shook. "It's Dad."

I pushed away from Beckett just as Fallon and Parker sprinted through the door.

"He's breathing," I said, trying desperately to keep my voice calm, to give the assessment as if I were in the emergency room and the patient wasn't someone I loved. "He's got a pulse, but it's slow and erratic. I can't see any injury. It's too dark."

Three flashlights slanted over my father.

"Goddamnit, Maisey," Beckett cursed. "That could be you!"

I threw him a look. "Be mad at me later. Right now, I need you to call for help. Whoever this is, they think they killed him. They think he's dead, but he's not—" My voice cracked on the last words, and I fought the tears that flooded.

"Where are they?" Beckett leaped to his feet just as Parker

whipped around to scan the detritus and refuse for the unseen enemy.

"He's not here!" I told them. "But there's a phone. None of that matters! Dad needs help! Now!"

Fallon made the call to Sheriff Wylee while the two men tore through the room, searching for clues, and I stayed by my father's side, my pulse thundering with fear. Not being able to properly examine him sent my panic spiraling higher. There were no visible injuries, at least nothing I could point to, so what had they done to him? Had they poisoned him? Was something vile coursing through his veins, stealing him from me one slow heartbeat at a time? Would he be gone before I could do anything to stop it? Our attacker had already assumed he was dead, so how much longer before that became true?

I caught a sob before it escaped. Crying wouldn't help Dad. I needed my wits about me. Vader whined again, pushing his body into mine, and I tried to soothe us both by rubbing a hand over his fur.

While Fallon talked with Sheriff Wylee, Parker and Beckett returned from their scan of the room. Parker held the attacker's phone in the sleeve of his jacket.

"We need to get Dad out of here," I said. "Now."

"Is it safe to move him?" Parker asked, handing the horrible phone with its robotic voice off to Fallon and crouching down next to us.

"I don't know. I don't know." I shook my head. "I can't find any injury, but that doesn't mean there isn't a break I can't see."

"Wylee can't get a helicopter here in the thunderstorm," Fallon said as she hung up. "We'll have to get him down to where the rescue ATVs can reach us."

"We can use the old bed frame," Beckett suggested.

He and Parker began pulling items from the stack of debris. A twin, metal bed frame and wooden planks became a makeshift stretcher we tied Dad to using the men's jackets. As Beckett and Parker lifted it, Dad's head lolled to the side, and my stomach lurched.

I reached for his neck, felt the barely-there pulse, and tried to swallow around the lump in my throat. "Stay with me, Dad. Please stay with me."

Fallon led the way outside, picking her way down the stairs that creaked and groaned. Beckett's foot broke through rotted wood, and we all held our breath while he pulled it back up. It was slow going, but we finally made it down. I stopped them at the base of the staircase, searching Dad in the better light for injuries. When I peeled open his eyelids, the way his pupils remained pinpoints, unchanging even in the light, made me want to cry.

The rain had slowed, and the clouds that had circled the tower when I'd gone inside were lifting, but it was still a long, arduous journey along the cliff down to the bottom of the watchtower's path. The horses waited for us, huddled together against the wet weather.

The hum of motors had us all turning to watch as two ATVs zipped through the trees toward us. The first quad had barely stopped before I was reaching into their emergency medical kit. Finding a syringe of naloxone, I ran back to Dad and plunged the needle into his thigh, delivering a dose, and hoping beyond hope it would help. Hoping whatever drug he'd been injected with was one of the many naloxone could combat.

Dad didn't wake. His eyelids didn't even flicker, but he was still breathing.

Keep breathing. Please, Dad. Keep breathing.

With the search-and-rescue team's help, Parker and Beckett transferred Dad from our makeshift stretcher into the Stokes basket and strapped him in. Then, I climbed up into the space behind it, where I could monitor his condition.

I glanced up to find Beckett watching me. His relief and anger and remorse were easy to read. They were the same emotions I was battling. Guilt so strong it felt like I was drowning. Dad had almost died…because of me. He still might not make it due to whatever had been given to him.

"I'll be right behind you," Beckett said.

I nodded and gripped the roll cage with a hand that shook as the ATV took off. I reached for Dad's hand with my free one and held it all the way back to the ranch, where the ambulance waited for us.

Sheriff Wylee met me at the back doors as Bugsy and the search-and-rescue guys loaded my dad inside, and I updated her on his status and the naloxone I'd delivered.

"They think he's dead," I told Wylee, choking on the words and rush of emotions that came with it. "Whoever this is, they think they killed him."

Wylee's lips flattened in anger. Over seventy years old, the large, white-haired, light-skinned man had always prided himself on keeping our community safe and didn't take it lightly when evil touched down in Rivers.

"If they believe he's gone, we may be able to use that to our advantage," he told me. "We'll keep Lewis secluded at the hospital for now."

The idea of actually losing my father, especially this way, to violence, had the world spinning around me. There was a good chance I'd been too late with the naloxone, or it might not have been enough, or permanent damage could already have been done to his body. And if I hadn't been fast enough to save Dad, that robotic voice mocking me would haunt me for the rest of my life.

Wylee squeezed my shoulder. "Don't worry about it now. Just concentrate on Lewis. I'll figure the rest out with my team." He looked over to where Josh was getting into his sheriff's vehicle. "Cleaver is following the ambulance, and he'll stay with both of you until I can work out a security plan."

Unable to find my voice, I simply nodded and climbed into the back of the ambulance to sit next to my father. Typically, they didn't let a civilian in the back, but I wasn't a civilian. I was a nurse, who Bugsy had seen in action many times in the emergency room. I wouldn't get in her way.

The door shut, the sirens came alive, and the vehicle took off.

I pulled my father's hand into mine again as Bugsy administered a second round of naloxone via a spray to his nostrils. He didn't wake, but he was still breathing. In an attempt to stop the tears that threatened, I bit my cheek so hard

I tasted blood.

Questions and doubts flooded me. About our attacker. About the promise I'd made so they'd give me Dad's location. I'd promised to leave Swift Rivers. I'd promised to vanish and never look back.

I'd promised to leave Beckett.

And just the idea of that tore through me almost as much as the idea of Dad dying. Because if I left Beckett, if I abandoned him like his mother and Liza had, it might not end his life, but it would kill his soul.

I'd be responsible for two deaths instead of one.

Chapter Thirty-one
Beckett

SOFTLY
Performed by Lonestar

ELEVEN YEARS AGO

HIM: Thought you were coming over?

Minutes later.

HIM: Maise?

Minutes later.

HIM: I'm giving you two more minutes, and then I'm coming to find you.

  HER: Sorry. I can't come. I had two escaped chickens to deal with, and the Helmers' dog thought it would be fun to chase them down to the creek. I'm a muddy mess, and once I clean up, I can't leave Mom alone.

HIM: Chelsea was supposed to be there tonight. She promised.

  HER: Randy called, so she went scurrying over to his place.

HIM: Cleaver's brother? Isn't he, like, twenty-two or something?

  HER: I think. Does it matter?

HIM: She's underage.

  HER: Chelsea knows what she's doing and what she wants. Believe me.

HIM: So you're alone. Again. I'm on my way.

PRESENT DAY

The whole time I was making my way back to the barn with Parker, Fallon, and the horses, my anger steadily grew. It only continued to morph as I drove my SUV through the windy back roads to town. It wasn't only directed at the asshole responsible for hurting Maisey's dad. It was at Maisey herself. For not trusting me. For trying to handle this on her own. For putting herself in danger and falling right into the attacker's plans.

I didn't know what had led her to the watchtower and her father, but it must have been whoever was doing this telling her how to find him. By doing so, she'd played right into their hands. They could have been there, waiting to hurt her as well as her dad.

She could have died.

It could have been her lying on that stretcher.

My heart didn't just ache…it bled.

When I pulled into the drive of my house, Sweeney stepped onto the porch.

"Once I heard you found Lewis, I came back here to check on things. The house is clear," he said.

"Thanks," I responded, but I couldn't keep my fury out of my voice. "I'm just here to drop Vader off, change, and grab some dry clothes for Maisey."

He nodded but didn't say anything else as I stormed into my house with my rage barely in check. By the time I threw off my drenched clothes, pulled on new ones, and found some things for Maisey, I'd only grown more aggravated. At myself. At her. At the entire screwed-up situation.

But mostly at whoever had done this.

As I came out of the guest room with a duffel over my shoulder, Sweeney stopped me. "You go to the hospital all half-cocked and ready to fight, you're not going to help our little

Maisey."

Jealousy roared. She wasn't his little anything.

I was being ridiculous.

And damn him, he was right.

I dragged a hand over my face. My distressed dog whined, pressing his body into mine, sensing my fury and fear. I didn't know how to calm down.

"Okay to leave him here with you?" I asked, bending low to give my dog the first whole-body rub he'd received since I'd shown up at the ranch.

"We'll be fine here," Sweeney said. His hand landed on my shoulder. "She will be too. We're all on this now, which means the snake won't be able to stay hidden forever. Not with all of us hunting him."

He was right, but what else would happen before his identity was uncovered?

I rubbed my dog again and said gruffly, "I'll be back soon, and I'm bringing our girl with me. We'll pick up the stupid cat, and we'll all be together again. Soon, bud. Soon."

Then, I headed out the door. I'd promised myself I wouldn't let Maisey be hurt again, but the asshole had struck at her through her dad and sliced home anyway. Worse, she'd faced it all alone.

She hadn't had to do any of it by herself. She could have trusted me to be at her side. But Maisey never wanted to put others out. She was more than willing to help everyone and anyone but hated to be on the receiving end. But this time was different. In trying to face this alone, she could have been killed.

Damn. My heart couldn't take this. Couldn't take the thought of not having her in my life.

But when I reached the hospital and saw her—despair carved into her face, pacing a deserted corner of the ICU, soaked to the bone and shivering under the sterile blast of the air-conditioning—my anger burned itself out in an instant. She was hurting. Scared. Fucking freezing.

She faced the room where the doctors fought for her father's life, so she didn't see me coming down the hall. But

Cleaver did. He just stood there, a useless sentry with a frown dug between his brows, doing nothing. Nothing to ease her panic. Nothing to stop her from trembling in those rain-drenched clothes. And my rage found a new home—this time at him.

"Maisey!" She turned, and the tortured grief on her face sliced through me more. In two long strides, I dropped the duffel and wrapped her in my arms. She buried her face in my chest and broke. Sobs shuddered through her, wracking her body. A body that was as cold as ice.

I glared at Cleaver over the top of her head. "You're freezing. You need to change."

"I can't leave. I need to know as soon as they walk out what's going on," she said as her teeth chattered.

"If you get sick, you won't be any good to him," I shot back. "I brought you some clothes."

I grabbed her hand as I picked up the duffel and then hauled her, protesting, down the hall to the nearest restroom. After dragging her into the single-stalled room, I blocked the door, unzipped the bag, and pulled out clothes.

"Take those off, or I'll do it for you," I demanded. Relief flooded me when anger sparked in her expression instead of the tortured grief I'd seen.

She did what I'd ordered, toeing out of the soaked sneakers, ripping off the drenched tee and yoga pants, and letting them drop with a wet slap to the linoleum. She stood there, completely naked but gut-wrenchingly beautiful and full of fiery emotions.

She fisted her hands at her waist and scowled. "Better?"

"Not even close," I growled.

Stepping toward her, I pulled a sweatshirt over her head. It was an SRFD one I'd grabbed from my go-bag at the last moment. The hem hung down around her thighs, and I found myself inappropriately turned on by the sight of her.

The memories of what she'd tasted like and sounded like and felt like when we'd been wrapped around each other last night flooded me.

Angry with myself now, I reached into the bag for the underwear and jeans I'd grabbed from her room. She yanked them on. "I don't have time for your overprotective bullshit, Beckett. So save it. I need to get back to my dad."

"Standing outside the hospital door isn't going to change whatever is going on beyond it," I snapped. "Tell me what the hell happened and why you went up there on your own!"

She crossed her arms over her chest and looked down at her toenails that were painted the same color as the dress she'd worn to the ball.

When she didn't respond, my heart cracked open a little more.

"Tell me what happened. Why are you shutting me out?" It was a quiet plea, one she didn't heed.

After several long seconds, when she still wouldn't look at me, a different fear wound through me. I hadn't lost her physically. She was there in front of me—stunning and brave and so fucking stubborn—but something had happened to cause her to retreat emotionally.

She trembled. She wasn't in the wet clothes anymore, but she still had to be cold, her bare feet icy. I crouched in front of her, tugged one foot onto my knee, causing her to catch her balance by placing a hand on my shoulder. I rubbed her toes, trying to bring some warmth to them, before dragging a sock on. I repeated the process with the other foot before I risked looking up at her.

Her fury had disappeared once more, and in its wake, the grief had returned. A sadness so deep I could almost taste it in the air. I'd seen this look on her before, after her mom had died, when I'd found her, holding her dead mother's hand in her parents' bedroom.

I'd been there for her back then, just as Fallon had, but I'd pulled away a bit after that. I hadn't liked or wanted the feelings she'd raised in me. I knew now it had been one of the many mistakes I'd made with Maisey over the years, and I wouldn't ever repeat them. I wasn't going to step back and let dead space take up room between us ever again.

I snagged her hand, brought it to my mouth, and kissed the

palm. "Don't disappear on me, my Maisey-girl. I'm here. I won't let you down. I swear on everything I hold holy, I won't let you down. Trust me to help you through this."

The tears came again—slow trails down her cheeks.

"They want me to leave." She said it so quietly I almost couldn't hear the words.

"Who? What do you mean?" I asked, standing up and watching every emotion as it flitted across her face. Grief. Fear. Remorse. Resignation.

She finally shook her head, looking down and away before shoving her feet into the slip-on sneakers I'd brought for her. "The person who did this to Dad. They made me promise to leave Swift Rivers. To leave and never come back. It was the only way I could get them to tell me where Dad was."

"Screw that." Even to my own ears, my voice sounded threatening. Dark.

Wide eyes met mine as she brushed at the tears still littering her cheeks. Her voice broke as she tried to explain, tried to justify leaving. "They said they'd hurt everyone I love. You. Fallon. Lila. They said they'd start another fire and burn down the ranch if I didn't go. All I have to do is leave, and everyone is safe."

Surprise winged through me. Surprise and hurt and rage.

She was trying to leave.

Like my mom. Like Liza. I'd given her my heart, because I'd sworn she'd never do what they had, she'd never slice me open and leave me bleeding the way they'd done to my father. To me—

No. I cut off all my thoughts.

I wasn't letting her go. I wasn't letting the cycle of abandonment repeat.

More, I wasn't letting her give in to some fucker who thought he could manipulate her into getting what he wanted.

I reached for her, and she stepped back.

"I won't risk everyone's lives, Beckett. I can't!"

"You're not leaving, Maisey. I. Won't. Let. You."

"So, everyone just dies so I can stay?"

I shook my head, brushing aside the fear that still remained at the idea of losing her, even as another idea took hold—one that gave me a sense of hope. "No one is dying. No one is leaving. The truth is, they screwed themselves over by demanding it."

Her brows furrowed. "What do you mean?"

"All we have to do is figure out who benefits from you leaving, and we'll know who this is. They tipped their hand." I reached out and hooked her pinky with mine. My chest loosened another hair when she didn't pull away this time. "Were those their exact words?"

She frowned. "Which ones?"

"*Another* fire?"

Realization dawned. "Yes."

"So, the fire at your dad's house was them. That happened before I heard about the chief retiring and we told folks we were engaged. This gives us even more information. This is someone who would benefit from you being gone and the house burning down."

She met my gaze, both of us thinking about how Carter had been pushing us to sell. The story unfolding was an old one—if the owners wouldn't sell, you threatened them, burned them out, or found another way to get them to leave.

Before we could talk about it further, a loud knock on the bathroom door was preceded by Cleaver's voice. "Maisey, the doctor wants to talk to you."

More doubts pummeled me. Cleaver hadn't made any progress on any of the notes and attacks. Was it on purpose? Carter was his cousin—their mothers were sisters. Were they working this together? I didn't want to believe it. Cleaver had all but threatened my life at the idea of me even hurting Maisey. But had it been an act?

She took a step toward the door, and I stopped her. "We're in this together, Maisey. Together. You and me. You're wearing my ring. You promised me forever. I'm holding you to it."

She didn't respond, and fear spiked its ugly head, but I did my best to force it down and away.

Opening the door, Cleaver's face was grim, and Maisey panicked, thinking the worst. "Dad!"

Cleaver shook his head. "No. They stabilized him for now."

Maisey broke away from me and rushed down the hall.

In her absence, Cleaver and I stared daggers at each other. I was the one to break the silence. "You've done a shit-poor job at finding out who's doing this."

Cleaver's jaw tightened. "I've been working my ass off to follow the leads. The problem is, we just don't have enough of them."

"Well, good for you, then, because this has given you a bunch more to follow."

And then I shared everything Maisey had just told me with him.

"Carter wants our land. He's been pressuring Lewis and me to sell. I didn't really think of it before because this person has been targeting Maisey and not her dad or me."

Cleaver's face darkened, and that eased my doubts about him, but only by a hair.

"I'll get the phone records for Lewis's phone and hers. Plus, the phone they left in the tower will lead us back to them as well."

"Parker has a pal on the SEALs who has a way with tech. If you don't have the resources or your team doesn't have the skill, I'm sure we could get his help."

Cleaver bristled. "We know what we're doing."

"You may *know* what you're doing, but will you follow through?" I demanded.

"What are you trying to say, Romero? Just spit it out."

"If this is Carter, your cousin and friend, will you still put the cuffs on him?"

"You think I'm working with him? Screw you. If he committed these crimes, he'll do the time."

I spun around and started down the hall after Maisey, tossing back over my shoulder, "Forgive me if I withhold judgment until you actually do something to stop this asshole."

When I joined Maisey in the hospital room, it was to find Wylee with her. The doctor was giving them a rundown on the blood work. Lewis had been given heroin laced with fentanyl—a deadly combination in a lethal amount. The doctors had placed him on a ventilator because his breathing hadn't returned fully, and he hadn't woken up.

"No one can know he's made it through," Wylee said sternly.

"There's a good chance he still won't make it," the doctor responded and then grimaced as she met Maisey's stricken face. "You gave him the naloxone as fast as you could, Maisey. We can hope he regains awareness and starts breathing fully on his own. We can hope the side effects will be minimal, but with what his mind has already been through in the last month, it'll be touch and go."

Desperate to somehow comfort her, I pulled Maisey up against my chest and wrapped my arms around her. If nothing else, I could make sure she felt loved and protected for the moment.

"We need to register him under a fake name and change rooms. I'd really like to move him over to the county hospital, if you think he's stable enough," Wylee told the doctor. "Call Bob with hospital security. Get him down here so we can discuss it."

The doctor and the sheriff stepped out of the room, and Maisey pushed away from me to take a seat at her father's bedside. She pulled his hand to hers, kissed the palm, and then held it tight.

I sat across from her, where I could see the door and the nurses' station outside. I watched as Cleaver and Wylee talked with the doctor, and a man in a suit joined them. Eventually, another deputy arrived, carrying several evidence bags.

The sheriff grabbed one and stalked back into the room. "Maisey, you don't happen to know your dad's passcode, do you?"

She reached for the bag and typed the code in through the plastic. As the sheriff was adding the code to his notes, Maisey brought up her dad's messages and then stilled.

Her voice, already raw with emotions, trembled when she said, "There's a text from…me…asking him to meet me on the back porch of Lauren's place. It's not my number, but it's labeled as Maisey in his contacts. How is that possible?" She was pale as she continued to scroll through the messages. "Yesterday. Someone texted him and said it was me. That I'd gotten a new phone as a security measure."

Sheriff Wylee leaned over and gently took the phone away. "Don't feel guilty, sweetheart. None of this is on you, but it might lead us back to the bastard. The phone number will lead somewhere. Even if it's a burner phone, we can trace it to the store where it was bought. They'll have security cameras. People forget it's almost impossible not to leave some kind of digital trail these days."

Silence descended, making the sounds from the ventilator scream.

"We need to look at your phone and trace the calls you received as well," the sheriff said.

Maisey's gaze met mine, and for a moment, panic flitted over her face. "You'll read my messages?"

Wylee's brows drew together. "We'll keep it to the ones from the unknown number Beckett told Cleaver about, but I want to have the phone checked for tracking software and cloning apps."

Maisey's cheeks turned pink, and I realized what she was worried about. It brought the first spark of amusement I'd felt in hours. "Darlin', don't worry. I'm sure Wylee here has sent similar messages to his wife."

My comment didn't help. Maisey flushed even more. The color spread down her neck, and I knew exactly what it would look like all over her body now. I'd watched the delightful red coat every inch when I'd whispered words of encouragement to her last night before she'd come apart under me and over me repeatedly.

The sheriff finally caught on to what the issue was and hid a smile behind his hand. "Ah. Yes. Well. No need for us to look at those. We'll concentrate on the texts you got today and use a keyword search for anything else we think is relevant. We'll do our best to maintain your privacy while also ensuring the phone is safe for you to use. I'll try to have it back to you by the end of the day, tomorrow morning at the latest."

Maisey's throat bobbed again before her shoulders went back, and she dragged her phone out of the pocket of her jeans. "Whatever it takes."

Wylee combined hers with her dad's phone and then said gently, "Now comes the hardest part, sweetheart. I need you to leave the hospital."

"What? No!" She shook her head vehemently, grasping her dad's hand. "He needs to hear my voice. He needs to know I'm here waiting for him, so he'll fight harder."

The sheriff patted her shoulder and then squeezed. "If we want the bastard to believe they won this round, they need to think your dad is gone. You wouldn't stick around if that were the case."

Sadness rippled across her face. "You're right." She rubbed her eyes, the glassy look in them worse than it had been before. She glanced from me to the sheriff. "I should leave town too, right? Like they asked? To protect everyone?"

"No," I insisted.

She ignored me. "It's not just me. If I stay, it puts Beckett and Fallon and Lila at risk too. The entire ranch. Think of all the people staying there right now and all the people from our community who will be there tomorrow for the Fourth. It's stupid to endanger everyone when I can easily do what they want and leave."

I made some inarticulate noise of objection, and her face softened. "Just until the sheriff catches whomever this is, Beckett. You know this is the smart play."

"You're not leaving. I'm not letting you out of my sight, Maisey. Not for one damn minute with some whack-job out there targeting you," I growled.

Wylee dragged a hand over his white beard. "Let's all take a breath. Truth is, we might get more out of whomever this is if you stay, Maisey. They'll be pissed if you don't follow through, but it also puts you at greater risk."

Maisey pressed a hand to her stomach. "I won't be responsible for someone else I love getting hurt…or worse."

"We can count on Steele to protect his wife, family, and the ranch," the sheriff said. "He's done a mighty good job of it in the past. Once he knows about this threat, he'll increase the security there, even more than he normally does for the holiday. Anything suspicious will raise a flag with his team and mine. And when you don't leave, the bastard will reach out to you again, and we can trace the calls or texts in real time."

Every fiber of my being hated the idea of her staying and being bait for a killer as much as it did the idea of her leaving. But I wouldn't let her out of my sight, and we had a retired Navy SEAL at my house, with even more SEALs at her father's place, where Parker had placed them.

As long as Maisey didn't run off again, we could protect her.

Uncertain, she stood, kissed her father on the forehead, whispered something in his ear, and then squeezed his hand. I met her at the foot of the bed and tucked her close to me once again. At the door, she looked back, and tears pooled once more.

"It hurts to leave him." Pain rippled through the words.

"I know, Maise. I know."

As we left the room, Cleaver stepped in beside us, and Wylee said, "Steele told me about his teammates hanging out at your dad's and Beckett's. I'm sticking Deputy Cleaver outside your place too. We're also trying to get a hold of the Helmers to see if we can move their renters out and put in an undercover unit there. I'm hoping we'll have them situated by tonight."

The four of us exited the hospital together, and by the time we did, the tears were traveling down Maisey's face unchecked.

While I'd always hated her tears, this time they served a purpose more important than emotional release—one I wasn't sure she'd even realized. If this asshole was watching, they'd see a distraught Maisey leaving the hospital, just like they'd expect if her dad had really died.

Still, my chest tore at her anguish.

I desperately wanted to hand some pain back to the person who'd done this to her. I wanted to hand them hours of torment for every second they'd caused her. If I had my way, they'd never escape pain again. They'd live with it until they took their very last breath.

Chapter Thirty-two

Maisey

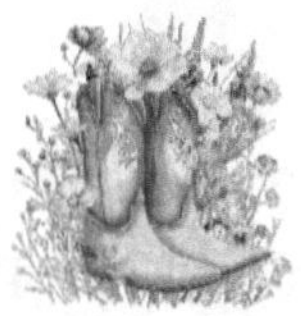

HOW MUCH A HEART CAN HOLD
Performed by LeAnn Rimes

THREE YEARS AGO

HIM: Fallon okay?

> *HER: Yes. Shaken. But grateful it's over now.*

HIM: When I saw Parker at the airport and he told me she'd been kidnapped, I'm not sure I've ever seen that level of devastation on another human. Not even on my dad's face when Liza left.

> *HER: He loves her.*

HIM: It might not have happened today, but one of them is eventually going to be left behind. Even if one of them doesn't betray the other, someone will still die, and someone will still be left alone.

> *HER: You always focus on the tragic ending, Beckett. But you forget the important part. You forget they'll have years and years and years of beautiful, loving, happy moments together before death takes them.*

HIM: And you're assuming it'll be years and years and years. Life isn't that predictable, Maise. Cancer. Heart attacks. Some loser who shoots up a bar, and poof, it's all gone. And you're left with half your soul ripped out.

HER: I'd still risk it. I'd give up just about anything for a few moments of truly feeling loved the way Parker loves Fallon.

PRESENT DAY

By the time we got to Beckett's, I felt like I was dragging a thousand-pound weight with me. The stress of the last few weeks, that had been eased briefly by Beckett's beautiful proposal and the even more beautiful night I'd spent in his arms, had been chased away by this godawful day. A day that rated up there with finding out Mom had stage-four cancer and closer to the day she'd passed.

But I couldn't let myself think about burying another parent now, or I'd dissolve into inconsolable tears.

I barely registered Sweeney or Vader once we walked into the house. I headed straight to the shower in the guest bathroom, turned the hot water on full bore, and stood there, trying to chase away the cold, but it didn't work. My body ached, my throat stung, and even though I bundled myself in sweats, I was still freezing and couldn't seem to banish it.

Maybe the cold went hand in hand with the emotional numbness that had blanketed me again, much like it had the night I'd been attacked in the drive. And just like that night, I had no intention of fighting it. I needed it with me so I could keep moving.

When I walked into the kitchen, Beckett was heating soup, and Sweeney was nowhere in sight.

"Can I use your phone?" I asked, already missing mine more than I'd ever imagined I would.

"You don't have to ask, Maise. What's mine is yours."

I dialed Fallon and gave her an update. Wylee had already called them, and Parker was increasing their security. She promised me none of them would be moving about the ranch without protection, especially the kids.

"I'm so sorry, Fallon," I said, exhaustion creeping over me.

"This isn't on you, Maisey. This is one-hundred-percent on the shithead who took your dad."

"My brain knows it, but my heart is having a hard time catching up."

"I take it you aren't going to be here for the show tomorrow morning."

Indecision warred. What would I do if my dad were really gone? Would I even be able to concentrate enough so I wouldn't end up hurting myself or Titan?

What would Fallon do to fill the gap in the show schedule? I was sure one of the kids from the riding school would be happy to fill my slot.

But what would I do if I didn't perform? Sit here, worrying about Dad? Worrying about the people I loved? For hours? All while I waited for our attacker to strike again?

I pressed my hand into my stomach and let out a shaky breath. "As long as you truly believe Parker and the security team have the ranch and all of you protected, I'd still like to do the show." Beckett's eyebrows rose in an unspoken question. "The sheriff is right. If this asshole sees me going about my life as normal and not leaving like they wanted, they'll come for me again."

Fallon wasn't any more thrilled about the idea of me being bait than Beckett had been. But I'd do just about anything, except risk the people I loved, to lure the enemy out of their hiding spot. If they came for me, they wouldn't be coming for anyone else.

After we hung up, Beckett insisted I eat. When I could barely push my spoon through the broth, we both gave up, and he pulled me to the couch, tugging me up against him. Vader leaped up next to us, pressing against my opposite side and resting his head on my thigh. I petted him, trying to soothe us both as Beckett flicked through channels on the television.

The ring on my finger grabbed my attention. I twirled it around. I'd felt elated, on top of the world last night. I hadn't dreamed the words he'd given me, right? I hadn't made up the "I love you" he'd whispered in my ear as I'd come apart?

Yesterday, I'd been determined to fight for forever with

him, all the while having no clue he'd already taken the leap all on his own. When had that happened? When had he decided to unlock his heart and hand it to me for real?

But in taking it, was I risking doing exactly what he'd always feared? Would I hurt him? Abandon him? Not of my own free will but because someone ended my life the way they'd been determined to end my father's?

I blinked furiously, fighting the tears that rose again. As if he'd read the quagmire that had become my emotions, Beckett slid a finger over my cheek and tucked a strand of hair behind my ear. "We've worked too hard to get here, my Maisey-girl. We're not letting some bastard take it away from us."

I didn't respond. Couldn't.

"For years, I thought opening your heart, letting someone in, was the most foolish thing anybody could do. That love was a weakness. Something that doomed you to pain. But I was wrong. Love makes us stronger. It's made *me* stronger."

"Beckett—"

"I love you," he said firmly, resolutely, and the tears could no longer be stopped. "But I swear on my life, if you ever do something that stupid again…"

I bristled at the word stupid, and he saw it.

"Wrong word choice," he amended. "You've never been stupid. So, tell me why you thought you had to go to the watchtower alone. Tell me why you thought we shouldn't face the danger together after you let me slide that ring on your finger, after we'd spent hours merging our souls and our bodies together, and after you'd whispered 'I love you' back?"

"I knew Fallon would use the Find Family app to locate me. I trusted you both to come after me."

His brow raised. "You knew we'd come?"

I nodded, and for the first time since we'd woken up to our phones going off, Beckett leaned in and kissed me. It was slow and sweet and full of the overwhelming emotions we'd had beating through us all day, and it temporarily thrust aside the numbness to write itself on my heart in a new and almost impossible way. It was a brand that wove onto the very fiber of my being.

"I'm scared," I told him. "Scared for everyone I love. Scared of staying and you being hurt. Scared of leaving like they want and destroying us both."

He tugged me closer, stroked my back, kissed my forehead. "You're not leaving, Maise. We're not letting them win. We've got something they don't."

I just looked at him in confusion.

"Family and friends looking out for us. People willing to battle at our sides."

It reminded me of what Andie had said about trying to fit our wedding in Beckett's backyard. We did have family here. Maybe more than I'd ever realized. Family were the people you could count on to show up when you needed them most. It was the people who'd shown up for us today. The ones who did the unfeasible on your behalf when the people you shared DNA with couldn't or wouldn't.

Like my father might not ever be able to show up again.

The pain that ripped through me at that thought left me raw and exposed. After last night, I should have spent the day reveling in the pleasure of having gotten what I'd always dreamed of having. Instead, I was grappling with the potential loss of another parent. All the things I still wanted to say and do with Dad, that I might now miss out on, cut like a knife, slicing me in ways I wasn't sure I could handle at the moment. So I welcomed the numbness back. I'd let it shelter me for a while longer, at least until I could handle the full brunt of these new cuts to my soul.

♫ ♫ ♫

Amazingly, I'd actually fallen asleep for a few hours tucked up next to Beckett. And when I woke, groggy and somehow impossibly still cold, Beckett insisted on making us dinner. Neither of us ate much, and I cleaned up, storing the leftovers while he went to check with Sweeney and Parker's friends, who were holed up in Dad's house.

I used Beckett's phone to check on Dad. Wylee and the hospital administrators had transferred him to the county hospital under a fake name. He was still in a coma, but he was breathing better, so they'd removed the ventilator. It was progress. But not enough for my worry to ease. I wished desperately I could be with him. I knew if he heard me there, talking to him, telling him how much I needed him, it would increase his chances.

It hit me how true my thoughts were. I did need him.

Maybe not in the way I'd once needed him as a child for food and shelter. Not even for the emotional support he'd failed at giving. But I did need him. He loved me in his own, incomprehensible way, and he was trying to make amends for how he'd checked out on us—on me. We had a chance to build a relationship we'd never had before, and I needed a relationship with my father that would bring back those early childhood memories of laughter and games. We'd eased toward that while staying at Beckett's, and I wanted it to continue so if and when he did pass away, I'd have a host of good memories layered over all the bad.

Beckett returned from checking in with the SEALs, saying they had nothing new for us. No one had showed up on any of the cameras they'd installed. No one was physically lurking in the shadows.

And yet, I still felt them there. I could almost feel their breath on my shoulder.

When we headed for bed, Vader followed us with his tail down, and I realized it wasn't just the emotions he felt zipping through the air. He whined as he sniffed at the blankets where Dorothy had been.

"He misses the cat," I told Beckett.

He rubbed his dog from head to tail. "I know, bud. Things have been chaotic. Dorothy will be back with us soon, and you two can cuddle all you'd like."

The dog settled at the bottom of the bed, still looking distraught.

Under the covers, Beckett tucked me up against him and kissed me. It held the same fierceness as the kisses last night, the same promises I'd felt embedding themselves deep inside me, and yet it was also incredibly tender. A kiss goodnight rather than a kiss that led to more.

Longing flared to life, pricking at the shell I'd forced around me. This was what I needed even more than the numbness. I needed his touch. Not only to feel alive and loved but to chase away the worry and fears and guilt that were clinging to me from this awful day. I craved a few minutes of bliss to hide the pain.

I slid my hands and mouth along his neck and his chest before trailing hungry, frantic kisses lower, tugging at the waistband of his boxer briefs.

He stopped me, dragging my mouth back to his and kissing me tenderly. "Maisey—"

"I need you to make love to me, Beckett. I need to forget everything but your touch for at least a few moments. Remind me I'm yours. That this is real. That our fake relationship isn't fake at all."

His Adam's apple worked overtime, and unshed tears welled, but he did just what I'd begged. He made love to me. It wasn't with the insatiable hunger of last night. Instead, it remained slow and sensual. Each stroke, each touch, each kiss was another vow. An oath he was uttering to me in the silence.

I hated that as we moved together, as he filled me up body and soul, my mind went to just what this might cost us. Hated that whoever had come for us had me wondering if Beckett had been right all along, and all relationships were doomed.

When we'd both reached the top and come down the other side, tears were running down my face. Beckett caught each one, gently wiping them away.

"Don't cry, my Maisey-girl. When you do, it guts me."

"I'm happy, Beckett. This time with you makes me so happy." While it was true, I could already feel the emptiness swirling back in. "But I'm also sad and terrified."

He kissed me on the forehead. "I know, darlin'. I know. But right now, you're here, safe. Your Dad is safe. All the people you love have others watching over them. So try to get some sleep. Everything will seem better in the morning."

But it didn't.

I woke with the same hollow heaviness hanging on me.

Dad was still in a coma. No one had caught the attacker. We had no answers or solutions or end in sight.

Instead of looking forward to a day I'd always enjoyed—a day that had always brought happiness to me and our town—I felt the weight of the world pressing down. It tagged along with us as Beckett and I drove to the ranch with a sheriff's deputy following close behind.

Fallon and her family had done their best to turn the often-questioned holiday of the Fourth of July into a true community celebration. Each year, they hosted the festivities at the ranch, starting with a trick-riding show that drew in the crowds before everyone wandered through the craft, food, and game booths. Throughout the afternoon, friendly teams faced off in sports and riding challenges, and when evening fell, the family capped it all off with a classic summer barbecue—free for the hotel's guests and the entire town.

It was typically a joyful day for the residents of Swift Rivers.

I was determined to shake off the heaviness holding me down and concentrate on the goodness the day brought rather than the person waiting somewhere in the shadows.

I'd barely finished braiding Titan's mane and putting on his trick saddle with Beckett's help when Sheriff Wylee strode into the barn. He looked ragged, like he hadn't slept at all, and more guilt zeroed in on me. The man was over seventy and running himself into the ground trying to solve my problems. Even though it was his job, I still despised that my troubles were the reason for it.

After greeting Beckett and me, the sheriff handed me my phone. It was a relief to have it back. I pocketed it, and Beckett grabbed my hand, tugging me into his body, as if just touching could soothe us both.

"According to the tech guys, it didn't have any spyware or tracking apps. The number that called you was the same one that texted your dad. We've traced it, as well as the phone left at the watchtower, to a batch of burners bought from a box store in LA. Judge Farling has already issued a warrant, and I've asked Coop to swing by the store this morning and grab the surveillance videos and purchase records on our behalf before he heads here tonight."

"Cooper's coming?" Beckett asked, and Wylee nodded.

"Told him I needed all the hands I could get."

Hope flared. Wylee's son was a detective with the LAPD. He hadn't lived in Rivers since he'd graduated from high school, but he visited often enough that everyone in town still knew him. He'd become something of a hometown hero over a decade ago after he'd saved a movie star from a stalker, and the media had become obsessed with the relationship that had bloomed in the aftermath. Maybe his experience with situations like this might give him some insight into what was going on here. Maybe he could give new ideas to his father and Josh.

"You got any more leads?" Beckett demanded, and I could practically feel his irritation through our connected bodies. "Or are we pinning our hopes on a box store's security cam?"

The sheriff ignored Beckett's sarcasm. "If you'd told me about Carter pushing his development sooner, I would have looked harder at him. Instead, I've been playing catch-up."

"I didn't think anything about Carter's offer. It didn't raise any red flags because Dad and I have had multiple offers over the years, just like I'm sure Lewis has."

"Well, I went by his place this morning, and he insists he was with Delilah the night Maisey was attacked in your driveway. He said he'd give me the receipts for the restaurant in Visalia where they had dinner. I'll pull video footage to confirm it, but he also wasn't in town yesterday. He was in Tulare, scoping out alternative building sites for his development, seeing as you and Lewis refuse to sell. I'm working on a warrant for his phone. If we can confirm it pinged off the towers near Tulare, we'll be able to confirm his story."

The slight hope I'd felt started to fade again. If Carter and Delilah had alibis, we were back to nothing. Back to zero leads. Frustration bloomed, and tears pricked my eyes.

"But how can we be sure Carter was really in Tulare and not just his phone?" Beckett asked. "He and Delilah could be working together, right? Or he could have had his assistant take the phone out of town to ensure it pinged elsewhere."

Wylee stroked his beard. "You're not wrong, but all we can do is follow the leads one step at a time. I can't lock him in a cell just because you suspect he might be behind this."

My frustration finally leaked out of me, and I threw my hands up. "So what? We just allow them to keep coming at us while we wait? While more people I love get hurt?!"

"I understand how you're both feeling—"

"No. I don't think you do, Sheriff," Beckett bit out. "If this were Lydia, would you only be taking these careful, measured steps, or would you be burning the fucking town down to make sure she was protected? That the person who attacked her was behind bars?"

The sheriff's face darkened. "Don't use my wife against me, son. We're doing what we can, within the law, so we can put this bastard away for good when we finally arrest him. If it were Lydia, I'd want the same thing. I'd want the asshole locked up with no loophole allowing him to escape. So yes, I'd still be doing things by the book, but I'd also make sure I didn't let her out of my sight."

The men glared at each other for a long moment before Wylee's face softened, and he sighed. "Between you, Parker's team, and my men, we have Maisey covered. Cleaver is on his way here as we speak. He's hardly slept since this all started."

I hated this. Hated every second of this. The burden I was to the people around me. The threat hovering over all my loved ones. The guilt dragging me down into the abyss.

"Forgive me if I don't want to put Maisey's life in the hands of Carter's cousin." The sarcasm and doubt in Beckett's voice pushed Wylee right back over the edge.

"Now, you listen. Josh Cleaver is a good man and good deputy—"

As the voices raised, Vader barked, easing up next to Beckett with the hair on his nape rising. And all that pain I'd been holding back tried to slam back into me.

"Stop!" I shouted, instantly regretting it. Quieter and calmer, I repeated, "Please stop."

Remorse instantly washed over Beckett's face, and he squeezed me to him tighter, but his guilt only ended up adding to mine.

The sheriff ran a hand over his white beard, and when he spoke, he was once again calmer. "I'm not taking any of this lightly, Beckett. It's been difficult for me to find any department nearby willing to send officers to help us out due to the holiday, but Cooper is on his way, and the Steeles have sent more folks from their Vegas security team. We've got Sweeney and his friends at your house, and I've been told the renters at the Helmers will be leaving this morning, so we can put someone there too."

I frowned. "Has anyone even really been staying at the Helmers'? We haven't seen any cars all week."

Wylee flipped through his phone. "Yeah, it was rented by some movie production company that goes by the name Lost Acres Productions. Supposedly, the CEO and his girlfriend are here, but I worked out a deal with Fallon for a future stay at the resort if they agreed to cut their vacation short to help us out by leaving early."

My stomach bottomed out as his words rang through my mind.

A movie production company.

A chill ran up my spine.

A man and his girlfriend.

No. No. It couldn't be.

My voice shook as I asked, "What…what was the company name again?"

"Lost Acres."

"Oh God…" I felt all the blood leave my face, and the barn spun around me. I didn't want it to be true. I could believe she'd leave childish notes… I could believe that much, but to actually attack me? Drug Dad? She wouldn't have…

"Maise." Beckett's worry sifted through me.

The unknown number that had been bugging me seemed to swim before my eyes, and with a shaking hand, I pulled my phone out of my pocket, scrolling backward to the awful text she'd sent the day Beckett's door had been painted. When I found it, bile curled up my throat. The number was only a few digits off the one that had sent Dad and me messages. Easily part of a batch of burners.

The trembling in my hand grew until it consumed my body. Until it shook loose the numbness I'd kept close since yesterday, ripping it completely aside. Hot fury filled in behind it.

Beckett saw my reaction, and he reached for me. "Maisey?"

Thousands of memories flooded me. The disgust in her tone. The cold words. The toxic gaslighting I'd wanted to believe was actually caring and worry.

Furious tears swarmed. I'd never felt rage this strong. Not ever. Not even when my therapist told me I had a right to be angry. Not even when she'd told me if I didn't confront it, it would someday explode on me.

That day had arrived.

It was here in violent, living color, and I'd never be the same again.

"I know who's doing this."

Chapter Thirty-three
Beckett

WITH MY EYES OPEN
Performed by Lonestar

ONE YEAR AGO

HIM: The way you move on Titan is a bit of a miracle. Beautiful. The art of a goddess coming alive right before our mortal eyes.

> *HER: I'm not sure how to respond to that.*

HIM: No need. I just wanted you to hear it. You've always been beautiful, Maise, but seeing you with your horse is something really special.

> *HER: *** eyeroll emoji *** We both know I haven't always been beautiful, but I will concede that Titan and I put on a good show.*

HIM: What will it take for you to realize the image you had of yourself as a kid was not how the world saw you?

> *HER: I'm not getting into this with you. I'm happy with who I am, but we both know how the world saw me.*

*HIM: *** a series of pictures of a much younger Maisey, laughing at the lake, pirouetting on horseback, and swinging in a tire swing, hair flung out around her ****

HIM: Look at those and tell me you don't see a beautiful girl with light pouring out of her. As much as I don't want love for me, I hope you find it, and that whoever the man is takes his job seriously and reminds you every single fucking day how stunning you are.

PRESENT DAY

When Wylee left, fury followed Maisey to the restroom as she went to change into her show outfit. And while I was glad to see something more on her face than a blank mask, I loathed the reason for it, detested that Chelsea was once again chipping at Maisey's happiness. She'd wrought a lifetime of trauma on Maisey, for what? Jealousy? Rivalry? Money? The anger I'd barely tamed yesterday returned, simmering into a burning rage.

I was tempted to storm out of the barn, go find her sister myself, and end this by strangling Chelsea. But if I left Maisey to go find Chelsea, and we were wrong about who this was, I would have left my girl unprotected. I had no intention of doing that until I had no other options. So as little faith as I had in them at the moment, I had to hope Wylee and his team would do their job, find Chelsea, and bring this chapter of our lives to a close so we could focus on our future.

I was still wading through those thoughts and emotions when Maisey came out of the bathroom. And as soon as my gaze settled on her, every single thought left my brain except one—she was stunning.

The body-fitting outfit showed off all her delightful curves while covering her from head to toe in red. The material was cut in crisscrossing slashes, varying in texture from glittery sequins to smooth silk. The tank-style top left her arms bare, but she wore sparkling red cuffs from wrist to almost elbow. The soft-soled shoes she wore while performing blended in with the rest of the outfit. She'd tied her hair back in two long, intricate braids woven with the same ribbons she'd used in Titan's mane.

She looked like a superhero.

And I knew from experience that watching Maisey perform on Titan would spark the same awe as seeing Wonder Woman whirl her lasso or flick bullets off her bracelets.

Before I realized what I was doing, I'd closed the distance, put my hands on her waist, backed her up against Titan's stall door, and planted my mouth on hers. The kiss wasn't sweet. It wasn't the devotion I'd tried to convey last night. It was a furious passion fueled by the anger the morning had wrought.

It tore at my soul, knowing we'd given Chelsea the power to touch us here. To impact our embrace. But the longer the kiss went, the more I felt the essence of us take back over.

Maisey's sweetness and strength would always be more powerful than her sister's bitter hate.

By the time Fallon's chuckle came from behind us, we'd found our center again. It allowed me to focus on the simple truth of me and Maisey and our love.

And when I stepped back and saw Maisey's face flushed, not with fury but with that soft, sated smile she wore whenever I touched her, everything felt like it was going to be okay.

Her sister would be found. This would be over. And I'd forever have Maisey at my side.

"The schedule we made has you up first, but we can swap spots if you think you need a few more minutes here." Fallon's voice was full of humor.

I turned to see Fallon wasn't in a fancy trick-riding outfit like Maisey wore. She was in more sedate, typical western wear, which meant she wouldn't be doing the same level of tricks my Maisey-girl would be—at least not today.

"No need. I'm ready now," Maisey said. She shot me an impish smile that both relieved me after the hurt and anger I'd seen minutes before and made me want to pull her back into my arms and kiss her senseless.

Maisey led Titan out of the barn with Fallon and me following her.

Just like Wylee had promised, Cleaver had shown up, and he tipped his hat in our direction as he took up a post near the barn. From his position, he could see the entire corral and the packed bleachers on the far side. The quiet hum of voices filled the air, anticipation building as they waited for the show to start.

At the entrance to the corral, Maisey tossed herself up onto Titan's back and then looked down at me with that soft smile I adored. The one I liked to believe was just for me. "Wish me luck."

"No luck needed, darlin'. You're going to knock everyone's socks off."

The light in her eyes grew, the hurt and anger diminishing yet again, and the tension in my heart eased. Maisey headed into the ring, halting Titan just inside the gate while Teddy played emcee and welcomed everyone to the ranch.

"I have to get ready," Fallon said, worry creasing her forehead as she watched Maisey. "Just tell me she's holding up."

"She's holding up." When she turned to me, giving me a look full of doubt, I did my best to reassure her. "Really, Fallon. You know our girl is one of the strongest humans on this planet."

"I don't want her to have to be. She's been through enough."

I nodded as a ball wedged itself into my throat again. After another beat, Fallon whirled around and headed back to the barn to get her horse ready for their act.

I leaned up against the rail, taking in a deep breath. Yesterday's storm had finally blown itself out in the evening, heading over the mountains and cleaning the summer dust from the air, but puddles and humidity remained in its wake. The damp mingled with the scent of pine and redwoods. Scents I loved in a place I loved.

But I loved Maisey more than any of it. I may have denied it for twenty years, but she'd always been the center of my world. The grounding force. The most important reason why I'd stayed in Rivers when I could have gotten a job in a department just about anywhere.

Teddy finally announced Maisey, and I watched as she and Titan rounded the ring in a warm-up circuit. Graceful…moving smoothly together from years of practice. As they went by me,

Maisey shifted up from her seat to a standing position before literally falling in a fluid, dance-like move so her feet were all that remained on the horse. The rest of her body was stuck straight out from Titan's flank, and as they rounded the corner, her hand brushed the dirt where she picked up a sparkling red lasso she'd left on the ground. The audience oohed and aahed and clapped.

As Maisey rolled up onto Titan's back, danced to her toes, and swirled the lasso in the air, a body leaned up next to me, elbows rubbing against mine.

"She looks good up there," Dad said.

I shot him a quick glance, noting he was wearing his good hat today and his best shirt with the pearl buttons, before my focus returned to Maisey. She was a fiery star like this, but even when she wasn't performing, she was a bright flame in the dark of night. A blaze I would always seek. A flare I wanted to fan and watch grow until it illuminated the entire town with its brilliance.

A year ago, I'd been watching her do a similar performance, and I'd been struck by how magnificent she was. I'd texted her afterward and told her just that, and she'd brushed the compliment off, but I also remembered telling her she deserved to have a guy in her life reminding her every day of just how stunning she was. How beautiful—inside and out. And I remembered the twinge I'd felt in my chest at the idea of some unknown man being the one to tell her all of the things I wanted her to believe about herself. Why hadn't I realized then that I wanted to be that man? That I wanted to give her everything she dreamed… I'd wasted a year.

No, I'd wasted more than that. Dozens of years.

But I couldn't continue to beat myself up forever. If I did, that bitterness would leak into us like it had leaked into Chelsea. So I'd simply do what I should have always done. I'd shower Maisey with compliments and love and adoration. And if and when one of us passed, we'd have all these moments we'd made together to hold us up until we found each other again in whatever afterlife followed this one.

"I'd say I was surprised to see her out there after losing her dad, but then our Maisey-girl has never wanted to let anyone down, has she?" Dad asked as we both watched Maisey execute another flip, this time under and around Titan's barrel, perfectly.

I looked behind me at Cleaver, who at least seemed to be taking his post seriously, and then leaned in to Dad so I could keep my voice as low as possible. "He's not dead. We're just letting everyone believe that until we can catch the person responsible."

Dad's thick brows went up, meeting the brim of his hat. "You know who it is?"

I caught him up on everything that had happened the best I could, quickly and quietly. I could feel his gaze fixed on me rather than on Maisey, but I didn't take my eyes off my girl, and I knew what Dad saw while watching me—the love that was all but pouring from me. And I didn't care. I didn't want to hide it. Instead of thinking it was foolish to love her, to love anyone, I was honored she'd accepted what I'd offered.

Dad's hand landed on my shoulder. "Damn, Beck. You finally did it. You finally opened your heart and let her in. I'm so proud of you."

My chest nearly burst. My father had always let me know when I did things right and wrong. He'd always been proud of me, which was why his words from our day at the lake had lingered with me like a bad taste. The disappointment in them had haunted me.

"I love her. With everything I have." My lungs were completely clear. The only thing there was an overwhelming rush of love. "I just hope I don't screw it up."

"You won't. You'll do the one thing I didn't, Beckett. You'll fight for that girl with every breath in your body," Dad's voice cracked, drawing my attention from Maisey to him. The sadness there, the utter remorse scored into every wrinkle, tore at me.

"Mom and Liza leaving weren't your fault."

"I knew your Mom was unhappy in Alabama. I could have followed her and allowed her to go after her dreams. Instead, I insisted on staying. Dug my heels in and wouldn't drag them out again. Doesn't make anything she did right. The cheating. The fire..." he choked, and I wondered if the smoke tortured him as much as it had tortured me. "As for Liza, I should have gone after her. I could have let her know we'd be waiting when she was done building those schools in South America. But instead, I told her that if she left, she should never come back, even though all I really wanted was for her to do just that. To come home to us."

Emotions overwhelmed me. Sadness for the love we'd both lost out on because of wounds that had taken too long to heal. But mainly for Dad, because I knew he hadn't gone after Liza for me. He'd chosen the love of his son over the love of a woman.

"I'm sorry you had to stick around to take care of me when you should have gone after Liza. If I had it to do over again, I'd..." I didn't know how to finish my thoughts. Would I have told him to go? Would I have gone with him? Left Maisey and Swift Rivers behind? I would have hated it, and my father had known that and made the tough choice so I didn't have to.

When I lifted my gaze to his, it looked like I'd sucker punched him. "Beckett, is that what you thought? That I had to give them up to keep you?"

I shook my head, but it was halfhearted. He'd never known I'd overheard his conversation with Liza. Didn't know how much my heart had been shattered, not only at another mother figure abandoning me but by the knowledge I'd been the reason my dad had lost the love he'd finally eased back into his life.

"Beck, you weren't *ever* the reason my relationships failed. Not once. I didn't have the guts to go after Liza. That's on me. But if I had gone after her, you can be sure I would have dragged you with me, even if you were kicking and screaming. You and me, we're family. Tied together in unbreakable knots. Always have been. You got that?" He looked back out at Maisey as she leaped through her lasso and landed on Titan with ease, and the crowd applauded. "That young lady there is just adding another knot to our rope. Liza could have added one too if I'd gone after her and apologized, but I didn't." He took a breath. "So, you do what you need to do to keep those knots secure, and if they try to unravel, you do whatever it takes to pull them tight again. You got me?"

My throat relaxed, and the pressure in my chest that had built while we talked eased. I nodded. "I got you."

Maisey executed an elaborate turn and a giant bow as the crowd cheered and shouted her name. Dad and I added our own claps and shouts to the avalanche of applause my girl was already getting.

Dad patted me on the shoulder. "Gotta head down to the lake and make sure the bleachers are set up. Tell Maisey I thought it was her best show yet."

He started to walk away, and when I called after him, he looked back over his shoulder. "Is it too late?" I asked. He frowned. "For you to go after Liza? Is it too late?"

He lifted his cowboy hat off his head, ran a hand through his hair, and then set it back down. "It's been fourteen years, so…maybe…I don't rightly know."

"Think about it," I told him and then turned as the corral gate opened, and Maisey walked out leading Titan.

I caught her in my arms, planted a kiss on her lips, and whispered in her ear just what I wanted to do with her in—and out of—that sparkly outfit.

She flushed until her skin nearly matched the red of her clothes, and for the first time all day, for the first time in two days, my heart actually felt light.

♫ ♫ ♫

After Maisey rubbed down Titan, she changed out of her show number back into the dark jeans, sleeveless button-down, and worn brown cowboy boots she'd had on before. She'd been more relaxed after the performance. Her time on Titan's back had been the same salve it had been when she'd been growing up, and I was glad she'd gotten a moment of reprieve.

But as people filtered into the barn, each one stopping by to express their sorrow over her dad's supposed death, her relaxation disappeared.

She may have needed the distraction of the show this

morning, she may have needed to be with her horse, but she didn't need to hang out amongst the booths and festivities, lying to people about her dad while worrying if their words would become the truth.

So I made the call to end it. "We're heading up to Fallon's to pick up Dorothy, and then we're going home for a few hours.

She rubbed her forehead, and she whispered, "I wish I could see Dad."

"I know, Maise. I know."

When we got home, I did my best to distract her again, this time with my hands and mouth, and then afterward with taunts about Vader and the stupid cat. My hard work paid off. Eventually, I saw her expression soften and her shoulders ease. But as the afternoon started to fade, and the sun cast long shadows over my backyard, and the time to return to the ranch arrived, the tension slammed back into both of us.

While, technically, Stoney's crew was on call at the firehouse, the small size of our station meant we were all-hands-on-deck for the Fourth of July. We always divided the coverage up with half remaining in town to battle fires set by idiots using illegal fireworks, and the rest at the ranch, ensuring the pyrotechnic display didn't catch wind and spark a blaze in the dry summer foliage.

Usually, I didn't mind being on call for the holiday, but tonight it meant, for at least a few hours, I wouldn't have Maisey in my sights. I'd have to trust the other people Parker and Wylee had arranged to protect her, and I knew it was going to be nearly impossible for me to relax.

Reading me the way I usually did her, Maisey said, "It's going to be okay, Beckett. I won't leave the grandstands. I'll be safe in the crowd."

"I'd hoped we would have heard something from Wylee by now."

"Me too," she whispered, grabbing her bag and heading for the back door.

I whistled for Vader, who looked from me to the cat, clearly torn. I chuckled. "You can't take her with us, bud. But she'll be here when we get home in a few hours, and I need you to stick with Maisey tonight."

As if he understood, the dog gave Dorothy a huge lick and then trotted over to us.

He had his head out the window, tongue lolling in the breeze that had picked up as we drove through the gates at the ranch. It was busier than it had been this morning, with the entire drive now lined with cars, and the two makeshift parking lots the staff had set up in fallow fields packed to the edges. The ranch's golf carts whizzed by with people, shuttling folks from the designated parking areas down to the beach and the temporary stage, dance floor, and bleachers.

I'd wanted to wait until the last possible moment to show up so the barbecue was pretty much over. But the grandstands were nearly full. Some folks sat listening to the band, and others danced, all while waiting for night to fully descend and the fireworks show to begin.

I parked my SUV off the road next to the fire truck, and Cleaver, who'd dutifully followed us back and forth today, pulled in behind us.

I turned off the car and twisted in my seat to take in Maisey. She was staring out the windshield, watching the sky turn from burnt umber to teal to black above the lake. She tugged at her hair that she'd let loose from its braids after an afternoon spent tangled in bed. The nerves had returned, and I hated seeing them.

Feeling the weight of my stare, she turned, green eyes hitting mine with a sadness I wanted to wipe away. I took her left hand in mine and caressed the *toi et moi* ring. Two becoming one. The truth was, we'd never had to *become* one. We'd just always been one.

"There's a piece of me that still hopes I'm wrong."

She wasn't. As soon as she'd said it to Wylee this morning, I'd known she was right.

I couldn't lie to her, couldn't reassure her that the worst hadn't happened to her family, so I did my best to soothe her in other ways. I leaned toward her, put a hand on the back of her neck, and kissed her before resting my forehead against hers. "Whatever happens, whatever way the chips fall, there's one thing I'm certain of—you and me are together, forever."

Her hand caressed my cheek, throat bobbing and eyes swimming. Then she gave me a weak smile and reached for the door handle. I climbed out and joined her around the hood of the car, twining my fingers with hers.

Heads turned in our direction, proving we'd continued to be the center of our small-town rumor mill, maybe even more so with the talk of her dad's death.

Vader trailed us with his leash in Maisey's hand. His tail was up, on alert. The emotions he'd sensed bleeding from us for two days were keeping him on edge just like us.

When we reached the bleachers, we drew to a halt, watching people dance to Watery Reflection. The band members may be in their fifties, but you'd never know it from their energy on stage. The eclectic mix of rock and pop and folk meant their songs had something for every type of music lover.

All I wanted to do was swing Maisey into my arms, dance with her, and kiss her under the fireworks. I promised myself, next year, things would be different. If I got the fire chief position, I'd be here, supporting my crew, but I wouldn't have to stand watch. I'd be able to tuck Maisey up against me and make sure she and the whole damn town knew just how permanent we were.

Cleaver eased up next to us, and I asked, "What's the news from the sheriff?"

"The movie set broke up two days ago, and the cast headed back to LA. But they aren't picking up filming there until after the holiday weekend. No one knows where Chelsea and Gavin are staying, and the Helmers' place is empty. We have a deputy sitting on it, but he may get pulled away if things get hectic downtown."

I thought about our chat with Chelsea at the mall. She'd said they were on a break from filming but were due back. It wasn't a lie. It matched this story, but she'd made it sound like they were still filming here in the mountains.

"What's next?" I asked.

"We've got an APB out on Gavin's car and are running their credit cards, but we have to find them before we can question them."

Every time we talked with the sheriff's department, we got a wait-and-see kind of answer, and I had to clamp my teeth to stop myself from biting out an angry retort.

"Maisey!" a voice called from the bleachers, and we whirled around to see Andie waving at her to come join them.

Maisey squeezed my hand and then let it go, heading toward the stairs.

"Don't go anywhere," I called after her.

"I won't," she said.

I looked down at Vader. "Protect Maisey. Go with Maisey, boy." He barked, accepting his task, or maybe he was just as much in love with her as I was. All I cared about was that he went after her, adding another layer of protection.

I shot Cleaver my deadliest look. "Anything happens to her on your watch, I'm holding you responsible."

He started to respond, but I didn't wait to hear it. Instead, I headed for the engine and my crew, who were all waiting for me in their turnout gear. They shifted on their feet in discomfort, but it was Tejas who asked the question.

"How are you and Maisey holding up?"

"We're okay. We'll be better once the sheriff catches the person responsible, and we're hoping that happens tonight. Right now, I need to concentrate on getting this done so I can get back to her."

I handed out assignments, ensuring we'd be spread out as wide as possible to catch any ember that sparked, before returning my attention to the grandstands.

Maisey was sitting with Andie and some of the other staff from the resort. She was safe, with Vader lying devotedly at her feet and Cleaver watching her from the foot of the bleachers, and yet my gut was screaming at me in warning.

Was it Cleaver I didn't trust or just the entire situation? Maybe it was simply not having her next to me, where I could step between her and her enemies if need be.

The sun finally slid completely past the mountains, and the stars winked into existence, their reflection sparkling in the smooth ripples of the lake. The smell of pine, wildflowers, and hay that always surrounded the Harrington resort was almost hidden beneath the aroma of barbecue and beer. It mingled with the sweat and suntan lotion of bodies who'd spent a day in the sun and water—a day celebrating community—while Maisey had spent the day anxiously worrying. The unfairness of it pissed me off.

As I stepped into my gear, my mind should have been on the potential fire danger. Instead, all I could think about was Maisey and the danger to her life.

I grabbed my lid, tucked it under my arm, and slammed the storage compartment on the engine shut before peering around the cab once again to reassure myself Maisey was still sitting right where I'd left her. I groaned inwardly when Delilah blocked my view.

She was in a red-white-and-blue sundress that flirted with her knees. Her dyed mahogany hair was drawn back in a graceful bun. It was hopeless to think I'd escape her, but I also didn't want Maisey worrying about whatever conversation I was having with Delilah, so I stepped back into the shadow of the engine. I leaned up against the truck as Delilah crossed her arms in front of me.

"I'm tired of you and Maisey pointing fingers at me, Beckett."

For two seconds, I felt bad for doubting her. Delilah was messed up, but she'd never really harmed anyone but herself.

"I'd say I was sorry, but the truth is, I didn't know who else to look at, Del. And I'd do anything to protect Maisey. Anything. I'm hopeful after tonight—tomorrow at the latest—it should be over, and we can all just put this behind us," I explained.

She studied the lake before turning her face back to me. Then, she sighed and moved to lean up next to me against the truck.

"I didn't get it, you know," she said. "I knew she loved you, but I didn't get how much you loved her right back. I guess I wanted to believe the act you put on about having no interest in any kind of long-term relationship. And I guess what *you* didn't understand was how tempting that act was to us mere mortal females."

Surprise shifted over me. Seeing it, Delilah shrugged and gave me a wry smile, as if I'd said something witty when I hadn't opened my mouth at all.

"After all, what woman can resist the challenge of changing a self-proclaimed bachelor into a lovesick fool? I thought if I could just get you to spend enough time with me, I'd have you on your knees, declaring your love. But that was never going to happen because you'd already given your heart to Maisey when we were kids."

"There's never been anyone else for me," I told her truthfully, knowing that even those words couldn't adequately express the full depth of my love for Maisey.

Silence dropped down between us for a long moment.

Delilah inhaled deeply and then asked, "So they found out who drugged her dad?"

I wrestled with telling her the truth, because if Maisey's guess was right, both Delilah and Carter were in the clear, but I wouldn't bet Maisey's life on it. I'd let the cards fall where they would, and Del could hear about it later

"Captain. You about ready to head to the lookout spot?" Tejas asked, coming around the truck.

I stepped away from the engine. "Yeah. Give me two seconds."

He moved off, and I looked down at Delilah.

"I'm sorry if I ever led you to believe we could have been more than friends, Del."

She shook her head and grimaced. "You didn't. I can't count the times you told me you weren't interested."

The sadness in her voice brought back the teenager I'd found under the bleachers. The one with blood pouring from her wrists, who'd sobbed that no one loved her. That no one would ever love her. She'd gotten better at hiding it, surviving with it, but Delilah was still carrying those wounds with her, just like I'd carried my childhood traumas with me. I hoped she could get past whatever her version of the smoke was to truly open herself up to someone.

"If I hadn't already given my heart to Maisey, Del, you would have been at the top of my list."

She scoffed. "Thanks for trying to make me feel better, Beckett, but you and I both know that isn't true."

"If you can't believe that, then at least believe this—there is absolutely someone out there for you. Someone who's going to fall on their knees just like you want, adoring you for your relentlessness and determination. Someone who will return all that love you have in you."

She put a finger to the corner of an eye, as if holding back tears.

"Is there any hope of you turning your thing with Carter into something more?" I asked, even though I hated the idea of her with him. Even if he was in the clear when it came to what was happening with Maisey, he was still a smug bastard. A slick and oily creep who, according to Maisey, was using drugs.

Delilah laughed. "No. He's worse than Dad when it comes to keeping his dick in his pants. He's someone you scratch an itch with, but not someone you want to be the father of your children." She looked out at the lake. "Plus, I think he's going to be hightailing it out of town soon. Carter was counting on you and Lewis selling your properties to him for the Meadow Lane development he had planned. He said he had a sure way to get you both to sell, but you didn't. Now, Carter is running scared because he has no way to pay back the loans he took out from Lorenzo Puzo. And we both know how the Puzo family deals with unpaid debt. I'd be shocked if Carter is not in Mexico by morning."

Every single breath left my body. Had Maisey been wrong? Was this actually Carter? Desperate and afraid?

Fuck.

Fear coursed up my spine. I stepped around the front of the engine, frantically searching the bleachers for Maisey. My heart nearly stopped when I found the spot where she'd been empty. Andie was still there, laughing and chatting with Francois, the resort's head chef. But no Maisey. No Vader.

No Cleaver either, and it should have eased the tension

racing across my shoulders, but it didn't. Where the hell had they gone? Maisey had promised she'd stay in the stands, where not only Cleaver but the other deputies and Parker's security team could watch over her.

"I gotta go."

I left Delilah calling my name. I moved in the direction of the shore and my team, but it wasn't them I was seeing. I was desperately scanning the crowd for my fiancée.

The pyrotechnic crew had already taken the motorboat out to the temporary dock in the middle of the lake and were minutes away from setting off the fireworks. The band was no longer playing, but music still blared from the speakers that would soon match the bursts of light in the air.

My team had taken up their positions, spread out along the shore as planned, and I should take up mine, but my heart and soul screamed at me to leave. To run. To go find Maisey.

Dread pooled, growing until it was a painful ache.

I fished out my phone from the depths of my gear and sent a text to Maisey. When she didn't respond, I called Cleaver and tried not to panic even more when he didn't pick up.

By the time neither Wylee nor Parker picked up either, the feeling of dread had grown until it was ringing in my ears like an engine's siren.

Nothing was right.

Then it hit me. *You're a fucking idiot, Romero.*

I knew how to find her. Just today, I'd insisted she add me to the Find Family app. I brought it up, held my breath while the circle spun, searching for Maisey's location.

When I saw it, the panic grew to full-out terror. She was too far away. Too damn far.

I ran, the heavy turnout gear weighing me down.

Tejas and Kasey called out after me in confusion.

But I didn't care about my job, or the people under my command, or potential flames.

I only cared about finding her before the worst happened.

I only cared about preventing another knot in my life from unraveling.

Chapter Thirty-four

Maisey

CASSANDRA
Performed by Taylor Swift

SIX MONTHS AGO

HIM: Movie?

> *HER: Not today. I'm finishing a series.*

HIM: Which one?

> *HER: It's romance. You wouldn't be interested.*

HIM: We're too big for the treehouse, but maybe we should reinstate reading time.

> *HER: You could join the book club Fallon, Andie, and I started up.*

HIM: You're missing the point, my Maisey-girl. It's you I want to spend time with.

PRESENT DAY

I laughed as Andie and Francois teased each other, all the while drooling over the Watery Reflection band members. The men may have been old enough to be our parents, but they were still attractive. Still had that enticing rock star energy.

Beckett had that same dynamism that drew people to him like wildlife to the river. If he'd ever had any interest in music, it would have served him well. It was perhaps the one and only way he'd ever been like my sister.

Chelsea had the same vibrant pull.

My soul ripped a bit more, thinking of my sister.

Maybe I was wrong. Maybe I was seeing the worst in her instead of the best.

But I hadn't received a single text from her today, when I'd expected something. Even though I'd told her to lose my number, if she'd heard the false rumor about Dad having passed away, she would have called, right? Maybe it simply meant she hadn't heard? But then again, she'd heard about my engagement to Beckett before I'd even been able to tell Dad.

The tension that had been released momentarily as I'd spent an afternoon twined in Beckett's arms returned, hammering into me until my shoulders felt like bricks were stacked on top of them. I desperately wanted to hear from the sheriff. To finally know where things stood.

My phone vibrated, and I swiped, hoping it was Wylee, only to see that, somehow, I'd missed a call from the county hospital.

My stomach fell…until I read the translated text of the voicemail. Dad was awake! He was awake and asking about me. He wanted to know if I was okay and if they'd caught whoever had done this to him.

Thank God… Thank God… He'd pulled through.

I wasn't going to lose him too. Not now. Tears of relief washed over me.

I needed to leave. I needed to go see him.

My phone vibrated again, this time with a text. And when I read it, confusion bled into the relief and joy I'd felt over the news about Dad.

> *BECKETT: Wylee needs us up at the barn. Come right away.*

I searched the dark, scanning the area by the fire truck where I'd last seen Beckett with his crew. While I couldn't see any of his team clearly, I did catch the reflective stripes on the jacket of at least one firefighter as he strode down toward the lake.

Would Beckett really leave his crew to go to the barn? As soon as I thought it, I knew the answer was yes. If he thought I needed him, he'd go, no hesitation, no questions asked. But would he leave me to do it? Again…yes. He'd leave me with Cleaver if he thought he could end this for me. He'd do anything to make sure I was safe.

I stood, and Andie glanced up at me, brows drawing together. I wasn't sure how much she'd heard from Fallon and Parker about what was going on, but after what had happened with my dad the day before on the ranch, she knew enough to be worried. "Where are you going?"

"The sheriff needs to talk to me. I'll be back."

She studied me anxiously as I made my way down the grandstands with Vader on my heels.

I expected to find Josh, expected to find him waiting at the bottom of the stairs for me, but the spot where he'd been was empty. I scanned the area, pulse rate picking up. I didn't understand… He'd promised Beckett he'd be at my side all night. So where was he? Why would he leave?

That creepy feeling I'd had off and on since finding the very first note, crawled up my back and over my neck like a ghost walking on my grave.

> *ME: I can't find Josh. Should I come alone?*

> *BECKETT: Cleaver is handling something for the sheriff. You're safe. It's almost over, but Wylee needs us to hear this for ourselves.*

I should have felt relief. Should have felt glad that it was nearly over. But if it was, it also meant a permanent tear in my family. What was I going to tell Dad when I saw him? That his daughter had tried to kill him? That she'd cared more about whatever she might inherit from him than his actual life?

I clenched my jaw, trying to hold back the tears.

Vader and I made our way to the dozen golf carts and the group of teens hired to drive them throughout the day. I was thankful when I saw Chuck with them, because he knew me well enough to let me take one on my own.

"Hey, I need to zip up to the barn. Is it okay if I take a golf cart?"

Chuck scratched his head and looked out at the dock where the fireworks would be going off any second. "We'll just need it back after the show to shuttle everyone to the parking lots."

BECKETT: Do I need to come get you? Or can you handle getting here by yourself?

Unease sifted through me again. Nerves rattling like chains on cement.

Something was wrong.

What if this message wasn't really from Beckett? Worse, what if they'd somehow grabbed him like they'd grabbed Dad? What if, even right now, he was waiting for a dose of naloxone to save his life?

I pressed a hand to my stomach, doubts and indecision warring with my first instinct to race to the barn to find him. To help him. I could be walking into a trap. But if Beckett was at the barn, lying on the ground, drugged… I had to go. There was a med kit at the hotel. I could save Beckett's life and call for help.

Saving him was all that mattered.

Saving him but also making sure we had help on the way.

I put a hand on Chuck's arm. "Can you do me a favor? Find one of Wylee's deputies and tell them to meet me at the barn."

Chuck's eyebrows lifted. "You okay? You need me to come with you?"

"No." I shook my head violently. "What I need you to do is find an officer to come to the barn."

He took off at a dead run, and I slid into the driver's seat of the nearest golf cart, hands trembling as I turned the key while Vader leaped up next to me.

The cart's headlights barely made a dent in the dark as I headed back up the hill to the main buildings. A partial moon shone over the fields and trees, turning the landscape into a weird panorama of shadows and light. The hot day hadn't quite rid the earth of the damp from the storm, and the air smelled of both.

As I pulled the golf cart into a slot by the barn, the quiet of the hotel and outbuildings felt eerie. Almost like it had felt when I'd approached the watchtower yesterday. Like a horror movie on repeat—one nearing the climax. A shiver went up my spine in the silence.

The fancy lanterns on the outside of the barn made triangular, yellow shapes on the ground, broken by the shadows Vader and I cast as we approached.

Only one of the large barn doors was open, and I hesitated at the entrance. My instincts were screaming at me to run, but my head and heart weren't listening.

Beckett was here, and he might need me.

But Vader hadn't gone running inside to greet Beckett like he would have if he'd smelled him. Instead, the dog was pressed up against my leg, and the fur at the scruff of his neck was raised. My entire body trembled as I called Beckett's name. I got nothing in return but the quiet greetings of the horses. Soft nickers and snorts. Sounds that should have been reassuring but weren't.

I looked down the road toward the lake and up the other way to the castle. Should I wait for whoever Chuck grabbed? My nerves tightened more, fear traveling along them. I'd promised Beckett I'd stay at the grandstands. That I wouldn't go anywhere alone, and yet here I was…alone.

Stupid, Maisey. You're so stupid. The hissed taunt from my past almost felt real.

A noise hit me. A quiet groan followed by the rustle of movement in the hay.

Beckett!

My feet flew toward the sound.

Behind me, Vader yelped in pain, and I whirled around to see him lying on his side in a stall just as a blond-haired woman I didn't recognize slammed the door shut. Fury bled through me. At him being hurt. At this person, who I didn't know, coming after me and my loved ones.

"Don't you dare hurt him!" I raged, stepping toward her.

The scraping of shoes behind me screamed a warning, but

I had no time to react. Strong hands grabbed my arms, twisting them backward. The brutal force shot pain through my shoulders, and I cried out just as a firework exploded.

The horses whinnied nervously, pawing at the ground uneasily.

"Stupid choices, Cornlette." My sister's voice came from a face I didn't recognize. The woman reached up and pulled a silicone mask, hair and all, from her head, revealing the person I'd grown up thinking was beautiful. Chelsea dropped the mask at her feet and pulled pins from her hair before brushing it out with steady hands.

"You've made a series of stupid choices in the last two weeks." My sister's voice was cold. Detached. "Why in the hell did you decide *this* was the time to leave your saintly obedience behind? Why didn't you just do what you were told and leave?"

It was hopeless to talk to Chelsea when she was like this. For twenty-six years, she'd always walked away the winner of our arguments. But perhaps I could talk some sense into Gavin.

I twisted, desperate to catch his eye, but pain lanced through my shoulders at the movement. My captor yanked my already strained joints higher just as a familiar, overpowering cologne hit me.

By the time I caught sight of him, the shocked acknowledgment was already ripping from me, "You!"

"Hello, metal breath." Carter's sneer matched the feverish mania gleaming in his eyes.

A cold weight settled in my gut as I watched him—sniffing, rubbing his nose against his shoulder, but never loosening his grip. He was high. On something potent. Maybe the same heroin they'd pumped into Dad, except a smaller dose.

There'd be no reasoning with Carter either. Not like this.

I whipped my head back around to Chelsea, warily eyeing the items she now held.

She'd always been deathly terrified of needles. So afraid that she'd passed out at the mere sight of them when Mom was sick—unless that had just been another act in a long list of skilled performances. But it was the whip she gripped that really confused me. She'd never been a horse person. Never learned to ride. What could she possibly want with it?

As if answering my unspoken question, she drew closer, clumsily slashing the whip through the air. Even with her poor form, it was enough for the tip to nick my chin right at the spot still healing from hitting the pavement. I gasped in pain.

Behind the stall door, Vader had recovered and was barking and snarling, hurling his body against the wood. Relief flooded through me knowing he was okay, but fear quickly followed— if he broke free, Chelsea might hurt him more.

"I promised you'd regret not leaving," Chelsea said. "Now, you'll die, the barn will burn, and maybe even the entire Harrington resort if your *fiancé* isn't quick enough."

Even as she said it, she kicked over a red container I hadn't noticed. The scent of gasoline filled the air, running in rivulets along the floor.

"Why, Chelsea? Why would you do this? You can't possibly hate me this much."

"I don't hate you. I just don't give a shit about you either. And you only have yourself to blame. It would have been simple if you'd just done what you were told. With Dad dead and you disappearing where no one could find you, all the money from the sale of his property and his life insurance would have been mine and mine alone."

I shook my head in disgust. "Dad doesn't have life insurance, Chelsea. He's broke."

She laughed, and it reminded me of the time she'd played the evil queen in *Snow White*. It had been dark and ugly and terrifying, even when I'd known she was acting, and now it was all the more frightening because I knew just how real it was.

"He actually does have insurance. I've been paying for it for three years, just biding my time. When I saw Carter in LA and he told me about the deal he'd been trying to make with Dad, I knew it was the perfect time. I just had to get you out of the way."

"I can't believe you're willing to actually kill your family for money."

My chest ached, and my shoulders burned as Carter yanked them back farther.

"Family. Some family. That poor, innocent Maisey routine you played at the mall almost cost me Gavin!" She slashed the air with the whip, but this time, I jerked to the side before it could hit me and almost struck Carter.

"Hey, watch it," he snapped.

Chelsea acted like she hadn't even heard him as she came closer, swirling the whip. "Gavin left. He fucking left me in that shack of a rental all because your idiot fiancé somehow convinced him with one sentence that I was a horrible person."

"If he finally saw the real you behind your act, don't blame me or Beckett. Maybe you just aren't as good an actress as you like to believe."

Fury flared across Chelsea's face. She flicked the whip, but for the second time, it didn't reach me.

"I should have already won an Academy Award for all the years I pretended to be your loving big sister."

I snorted in disgust, even though the truth was, I had believed her for years. I'd believed her over Beckett trying to show me the truth.

"Chelsea, let's just get this done," Carter said behind me.

"Don't tell me what to do," she hissed at him before staring daggers at me again. "You may have tried to ruin my relationship, Cornlette, but Gavin will come back to me. When I wave a check for a million dollars in front of him, he'll be begging me to be his again. Begging me to hand it over so we can finally film the movie we wrote together."

"You're never going to get that chance, Chelsea. Sheriff Wylee is already investigating you."

"I have a plan," she said, glancing behind me to Carter.

He didn't seem to register the look, but I did. With a fresh wave of horror, I understood. Chelsea was going to lay this all at his feet. She'd kill me, set the barn on fire, and make sure Carter died in the process. She'd make it seem that he'd been the one behind all of it.

But Chelsea seemed to have forgotten one thing. I wasn't

alone.

I'd sent Chuck for help, and my absence would be noted at the lake. An entire team of people would be looking for me, and Beckett would be heading them up. He had my location on his phone. He'd be here.

I just had to delay, put up enough of a fight that Chelsea and Carter concentrated on me until help arrived.

I did what Parker's dad had taught Fallon and me to do if attacked. I slammed my head backward and was rewarded with a grunt of agony as I connected with Carter's nose. Then, I dragged the heel of my cowboy boot along his shin.

He screamed, "Fucking bitch!"

His hold on me loosened just as I let my muscles go slack, becoming dead weight in his hold. He dropped me, and I hit the ground. I rolled and kicked at the same time, my foot landing another blow to his leg.

Carter retaliated, his foot landing in my rib cage, as Chelsea flicked the whip again. It slashed through my biceps, drawing blood, and I screamed.

Vader's bark was desperate as he leaped up against the door of the stall. The wood cracked, the sound mixing with the bang, bang, bang of the fireworks and the stomping and snorting of the horses.

The scent of gas and the sting of it on my hands increased my fear. Not just for me, but for all the animals. Vader and Titan and the dozens of horses housed here.

"Idiot!" Chelsea snapped at Carter. "You couldn't even hold on to her for two seconds?"

The whip hit me again, this time on the thigh, ripping my jeans. I bit back a cry as Vader's barks grew even more frantic.

"This is a lot more fun than I was expecting it to be," my sister said, flicking the whip again and laughing when she saw me flinch. She glanced up at Carter. "What are you waiting for? Dose her."

She tossed the needle at him, and he caught it deftly. My mouth went dry. My heart thudded.

I kicked again as he got closer, and the whip slashed,

missing me but shooting dust into my face. As I coughed and blinked, Carter grabbed my ankle in a viselike grip and used his mouth to uncap the needle. He had the point pressed against my thigh as my sister closed the distance.

He hadn't even had the chance to realize she was there before she plunged a second needle into the side of his neck.

Shock coated his face. "What the hell, Chel—"

He fell on top of me, his lifeless body making it almost impossible to move, as his needle rolled away. I stretched my arm, desperately trying to reach for it, and the whip hit the back of my hand.

"I can't believe he fucking missed!" Disgust dripped from her voice. "He had one job and couldn't even get it right."

She swept the needle up as Vader tore at the wood of the stall. Chelsea shouted, "Shut up, you mongrel!"

The dog didn't listen. If anything, he became more savage.

With her attention turned toward Vader, I pushed Carter off me and rolled over, rising to my hands and knees. The whip hit my shoulders, and I screamed again.

Another series of booms filled the sky outside the barn as the fireworks show moved toward its finale, and tangled in with the noise came another. A noise that made me want to weep. A deep voice filled with deadly intent.

"Don't take another fucking step."

Chapter Thirty-five
Beckett

WE DON'T RUN
Performed by Bon Jovi

ELEVEN YEARS AGO

HIM: You sleeping?

> *HER: Can't. I keep hearing that sound Dad made at the graveside. It was unearthly. Horrible.*

HIM: You're right, it was horrible. Worse than the sounds my dad made when Liza left. But it just reinforces what I already knew—love is pain.

> *HER: Maybe it is. But I also saw the joy they had when they were together. The smiles and laughter. The way he held her pinky when they walked together. The way she kissed him goodbye before each gig. So maybe having that is worth the pain later.*

PRESENT DAY

Fury filled me as I saw the tip of the whip collide with Maisey's shoulders and heard her pained cry as she fell forward into the dirt. Her shirt was torn. Her skin bled. And white-hot rage pumped through my veins like a wildfire out of control as I strode into the barn.

"The prince has finally shown up on his white steed. Come

to save the pitiful freak as usual?" Chelsea's voice was full of scorn as she raised the whip again.

"You move that hand again, and I promise you, I'll break every finger on it." The threat in my voice did nothing but make Chelsea laugh, the sound bitter and cruel, with an edge of malevolence.

She dropped the whip, and as I started to close the distance, she reached behind her and came back with a pistol. It was small caliber but enough to do severe damage at this distance to me or Maisey.

Vader barked frantically, desperately trying to get out, to protect Maisey and me. He'd gnawed through a chunk of the wooden stall door. I moved toward him, and Chelsea put a bullet in the ground at my feet.

I stilled. Vader snarled.

"It's over, Chelsea," I said, taking another small step.

She fired again, this time right next to Maisey's head. Maisey's face paled, and when she looked at me, the raw fear in her eyes made my stomach churn.

"Keep moving, Romeo Romero, and you'll be the reason she dies painfully with a bullet hole in her instead of painlessly with drugs and smoke inhalation."

"You've got about a minute before this place is swarming with officers."

Chelsea's face warped into a grotesque grin that hid inside a mask of beauty. "Let's see. Do you mean Sheriff Wylee? Because Carter tied him up in the trunk of his own car and drove it into the forest. Someone might find it before he dies, but who knows? And Cleaver? The sappy freak who had the hots for Cornlette his whole life? He's knocked out and handcuffed to his own steering wheel. See, he came running when Wylee sent him a text."

Outside, the fireworks show was coming to an end. The booms were right on top of each other. The music from the lake vibrated through the valley, the words impossible to hear, but the beat thudded rhythmically as this strange, hypnotic movie scene came to a head.

"Just like my stupid sister came running when you texted her. People really shouldn't believe everything they read, even on their own phones," she laughed.

Chelsea dug in her pocket and came out with a cigarette lighter. The smell of gasoline hit me, and my eyes fell to a spilled jug, the liquid running over the dirt and straw all the way to Maisey. My stomach sank. Maisey's clothes were wet.

My attention returned to the lighter in Chelsea's hand, wondering if I could catch it before it fell.

"I drop this, and she'll go up in flames. You'll try to rescue her and end up with a bullet in your head for the effort. I'd offer you a bribe to walk away, but we all know the heroic Beckett would never take one. You can't save her this time," she said, raising the gun at the same time she flicked the lighter and lowered it.

"Drop the weapon!" a voice from the back of the barn had Chelsea whirling toward the sound just as she dropped the lighter. The gasoline went up, and I lunged for Maisey. I landed on her, trying to hold back my full weight but shifting so my turnout gear was facing the flames.

Chelsea's pistol went off as Cooper Wylee stepped fully into the light and returned fire. Chelsea screamed, blood blooming along her shoulder as the gun fell to the ground amongst the flames. I watched in horror as she stumbled backward, the fire licked her legs, and she shrieked in agony, twisting to try to escape.

I rolled with Maisey, whipping her away from the fire as Chelsea continued to writhe in pain.

Smoke alarms sounded, and dozens of fire sprinklers kicked in, drenching the barn with water.

Cooper ripped a Class A-B-C fire extinguisher off the wall and sprayed it over Chelsea's body and the flames. Black smoke spiraled upward, causing Coop and Chelsea to cough furiously.

The horses stomped and snorted in fear, kicking their doors. Vader howled.

I had to clear everyone out. I had to get rid of the fumes.

But first. Maisey. God. Maisey. Clutching her to my chest,

I found my feet and ran for the door. When I set her down, I briefly met her terrified gaze, and my heart nearly collapsed. The grief and sadness there were too much. Too much for one person. All I wanted to do was hold her, catalog every injury, and wipe away every bead of blood, but instead, I headed back into the barn.

I snagged a second extinguisher from near the exit and joined Cooper. His sports coat and cowboy boots wouldn't keep him safe if the fire kicked back up, but thankfully, it disappeared in a hiss. I tossed the empty canister aside and grabbed Chelsea's arm to haul her out just as a dozen bodies burst into the barn.

My fire crew. Parker's security team. A handful of sheriff deputies.

"Get the animals out of here," I told them as I hauled a screaming and struggling Chelsea toward the door.

She was ranting about her skin, and her career, and her "stupid sister." And that rage that had been momentarily pushed aside by fear for our lives returned in full force. I wanted to accomplish what the bullet and flames hadn't—I wanted to end her life. I wanted to forget the oaths I'd made to save lives and property and do to Chelsea what she'd intended to do to my Maisey-girl.

As we stepped outside, I nearly ran into an out-of-breath Kasey, hauling a line toward the barn. I all but tossed Maisey's sister at her, saying, "Take her. Take her before I do something I'll regret."

Chelsea slammed her foot into my kneecap, loosening my grip before Kasey could get hold and allowing Chelsea to run. But she only got a foot away as Cooper grabbed her, his brown hair sticking up at angles and blue eyes deadly cold. Even though he'd grabbed her uninjured arm, she still shrieked in pain and frustration.

Cooper pulled a pair of handcuffs from his back.

"Chelsea Campbell, you're under arrest for the assault and kidnapping of a police officer, the attempted murder of Lewis Campbell, assault and attempted murder of Maisey Campbell..." he continued the list and moved on to her Miranda rights.

It wasn't enough. Her arrest wasn't nearly enough for what she'd done to my girl. The years of gaslighting. The years of trauma she'd wrought. For the pain she'd caused Maisey this week.

Maisey.

Maisey was all that mattered.

I spun around to see her leaning up against a golf cart. As I started toward her, my dog bounded out of the barn and straight for her, colliding with her legs. As she put her hand on top of his head, she whispered something to him I couldn't hear.

I jogged over, scanning every inch of her. My heart thudded, fear racing over the rage as I grabbed her hand and realized it was bleeding. Goddamn it. She was covered in blood from her chin down. It was all over her. Not enough for her to be in danger of bleeding out, but the whip had left its mark in multiple places.

That bitch. That fucking bitch.

I started to turn, started to head back to Chelsea and Cooper, but Maisey twined her fingers with mine and jerked me to a halt.

"Beckett."

That's all it took to draw me back to her, and the sadness and pain I saw etched over her face had me swearing all over again.

I put one hand on the back of her head—uncertain if it was to steady her or steady me—as I leaned in and took her mouth with mine. I kissed her with an abundance of stored-up terror and worry and anger. I kissed her violently for going off on her own after she'd promised she wouldn't. I kissed her furiously for almost dying. I kissed her because we were both alive to do just that.

When I pulled back ever so slightly, she touched my cheek tenderly before catching sight of someone over my shoulder. I turned to see Cleaver holding an ice pack to his head and rocking on his heels.

"The sheriff!" Maisey said. "Chelsea said they locked him

in his trunk and left the car somewhere."

"Cooper handled it," Cleaver said, nodding in the direction of the man reading Chelsea her rights. "He showed up at the station with the surveillance videos, and when no one could find the sheriff, Cooper had the office track the GPS on his rig. Did your sister actually think no one would find him?"

"I don't think she cared," Maisey said, looking over to where Kasey had started working on her sister with a med kit from the rig. Cooper stood watch, with his arms crossed over his chest and a dark scowl on his face.

Chelsea was still writhing in pain from the burns up her legs and the gunshot wound, but I didn't feel an ounce of empathy. She'd earned that pain and much more.

Parker sprinted out of the darkness, sliding to a stop next to us. He was out of breath, and his clothes were in disarray, even his shirt was on backward. He and Fallon had been noticeably absent from the firework show, and it was clear the ranch's fire alarms had drawn him from the alternate activities in which they'd been engaged.

"Fuck," he breathed, taking in Maisey's cuts and the smolder still emanating from the barn. He jerked his phone out and texted out a message as he said, "Fallon stayed with the kids."

"Stayed, or you tied her up and forced her to stay?" Maisey said, and when her lips turned upward ever so slightly, the heaviness in my chest eased slightly.

"She stayed. Just until Lauren could get over to the house," he replied. He took in the scene again before settling his glare on Cleaver. "I thought you weren't letting Maisey out of your sight. You promised that was your only job."

"And I thought you had people and cameras searching for Chelsea," I grunted out. "And yet she still got in. Got her hands on Maisey."

"Stop!" Maisey yelled, and the three of us went silent, anger and frustration and regret spreading in the air between us. "It isn't Parker or his team's fault. Chelsea was wearing a mask."

"A mask?" Cleaver repeated.

"Yeah, it's somewhere in that mess," Maisey said, nodding toward the barn.

"Shit. With her acting career, we should have expected that," Parker swore, remorse clear in his tone, his face grim.

"What's your excuse?" I demanded of Cleaver.

"Wylee texted me. Said he'd apprehended a suspect in the barn and Sweeney would be watching Maisey so I could assist. I'd barely gotten into my car when I got hit from behind." He shuffled the ice pack around and then grimaced. "Idiots didn't take my key when they handcuffed me though. Once I woke up, I got here as fast as I could."

Irritation bled through me. Everyone had fallen right into Chelsea's hands.

"I shouldn't have left the grandstands." Maisey's voice drew my eyes to her. To the cuts that still hadn't been treated. To the sadness that still hadn't faded from her face. "I knew better, Beckett. I knew the texts yesterday were faked. Every part of me was telling me it wasn't you who'd messaged me, but I couldn't find you anywhere…and I thought maybe they had you…that they were actually using your phone, and that they'd drugged you like they had Dad…that you might die…"

Her voice cracked, and her whole body shook as emotions poured out of her.

I wrapped my arms around her, squeezing tight. Any frustration I'd felt at her leaving the bleachers and the lake vanished. How could I accuse her of breaking her promise when I would have done the same? Had done the same. She'd come because she thought they had me, just like I'd come when I'd realized she was in danger.

Instead, I focused on the relief that came from knowing we were all alive. That we'd survived. This was over. Chelsea would never hurt her again.

The ambulance had shown up while we'd all been pointing fingers at each other, and when Bugsy started to load Chelsea into it, Maisey pulled away from me. I tried to grab her hand and stop her, but she just jerked away, stalking over to her sister.

Seeing Maisey approach, Chelsea started screaming. "Get away from me. Get the hell away! I lied before. I do hate you.

Hate you and your ugly face and the way everything in your life was handed to you on a silver platter."

I was right behind Maisey and started to say something, but one scowl from her had me biting my tongue. She turned back to Chelsea and said, "I just want you to know that you didn't just fail at killing me tonight. You failed yesterday too. Dad isn't dead. He's alive. He's awake and asking for me. Not you. Me. Because you've never really been part of our family. You always made me feel like I was broken." She stopped, swallowed hard, and then continued. "But the truth is, you're the broken one, Chelsea. Broken inside in ways far more twisted, more ugly, than my jaw ever was. In hindsight, fixing me was easy. Fixing you…" She shook her head. "That will be a different kind of pain, and I'm not sure you'll survive it."

Then, my girl turned on her heel and walked away from her sister.

My dog leaped after her, running in ecstatic circles, as if the last few minutes of terror had never happened. As if he hadn't been snarling and howling, ready to kill someone just moments ago. I wanted to be able to do the same, to forget. To leap around Maisey like an idiot, proving my love. And I would. I'd be just what Delilah had said—a lovesick fool. But before I did, I needed to get something off my chest.

So, I stepped closer to Chelsea, her beautiful face twisted with agony and hatred and just a flicker of fear that I rejoiced in.

"You're going to jail, Chelsea. For life." My voice lowered, deepening with emotions as the truth of the vow I made ripped through me. "You wanted fortune and fame? Well, I'm going to do everything in my power to make sure your name and your story *never* see the light of day. That you don't get one ounce of infamy out of what you did to her, to your family. You're going to die, and no one is going to care. No one will remember who the hell Chelsea Campbell was. I'm going to make it my life's mission to make sure not even Maisey spares you a thought. I'm going to fill her life with so many happy memories she won't have time to even wonder about you. Enjoy your stay in a federal prison."

As I walked away, Chelsea gave a horrific scream, and my mood lightened, pleased I'd done exactly what I'd intended—given her a dose of pain that wouldn't disappear anytime soon.

♫ ♫ ♫

Maisey was exhausted and hurting by the time we were able to leave the ranch—bone tired, swaddled in bandages, and still smelling of gasoline, even though Fallon had brought her a change of clothes when she'd finally made it down to the barn.

In addition, Maisey's throat had become raw and scratchy the longer she'd been forced to repeat what had happened and answer stupid questions. I wasn't sure if the rawness was from the smoke, the stress, or if the combination of everything had weakened her immune system and allowed that virus that had been running through Swift Rivers to finally claim her. All I wanted to do was to take her home, tuck her into bed, and keep her there for a week. But instead, she'd demanded I drive to the county hospital so she could see her dad.

It was well past visiting hours, and our smoky, dusty appearance coated with the smell of gas didn't bode well for the nurses letting us into Lewis's room. But after a call from Cleaver and the doctor, they reluctantly relented.

The television was on, and Lewis had his eyes on the screen, but his mind seemed elsewhere.

"Dad," Maisey called.

His focus shifted to her, and he started to smile until he really took her in. "What happened?!" he demanded.

She ran to him, sat in the chair beside him, and brought his hand to her bandaged face. "I'm okay. I'm okay, Dad. Better than you. These are just some scrapes that'll heal in no time."

She'd needed stitches for the cut on her biceps, but leave it to Maisey to downgrade her own injuries so she wouldn't worry anyone.

"Why do you smell like gasoline?" he demanded, the worry on his face growing.

"It's a long story…but I swear I'm okay," Maisey told him, fiddling with his blankets.

Because I knew she needed a minute to get her emotions in check and decide exactly how much she was going to tell her father, I intervened by asking, "How are you feeling, Lewis?"

"Fine, fine. I've been telling the doctors and nurses for hours. I was just worried when no one would let me even talk to you." He patted Maisey's cheek, tears pooling. "I thought… I thought something bad had happened, and they just didn't want to tell me." He scanned her again, his sorrow increasing. "I should have been with you, Maisey. Whatever happened, I should have been there."

"Dad…" Her throat bobbed, and the look she shot me was full of helplessness. She was going to hurt him by telling him what had happened, and it went against everything in her nature to do so.

I squatted down next to her, hooking her free hand with mine as I faced her dad. "Lewis, they've caught the person who did this to you. It's the same person who attacked Maisey outside the house and tried to hurt her again tonight."

Lewis's face turned dark. "Thank God, they caught them." He shook his head. "I don't remember anything about what happened to me. The doctors said you found me at the old watchtower at the ranch, but I have no clue how I got there." His eyes landed on Maisey, taking in her obvious distress, and his face turned even grimmer. After several long seconds, he let out a resigned sigh. "Was it Chelsea?"

The surprise that rolled through me was reflected on Maisey's face.

"Wh-why would you think that?" she stammered out.

"All of this started after she showed up unexpectedly with that slick actor at her side. The timing of it just felt off." He looked away, toward the television screen, deep in thought. "And when I woke, I had this feeling…this thought that wouldn't leave, telling me Chelsea was in a heap load of trouble."

Maisey took a deep breath and then rushed out, "It wasn't Gavin who helped her, Dad. It was Carter Smythe."

Her father snorted in disgust. "That weasel is even worse than the actor. How'd he hook up with her again?"

Maisey glanced up at me, a helpless look on her face that was rarely there, so I dove in to explain. I told her dad what Maisey had told Cooper Wylee and Deputy Cleaver about the life insurance and the property deal. I added in what Delilah had told me about Carter's loan from the renowned mafia family, and Lewis's face grew impossibly darker.

"That girl was money-obsessed from the time she was a toddler," Lewis said, shaking his head. "I told your mother that someday something bad would come of it." He looked up at the ceiling. "I can only be glad Marge didn't live to see it. It would have torn her apart." He squeezed Maisey's arm. "Like it's tearing you apart. Your sister was never your responsibility, Maisey. Just like your mom wasn't, and taking care of me wasn't either. I'm sorry. Sorry we all became your burdens at such a young age. If I had it all to do over again…"

His eyes filled as he trailed off, and the tears Maisey had been holding back rolled silently down her cheeks.

"I love you, Dad. If I had it to do all over again, there's nothing I'd change."

"That's because you've always put others first and never done anything worthy of regret. But it's time you concentrate on yourself now. On you and the life you're building with Beckett."

They both cried, and as much as I hated seeing Maisey's tears, I knew these were ones well spent. Well earned. You had to grieve before you could move forward again. If I'd learned nothing about relationships, I'd learned that much.

Lewis was the first to gather himself. He looked down at her hand and rubbed the ring I'd given her.

"I see you picked out a good one."

Maisey's face softened, turning into the first real smile I'd seen in hours. "Beckett picked it out, Dad. Your words must have struck home because he chose the perfect one and surprised me with it."

Lewis's lips quirked upward. "I figured, with all those romance books you read, he had to have a romantic bone somewhere in that body to have won you over."

A little laugh escaped her that turned into a yawn she tried to hide.

"Beckett, take our girl home and make sure she gets some rest."

I pulled her up out of her seat. "Happy to."

"I'll be back tomorrow." Maisey leaned in and kissed his forehead.

"Don't you dare. I don't want to see you back here until those bags under your eyes are gone and you're bandage free."

Maisey shook her head in amusement. "That could take weeks."

He shrugged. "At least a few days, then. I'm good with staying here and letting someone other than my little girl take care of me for a while."

"That's not how it works, Dad. This isn't a hotel. You don't get to choose to stay or not."

Lewis shrugged. "We'll see. I think I'm feeling awfully weak. Faint, even. Definitely not sure I can get out of this bed."

I couldn't help the snort that escaped me.

"Go," Lewis said, turning somber once more. "Rest."

And finally, Maisey let me tug her out of the hospital.

I hadn't wanted to come, but in the end, it had been the right thing. Like always, Maisey had known what was best for her and her family. If she'd waited, all she would have done was worry about telling Lewis what had happened with Chelsea. Now, it was over. They still had a lot of healing to do. But they had a chance to fix their relationship.

We all had a chance to do so.

I'd told Maisey love wasn't a weakness, that it actually made me stronger, and I'd meant it. But what I hadn't said was that only *real* love had the power to be that strong. My mom hadn't known real love any more than Chelsea had. They'd tried to weaponize it. They'd try to use the love others had for them to their advantage, but it had backfired. Chelsea was going to prison, and my mother, the first and only time I'd checked up on her, was barely hanging on by a thread, working in some dive in New York, a step away from the street.

Both my dad and Maisey had known and given love freely,

without restraint, and it had strengthened them. I wanted to be just like them. I wanted to love, to give it freely, and hope it made me even one-tenth as strong as them.

Chapter Thirty-six
Maisey

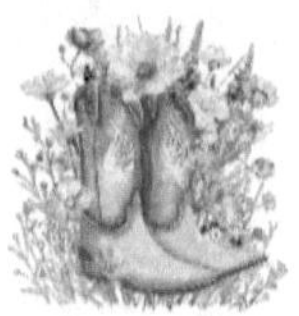

OPALITE
Performed by Taylor Swift

PRESENT DAY

HIM: Pancakes or waffles?

HER: Neither.

HIM: You need to eat.

HER: I need you.

By the time we got home, it was almost stupid to go to sleep. The sun would be up in just an hour or two. I was supposed to be heading into work in a few hours, but I wouldn't make it, and I had to hope Meredith wouldn't let me go after all my absences, excused or not.

With the way my entire body was screaming at me, I figured it would be a few days before I could withstand the rigors of a twelve-hour shift. The slashes from the whip were raw and achy, my throat was burning, and my eyes were gritty from smoke and gasoline and tears.

When I walked into Beckett's, I could have fallen straight into bed and slept for a day straight, but instead, while Beckett hosed off Vader and fed him, I headed for the guest bathroom to shower. In a repeat of the day before, I stood under the full heat and tried to wash off more ugliness. Dirt, gasoline, and blood, as well as heartache.

My sister had tried to kill me. Kill our father.

I wasn't sure I'd be able to process that without another round of therapy.

Surprisingly, I wasn't numb tonight as much as I was simply exhausted. I felt it all the way down to my bones. Deeper than I'd ever felt it before. Just climbing out of the shower made me feel like I was a hundred years old and riddled with arthritis.

I palmed some over-the-counter pain meds and then sat on the closed toilet, slathering all my cuts and scrapes with antibiotic ointment and bandages, taking extra care of the stitches on my biceps. Once I finished, I just sat there, trying to find the energy to move, to make my way down the hall to the bedroom.

The adrenaline crash from the events of the last days and weeks of sleepless nights had finally taken its toll. Add to that, I was pretty sure the virus burning through town had finally worked its way into my system. It left me feeling like I'd never be able to stand again.

The bathroom door flew open, banging against the wall, and Beckett stormed in with a frown between his brows and frustration spread across his face. Whatever it was, whatever had happened now, I wasn't sure I could take it, because I was tapped out. I'd reached the end of my strength and sanity.

Somehow, I mustered up the energy to ask, "What's wrong? Is it Dad?"

"Your Dad is fine. I want to know why you're still showering in the guest bath?"

"My stuff is here."

"Move it. You aren't a goddamn guest."

When I didn't reply, he stepped toward me, and in one smooth move, he swept me off the toilet into his arms. "What are you doing?"

"Showing you, once and for all, where you belong," he insisted, stalking down the hall and into his bedroom. I was too tired to fight him, and truthfully, I didn't want to. I was grateful for not having to move myself, and I loved spending the night tucked up against Beckett.

He yanked the covers back and gently set me down.

The heaven of his mattress greeted me, instantly tugging me closer to sleep. My eyelids were already closed by the time he shut off the lights and joined me. When he pulled me to him, I didn't resist, resting my head on his chest, feeling safe and loved in his arms—a warm cocoon of Beckett's making.

"I need to know, Maisey," he said quietly.

I tried to drag myself back from the edge of sleep, tried to mumble, "What?" but wasn't even sure if it made it from my thoughts into actual words.

"Are you having second thoughts? About us? About getting married? Is that why you refuse to move your stuff into this room? To make it ours instead of just mine?"

I tried to shake my head, tried to reassure him, but I just couldn't open my eyes. Couldn't talk. I thought I said no. Wanted to add on that I wasn't having any doubts about him or us or the future I wanted with him, but my body wasn't cooperating.

From somewhere close to the abyss of sleep, I felt the kiss he placed on the top of my head and heard the *I love yous* whispered in my ear, but then there was nothing but a dark, deep, dreamless sleep.

♫ ♫ ♫

The light was shimmering through the blinds when I woke alone. I felt not quite hot and feverish, but still achy and raw. I sat up and found a tumbler on the bedside table along with a bottle of pain medicine. I took a couple, grimacing at the pain as I swallowed, and then continued to sip at the honeyed tea, trying to soothe my aching throat.

I turned my phone over to check the time, astonished to find it was nearly noon.

As if he'd somehow heard me barely moving, footsteps echoed down the hall, and Beckett appeared in the doorway with Vader trailing after him. When Beckett leaned up against the frame, the dog pressed into him, as if afraid to leave his side again.

"How are you feeling?" Beckett asked.

"Like my throat got stung by a thousand bees and I took a fall from Titan at a gallop."

"That good, huh?" His lips quirked. "You feel like eggs? Toast?"

"Not really," I said and started to slide out of bed.

"Where are you going?" he growled.

"To get ready. Go see Dad. Deal with whatever we need to after yesterday."

In two strides, he'd reached the bed, taken my legs, and shoved them back under the covers. "You're not going anywhere today. You need to rest and heal. Everyone can fucking handle things on their own for one day without you." When I started to protest, he put a finger over my lips. "Don't make me tie you to the bed."

The warning landed in my stomach with an unexpected heat. When my eyes found his, I saw a mirror reflection of the desire that had rushed through me.

But as he leaned in to kiss me, I put my hand up between our mouths.

"No kissing, Beckett," I said and nearly laughed at the disapproving look on his face. "I don't think this is just the smoke messing with my throat. I think I've finally succumbed to the cold going around, and even with your rock-solid immune system, you're bound to get sick if you keep touching me and breathing the same air as me."

He shrugged. "If I do, I do. It'll be worth it."

"You say that now, when your throat doesn't feel like you're training to be a fire eater."

"That's an interesting notion. A firefighter who's also a fire eater. Fireball absorbed the flames, but I could swallow them instead." He was smiling, the large smile that always landed in the pit of my stomach and made his dimple pop. Over the years, I'd gotten good at pushing aside the longing that look brought, but now, I let it hit me fully, relishing it.

The longer I stared at him, the more the tease in the air disappeared, replaced with the electricity that zipped between us. He sat on the mattress next to me and tugged my hand into his.

"As much as I'd love to stay here with you and Vader and ignore the world," I said softly, "I don't think that's going to be possible today."

"Just today? Or has something changed that's making you want to run from me?" he asked, and I heard behind his calm voice the teenage boy who'd once been abandoned. The man who'd shielded his heart, even from me, for twenty years. I hadn't been able to drag myself out of the abyss last night to respond to his questions, and now he'd had an entire morning to doubt me. Doubt us.

"Since the moment you entered my life, Beckett. The thing I wanted most was you. That has never changed. It was the same yesterday. It's the same today. And it will be the same years into our future."

Relief softened every line on his face. "Then move in here. Truly move in here. I want you in my bed, in my bathroom. I want your books strewn across my living room. I want you to turn this house into something that's ours and not mine. And I desperately want to be the person who makes all your dreams come true, if you'll have me…if you'll let me."

Emotions bloomed, filling my chest to their limit and making it difficult to talk. How long had I wanted to hear just this from someone? No…not from just anyone…from Beckett. I'd always wanted him to look at me just this way and offer me himself. Offer me the love I'd always known he had inside him to give. Now that I had it, now that he was mine, it felt unreal. And yet it wasn't.

Forever after wasn't just for romance novels.

The intensity of my joy nearly left me breathless, and it took far too long for me to finally respond. "Okay. I'll move all my stuff out of the guest room and bath today."

The happiness in his eyes matched my own, but he shook his head, humor twinkling in his eyes as he said, "No. You're not doing anything today but resting. I'll move your things."

As much as I would have liked nothing more than to not move a muscle from Beckett's bed, I longed to see my dad. To make sure he was okay. When I said that, Beckett just shook his head again.

"You heard him last night. He wants you to rest. When I talked to him this morning, he made me promise I'd make sure you did just that." When I started to protest, he covered my lips with his hand. "I talked to the doctor too. He said there's no way they're releasing your dad for at least two more days."

"But the sheriff—"

He pressed his finger firmer into my lips. "I also called Cleaver. He and the sheriff and Cooper are still sorting through all the details, but Chelsea is trying to lay as much of the troubles as she can at Carter's feet, hoping to keep the charges against her down. She says it was Carter who spread the Sterno at your dad's. He thought your dad wasn't home, and when your dad walked into the kitchen, Carter knocked him over the head, thinking he'd die of smoke inhalation and that would be that. When the house didn't burn to the ground, they changed their plan of attack. They wanted you out so you'd stop helping your dad, but also so you couldn't claim your half of the estate when your dad died.

"The sheriff got even more information when Gavin showed up at the station, wanting to file a missing persons report for Chelsea because she hadn't shown up at the studio. When they questioned him about Chelsea's whereabouts for some of the incidents, they were able to piecemeal most of what happened. It's likely she was the one who smashed your windshield. And Cleaver found a pair of steel-toed boots at the Helmers' place, so we think she attacked you too, trying to place the blame on a firefighter…maybe even me."

My insides squeezed tight. Beckett saw it and hurriedly rushed through the rest. "Anyway, it looks like Delilah is in the clear. She wasn't lying or covering for Carter. It was just that he and Chelsea were tag teaming, so they'd each have alibis for some of the events, making it nearly impossible to pin the whole thing on either one of them."

"So, the sheriff doesn't need me…for anything else?"

"They have your initial statement, but you'll likely need to talk to the DA about how she killed Carter. I told Cleaver they'd have to wait until at least tomorrow. We need a break. We've earned it. You've earned it. You've spent your life caring for others, my Maisey-girl. For one damn day, let someone else— let *me*—care for you."

I wasn't exactly sure why, but it was those final words that caused the tears to finally break and pour down my cheeks. Maybe it was simply the entire emotional roller coaster finally screeching to a halt and allowing my mind and heart to catch up.

Beckett's expression softened, and he wiped my cheeks tenderly. "Have I told you how much I hate it when you cry?"

"It makes me look even more ghastly, but I can't stop."

"You'd know I was lying if I said you looked perfect," he said, running his thumb along my jawline. "But even exhausted and hurt and sick, my Maisey-girl is still the most beautiful soul in the room."

I wasn't sure how that was possible when I knew I looked a mess. I hadn't dried my hair last night or used any of the products I usually did to fluff it up, which meant it was clinging to me like a sheet of plastic wrap, only dark and stringy. And I was sure my face was pale and shadowed, eyes red-rimmed from tears and whatever virus had taken hold of me. I was probably the most unattractive I'd been in a really long time, especially in front of another human.

"As I'm the only soul besides yours in the room, it doesn't take much to be the prettiest," I tossed back.

Beckett chuckled, and the smile that accompanied it hit me square in the chest again. "You have a gift for that." I raised a brow, and he continued, "For qualifying compliments. Making them seem less."

He was right. It was a bad habit I hadn't broken, even with therapy and years of trying. But knowing Beckett thought I was beautiful, knowing he still wanted me regardless of how I looked or how screwed up my life was, helped push those destructive thoughts to the background. Not in a bad way that meant they'd bite me in the butt someday, but in a way that said they were truly healed. Not just scabs that would crack open, but scars that proved I'd survived.

"You're right. Say it again," I said softly.

His brows lifted. "You're the most beautiful woman I know. Not just in this room, but in the entire world. You're the only one who turns my head, Maisey. The only one who makes me feel like I've just climbed a mountain in full turnout gear and as if I could soar through the sky at the same time."

"Thank you," I said, heart thudding, body going loose and heated. "For seeing me as I want to be seen."

"That's closer." He leaned in and kissed my forehead. "I'll be right back. Don't move, and drink your tea."

He looked at his dog, who had moved from Beckett's side to curl up at my feet next to Dorothy. "Make sure she doesn't move, Traitor Vader." The dog lifted his head and woofed. "Good boy."

When he left the room, I slid my feet out of the blankets, and the dog sat up and whined.

"A woman's gotta pee, Vader. I'll be right back. I promise."

When I stood, Vader barked his disapproval.

"Maisey!" Beckett hollered a warning from the other room.

"Bathroom!" I yelled back, grimacing at the pain that slanted up my throat before patting the dog's head and whispering, "Tattletale. See if I buy you any more of those jerky strips you love."

Vader butted my hand with his head as if in apology and followed me to the bathroom and back, while the kitten watched us with lazy eyes. Just the short little jaunt to the restroom wore me out, so I did exactly what Beckett and his dog wanted and lay back down.

Vader joined me again, doing three complete circles before lying down with his chin on his paws, watching me carefully, as if he was ready to bark again if I moved.

"You really are a traitor," I teased.

The kitten, obviously tired of rest, crawled up his back, played with his thumping tail, and then went scampering off to find some mischief. Vader looked at me, then in the direction the cat had gone, and back to me.

"Go play, I'll be good," I promised. But he didn't budge.

I grabbed my phone, called the hospital, and talked briefly

to Dad, who said exactly the same thing as Beckett. Stay home and rest. After hanging up with him, I texted Fallon. She replied she'd heard from Beckett and to not worry about anything but healing.

I was just putting the phone back when Beckett returned with a tray piled with food and drinks and books.

"Whatchya got there?" I asked.

"Just your standard bed picnic requirements."

My heart swarmed with more happy memories. "I haven't had a bed picnic in…" I shook my head. Maybe since before Mom had died.

Beckett put the tray down on his side of the bed, sliding under the covers. "Snack?" he asked, waving a package of Pop-Tarts.

I shook my head. "Not yet. Maybe later."

He stacked the pillows so he could sit up against them and the headboard before pulling me closer so my head rested on his chest. He pulled a book from the tray, opened it to the middle, and just as I was about to complain he hadn't brought a book for me too, he started reading aloud.

I realized it wasn't just any book, but one of my favorite comfort books—*On the Ropes*. It was a swoony, friends-to-lovers story with a retired boxer and a filmmaker by Kathryn Nolan. It had a great message about community and a smoking-hot sex scene in a car at the famous Philadelphia *Rocky* museum steps.

"What are you doing?" I breathed out.

He raised a brow, lips quirking. "I would think it's obvious, darlin'. I'm reading."

"But you aren't starting at the beginning."

"I've already read the beginning. And as beat up as this copy is, I'm assuming you've read it a few times too. So, I figured I could start where I left off, and you'd still be able to follow along."

I swallowed hard, and this time it wasn't because my throat was sore. This time, it was because I knew the book well and was aware of just where we were at in the story. My cheeks flushed as he started in just before the steamy scene. And when he got to the hottest part, I couldn't help my body's reaction to not only the words but to Beckett saying them. I shifted against him, starting to pull away, but the arm he'd draped around me tightened.

"You're making it hard to read, darlin'."

"It's just weird…not only knowing you've been reading romance for years but having you read it *to* me."

He looked down, lips quirking. "Not ashamed, are you?"

"No!" I snapped back. "There's nothing shameful about romance."

"Do you get turned on by them?" he asked, setting the book on the other side of him.

I shrugged, my cheeks flushing.

"I'll take that as a yes," he said, lips widening into a full-blown smile. "Me too. There was this shower scene in one that had me hard as a rock." I inhaled sharply. "And the entire time I was taking care of myself, I was wishing it was you there, in the shower with me, doing just what that couple had done."

Sore throat? What sore throat? I felt nothing but heat and desire. Nothing but want at his words so casually spoken. So casually offered. Beckett had always been that way, making sex and desire and lust seem normal. Not mundane, but acceptable.

"This scene. The way he's working her up, making her come apart. I like that too." He studied me with a heated look full of the desire I felt. "Shall we try it ourselves?"

My mouth popped open, and he chuckled before reaching over to push my chin closed and skating his thumb over my lips. "I've heard the dopamine release that comes with an orgasm is good for the immune system. An elixir, even. Might make your cold feel better quicker."

My heartbeat ratcheted up a notch, slamming into my ribs with a thud, thud, thud. A sensual pounding that thrummed all the way through me.

"There's no scientific evidence either way," I managed to tell him.

I was flat on my back with him above me in a flash. His

hand skated down my T-shirt, finding the hem and gliding underneath it. My skin lit up like sparklers going off wherever he touched.

"Let's test the hypothesis," he said.

I put my hand over my mouth and spoke from behind it. "I'm serious, Fireball. No kissing."

He stared at me with eyes that looked like he'd already eaten fire. They were ablaze with want. Passion. Desire.

"Fine, no kissing…on the mouth," he said and then proceeded to touch me everywhere else with fingers and lips and tongue. He traced patterns along my ribcage and over my belly, and in a flash, my shirt was gone, and he was paying homage to my breasts, igniting me from the inside out. The fire in his eyes leaped wild and free through me, my body responding to every stroke and lick in a way I'd never realized it could, never quite believed was possible, even when I read about it in my stories.

"Beckett." The word tore from me. A whispered plea. For more. For less. For this feral climb to the summit to last for an eternity. For the cataclysmic release to wait a little longer, just so these perfect minutes with him could be dragged out. So I could savor them for a lifetime.

He grinned up at me, slowly moving downward, taking my sleep shorts and underwear with him and leaving me bare right before he put those long, muscled fingers to use once more. Before he put that delightfully sexy mouth to work again on my hip bones, my thighs, and finally, where I longed for him most.

The moan I let out sounded otherworldly, as if the veil had been crossed.

He took me up, up, up with skilled precision. With dedication. With determination.

And when I shattered, when I burst over that top and cried out his name, there was nothing but joy and love in the air.

Chapter Thirty-seven
Beckett

WORST WAY
Performed by Riley Green

FIVE MONTHS LATER - DECEMBER

HIM: Did you read the scene in the book I sent to you?

HER: I read it at work! You were supposed to warn me!

HIM: Tonight. That's you and me.

HER: If you can make me beg like that, I really will petition the city council to build you a statue.

HIM: Better get your speech ready, darlin'.

"Maise, we gotta go, or we're going to be late," I hollered down the hall toward our bedroom as Vader scratched at the back door to get back inside.

I'd barely opened it, letting in a biting wind and a flurry of flakes, before Vader was brushing past me and heading toward the living room.

"Vader. Feet," I commanded, waiting for him to come back and wipe them off on the towel we had sitting by the door. It had been Maisey who'd trained him to use it, but it had saved me from mopping up his mess a dozen times a day.

When he turned around, I groaned. "Oh, hell no."

I swore he grinned at me around the kitten he held gently by the nape of its neck between his teeth.

He whimpered, and the cat mewled a pitiful plea right as Maisey walked into the kitchen.

"Oh, Vader! Not another one."

As if sensing a disturbance in the force, Dorothy came scampering into the room with Todo, the wiry-haired black cat that Vader-the-Cat-Whisperer had brought in two months ago, right on her heels.

As my ridiculous dog with a savior complex held out the new, orange kitten, the other two cats sniffed and hissed and snarled before losing interest. They headed to the automated feeders that were ready to go off at any second.

Vader sat on his haunches and whimpered again.

"Oh, for the love of—" I started as Maisey said, "He's so little and sweet."

And I knew we were going to end up with another stupid cat. At this rate, I was going to have to add on another room to the house just for the herd of cats we were collecting. Were they called a herd? Or were they a litter?

"We don't have time for this. We're going to be late," I said again.

Maisey leaned down to kiss Vader on the top of his head. "You'll have to get him settled in all on your own. Make sure he doesn't tear up the couch."

My dog nodded as if he understood every command.

Maisey grabbed her coat off the hook, and I stepped up to hold it while she slid into it. That was when I really noticed what she was wearing. A deep-maroon sweater that clung to her curves and ended just above her belly button, showing a hint of skin before it disappeared below the waistband of dark jeans. I groaned again, this time in agony for an entirely different reason.

"Did you put that outfit on just to torture me?" I breathed out as I swept her hair to the side and dipped my head to place a kiss on the smooth skin of her neck. I made the mistake of inhaling, and the water-lily scent of her went straight to my groin.

She laughed softly, turning to face me. She hooked her arms around my neck with ease, which had me eyeing the spiked boots that made her a good three inches taller than normal.

"That's it. I'm calling Dad. We aren't going to make it to some stupid happy hour," I said as I slid my hands beneath the hem of the sweater.

Her breath turned choppy as my fingers teased the edges of a lace bra. I swallowed her little gasp, setting my mouth on hers and licking inside the sweet heat. She responded by pressing into me, tangling her fingers in my hair, and nipping at my lower lip.

Just like it always did when I touched her, when we were lost in each other like this, time slipped away. Nothing existed but her. The smell and taste and feel of her. Of us. My body ignited. Ached. Yearned. I picked her up and set her on the counter, stepping between her thighs, and angled my mouth to go deeper. To show my devotion, my absolute surrender to anything and everything Maisey.

I'd just pulled aside the cup of her bra, gotten one nipple between my thumb and forefinger, when my cell phone burst to life in my pocket.

Dad's ringtone.

Damn.

Maisey laughed, but when I pulled back, her eyes were dark green, full of the same heat and longing that was zipping along my spine, over my shoulders, and through my chest.

As I yanked the phone out and swiped at the screen, Maisey brushed at my lips to remove her deep-red lipstick.

"Yeah?" I grunted out.

"Hey, Beck. Just checking. You're still coming, right?" And the nervousness in Dad's voice had guilt slamming into me.

I had Maisey with me every single day. I could make love to her anytime I wanted—and I did often. Fiercely. Tenderly. Slowly and sensually. Fast and hard. My fiancée was in my bed each night and in my shower every morning. But Dad had only this one time to make amends with Liza.

He only had this one moment to see if fourteen, going on fifteen years, was too much of a divide to cross or if the love they'd had all those years ago could somehow find a home in them again. And I'd promised I'd be there to break up the tension, to ease the reconnection.

"We're running a little behind because Vader brought another goddamn kitten home."

Dad laughed, but it didn't hide his nerves. I glanced at the clock. We had time to make it before Liza showed up at the ranch, but I'd have to push it a little faster than I'd wanted to in the light layer of snow that had drifted through last night.

"We're on our way now."

"Okay. See you soon."

Before I could hang up, Maisey took the phone. "Don't be nervous, Kurt. One look at you, and she's going to remember all the reasons she loved you."

My dad responded, but I couldn't hear what it was as I hadn't put the phone on speaker. Maisey laughed, and they hung up as I lifted her off the counter.

I held her arm as we made our way to the SUV so she wouldn't slip in those sexy boots on the snow. Once we were on the road, with our windshield wipers brushing aside the wet flakes, Maisey darted me a worried look.

"She's going to be kind, right? She's not going to be a bitch and say something mean?"

I thought back to the Liza I remembered. She'd never been cruel, not even when Dad told her if she left to never come back. She'd been sad and heartbroken but said she'd respect his wishes.

I shook my head. "I don't think she'll be mean."

"Good. I don't want to have to go all Fallon on her."

I snorted. "Let's leave all the Falloning to Fallon."

"If there's time, after we have lunch with Kurt and Liza, Andie asked us to stop by her office. She's got some more flower samples for us to look at."

I didn't groan aloud, but I swear Maisey heard me anyway.

She laughed and said, "I know. I know. This wedding planning stuff is more intense than I even thought. I'm almost ready to say screw it and elope the way Fallon and Parker did."

"No," I responded instantly.

"What? Why not?" she asked.

"Maisey, I'm not sneaking off to Vegas to say I do. I'm standing in front of the entire damn town and claiming you as mine."

"You already did that when you put a ring on my finger at the Firefighters Ball."

"And I'll do it again at our wedding. And maybe again on our first anniversary. And our five-year, ten-year, and twenty-five-year anniversaries. I'm going to say it over and over again so no one, not Cleaver or Sweeney or any of the guys out there waiting with bated breath for me to screw up, thinks they can steal you away from me."

Her expression turned soft and emotional.

"Don't you dare cry."

She put a finger to the corner of each eye. "Then stop saying such sweet things, Chief Romero."

The name went straight to my chest and down to my dick. I loved it when she said it. Loved it when she screamed it too. I'd thought the best part of being the fire chief was going to be making the changes I'd been itching to put in place for years. But the best part was, hands down, hearing Maisey call me Chief in the privacy of our own bedroom.

"You really are determined to torture me today."

She winked. "I'll be sure to reward you for your exemplary patience and control." She reached over the center console to brush a finger along my cheek. "I have a new book for us to read."

The situation in my pants took a decidedly dangerous turn. "Well, reward or not, I'll be delivering some well-earned payback."

She tapped her lips. "Hmm. Want to make a little wager? See who begs first?"

I stared far too long at her and had to jerk the steering wheel so we didn't go off the road. Our back end slid slightly on the icy road. "Stop distracting me."

She only laughed. The laugh that sounded like bells on the pearly gates.

I wouldn't change a moment of the life we'd made together. The life we'd made completely and utterly ours.

When we pulled into the ranch, Dad was waiting at the doors of the castle. He was pacing, tipping his cowboy hat forward and then back. Maisey leaped out of the SUV and headed toward him in a hurry, sliding in those spiked heels in the snow. I swore, shoving out of the car and catching up to her in time to keep her from hitting the ground.

She smiled up at me. She did that a lot these days—smiled.

At me. At the menagerie of animals we'd inherited. At her job in the Labor and Delivery Ward. At Fallon and her two kiddos and the one on the way. At her dad, when we went to visit him in the senior living complex he'd moved into a month ago. The repairs on his house were still a work in progress, but he'd been determined to give us the space we needed. So he'd cashed in some of his retirement and jumped ship. Maisey hadn't been thrilled, but he'd promised he'd be able to right it once the house was renovated and sold.

Maisey hugged my father, tucked her arm in his, and dragged him into the hotel as I followed. She murmured something to him, quiet words to calm him down, as we made our way to the tiny speakeasy in the attic of the hotel.

To get there, you had to enter what had once been an old walk-in safe, through a half-open shelf that concealed the tunnels that crisscrossed behind the walls of the castle, and up a dozen stairs to the room tucked up in one of the spiked towers.

The jazz music filling the room was a perfect complement to the speakeasy. Just as the bar's dark and moody lighting and the handful of booths made of blue velvet tossed you back in time to the 1930s.

Normally, you had to reserve a spot here weeks in advance, but Andie or Fallon could usually swing something for us when we needed it. And both those ladies would do anything for my dad, so after he'd chosen the location for the meet with Liza, because she loved Gatsby and gangster movies, they'd made sure we had a booth.

We'd barely ordered drinks when my dad let out a breath and said, "I don't know what I was thinking. Why did I invite her here? It's been almost fifteen years. If she wanted to forgive me, she would have reached out by now, don't you think? I don't blame her. I said unforgivable things. I'm not sure why she even accepted my offer to come. Maybe she just needed a vacation—"

"Dad," I said, reaching across to grab his hands and cutting him off mid-ramble. "All you have to do is tell her what you told me this summer."

His brows furrowed together, thinking back.

"Tell her the truth. That you made a mistake. That you've regretted your words to her ever since. That all you really wanted was for her to come back. Tell her she was part of our unit and that when you felt the knots fraying, you didn't do what needed to be done to tighten them, and you let her slip away because you hadn't done the job you needed to do to heal yourself."

Dad scoffed. "Even if I could say all that, why would she believe me?"

Maisey squeezed my thigh under the table and held my gaze. Behind my dad stood a woman, younger than him but not by all that much. Her dark hair had broad stripes of gray that matched her eyes. Nervous eyes above a kind smile.

My heart thudded. Dad hadn't seen her. And I knew once he did, his tongue would be stuck to the roof of his mouth. So instead of warning him, I prodded him.

"Have you ever once stopped thinking about her since she left?

"Not once."

"You told me I deserved a love so consuming that all I could think about each day was getting back to that person. Is that how you felt—feel—about Liza."

He nodded.

"Do you believe passion and love are gifts and not

burdens?"

"Beck, what's your point?"

"Just answer me."

"I do. Love is a beautiful, precious gift. But I wasted it with Liza. I pushed her away because of what happened before she entered my life. If I could change any one thing in my past, it wouldn't be meeting your mother, because she gave me you, but I would change what I said to Liza that day. Instead of pushing her away, I'd tell her she would always have a home here, no matter how long she was gone or how far she needed to travel. When her feet were tired and her back weary, when she'd done all the things she needed to accomplish, she could come home, and we'd be waiting with open arms."

The woman behind him brushed at her eyes and then straightened her back. "Well, I've got some pretty tired feet and could sure use a pair of open arms."

Dad jumped out of the booth as if a rattlesnake had bitten him.

His expression was stunned as he took in Liza's smile that had softened around the edges with age but hadn't really changed at all.

"Liza…" his voice died.

"Well, Cowboy, you going to open those arms or not?"

He didn't hesitate. He just opened wide, and she stepped right into them.

My throat nearly closed up at the beauty of it. When I looked down at Maisey, she was brushing at tears. I leaned in and kissed her cheek, whispering, "You know how I feel about your crying, my Maisey-girl. You're gutting me."

"I'll make it up to you."

"You have a lot of making up to do."

She huffed out a laugh.

Dad finally let go of Liza, and when he did, she turned and opened her arms to me. I stood and hugged her. And damn if tears didn't fill my eyes. She squeezed me tight and let me go. Then she patted my face. "You've grown up just as I thought you would, Beckett. Strong and handsome, and right next to your Maisey-girl."

Maisey slid out of the booth. "Hey, Liza."

The women hugged, and my dad and I exchanged a glance over their heads. It had taken us a long time to finally get to this point—to accepting and holding love in our lives. But we had it, and I knew neither of us was ever going to let it go.

We'd fight to keep it. Fight with every breath to stop those knots from ever unraveling again.

♫ ♫ ♫

That night, after I'd gotten payback for the sinful sweater and the lace bra, for the taunts and teases and tears, by making my Maisey-girl beg multiple times, I lay with her sweet body on top of mine and thought what a lucky bastard I was.

Lucky she hadn't found some other dickhead to marry before I'd pulled my head out.

Lucky she understood the wounds that had made me so she could call me out on my shit when the smoke occasionally tried to return and choke me.

Lucky to have had an angel reach out to grab my hand.

She moved, and I growled. "I'm not sure I'm done with you yet."

She laughed. "Fine, you open the drawer."

"What?" I frowned.

"Open the drawer, Beckett," she said, nodding to the bedside table.

"Is that where you're keeping the new book? I'm not sure anything in it will be better than what we just did." But I still opened it because I would always do what she asked for the rest of our lives.

I pulled out a black bag. It was pretty hefty, holding something solid.

I raised a brow again. "You know how I feel about toys, darlin'. We don't need them. We got each other, and we work just fine on our own."

When she laughed this time, it was with something close to pure joy. "It's not a sex toy. Well…not really. Open it."

I shifted a little, trying to keep her right where she was on top of me, while I tugged at the drawstring. I was even more confused when I pulled out a trophy. Like the kind you get in middle school—a participation trophy.

It took me a minute to realize it was an R-rated trophy. Well, maybe not R-rated, but definitely PG-13. The figure at the top was two people twined in a very heated kiss. They were clothed, but he had one hand on the back of her head and the other on her ass, holding her up against a wall. She had one hand in his hair, and the other was hidden, tucked up between them, but was likely on his junk.

"Maise—" I was confused and slightly turned on by a damn bronze trophy.

"Read the plaque, Fireball."

I squinted, and it took me a minute for it all to set in. And then a laugh rumbled out of me from deep within my core. The inscription said, *To Chief Romero, for his exceptional expertise in the bedroom. He is hereby awarded this trophy as King of Inciting Orgasms.*

"Took me longer than I thought it would to find the right reward. It's not quite a medal, but..." Maisey shrugged. Her face was lit with a joyfulness that bordered on mischievous.

I tossed the trophy on the floor, and she made the same noise she did when Vader did something wrong, but I didn't care. I put a hand to the back of her head and pushed her face to mine so I could nip at her lower lip. "'Bout time you recognized my expertise."

She laughed again as I trailed kisses over her jaw, her neck, and down over the curve of a breast.

She sighed. "Keep earning it, Chief Romero, and maybe you'll get another, better reward."

The sweet tease hit home differently than she'd intended, igniting not my libido but my heart. The fullness I felt in my heart, in the muscle that beat freely for her, had me leaning in to give her another tender kiss. "I already have the best reward anyone could ever give me, my Maisey-girl. I have you."

She flushed, pink coating her skin. I loved how I was able to trace my fingers over it, following the trail all the way down to the places that made her gasp.

"Tell me you love me," she whispered.

"I love you. I loved you yesterday and today, and I'll love you even more tomorrow."

I rolled so she was below me, staring into eyes that had darkened like the forest out back. As I continued to stroke and caress and touch and taunt, I demanded, "Your turn, darlin'. Tell me you love me."

Her breath turned thready again, but she gave me what I wanted, saying, "From the moment you tumbled into my backyard, I've been yours, Beckett. Saying I love you isn't enough, but they're the only words we humans have been able to invent to try to convey it. So why don't I show you instead?"

And that was precisely what we did, showed each other, with not only our bodies but our hammering hearts and shimmering souls, we belonged to one another. That our knot would never fray. That we would be one of the lucky couples who beat the odds by finding our forever after right next door.

Epilogue
Maisey

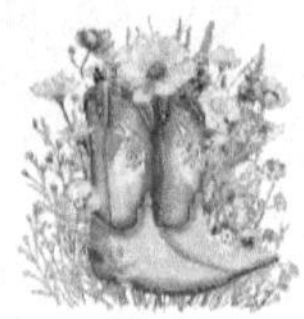

WORKIN' ON THIS LOVE
Performed by Lady A

ANOTHER TEN MONTHS LATER - OCTOBER

HIM: I need a new trophy.

HER: Hmmm. Do you? Do you really? What did you do to deserve one now?

HIM: I've exceeded the human capacity for patience.

*HER: *** eyeroll emoji ****

HIM: That dress… It isn't going to be salvageable when I'm done with it, darlin'. I'm absolutely not wasting time undoing each of those buttons. I'm just going to rip it right off.

HER: It's got a side zip, but it's too bad you won't be able to use it. We agreed I'd spend the night in the bridal suite, and you'd be with Kurt.

HIM: That was before you decided to wear that dress. All bets are off.

The wedding rehearsal down by the waterfall had gone smoothly and quickly. What was even better was how the clouds that had lingered overhead had broken up and shifted off into a glorious orange-and-pink sunset.

We'd known it was risky to schedule an outdoor wedding in October, but it had been our own fault for waiting so long to book something with Andie. By the time we'd actually gotten around to talking to her about a date, this had been her best available, unless we'd wanted to wait another six months. We hadn't. So, we'd paid the deposit and hoped for the best.

And the weather seemed to be smiling down on us.

With the rehearsal behind us, we were now in the dining room at the castle for dinner with our family and closest friends. The table had to be extended to its full length to accommodate the fifteen people sitting around it, in addition to Beckett and me.

Our fathers sat side by side, making jokes about us as kids, while Liza laughed softly, her fingers twined with Kurt's. Fallon was feeding the baby, and Parker had wrangled Theo and Lila into chairs. Tejas was flirting with Andie, and she was keeping him at arm's length, like she did most men. And then there was Fallon's family, who'd done so much for me over the years, not just monetarily, but by extending their kindness. Lauren, Teddy, Rafe, Sadie, and Fallon's siblings were all chatting and smiling.

A relaxed happiness was in the air that felt contagious.

That first night Andie and Fallon had shown up at Beckett's to talk about the wedding, before we'd made it real, I'd imagined this would be the extent of people who'd show up for it. But tomorrow, the ranch would be bursting with at least a hundred people. In addition to some of the hospital staff and his fire crew, Beckett's role as fire chief had forced him to include the entire city council and their plus-ones just to avoid offending anyone, as well as both the old and new mayors and sheriffs.

As much as it made me nervous to think about all those people watching me as I walked down the aisle tomorrow, I'd happily do it because it meant Beckett's dreams had come true. I'd do just about anything to show him how proud I was of him. How proud I was of the role he'd already started to play in Swift Rivers, improving not only the department but the community itself.

I was even prouder of the way he'd changed in his private life and the love he gave freely now. The love he'd never once shied away from since sliding the engagement ring on my finger.

My chest filled with a glorious mix of joy and love and lust as I watched Beckett laugh at something Parker said. He'd worn his Class A's tonight after deciding to wear a tuxedo in our actual ceremony. I hadn't cared what he wore. I'd just wanted him to be comfortable.

When I'd told him as much, he'd said, "I don't think I should show up in my boxer briefs, darlin'." I'd laughed, as he'd intended. But then I'd slowly divested him of his clothes, including the boxer briefs, and neither of us had been laughing. We'd been lost in the heady touch of skin on skin and the slow-building roll to the summit.

My skin flushed simply thinking of it. As if sensing my stare, Beckett looked over at me, gaze stalling on the pink coating my skin. Then, he dragged his eyes down the deep-green dress I'd worn tonight. It had a thousand little buttons running along the front, from the sweetheart neckline all the way down to where it flared just above my knees. When his look finally returned to my face, the blaze in it only made my blush deepen. He smiled a slow, seductive smile that was big enough to make his dimple pop. He pulled out his phone, fingers flying over the screen.

My phone buzzed not even a second later. The text exchange did nothing to help my blush disappear, and when I looked up at him, Beckett winked.

I moved around the table, leaned in, lips brushing the cuff of his ear, and said, "Payback is hell, *Chief* Romero."

When he went to grab me, I danced out of reach with a laugh just as dinner was served.

We made it through the courses, with laughter and jokes and love floating around the table. And that full feeling in my heart grew and grew until I thought it might burst. Beckett and I were living a beautiful, delightful dream. Fiction made real.

Child Maisey had always felt loved by her parents, even if Dad's love had been hard to see with his absences. And she'd always felt loved by Beckett and Kurt and Fallon's family, who accepted her as one of them. But that little girl with the broken jaw, who'd turned into the teen with the scars, had always felt like she wasn't quite enough. At least, not enough for someone to choose to live happily ever after with.

Now, I realized I'd been looking for my happily ever after in all the wrong places, because the one person I'd really wanted had told me he could never love anyone in that way. I'd let us both believe it. I hadn't fought for him or us because I hadn't believed in my own worth enough.

So tonight, I was celebrating the ugly little duckling whose dreams had finally come true and the wounded little boy who'd learned to love, as much as I was celebrating the grown-up versions of us having grabbed hold of each other. Those little kids had survived. Had not only survived but excelled at life and love.

And now we'd make a family together.

Sooner than we'd planned.

My hand rested on my flat stomach, and a wave of love shifted through me so strong I thought I might cry. It was happening so much sooner than we'd discussed, but I knew Beckett would take it in stride just like he'd taken everything else in our lives. Better yet, he'd be the perfect, doting father.

My gaze traveled to my dad. Our relationship was deeper and fuller than ever before. He'd get a kick out of being a grandfather, sharing pictures and bragging on him with all the friends he'd made in his retirement community. And I finally didn't have to worry about where he was getting the money for it as his property had sold just a few weeks ago to Cooper Wylee. The sheriff's son had returned to town after the sheriff had a heart attack, and the city council asked him if he'd temporarily take over the role. He'd astonished everyone by giving up his job in LA and moving back to Rivers permanently with his tween son.

Coop moving in wasn't the only change on our street either. The deal on the Helmers' place that Carter had tried to put together over a year ago had obviously fallen through, but their kids had still put the house on the market, and we'd all been surprised when Andie had purchased it in the spring.

It had been fun to have a girl friend living on the street. Plus, she'd been over to the house a lot getting Beckett's opinions on renovation ideas.

Just as dessert was being cleared away, Fallon stopped by the head of the table, dropping off a wrapped box with Beckett. I frowned at it as he stood, raising his glass. Seeing my confusion, his faced softened with love, and he leaned in to tuck a strand of hair behind my ear and whispered, "Don't worry so much, darlin'."

He cleared his throat and said, "If I could have your attention for just a moment."

The room grew silent, our loved ones concentrating solely on us.

"I wanted to take the opportunity before the chaos of tomorrow to say thank you to all of you. Not only for being here to celebrate this moment with us but for showing Maise and me the real value of family…of love."

His voice grew scratchy, showcasing the emotions Beckett so easily gave these days.

"I'm grateful beyond words to have learned from all of you. So thank you." He raised his glass in a silent toast. Then, he turned to me, drew me up from the table by my hand, and picked up the box Fallon had left. "But I also wanted to take the time tonight to say thank you to my bride-to-be.

"Maisey, from the moment you took my hand as a little kid, you've shown me what true love and acceptance looked like. You've given freely and quietly of yourself, giving far more than you ever took so the people around you could be happy. Could have everything they needed. Could have love. I wanted to give you something in return, to thank you for showing me exactly what forever after looks like and for never giving up on me before I finally realized I wanted my own happily ever after."

Tears pooled. Ones I knew he'd hate, but I couldn't stop them. It was his own fault for saying such sweet things. For hitting right on the sore spot Chelsea had left so long ago and that was still taking time to heal. She'd beaten it into me, with sharp words, that I was greedy and selfish, and I was still learning to counter those words with healthier ones.

Beckett brushed at my cheek.

"I wasn't sure what gift I could give you that would adequately express how much I, and everyone around us, see what you've done for us. It took me a while to find the first part and a bit longer to convince someone almost as stubborn as you that you needed your name on what I put inside it."

He handed me the gift.

"Beckett…I don't need anything." I shook my head. "I don't want anything. I have you." I ran a finger over his lips and then looked out at the table full of people. "And I have my family. That's all I need."

"Just give the man his moment, Maisey," Fallon teased, "and open it."

A chuckle ran through the room.

When I tore the paper off it, my heart nearly stopped, and the tears came unabated.

I traced my fingers over the butterflies and hummingbirds carved into the top of the jewelry box just as I had as a kid.

"What? How?" I shook my head.

Beckett brushed at my tears. "Gavin helped me track it down."

When Gavin had shown up in Swift Rivers, looking for Chelsea the day after her arrest, and heard about the full extent of her crimes, he'd been horrified. He'd come to Beckett's house—our house—and apologized for not seeing the truth of her sooner. I told him a year was nothing. That I'd been blinded for much longer than that, nearly our entire childhood. And even after I'd known the truth, I'd still hoped there was good in her.

Since then, Gavin had kept in touch with Beckett, checking in to make sure our lives were still going okay. It was sort of sweet and made me realize there was a lot more to him than the fake façade I'd first encountered at my dad's house that first morning. The fact that he'd helped Beckett track down Mom's jewelry box only proved it more.

"After we finally found it and the woman who'd bought it from the pawn shop agreed to sell it back to me, I checked with your dad," Beckett said, glancing over at my father, who was fighting his own tears. "And he said he wanted you to have it. I'm sorry to say we couldn't track down any of the jewelry. We're still not sure what Chelsea did with the pearls, so I put something inside it that might be just as important to you."

"There's more?" I croaked.

"Open the box, my Maisey-girl."

When I snapped the lid open, it took me much longer than expected to understand what was inside.

It was a certificate. A certificate of ownership.

More tears flowed unchecked.

Beckett had given me back Titan.

He'd bought him from Fallon and handed him over to me.

My friend had never once made me feel like the American Paint wasn't mine, but I'd still felt the gap. Still felt the wall between us. Still wanted to pay her and her family back for nearly twelve years of stabling him, feeding him, and exercising him. For caring for the animal who'd always felt like an extension of myself.

I flung my arms around Beckett, buried my face in his neck, and tried to get a grip on the tears. My body shook, and Beckett's grip tightened.

"Don't cry, my Maisey-girl. Don't cry. It was supposed to be a good thing."

I pulled back, looked up into his face, and said, "It's the perfect gift, Beckett. The most perfect gift."

He kissed me, and the little group of family we'd gathered all cheered and clapped.

"Thank you, Beckett, for showing me love isn't something that happens to you. It isn't magic or a miracle, but it *is* a gift. And I will always be grateful for the gift of you in my life."

And the other present he'd given me that he didn't know about yet.

But I couldn't tell him that now. I wouldn't lessen what he'd done by overshadowing it. I'd tell him tomorrow, after the wedding, in a moment shared with just the two of us.

"I love you, Fireball. With all my romance-loving heart," I said, kissing him again.

"And I love you back, my Maisey-girl, with all I am and all I hope to be."

There'd never been a more perfect happily ever after in any book I'd ever read than this one, simply because this was *my* happily ever after.

No. It was *our* happily ever after.

One we got to live every single day.

♫ ♫ ♫

Want to know how Beckett responds when he finds out Maisey is pregnant? Catch the entire scene in a free bonus epilogue on the night of the wedding.

DOWNLOAD TMWMO'S FREE BONUS EPILOGUE HERE

And if you if want a sneak peek at what's coming next in the *Swift Rivers Series*, keep reading for **a look at Andie and Cooper's HEA**.

The Moments We Chose

Love

Andie

LET IT BURN
Performed by Shaboozey

The last of the guests were piling into their cars, and the waitstaff was collecting a few remaining glasses and plates, turning off the faux tealights that glimmered in the antique lanterns tucked into the flower arrangements on each table. Another successful wedding in the books. The wooden dance floor and marquee we'd put up by the river near the barns would come down tomorrow morning, and it would look like nothing had ever happened.

Until the next wedding. A holiday-themed one in the middle of November.

I really needed to talk to Fallon about building an official venue. It might be more expensive in the short term, but it would save the labor of putting up and taking down the tents and dance floor every week during our heaviest season. And it would mean we could hold weddings year-round without the weather impacting us quite as much.

I had a vision of a large building made almost entirely of glass, so it would feel like the attendees were dancing amongst the trees and fields… Or maybe a crystal ballroom built in the middle of the lake, so it felt like you were dancing on the water. Although, that would require boats to shuttle the guests back and forth, so maybe not.

Something would come to me. I needed to wait until I had the plan fully formed before presenting it to Fallon. Knowing her, if she liked it, she'd run full speed with it and miraculously make it happen before June hit.

Her determination, grit, focus, and speed were some of the things I respected most about my boss…my friend.

Four years ago, I never would have expected to say the twenty-something owner of the five-star resort I worked at would become my best friend. Back then, she'd been in and out of the ranch while attending college, and her mother had primarily been in charge. Every one of the employees had watched Lauren struggle on and off with a prescription drug problem and had looked to me for leadership.

So I hadn't exactly been thrilled at the idea of handing over my control when I'd realized Fallon was returning home and staying permanently, intending to take up the reins her mother had wielded loosely. And maybe if the attacks on her hadn't started right after Fallon had arrived home, if I hadn't been overwhelmed with an empathy I'd never express, we wouldn't have become the friends we were now. Maybe I would have been bitter about her taking back what I'd essentially come to think of as mine. But instead, in doing everything to help her weather the storm, it had bonded us.

Over her traumas. Not mine.

To this day, Fallon hadn't an inkling of my past. And it needed to stay that way.

When I stepped out of the tent, it was to find Vader sitting, wistfully staring in the direction that Beckett and Maisey had disappeared inside the castle-like hotel. The large black dog still had a cute little bow tie attached to his collar, and a boutonniere to which the wedding rings had been attached.

I ran a finger over the silky fur on his head, and he whined. "Give them a night, Vader. Just a night. They've earned that. Come on, we'll go home, feed your cats, and then you can keep me company if you'd like."

He followed me toward the parking lot at the back of the castle.

I'd given up my staff room here at the ranch almost a year ago now, buying a house on the same street where Maisey and Beckett lived. I still got goosebumps whenever I thought of purchasing it. The house had been a risk. Not only monetarily but because it left a trail that someone could follow if they really wanted to find me.

My mouth went dry, and my palms turned sweaty just thinking about it. I had to force myself to breathe, to relax.

I'd been here eight years now. Eight years and no one had come for me.

I was safe.

If I weren't, I would have heard from my stepbrother. He was keeping tabs on things. He'd know if there'd been any movement on that front.

I was almost to my mid-sized SUV, when I realized the streetlight above it, the one I always parked under when I was going to be here late, was out. I had to force myself to breathe, to relax. It was just a broken light. These things happened all the time. Maintenance would fix it tomorrow. The dark wouldn't be waiting for me when I came out tomorrow.

But the shadows now surrounding my SUV still made my pulse race. I opened the back passenger door, and Vader jumped in. I clipped his seatbelt with rushed hands, shut the door, and nearly jumped out of my skin when a gritty, irritated voice came at me from the dark.

"I'm tired of leaving you messages that go unanswered."

All the air inside me vanished, and my limbs shook violently. I forced myself to whirl around and face him, using the car to steady myself.

The person who stepped toward me wasn't the villain from my nightmares.

But even knowing that—even recognizing the truth—I couldn't calm the wild beat of my heart. I couldn't draw a full breath. I remained winded, chest locked tight as if I'd been thrown from a horse at a dead run.

Cooper Wylee moved toward me, brows drawn together as he studied me with an intensity that rocked me to my core.

The dim light that reached us from the hotel's windows turned his brown hair black. It was uncharacteristically slicked back tonight, his usual waves tamed for the wedding, and it put his strong jaw and a dangerously seductive cleft prominently on display. His eyes, usually a baby blue spiked with an icy fire, were nothing more than dark wells in the darkness tonight.

He'd already lost the suit jacket he'd worn to Maisey and Beckett's wedding, leaving him in a plain dress shirt that did nothing to hide the solid brick of his chest. He'd pulled off his tie and flung it over his shoulder, undone the top few buttons of the shirt, and rolled the sleeves up, showing off thick biceps. Somehow, seeing him like this felt incredibly intimate, as if I'd captured him in his room, undressing.

And it did nothing to help my poor frozen lungs. If anything, it stopped my breath further.

He was the most attractive man I'd seen off a movie screen.

More attractive than even—

Just the mere memory of the last man I'd thought to be this good-looking was enough to blur my vision and have me tilting back into the car.

And then Cooper was there, putting a hand to my elbow.

"Hey," his voice softened as he took in my obvious distress, gripping me tighter.

His touch scored me. Marked me.

And I'd promised myself I'd never be marked again. But I couldn't breathe well enough to tell him to back off. Instead, the world continued to spin, and I knew if I didn't inhale, I'd faint. I'd be on the ground…helpless.

That thought only increased my panic.

Increased the pulse of blood pumping through my veins and seeming to shove a cork into my throat, sealing it completely.

"Andrina. Take a breath before you pass out," he commanded. A man used to giving orders that were followed. But that thought only made matters worse.

I made a useless motion with a weak hand as more panic rolled through me, and an uncontrollable tremor added to the turmoil in my body.

It wasn't because of Cooper. He was the sheriff of Swift Rivers, for god's sake. He wasn't going to hurt me.

But then again, you never knew, did you?

I'd thought…

No. No. Thinking of my past would not help me recover from this panic attack.

Before I could register what was happening, Cooper had opened the front passenger door of my SUV, pushed me into the seat with my feet hanging out the door, and shoved my head between my legs.

"Breathe, damn it. Nice and slow."

Cooperate, body. Cooperate! With every ounce of willpower I had, I forced my mouth to unlock and accept the cool night air. And finally. Finally, my lungs received the breath they'd so desperately needed. I gasped at the pain, as if it really was the first burst of oxygen after a fall.

"Slow. Count to four as you inhale. Hold it for four, and then let out for four," Cooper insisted, rubbing my shoulder. He counted for me, as if I were a child and couldn't. And I did as he told me because I didn't have another option at the moment.

As my lungs slowly recovered, as my body finally stopped shaking, anger and humiliation filtered in. At my body for betraying me. At Cooper Wylee for witnessing it.

I pushed the hand on my shoulder away. "Back off," I snapped.

And he did just that, taking two steps away from me.

It helped to have him farther away. It eased the zap and hiss of electricity that sizzled through me whenever he was too close.

When my breathing was normal and the trembling had stopped, I gritted my teeth and finally sat up.

He was watching me, but I couldn't read the expression there. It was too dark, and he was turned away from the hotel's lights, leaving his face a mix of shadows.

"What do you want?" I hissed.

He shoved his hands into his pants' pockets. "Before this little show"—he waved at me sitting in the car, still forcing myself to breathe—"I wanted a response to my damn message. Now I want to know who the hell you're afraid of and what they did to you."

Tears threatened, and I blinked furiously, grinding my teeth together again.

No way was I going to embarrass myself more by crying in front of him. Tears I'd refused to shed for years now.

No way was I giving any man—let alone this cold, disapproving one—an ounce of my emotions ever again.

Cooper

BAD MOON RISING
Performed by Creedence Clearwater Revival

Someone had done a number on her. Someone had taken this confident, beautiful, tough-as-nails woman and broken her.

That pissed me off. But it also had a voice in my head screaming at me to run.

Because I couldn't afford one more broken woman entering and leaving my life.

I couldn't afford what came in the aftermath.

Scandal. Heartache. Loneliness.

Screw that. I wasn't lonely. I didn't have time to be lonely. Not with an entire town counting on me. Not with my dad watching over my shoulder so I wouldn't fail at the job he'd had for nearly three and a half decades. Not with a tween son rebelling against everything and everyone, including me.

And if I didn't have time for loneliness, I certainly didn't have time for Andrina Nealy, her once copper hair now dyed to a dark sheen that still glistened with licks of the former flames, or those storm-colored eyes that promised chaos.

I didn't have time for a woman whose past I'd already suspected was nothing but smoke and mirrors. A card house ready to tumble to the ground with the next slight breeze.

Unknown

ANNABELLE
Performed by Shaboozey

Fucking bitch. Fucking bitch putting out all those pathetic signals to catch her next mark.

But he couldn't fucking have her.

She'd already promised forever to someone else.

And I'd see her in hell before she broke those vows again.

ORDER *THE MOMENTS WE CHOSE LOVE*

🎵 🎵 🎵

Keep tabs on what's next in *THE SWIFT RIVERS SERIES* by subscribing to my newsletter.

Or following me in these places:

@ljevansbooks

Acknowledgments

I'm so very grateful for every single person who has helped me on this book journey. If you're reading these words, you are one of those people. I wouldn't be an author if people like you didn't decide to read the stories I so carefully craft, so THANK YOU!

To my husband, who never ever lets me give up on myself, even when the battles seem endless, thank you for your sacrifice, strength, and laughter that gets me through the darkest moments. And thank you for always believing in me enough to ensure we take each big gamble as they come along. I love you more than words.

To my child, Evyn, owner of Lycanthrope Media, thank you for helping me create the best stories I possibly can by carefully and kindly tearing them apart. And thank you for helping me to be a better human. Love you, kiddo.

To my parents, sister, and in-laws who listen to me gripe about publishing and then cheer me on as if I'm the greatest writer on earth, thank you for making me feel loved and valid every single day.

To my beautiful author friends, including my daily hype friends Stephanie Rose and Kathryn Nolan along with Erika Kelly, Aly Stiles, AM Johnson, and so many others, thank you for reminding me every day that my worth can't be found in a series of algorithms.

To Atlee Hayes for giving me the idea for the cutest firehouse dog who brought home kittens to Beckett.

To Jenn at Jenn Lockwood Editing Services, Karen Hrdlicka of Barren Acres Editing, and Stephanie Feissner, thank you for being on this journey since nearly the beginning and continuing to have faith in me. Your edits and proofs are always the perfect polish that my words need.

To Michelle Fewer at Brayzen Bookwyrm, thank you for always knowing just what I need to hear to push my story forward one notch and always being gracious and kind while you do it.

To Leisa C. and Stephanie F., thank you for being the best and most fervent cheerleaders I've ever had. Thank you, not only for your love and support but for helping me build a beautiful community in LJ's Music & Stories that brings a smile to my face every day. And thank you to every member of the group. I can't tell you how grateful I am for each of you and how surprised I am that you continue to spend a part of each day with me.

To the host of bloggers who have shared my stories, become dear friends, and continue to make me feel like a rock star, thank you for going above and beyond to share my stories with the world.

To all my ARC readers, who have also become friends and true supporters, thank you for knowing just what to say to scare away my writer insecurities.

To every person who has joined me on this wildly rocky bookish adventure, may the happiness and joy you've brought me be returned to you a hundredfold.

I love you all!

About the Author

Award-winning author LJ Evans lives in Northern California with her husband, child, and the three terrors called cats. She's written compulsively since she was a little girl, often getting derailed mid-task by a song lyric that sends her scrambling to jot a scene down.

A former first-grade teacher, she now spends her days deep in the pages of romance and mystery with a bit of the otherworldly thrown in. Her stories are known for fierce heroines, protective heroes, and found families, following characters who live resiliently—stubbornly and triumphantly navigating this wild ride called life with hope, love, and hard-earned happily-ever-afters.

Her novels have won multiple industry awards, including *Charming and the Cherry Blossom*, which was named Writer's Digest's Self-Published E-book Romance of the Year.

For more information about LJ, check out any of these sites:

www.ljevansbooks.com

Facebook Group: LJ's Music & Stories
LJ Evans on Amazon, Bookbub, and Goodreads
@ljevansbooks on Facebook, Instagram, TikTok, and Pinterest

Books by LJ

Cherry Bay Standalones

Heat, heart, and hints of magic bind women discovering their strength to men who guard them fiercely.

Cherry Bay looks like a charming college-town on the surface—but secrets run deep. As young women come into their own, magic awakens in unexpected ways, sometimes in them, sometimes in the men drawn to protect them. When mystery tightens its grip, love becomes both a shield and a risk neither can walk away from.

*After All the Wreckage_*— Rory & Gage
A single-guardian, snarky-P.I., romantic suspense
*Charming and the Cherry Blossom_*— Elle & Hudson
A surprise-inheritance, he-falls-first, contemporary romance
Lost in the Moonlight — Lincoln & Willow
A grumpy-sunshine, forbidden-relationship, romantic suspense

The Hatley Family

Come for the danger. Stay for the grumpy cowboys, bold heroines, and soul-deep love.

In the rugged Tennessee wilds, loyalty isn't optional—it's survival. The Hatley men are hardened by land, legacy, and threats that won't stay buried. The women who love them are just as fierce, standing toe-to-toe with danger and daring these cowboys to fall hard. Family is everything, and love is worth every fight.

*The Last One You Loved_*— Maddox & McKenna
A single-dad, grumpy-sheriff, small-town suspense
The Last Promise You Made — Ryder & Gia
A single-dad, grumpy-cowboy, small-town suspense
The Last Dance You Saved — Sadie & Rafe
A single-dad, grumpy-cowboy, small-town suspense
Perfectly Fine — Gemma & Rex
A fish-out-of-water, groveling, celebrity novella

Available on Amazon or FREE with newsletter subscription.

The Swift Rivers Series
A Hatley Family Spin-off Series

Where heroes fall hard, cowgirls fight back, and love is the bravest rescue of all.

Welcome to Swift Rivers, where danger lurks beneath quiet streets and every love story is forged under pressure. Broody first responders carry scars they can't outrun. Fierce women refuse to be protected quietly. When threats close in and hearts are on the line, love becomes the one risk worth taking—and the one thing worth fighting for.

The Moments You Were Mine — Fallon & Parker
A single-guardian, bodyguard, small-town suspense
The Moments We Made Ours — Maisey & Beckett
A firefighter, fake-engagement, small-town suspense
The Moments We Chose Love — Andie & Cooper
A single-dad, grumpy-sheriff, small-town suspense. Coming 2026

The Anchor Novels

Service bonded them. Love rebuilt them. And the family they forged saved them.

Heartfelt stories of military heroes shaped by duty and loss and strong women who refuse to be anything but real. Bound by brotherhood and loyalty, they build families not by blood—but by choice. Every romance is a slow-burn journey toward healing, hope, and a love that finally feels like home.

Guarded Dreams — Eli & Ava
A grumpy-sunshine, forced-proximity, military romance
Forged by Sacrifice — Mac & Georgie
A roommates-to-lovers, second-chance, military romance
Avenged by Love — Truck & Jersey
A fake-marriage, forced-proximity, military romance
Damaged Desires — Dani & Nash

A frenemy, bodyguard, military romance
Branded by a Song — Brady & Tristan
A single-mom, military-widow, rock-star romance
Tripped by Love – Cassidy & Marco
A bodyguard, single-mom, small-town romance
The Anchor Novels: The Military Bros Box Set
The 1st three books + an exclusive novella

The Anchor Suspense Novels

In a world built on lies, loving her may be the deadliest truth for these men leading double lives and the brilliant scientists they claim as theirs.

Secrets are currency—and trust can get you killed. Broody operatives and powerful men step into the shadows to protect women whose minds make them targets. When enemies close in and betrayal is everywhere, love isn't just dangerous—it's the one thing worth risking everything for.

Unmasked Dreams — Violet & Dawson
A friends-to-lovers, forced-proximity romantic suspense
Crossed by the Stars — Jada & Dax
A frenemies-to-lovers, forced-proximity romantic suspense
Disguised as Love — Cruz & Raisa
An enemies-to-lovers, forced-proximity romantic suspense

The Painted Daisies

Behind the spotlight, the fiercest battles are for love—and these rock stars find it in the arms of men who will burn the world to save them.

Fame brings fortune, obsession, and deadly secrets. When danger stalks from backstage to center stage, these fierce musicians find refuge in heroes willing to sacrifice everything to keep them alive. Love is raw. Stakes are lethal. And survival means trusting someone enough to hand them your heart.

Swan River — *The Painted Daisies* Prequel
A rock-star, small-town, romantic suspense cliffhanger

Available on Amazon or FREE with newsletter subscription.
Sweet Memory — Paisley & Jonas
An opposing-worlds, friends-to-lovers romance
Green Jewel — Fiadh & Asher
An enemies-to-lovers, single-dad romance
Cherry Brandy — Leya & Holden
A forced-proximity, bodyguard romance
Blue Marguerite — Adria & Ronan
A celebrity, second-chance, frenemy romance
Royal Haze — Nikki & D'Angelo
A bodyguard, on-the-run romance with a morally gray hero

My Life as an Album Series

It started with kids at a lake—and the kind of loss that changes everything.

These interconnected standalone romances read like your favorite album—raw, aching, and unforgettable. From first love to second chances, grief to redemption, this small-town series follows friends who grow up together, fall apart, and learn how to live again. Love heals. Family is chosen. And every story leaves a song behind.

⚠ Reader Warning: Tears are likely. Hearts will be claimed.

My Life as a Country Album — Cam's Story
A boy-next-door, small-town, sports romance
My Life as a Pop Album — Mia & Derek
A rock-star, good-girl-bad-boy, road-trip romance
My Life as a Rock Album — Seth & PJ
A second-chance, antihero romance
My Life as a Mixtape — Lonnie & Wynn
A single-dad, nanny, rock-star romance
My Life as a Holiday Album – 2nd Generation
Six New Year's Eve, surprise-party, short stories
My Life as an Album Series Box Set
The 1st four Album series stories plus an exclusive novella

Free Stories

Get these novellas and flash fiction stories for **FREE with a newsletter subscription at:**

Perfectly Fine — A fish-out-of-water, celebrity romance

He's a charming, A-list actor at the top of his game. She's a determined, small-town screenwriter hoping for a deal. They form an unexpected connection until heartbreak ruins their future. Also available on Amazon.

Swan River — A rock star, small-town, romantic suspense *prequel*

Bound by music, ambition, and unbreakable friendship, The Painted Daisies are a rock band on the rise. But when murder strikes one of their own, secrets unravel even as desire flares. Now the women must navigate love, loyalty, and loss before one wrong move destroys them all. Also available on Amazon.

Rumor — A small-town, rock-star romance

There's only one thing rock star Chase Legend needs to ring in the new year, and that's to know what Reyna Rossi tastes like. After ten years, there's no way he's letting her escape the night without their souls touching. Reyna has other plans. After all, she doesn't need the entire town wagging their tongues about her any more than they already do.

Love Ain't — A friends-to-lovers, cowboy romance

Reese knows her best friend and rodeo king, Dalton Abbott, is never going to fall in love, get married, and have kids. He's left so many broken hearts behind that there's gotta be a museum full of them somewhere. So when he gives her a look from under the brim of his hat, promising both jagged relief and pain, she knows better than to give in.

The Long Con — A sexy, antihero romance

Adler is after one thing: the next big payday. Then, Brielle sways into his world with her own game in play, and those aquamarine-colored eyes almost make him forget his number-one rule. But she'll learn—love isn't a con he's interested in.

The Light Princess — An old-fashioned fairy tale

A princess who glows with a magical light, a kingdom at war, and a kiss that changes the world. This is an extended version of the fairy tale twined through the pages of *Charming and the Cherry Blossom.*